ABOUT THE AUTHOR

Beverley Oakley is an Australian author who grew up in the African mountain kingdom of Lesotho, emigrated to South Australia when she was young, and married a Norwegian bush pilot she met while managing a safari lodge in Botswana's Okavango Delta.

Her romance writing career began as a way to amuse herself in the 12 countries she's lived as the 'trailing spouse' of a pilot husband, and when she worked as an airborne geophysical survey operator in the back of low-flying Cessna 404s and CASA 212s - often the only female crew member - in remote locations around the world.

The author of twenty-five historical romances laced with scandal, mystery and suspense, she also writes Africa-set romantic suspense, and psychological historical romances under her real name Beverley Eikli.

Her Regency tale of redemption **The Maid of Milan** was short-listed in the Top Ten Reads of 2014 at the UK Festival of Romance.

Beverley lives near Melbourne (overlooking a fabulous Gothic lunatic asylum) with the same gorgeous Norwegian husband, two daughters and a rambunctious Rhodesian Ridgeback.

www.beverleyoakley.com
beverley.oakley (at) gmail.com

For Eivind ~ thank you for believing in these stories.

The fact that, you, my own husband, have translated ***Saving Grace*** *into Norwegian is very special to me.*

FAIR CYPRIANS OF LONDON

THREE SIZZLING VICTORIAN ROMANCES: SAVING GRACE, FORSAKING HOPE, KEEPING FAITH

BEVERLEY OAKLEY

FOREWORD

Hello dear reader,

I hope you enjoy my *Fair Cyprians of London* series set in the 1870s about a group of young women enticed through trickery or genuine desire to work in Madame Chambon's high class London House of Assignation.

Their stories of love, betrayal, honour and redemption are inspired by the frank interviews given by 'fallen women' to nineteenth century journalist Henry Mayhew which he documented in his book **London's Underworld.**

Each story ranges in heat level from sensual to sizzling and each is a standalone, with **Saving Grace** a very short novella and the others full-length novels. I really hope you enjoy them.

Many thanks

Beverley Oakley

SAVING GRACE

CHAPTER 1

London, 1878

Reclining on a red plush sofa, Grace took a sip of her sickly sweet orgeat and forced a haze over any thoughts about the night ahead. Madame Chambon only allowed her girls champagne when the gentlemen were paying for it and although Grace was not a drinker she liked the way it dulled her senses to the present.

The others were gathered in companionable groups on the fashionable Egyptian sofas, their heavy scent perfuming the air, their soft murmurs imbuing the atmosphere with a falsely domestic air.

She glanced at Hope, another of those who, like her, kept to themselves. Hope was favoured by the gentlemen who patronised their St James's establishment for her milky white skin and delicate, elfin features. Grace had heard the girl had been a governess before she'd eloped with the squire's son who'd abandoned her. She'd been too ashamed to return to her family. Maybe it was the truth. Each girl had a story to suit herself.

To Grace, the only truth was that they were all on a path to hell. It didn't take much for a girl to lose her character but once it was gone there were precious few options for her to put food in her belly and keep a roof over her head.

An expectant hush fell as the heavy draped and tasselled curtain was drawn aside and Madame Chambon arranged herself theatrically in the opening, ready to address her *petites choux*.

"*Ravissement!*" she complimented them in thickly accented English, clapping her hands. Grace suspected the elegantly ravaged Madame came from Lambeth rather than the Left Bank. Not that it mattered. No one in this business was who they said they were.

Least of all, Grace.

The girls, awed and anxious, straightened their rich, colourful gowns nervously. Despite her appearance of bonhomie Madame Chambon could turn on a coin. And it was she who ensured the girls did not return to where most of them had been plucked from—the gutter.

"A great opportunity awaits one of you tomorrow," she addressed them, "for I have just been honoured by the visit of a woman of great discernment ..."

A couple of the girls tittered. "A woman?"

They closed their mouths at Madame Chambon's beady stare, attending as she went on, "who has requested I supply her with one of my loveliest ..."

She drew out the pause as several of the brothel's most popular young ladies preened.

"... most hard-hearted girls."

All heads turned towards Grace. She blinked, surprised to register shock when she rarely felt anything these days. Is that how they regarded her? Hard-hearted?

Surely she was not alone in a profession that demanded one's soul in return for the necessities to live? She simply had nothing left to offer once she'd done what was required in order to pay Madame Chambon her keep and just survive.

Madame Chambon levelled her expectant look upon Grace, whose mouth dropped open in protest. "A woman? But—"

"The woman wants to give her *son* a present to remember for his twenty-first birthday. She is obviously a very fond mother—" Madame Chambon allowed herself to share the girls' amusement, adding, "with very good sense in choosing our select establishment to provide him with the very best initiation—" Her smile grew cloying as she continued to look at Grace—"without fear of him being lured into a transfer of affections amidst all the other ... ahem ... transfers that take place." Though she made a gesture with her hands to indicate the transfer of money, the girls tittered at the double entendre.

Redheaded Faith, known for her noisy exuberance, leaned in towards the girl beside her. "Grace doesn't have a heart to lose." Her whisper resonated.

Nor did Grace have the heart to participate in the banter that followed.

So what if she'd been selected? It was just another job and a good thing she need not worry about eliciting the emotions of a twenty-one-year-old virgin. Pleasing, also, was the knowledge that any business with a virgin meant it would all be over in less than five minutes.

MADAME CHAMBON SELECTED HER DRESS FOR HER, IN ROYAL BLUE AND silver stripes to complement her dark hair and pale skin. Grace's slender form lent itself to the silhouette of the day: a close-fitting cuirass ending in a draped fan train emphasised with knife pleat ruching. The expensive gown was at the forefront of fashion and made Grace feel she was rubbing shoulders with those she'd once served.

She contoured the flat of her stomach with her hand, turning to look over her shoulder in the looking glass at the stylish figure she cut.

It was true she enjoyed wearing a gown the like of which she'd once not even been entrusted to fold and put away but of course, like everything else, it came with a caveat: she could take only mincing six-inch steps and Madame Chambon required that her girls pay for the clothes she insisted they wear.

"Lor', but yer look like a duchess," breathed her dresser, little Maisy, standing back to appreciate the ensemble.

It was nice praise, and not surprising the girl didn't add that she envied Grace.

Grace patted her on the shoulder and smiled. "Make sure you're in bed early, Maisy, not hurting your eyes with those penny dreadful novels you do so love."

Maisy need look no further than those she served for lurid tales of ruined girls to provide the same moralising warning she got from her beloved stories. Grace hoped Maisy found another situation before Madame Chambon 'elevated' her from serving tired and often ungrateful young women who'd been up all night, to eager, high-paying gentlemen.

CHAPTER 2

Another job in another grand, fashionable West End townhouse, Grace thought wearily as she paused on the step of the hansom cab the jarvey put down for her. Until desperation had forced her to London, Grace had spent her entire life in the country working for a family who, like their rich and titled friends, decamped to the capital for the sitting of parliament and to further their ambitions through the social pleasures of the season—probably peppered with clandestine visits by girls such as herself.

No doubt she was the icing on the cake for a spoiled rich boy destined for some dreary, horsey-looking wife.

She was surprised when the lady of the house answered. But then, absolute discretion would be required, Grace reasoned, slanting a glance up at her from beneath the little spotted veil which hung from her neat flower-festooned straw hat—a suitably concealing millinery confection she was immediately grateful for as she found herself staring into the familiar cold blue eyes of the woman who'd once paid her wages.

"Hurry now. I shall take you immediately to my son, Miss—?"

"Fortune." It came out as a thin whisper as fear of recognition skittered up Grace's spine. For a moment she thought she was going to faint. She gripped her reticule tightly and forced herself to drag in an even breath.

Oh God, of all the people …

No, she couldn't faint. Too much depended upon it, she warned herself as she forced steel into her spine. Fortunately her unlikely procuress seemed to have as much desire to further acquaint herself with her son's *special indulgence* as Grace did the woman who'd cast her onto the pavement after five years of loyal service three years before.

"Follow me, Miss Fortune." Her former employer led the way up a flight of stairs, not turning as she continued, "I'm assured my son will find you pleasing yet professional enough that he will be in no danger of forming an attachment. Not that there's any danger of David doing that."

David? Grace could barely keep up. Her feet felt encased in lead slippers. And yet, what was her alternative?

Shame weighed heavy on her shoulders. Oh no, David the Golden Boy had an idealised vision of women's virtue. He'd made clear his contempt and disgust for creatures like herself. No, this interview would not be long.

Passing a housemaid, Grace turned her head away, the fear of discovery almost debilitating. Although the fearsome widow Mrs Willowbank maintained two establishments, Grace knew her former employer took her personal dresser and at least one other servant from her Cotswolds estate to her London townhouse for the season. While Grace was no longer the Barton Manor parlourmaid they'd remember, she knew if one of the servants were to look more closely at her, like Brice the butler, or her old friend Jenny, they'd see through the trappings in an instant. Grace dare not risk eye contact with anyone.

Meeting David, of course, was unavoidable. Sick anticipation of his inevitable reaction made her heart thunder in her ears and sweat prickle her skin as they turned towards the sleeping quarters.

Breathe evenly and smile. Grace remembered receiving the same advice when she'd had to fill in for the footman at table during one of

Mrs Willowbank's dinner parties and when she'd first undergone training as one of Madame Chambon's "girls".

Now her carefully cultivated facade of disdain all but deserted her. For a moment she contemplated picking up her constricting skirts and simply fleeing for her very life.

But to lose courage now had consequences: her likely return to the dungheap of society, inevitably to become a diseased creature vying with the fresh dollymops to the capital who supplemented their poor earnings selling their bodies.

Nor would she ever know the answer to the greatest mystery of her life: the reasons behind the betrayal that had thrust her into this despised life of vice. For wasn't this her chance at last?

Mrs Willowbank stopped at a door at the end of a dim corridor and turned. "You know the rules?" She seemed reluctant to look Grace in the eye, for her gaze hovered just above the girl's head. "I was quite explicit. My son has reached his majority seemingly averse to the charms of the ladies."

Grace's heart hitched a little. That wasn't exactly true.

"However, he is to be married. It is a good match and the young lady worthy and apparently understanding of David's—" she hesitated "—deficiencies."

Even after all these years Mrs Willowbank's condescension fuelled Grace's anger. Better to concentrate on that, she thought, than her devastation at this latest piece of information..

She swallowed, the moment nearly upon her as Mrs Willowbank knocked then pushed open the door. It was not how Grace had imagined it, but finally she would find out why David had not been the loyal friend he'd sworn to be.

"David." Mrs Willowbank beckoned Grace to follow her. "I've brought you a visitor. Miss … Fortune is her name. She knows what is required of her." With a cursory nod she turned, closing the door behind her.

Blinking at the strong light that streamed through the windows, Grace took a moment to orient herself.

It was a large room, with a four-poster bed against the far wall.

Quickly scanning the familiar paintings on the walls she felt a confused pang to discover there were none of herself.

It was clear the room was more artist's studio than bedroom, for in the centre was a dais upon which was arranged a chair for the model. The very same chair in which Grace had sat for companionable hours while David painted her portrait.

A little distant was positioned an easel. Breathing in the familiar smell of oils and turpentine Grace blinked back the tears which burned her lids.

She breathed deeply, tensing herself against David's judgemental scrutiny, but though he'd risen at her arrival, his whole stance conveyed disinterest and his expression was trained upon an object in the far corner of the room.

While she waited for the shock of recognition to register on his face she tried to quell the spontaneous surge of longing for him with the reminder of what he'd done to her.

Proudly, she stared at him.

The silence continued.

With a sigh, David gripped the back of his chair, angled his body towards her and trained his gaze upon hers.

Through hers.

With horror Grace registered his vacant stare: the glassiness and the faint scarring around his eyes that nevertheless did not mar his fair handsomeness.

"A pleasure to meet you, Miss Fortune."

CHAPTER 3

Grace put her hand over her mouth to stifle her gasp. He could not see her? What terrible event had befallen him? Shock and pity coursed through her and she nearly burst out, *"David, it's Grace!"*

But she could not. Not like this. She could not even move.

"Not the man you were expecting?" His voice was bitter. Devoid of the energy and warmth she remembered. He made an expressive gesture with his hands. "My mother does not intend for me to disappoint my future wife. Of course, that's not the real reason she asked for … a professional. Apparently this is my birthday present."

When Grace said nothing he gave a short laugh, adding with a note of apology, "I am not in the habit of entertaining prostitutes. I'm not even sure what to do with you. Perhaps you'd care to take a seat and entertain me instead with your erudite view on the state of English politics." He shrugged, adding carelessly, "If I'm so very repugnant to you, you're free to leave."

Grace blinked, stupidly, only galvanised into action when he snapped, "Well, Miss Fortune, what's it to be? I can offer you nothing. Nothing you'd enjoy anyway."

Forcing aside the emotion, she managed to call upon the breathy, suggestive tone of the practised whore she was while she feasted her gaze upon him. "I don't do this for the enjoyment," she murmured, stepping forward and running her hands down his well-cut woollen coat, "but I believe in honouring a bargain."

He jerked at her touch and then laughed, a humourless sound that brought chillingly to mind David's cousin. The horrible thought that Laurence might be in residence made Grace drop her hands in fear. However the urgency to learn more of what had changed the young man before her from the ardent boy she'd loved compelled her to resume the charade . Seeing David like this, so helpless and vulnerable, unleashed a flood of tenderness which was fast eroding the bitterness she'd cultivated towards him. It was clear he'd met with some accident to his sight yet his dark eyes were still just as expressive. She was struck by the most powerful urge to touch her lips to his beautifully shaped mouth, just as she had …

… the night before they parted.

No, she could not afford to have him send her away. She twined her arms behind his neck and nuzzled him, adding, "So don't look a gift-horse in the mouth, sir. You'll have a wife, soon. Enjoy me in the meantime. That's what I'm here for."

"An honest whore," he said, crisply, though with less surety in his tone as he swayed, seemingly unwilling to touch her but not wanting to push her away either. "Still, lying on your back can't be too difficult a way to earn your living."

She was not surprised by the sentiment. David had been an innocent with a revulsion for women like herself. It appeared he still felt the same.

She was suddenly terrified he'd assert his moral compass and decide she should leave. That would never do. Not before she discovered more. She had to play on his fascination. Make him want to sample her wares now that her ridiculous longing for him had been so unexpectedly reactivated.

For she realised she was as susceptible to his vulnerability as she ever had been to his kind companionship.

"Honest toil is hard to come by when you've lost your reputation," she murmured, pressing herself to him and raising her hands to trace the contours of his beautiful face. "But an *honest* whore prides herself on giving value."

He swallowed and a nerve twitched in the corner of his mouth. It was clear by his reaction that he was struck by indecision, yet intrigued. The David she'd known would have been too disgusted by a woman of the night to suffer her touch. But then, he'd had Grace.

The fact he did not step away suggested that while he was prepared to give his future wife his name he'd not yet given her his heart.

Well, it would be a small victory for Grace to make him want her now, when she hadn't been able to make him want her enough to discover her whereabouts three years ago after his mother dismissed her.

Steadying herself with her hands on his shoulders she put the tip of her tongue to his throat, to his Adam's apple, as he swallowed his … Desire? Concern? Apprehension?

He shivered and with seeming reluctance his arms went round her, eventually straying to her lower back, as if he was both fascinated and afraid of moving beyond the realms of propriety.

Grace reached behind her and guided his hand to her lower back. Having been given permission, he gently skimmed his hands over the contours of her figure-hugging gown.

Yet it was she who had to stifle her arousal, forcing out the words, "Would you like to feel more of me?" as she placed his hands on her breasts.

He swallowed as he tentatively contoured the striped silk of her cuirass, making her weak-kneed with wanting as she rubbed herself against him.

His voice was full of doubt. "What will you do? What must I expect? I'm blind. A virgin."

"An honest whore will give you all the pleasure of which her body is capable," she murmured.

"Anything?"

She raised herself on tiptoe and ran her fingers through his fair hair, revelling in the springy softness she remembered so well. "Anything except a kiss."

He tilted his head enquiringly and Grace gave a soft, throaty laugh. "An honest whore does not tangle with a man's heart unless she's prepared to give him hers. A kiss is a dangerous conduit." She touched her mouth to his jawline, as close as she dared, whispering, "Now, if you like the feel of my breasts, you can unbutton me."

How different from the honest relationship she and David had once enjoyed—but if she were to survive this encounter she needed to block her mind to the past and maintain the charade.

He stiffened. "I'd rather start from the top," he muttered, groping helplessly before she grasped his wrists and brought his hands to her face. The face he'd caressed so many years ago. The face he'd called an angel's face.

A whore's mask. Smooth and ravishing on the outside, ravaged by experience on the inside. No longer the face he knew. She had no fear of being recognised. Only the desire to be close. To take what she could in the short allotted time and hope that her heart did not shatter.

Reaching up, she removed the hatpin which secured her veiled confection and placed it on the ground beside his chair. Angling herself to give him comfortable access, she guided his fingers to the neat ringlets trained to fall over one shoulder. Very different from the wild mane which used to cascade down her back when he'd beg her to loosen her housemaid's serviceable topknot.

At first he touched it tentatively, then he fisted both hands in it, his expression suddenly animated.

She drew back. "What is it?"

"The texture," he muttered. "It's the same texture." He shook his head, unwilling to say more until she pressed him, wanting to hear it. Wanting confirmation that the long hours of companionship they'd shared hadn't been only in her imagination.

"I loved a girl once—" His voice was barely above a whisper, "—who had hair like this."

"What happened to that girl?" Grace asked, willing him to recognise her and acknowledge that he had ruined her life. To say he was sorry for it so that …

She could forgive him.

"She betrayed me."

This was not what she'd expected. Gasping, she stepped back, causing him to drop his hand and say mockingly, "Yes, imagine it! I loved her yet all the while that she pretended to be my ally, urging me to stand up to my mother, promising to protect my most valuable possession, my most dangerous secrets … she was betraying me behind my back."

No, no, no … How could you think it? Grace's voice shook from the effort of reining in her heated denials. "How did she betray you?"

"I found a photograph—" He swallowed as he steadied himself with a hand on the back of the chair, his twisted mouth pushing out the words as if they were foul and bitter—"of *her* in circumstances no woman of any decency would allow."

Oh God. Grace stumbled backwards as she put her hands to her face. She knew which photograph. Laurence had forced her to sit for him. *Blackmailed* her. He'd spent the summer with his aunt and, to while away the dullness of country life, had indulged himself with the latest craze: photography. When he had her alone in the little room Mrs Willowbank allowed him to use as a studio he'd made her remove her clothes and drape herself over the plush chaise longue and then he'd …

David's voice was thick was emotion. He drew his hand across his eyes as if the image were still branded on his vision. "I saw what only *I* had ever hoped to see but here she was parading her body before … before the world." His voice dropped to a thread of bitter accusation. "It was the last thing I saw."

The silence drew out until she could bear it no longer. "What do you mean … the last thing you saw?"

David glared, seemingly oblivious to the hand she tentatively lay upon his shoulder. "I suppose it's part of your job to pander to me. To sound interested. To sound as if you care."

It was difficult not to betray the extent to which Grace *did* care.

She stepped forward and gently took both his hands in hers. "Whores have feelings, too."

This elicited a small laugh.

"And curiosity," she added.

Perhaps he needed an opportunity to unburden himself to a supposed stranger. Perhaps something about Grace made him trust her, for he went on, "My cousin invited me to his new photography studio to show me the portraits he'd taken of my mother. Of course it was his intention that I see more. *More* than just the face of the girl I loved. Laurence told me how much she'd wanted to be admired through the camera's lens … and more intimately. He told me how smooth and soft she was. How moist her lips were. Of the little mole on her breast."

Helplessly, Grace felt his pain as he twisted away from her, fisting his hands. "Her betrayal cut through me and I picked up the first thing that came to hand so I could hurl it at him and remove the gloating smirk from his face. A bottle. I had no idea it was acid. Something he used to develop his work. Laurence went for me. We fought and the bottle smashed, splashing liquid into my face."

Oh my God. Horror made her mute.

David had been blinded in a fight over *her*.

"But she'd already gone by then. The woman I loved. The woman I trusted." His voice hitched as he sat heavily upon the bed, hunched over with his hands covering his face. "Without a word."

No, that's not true, Grace wanted to say but she was helpless in the strange new emotional landscape she inhabited, caught between the urge to tell him everything while knowing the truth would only make things worse.

She heaved in a breath. "Do you see … *nothing*?"

He looked up, unseeing. "I'm aware of light and dark. Sometimes I wish I was dead … now that *she's* gone."

Grace fought to keep her voice steady, tears stinging her lids as she whispered, "Why did she leave?"

"Mother dismissed her when I went up to Cambridge for my first term."

Rage and hurt swept away her sympathy. Here was her chance to ask the question that had haunted her for three years—*Why did* you *do nothing?*—but his voice, harsh, bitter, cut in, giving her the brutal answer. "The girl who said she loved me had given herself to someone else. She was pregnant. Mother said her father told Mrs Medley, our housekeeper, that she'd run off to London with the blacksmith. I saw the way he looked at her in church but I never thought she returned his interest. But I was away at university and he was a handsome man, working now and perhaps persuading her I'd never marry her. I suppose that's why she took off her clothes for Laurence. So she could get money to be with her blacksmith."

She gasped aloud. *Lies! All of them! Well, except for her being pregnant.*

She reined in her emotions. Nothing she said or did would change a thing. It was some comfort David hadn't stopped loving her, though she forced herself to subdue the ray of hope that breached her hardened heart. Hope always had a bitter lining. In this case it was that the truth of what she'd become was worse than the fiction his mother had created.

If Grace told David his mother had lied, then what?

She'd only have to tell him that she'd descended to vice far greater than he could ever imagine.

No, Grace was not the girl he remembered. He loved the pure, idealistic Grace, full of hope for the future. Not the debased, ground-down whore before him who bartered herself, body and soul, to stop from starving. She might despise what she'd been reduced to but the fact was she was a whore.

Oh God, a whore who did this *with strangers for a living when all she'd ever wanted was to marry David and have his children.*

CHAPTER 4

"Forget the past." Grace forced the suggestive, sympathetic tone into her voice as she moved forward, drawing him to his feet so she could inveigle herself back into his embrace. "And enjoy the present. I can take your mind off your sorrows."

She might not have David beyond this evening but for the next hour he would be the lover she might have had if things had been different. It would be a bright memory to mitigate the miserable future which stretched before her.

Slipping her hands beneath his shirt she ran them up his smooth chest. No longer the chest of the sapling she remembered. Gently she rubbed his nipples, ridiculously gratified by his shivers of reaction. He was putty in her hands and his fascination for her and what she could do for him was growing. What would he think if she tried to entice him further down?

Dare she?

The Grace he'd known would never have been so bold and brazen but she was a woman who played on men's fantasies for a living. A whore who'd never experienced desire in the course of her work. Now, with the young, healthy body of the only man she'd loved showing increasing willingness, she was desperately conscious of her own lustful urges. They frightened her. How little time she had to revel in the intimacies she'd once hoped to enjoy for a lifetime.

He was highly aroused by the time she slid her hand into the opening of his trousers, his sudden hardening echoing her own need as she felt the rush of warm liquid pooling in her lower belly.

"Oh God, what are you doing?" he gasped, gripping her shoulders as she knelt in front of him and gently circled the end of his manhood with her tongue. Clearly he was caught between pushing her away and keeping her prisoner.

"I shall disgrace myself!" he warned as she trailed her tongue the length of his shaft before taking him deeply into her mouth, but she ignored him, caught up by her own responses to his growing excitement. She could feel her desire roaring in her ears. His breathing was coming fast and even, his body was tense and his hands fisted in her hair as she moved him deeper into the cavern of her mouth, flicking her tongue over the ridges of his swollen shaft, squeezing gently, pushing him back and forth.

"Oh God!" he cried, convulsing as he came. He could barely speak through his shame. "I'm sorry."

Exultant, Grace slithered upright and held him tightly, as if to comfort him, her heart pounding at the simple fact she'd elicited such powerful reactions. That *she* was responsible for giving her beloved David such pleasure. "A virgin does not have to apologise for the brevity of his first time," she murmured, her mind whirling, every sense on high alert as she kissed his earlobe, revelling in the intimacy, though he seemed caught up in confusion, not knowing where to put his hands.

She raised them to her breasts still contained by her low cut bodice. Again, so brazen. The Grace he'd known would never have done such a thing. The David she'd known would have been repulsed by such behaviour.

"You can undo me, if you like." She wriggled invitingly in his embrace and he seemed to gain confidence, his exploring hands fumbling with the row of tiny buttons down the front of her tight-fitting cuirass. Touching her lips to his right ear, she whispered, "There, I'll help you."

When the fabric fell away she quickly divested herself of her upper bodice, pushing him down upon the bed again and settling herself on his lap so he could feel her bare arms and the swell of her breasts above her corset.

At first tentative but with increasing surety he ran his hands over her skin, myriad responses reflected in his rapt expression. Grace closed her eyes and offered herself to him, her heart engaged like it had never been since she and David had been close.

"Is this how it's done?"

"Seduction?" she murmured as she snuggled against him and toyed with his nipples.

"Whoring."

Deflated, she froze. Whoring. Yes, that's all it was to him. She was a stranger. A woman off the streets sent to service him for an afternoon.

"Don't leave. I'm sorry." He pulled her back. "I didn't mean to offend you. You're very good and I need tutoring." Unseeing, he groped for her breasts, at first ashamed, then obviously enjoying their size and feel as he trailed his fingertips over their exposed fullness as if committing them to memory.

"Tutoring?" She heard the dullness in her voice. "You make it sound like a lesson when I thought I was here to *indulge* you. Would you like me to take off my corset so you can weigh them in your hands?" She did not add: *That's what many of the gentlemen like to do? It gives them satisfaction to weigh up the inventory.*

Without waiting for his response she stood up, guiding his hands to the strings at the back of the constraining garment. Twisting her head to study his concentration as he worked the laces, she was struck by memory. This was the way he'd once looked at her. Eyes bright with determination as his hands trailed over her—respectfully, lovingly—while vowing that the day he reached his majority and was free of his mother he would marry her.

"Very good. And now for my skirt. Here are the buttons. That's right. My, but you're very deft with your fingers." She took refuge in briskness, her tone falsely admiring. As her skirt slithered to the floor she kicked it aside. A shabby way to treat a garment which cost her what she'd have to earn through servicing more than two dozen clients.

Next, she attended to her princess petticoat, a simple, embroidered linen shift which she removed from over her head leaving her naked save for her stockings. A girl in her line of work had no need for the additional petticoat and combinations modesty required the respectable debutante or matron to wear.

"Sit down," she instructed. Once again she lowered herself onto his lap and brought his hands up to her breasts as she murmured in his ear, "Take your pleasure. It's your birthday, David. Enjoy the experience."

He jerked at the sound of his name but complied, smiling as he held first her right and then her left breast before kissing each nipple with touching reverence. "You liked that?" he asked in obvious surprise at her small gasp.

Grace nodded, her eyes closed as she surrendered to the unusual waves of pleasure elicited by his touch. He'd put his mouth to her breast and was stroking her nipple with his tongue. It sent a rush of feeling to her groin.

"Is there only pleasure on the man's side? I understand you must hate this work because it...degrades you, but is it true a woman does not enjoy sexual relations?"

Grace realised that he'd not seen her smile of pleasure. He'd taken her silence in answer to his previous question to mean she did what she had to.

Oh David, I've only felt like this in your arms, she wanted to say. But if he did not know who she was now, he never would. Grace wasn't sure which would be worse: to face his revulsion or to accept that she would never know pleasure from the touch of a man, again. "A woman can enjoy sexual pleasure immeasurably if her heart is engaged." Now she was again the professional he'd hired as she twined her arms about his neck and nuzzled his neck. But when she breathed in his familiar smell, the same sandalwood soap was a bittersweet reminder of happier times. *Don't cry,* she exhorted herself. Instead, she steeled herself to say, "You are to be married, David. Do you wish to please your wife?"

"Miss Lenders is a worthy young lady." His tone was uncertain as he stroked her naked back. "I'm told she's not unattractive. She's agreed to the contract, though I daresay I have the better deal." He gave a short laugh. "The least I can do is learn a thing or two to try to please her so she won't take a lover in the first year."

"Perhaps she loves you very much. You don't have much faith in a woman's constancy?"

"Experience has taught me to be mistrustful of what a woman says. I prefer to judge her actions." He tried to speak carelessly. "I like you, though. You feel … nice. Show me how to bring pleasure to a woman. To my future wife. Where should I touch you?"

Unconsciously, his hand was now gently trailing up and down the valley of her breasts creating whorls of sensation Grace had not experienced since David last caressed her.

It was difficult to restrain herself. She shivered with pleasure and longing, and whispered, "A woman's urges are just as strong as a man's if she desires him. Here, I'll guide you to her forbidden places. Those hidden, secret places she tells no one except those she trusts most in all the world."

Grace had used nearly those same words when she'd made her last promise to David. She'd not been referring to her body, of course, but to a hiding place for something they thought would guarantee their future; their joint happiness.

He stilled, frowning, as if his words had tapped into a memory, and his mouth opened slightly as if he would really ask the question Grace both desired and dreaded: *Who are you, really?*

But he did not and in the silence Grace guided his hand to her inner thighs. This was business and she'd do well to remember nothing more could come of it than the handsome fee David—or his mother, God forbid!—would hand her after she'd dressed herself and was preparing to leave this house.

As he resumed stroking her, Grace studied him, his remembered promise filtering through her body's growing sensitivity. "My annuity won't be much," he'd told her—it seemed a lifetime ago, now—"but it'll be enough for the two of us and I'll supplement it with my painting. I'll be a real artist, then." He'd patted the secret drawer of the escritoire where he'd hidden the letter upon which he'd pinned his future. Their shared future. The letter from Señor Borteli, a famous landscape painter in Florence who'd offered to make David his student for a year. The letter that would change both their lives in ways he would never know.

The past was the past, she reminded herself as she shifted in his lap to give him greater access to places he'd never before touched. No point in tormenting herself with it, though the physical was proving a greater torment than she'd thought possible.

She felt exposed as she'd never felt with any client. She was frightened to rest her hands on his head and feel his soft brown hair as he put his lips to the hollow beneath her shoulder blade.

He used to kiss her there when he stopped her after she'd fly in from the passage with a moment to spare between cleaning the drawing room and making the family's beds. Her contours would be different now, of course. She was no longer the scrawny servant he'd remember, with hands roughened from scouring pots and scrubbing floors.

"Are you cold?" he asked, and when she said she was not, he frowned. "Then why are you trembling?"

"You have a lover's touch. See?"

His pleasure was real when he felt her nipples spring to attention as he gently circled them before bringing down his face and again taking first one and then the other into his mouth.

Grace threw back her head and moaned softly, guiding his hand back to her inner thighs. "Feel what you're doing to me," she whispered and laughed softly at his surprise when he felt the slippery wetness between her legs.

"Is ... is it—?"

"It's called desire," she whispered in his ear.

"But how—?" He shook his head, unable to finish.

"It's something a woman cannot feign. The physical manifestation of desire comes from within. For a woman, that is," she added. "Men are different. If their desires were whipped up only by the women they loved there'd be no need for … whores."

Though he frowned, he was clearly enthralled by the responses he was eliciting through his increasingly bold exploration of the folds of her sex and the swollen nub at their heart. Excitement was fairly fizzing through Grace's veins, making her gasp and jerk as her sensitivity grew.

"You must be enjoying it. You're so wet," he marvelled. "Look at the effect it's having on me, too. I … didn't think I'd ever feel desire again."

Opening lust-heavy eyes, Grace grasped his growing erection, making him wince, his voice hoarse as he whispered, "You are obviously … practised at making a man feel he is your heart's desire. I hope you will want to come again."

Cradling him, Grace laughed softly, avoiding an answer as she murmured suggestively, "I would like to make *you* come again, but perhaps you'd enjoy it if our pleasure coincided. A woman's climax is as enjoyable to her as a man's. You've already seen how my pleasure escalates when you touch me here."

He laughed and increased the pressure on the area between her legs which most excited her while his other arm held her close.

"Oh, that is very enjoyable," she whispered, nibbling his earlobes.

Suddenly both his arms were around her and his mouth was moving against hers, his voice urgent as he pushed her back upon the bed. "I've been closeted from the world for three years. I know only a schoolboy's love." He squeezed shut his eyes as if he were in pain and added, haltingly, "I know you're accustomed to what we're *doing* now but…what about what you're feeling?"

"Never!" she told him with more sincerity than she had felt in three years, resisting the urge to arch up and touch her lips to his. "I have never been with a man as tender and willing to please a woman as you."

"It's your job to say that."

Before she could answer he added, almost roughly, "Why have you chosen this life?"

"In a brothel?" Rolling out from beneath him, she gave a bitter laugh as she stood. She had the strangest feeling she'd put him in danger of being singed by her wickedness. "At least it's better than the life I had."

"Which was...?"

"On the streets."

She did not miss the spasm that crossed his face. Revulsion. Yes, he ought to be repulsed. *She* was. She was half tempted to leave; to spare him and to spare herself. But bitterness got the better of her.

"The first time I sold my body was to get medicine for my baby."

"You had a baby?" His hand went out to her and she allowed him to draw her back, first to sit beside him on the bed. But then it seemed he wanted to hold her again and Grace had no reserves left to refuse.

"It's the reason I was dismissed from my position in a grand house." The familiar grief clawed its way up her gullet. "But the baby died."

"I'm sorry."

She could feel his sympathy as his hands roamed over her body, blazing a trail of sensation across her sensitive skin and scoring her vulnerable heart.

"Sorry that it died or sorry for me that it was born?"

"Both," he muttered. "The ... father didn't offer to marry you?"

She let out her breath derisively. "The father was a young gentleman visiting the house who believed he was as entitled to pleasuring himself with the servants as he was to the entertainments his hostess laid on for him."

He was shocked, clearly. Perhaps sympathetic, though her plight was common enough. He would know that.

She took a painful breath. "He forced himself upon me and when the housekeeper realised I was pregnant—before I did, myself, for I had no knowledge of these matters—she spoke to the mistress. My mistress dismissed me. Without a character." She trembled at the injustice, still just as raw as it ever had been. "And a girl without a character has little alternative but to become a prostitute, in case you weren't aware. So, take all the liberties you like, sir. There's nothing I haven't done and nothing that will shock me. Have you *really* never been with another woman since you lost the girl you loved?"

He shook his head, his expression bleak, his hands gently cradling Grace's face. "I'm sorry for your misfortunes. Mine are in a different league. Yes, I've lost my sight but often I think I'd still look towards the future with hope if I had *her* by my side. Despite what she'd done."

"Falling pregnant and running away with the blacksmith?"

"I would have forgiven her if she'd realised her mistake and wanted to come back," he muttered.

Grace stiffened. "Perhaps she was waiting for you to come after her and declare your love."

David gave another of his short, humourless laughs. "She'd have understood why I did not. Do you know, I kissed her for the first time the night before I left for Cambridge. The softness of her mouth and the way she breathed my name are the sweetest memories I will ever have." His tone changed. "And then she gave herself to another."

She could not tell him this was untrue so with the greatest self-restraint Grace asked carefully, "You say you've never felt desire since her betrayal? What about Miss Lenders?"

"I barely know her, but Mama arranged the match and Miss Lenders will be well compensated for being allied to a useless creature such as myself."

"Don't say that!" Grace cried, fiercely, jumping to her feet. "You're kind and handsome and you only need someone who loves you who'll be your eyes." She wished she could stop herself from trembling as she tripped out the platitude. "When Miss Lenders knows you better she'll be that person because she'll see you're a man who deserves a good woman's love!"

CHAPTER 5

"Please ... Miss Fortune!" David rose and pulled her back into his embrace, holding her tightly, muttering as he buried his face in her hair, "You are very kind to jump to my defence but I do not need championing. I am determined that when I marry I will forge a life independent of the one my mother has mapped out for me. She's always forced me to bend to her will."

Didn't Grace know that to her cost? Mrs Willowbank had determined David's future the moment he'd been born and studying landscapes with a master in Florence did not feature. It was why David had felt it safest to entrust Grace with Signor Bettoni's letter the night before he went up to Cambridge in his first term. He planned to visit a sympathetic cousin en route to borrow funds so that when he returned to Barton Hall he'd have all in order.

And Grace would go to Florence with him.

The letter. Oh God, if only there'd been no letter, thought Grace, none of this would have happened.

"I do not intend being an object of pity to my wife," David went on with growing emotion. "I intend to repay Miss Lenders for taking me on. So show me how I can do that. Show me how to make her desire me."

"Come with me," Grace whispered, reaching across to draw back the counterpane of the four-poster bed.

He seemed uncertain when Grace angled herself close and ran her hands down the front of his trousers.

"Let me take them off for you," she whispered, deftly working the buttons, enjoying the feel of his smooth flanks, resisting the urge to trail kisses from his ankles to his lips. She was too afraid their time would be cut short and she was determined, now, to be possessed by David in the fullest sense. The memory would serve as her protection when she succumbed to the inevitable with each future client. "Now climb onto the mattress. I'll join you there."

Almost desperate with need, Grace climbed onto the bed and laid her naked body over his. Instinctively his hands went to her rump, his palms cupping her bottom, sending spirals of heady desire coursing through her veins and making her sex throb with anticipation.

So many men.

She'd had so many men and now, at last …

"I think you feel sorry for me," he murmured. "That's why you don't regard me with the same revulsion you do your other clients." His breath tickling her ear. "I hope not, because …" He'd transferred his attention to Grace's inner thighs, where he'd enjoyed her responses earlier. His touch ravaged her with urgent desire.

"Because…why?" she whispered, pressing her cheek to his chest as she moved her body slowly, suggestively, over his. His erection pressed into her belly and she rubbed herself up and down upon it, sighing with the satisfaction of feeling it swell.

"There's something about you … I can't explain it. You remind me …"

The thrill Grace felt was truncated as he muttered, "Only it seems wrong to compare you."

"Because she was pure? And I am not?"

Grace raised her head and studied his face. His heightened colour was his only answer.

Forcing his painful words from her mind, she rose to a sitting position, reaching down to cup his balls. He gasped at the unexpected sensation, hardening instantly, holding his breath and clasping her shoulders as she gently squeezed.

"You like it?" Her voice was husky. Suggestive. The same tone she used on all her clients, yet what was in her heart was so different.

"I shall disgrace myself once more if you continue." His breathing was laboured. "Stop doing that. I want to feel you."

She remained sitting, straddled upon him as his hands roamed over her, as if he were committing her to memory. Grace registered his frown, his growing excitement as he contoured her with the concentration of a sculptor exploring the possibilities of his subject.

"I can feel you … like I can see you."

She breathed deeply and surrendered herself to his touching. How thrilling it was to again be the object of his enjoyment.

He raised his head as if looking for something, then pulled her down so he could kiss her breasts, gently suckling her nipples while he massaged her buttocks.

"I can imagine every part of you," he marvelled, drawing his head away. "I'm an artist. I can't paint you but I can … *make* you. I could make you in clay." His breath came faster.

So did Grace's. Electric impulses surged through her, excitement roiled in her lower belly and moisture bubbled between her legs.

"You can be my muse. I can sculpt you. I can."

Hope clawed at her, just a little more forcefully. Perhaps there really was a shared future for them …

"Tell me *everything*. Your hopes, your dreams, your disappointments. I need to know you from the inside. It's the only way I can create you."

His rising excitement coincided with the crashing of her hopes.

His muse? She'd told him enough, already. "If I tell you *everything*, sir, you will want nothing more to do with me."

At the dull resignation in her voice, he checked himself. "Are most whores as honest as you?"

Despite herself she gave a soft laugh. "We quickly learn when we must lie. But I am not lying when I say I want you to make love to me."

"You *really* want that?"

Ever so briefly she touched her lips to his mouth before drawing back in sudden alarm as the familiar longing surged through her. It was too dangerous. Before long she must leave him.

Probably forever.

"Yes, I want you." She heard the almost desperate note in her voice as she rose above him, rubbing her sex over his now rampant erection.

He held her tightly, his breath hot in her ear. "And I want you, too. Oh, God—"

She'd reached down to grasp his shaft which she was sliding the length of her slick entrance and back again. His breath was now coming in convulsive gasps which matched hers as she guided him into her slippery depths—and as he filled her she felt the most heightened sensation of coming home.

"David." She breathed his name upon the faintest of whispers as he withdrew slightly before thrusting into her again and she felt herself clamp over him as need and joy and pleasure swirled through her.

"Oh God!" he cried again as he re-entered her, his passions ratcheting up with unstoppable force on a journey she shared.

He was still little more than an untutored virgin and she didn't mind that he came quickly upon a final thrust for she was so ready, shattering around him, her brain whirling, her heartbeat pounding as she collapsed on top of him.

For a long time companionable silence enveloped them. The clock in the passage struck three o' clock and the sounds of carriage wheels from the street below lent a strange normality to the sensation that nothing and everything was changed.

David was the first to speak. Shifting her against his side so that her head nestled into the crook of his neck, he held her close as he gently stroked her.

He laughed softly. "I hope I can last a little longer the next time." He paused, then asked awkwardly, "Why did you have no one to turn to?"

Surprised by his interest, she decided to lay herself bare.

"My family refused to have anything to do with me after I … disgraced them. My mam gave me what savings she had and sent me to London, making me promise I'd never contact them again."

His warmth was comforting, the familiarity taking her back to the days when they could speak of so many things as he sketched or painted her: the many injustices Mrs Medley meted out and David's troubles concerning his controlling mama.

She snuggled closer and he reached across to pull the covers over her as she went on. "In London I became apprenticed to a milliner until she, too, dismissed me when I could no longer hide my growing belly. I used the last of my money to pay the midwife and was going to take the babe to the foundling home. I had no means of supporting either of us, of course, but the babe became sick and as I nursed it, I grew to love it. I couldn't let it die so I called a doctor but I couldn't pay him … or get medicine."

He frowned, indicating for her to go on. "The doctor suggested … I pay him in kind." She swallowed painfully. "I had no choice. He took me against the wall in the room where I slept because my baby was screaming on the bed. He came often after that—" She breathed deeply, "—until my baby died."

She glanced across at him. David's eyes were dark with sympathy as he lightly caressed her.

"Were you not able to get respectable work?"

"I tried." *Oh God, she wasn't going to cry, was she?* "But I'd been dismissed without a character. No one would employ me so I had to return to the streets until I was procured by Madame Chambon."

"Is she a good employer?"

"I can't complain, I suppose, though she knows how to make her money out of us girls. Nevertheless she's taught me how to hold my own with a duchess. I now speak like a lady, am fully versed in proper etiquette and I can converse on the current affairs of the day in order to entertain the customers. That's why Madame Chambon charges so much for one of her girls."

"And that is why you are here." Carefully he ran gentle fingers over her eyes, cheeks, jawline. "And for once I'm glad of my interfering mama and her high standards."

Smiling, he moulded her buttocks with the barest pressure. But the pressure she felt inside her was like nothing she'd known before. She'd been drained by the telling of her story but he'd not reacted with revulsion. He still wanted to touch her. The excitement she'd felt during their lovemaking was returning, and with even greater force.

She'd told him everything and it seemed he was ready to repeat the intimacies of earlier.

Now he raised himself, feeling his way over her until his body caged hers. One hand traced her hips. As if committing them to memory he stroked the jutting bones before sliding his hand into the juncture between her legs.

He grinned and murmured, "You really do like it when I touch you there." He slid his fingers deeper into her heat. They glided through her moisture and she shivered all the more.

He moved his face closer to hers and for a moment she thought he was about to kiss her, then he drew back, perhaps remembering her stricture, despite their earlier passion.

But, oh how she wanted to be seared by the heat of his desire—and it could be ignited by a single kiss, she knew it.

"That is …heaven," she gasped, opening her eyes to see his glazed with passion.

A great poignant need gripped her heart. She had him in thrall. He was her slave, and how she longed to enjoy him again in the fullest sense. To feel him stretch out his responses. To claim responsibility for tutoring him in how to be the best lover he could be.

She cupped his head and brought his face down to hers.

His response was immediate. Electric. His arms went round her, crushing her to him, his mouth encompassing hers completely. She could feel his heart beating fast and furious as he sucked her lip, burning her with the heat of his passion, his tongue tangling with hers, until she could take no more and thought she would drown of need.

"I want you," she whispered. "Now! Take me!"

"And I want *you*!" He felt for her entrance so he could position himself. "I want to show you I can be both willing slave and obliging master," he breathed with a touch of the old humour she remembered.

Over his shoulder her gaze raked the length of their bodies, so nearly joined as one. Just as she'd dreamed of for so long. He dipped his fingers once more into her silken heat before she felt the swell of his erection begin to breach her entrance.

"Oh!"

They gasped in unison, the sound a catalyst for the cataclysmic reactions that followed as he again sheathed himself fully in her.

"Dear God," he moaned, twining one hand behind her head to keep her face close to his while the other gripped her bottom. Her skin burned at his touch, her heart beat furiously and she thought she would die of pleasure as she felt his fullness inside her, a testament to his possession and, she could pretend for a brief moment, his love.

"Oh, David," she whispered on the faintest breath as together they bucked and rode each other to the summit of their pleasure.

With her cheek tucked into the crook of his neck she shuddered with him to the end.

"Oh, dear Lord, that was magnificent!" he crowed, holding her tightly, his breathing still heavy as he gently played his fingers against her sex as if her twitching amused him.

As if wanting to prolong the pleasure of their coupling at the same time as reassuring himself her responses were brought on by him alone.

She brought his face round so she could kiss him lightly, lingeringly on the lips.

He did not stop smiling. Reaching out, he touched her cheek, toyed with her hair.

Grace gazed into his eyes. They could not see, but they still registered the depth of his emotion. Did he feel this was more than the practised arts of a consummate courtesan? She'd certainly never felt this depth of feeling before.

David opened his mouth to speak and Grace tilted her head. This *had* meant something more to him. If she could feel it, surely he could, too?

Did she have the courage to speak the truth? Would he believe the woman he truly believed had betrayed him? A whore, what's more?

Resolve ebbed and flowed, deserting her as a loud voice sounded in the passage outside.

CHAPTER 6

"Good God, what den of iniquity have I entered?"

The sound of footsteps crossing the floorboards after the door was thrust open had David instinctively holding Grace to his chest in a gesture of protectiveness.

"Happy Birthday and all that, cuz. Is this the wicked little surprise Aunt Bertha funded for your majority? Let's have a look at her, then? I'll give you my verdict. You, after all, have only her word to go on—and your dear mama's—so neither are exactly reliable."

Burrowing against David, Grace gripped him as if he were her last hope. Horror clawed inside her like a frenzied beast. She didn't have to see who their visitor was. Laurence's arrogant drawl was ingrained in her memory. He was the man who had ruined her life. Ruined the life she and David had planned together. Destroyed her reputation, filled her with fear, sapped her of hope and now threatened to embroil her in his sick, poisonous power all over again.

"Can't you see I'm entertaining? Get out, Laurence." David spoke with more authority than Grace had ever heard.

She felt a tiny spark of hope. That she could survive this. Then she heard Laurence's laugh. Harsh and familiar. He never let anything go.

And he was not about to start now.

"Nice rump. Your mama chose a ripe one. Come on. Let's see what else she has to offer."

David's voice was crisp and Grace felt the effort it cost him to retain control.

"Get out, Laurence!"

She registered his cousin's advancing footsteps. David did too. And he was clearly concerned for her dignity for he rose from the bed, still holding Grace against his chest as he ordered, "Pass me the dressing gown from behind the screen. I'll be damned if you think you can thrust yourself in here with no requisite courtesies. Do as I say!"

To her surprise she heard Laurence's footsteps hesitate. Retreat.

Could she really be granted such a reprieve?

But no, he'd merely compromised to the extent of snapping the dressing-gown off its hook for now he was advancing towards them again.

The hated caramel tones filled her with revulsion as he protested, "No, no, allow *me* to help the lady regain her modesty."

The familiar arrogance, violence lurking just beneath the surface, made her tremble uncontrollably.

"I don't want your help." Grace buried her head further into David's chest and he held her tightly as if he really could protect her.

"She doesn't want you, Laurence."

"She hasn't seen me yet, little cuz. Why, I might be her next customer … if I like her. She gets paid by the client, doesn't she? Tell me, my coy maiden, was he good? It was his first time, though you probably know that already." He gave a mocking laugh. "I can promise you much more satisfaction."

David's fists clenched. For a moment Grace thought he would strike out, leaving her vulnerable, but he continued to hold her close.

She felt the coolness of the silk dressing-gown as it covered her shoulders.

Then Laurence's fingers digging into her upper arm as he jerked her away, forcing her head up to look at him.

The astonishment that swept away his arrogance held him frozen with shock, but not for long enough.

Not long enough for her to strike out, struggle from his grasp and make her escape.

Oh no, he was not going to let her go a second time. He was motivated by more than simple desire this time.

No, there was Laurence's pride. She'd fought against him when he'd first forced himself on her, screaming her disgust. Then it was just the two of them. Now he had David to consider.

"Oh my God, you little slut—it's *you*!"

His shocked exclamation was truncated by a burst of laughter as he gave her a shake to disorient her before holding her away from him, surveying her as a hunter might survey his prey.

"Presented to me on a platter, so to speak."

The relish in his tone was terrifying. "Dear me, but I did enjoy our last little encounter. I was so disappointed to hear you'd left without a word."

David put out a hand, his tone bleak. "You know her?"

Laurence jerked her out of reach, his mouth twisted in an ugly smile. "I've sampled her wares, yes. Tasty little morsel. I have a mind to have another go. What's your going rate these days?"

Grace struggled. For a moment she couldn't speak for the horror that was unfolding around her.

"Get away!" she managed to rasp. "I'd rather die than have you touch me again!" Her voice was rising. She could feel hysteria choking her. Laurence was in control. As he always had been.

David took a faltering step forward and Grace reached out, desperate to be within his protective hold once more, pleading with his cousin, "Let me go. You have no right to do this. You never had any right. You destroyed—"

Roughly, Laurence snatched her back to him, clamping his hand roughly across her mouth.

She bit into it sharply and with an oath he loosened his grip enough for Grace to pull away.

She turned, looking wildly for an escape, but Laurence was barring the doorway.

She was trapped. He would have her. Make her pay for belittling him. Then he would humiliate David by forcing himself upon her in this very room. She knew how he worked.

"What the hell!"

She jerked round. David had hurled himself upon the back of his unsuspecting cousin and the two now grappled on the floor, David on top. But a blind man would not hold the advantage for long.

Still, it would allow her time to escape.

Holding the silk dressing-gown about her, she ran towards the door. If she could just get back to Madame Chambon's she would be safe.

Her hand was already upon the doorknob when she heard David's cry.

Turning, she saw the determination with which he clung to Laurence, whose flailing fingernails had smeared bloody scratch marks across David's face.

No, she could not leave him. Not like this.

But what about *her*? Grace? The hatred in Laurence's eye should be enough to convince her that he would stop at nothing to satisfy his warped impulses. David was his cousin, his equal in rank. David would be all right.

But *she* wouldn't. An inferior from the gutter. Grace had to think of her own safety and there was too much at stake if she stayed.

She registered her expensive ensemble: cuirass and skirt, crumpled beside the chair near where the two men fought, her little veiled hat nearby. A sparkle of silver twinkled in a ray of sun that slanted through the window. She stared at it, confused at first before realising that here lay the answer. Protruding neatly from the brim of her hat.

Rushing forward, she seized the hatpin at the same moment Laurence grasped her ankle.

Oh God, she was going to fall.

Yet even as she felt her balance going she plotted how she could use the force of her fall and the angle of her trajectory to her advantage.

Her aim was not perfect but good enough.

With a scream of pain Laurence released her as the point of the hatpin drove through the thin flesh between his thumb and forefinger.

"David, hold him!" Grace shrieked as she sprawled beside them and with surprising agility David flung out an arm which found its mark, though Laurence would be only temporarily overcome.

Grace scrambled to her feet as she sought an escape for both of them, knowing Laurence's wound was not debilitating and that once he tore the deadly point from his flesh he'd be like a mad dog.

She lunged for her high-heeled half kid boots. Grasping the chair to balance herself she brought the right foot down sharply upon his hand, then bent quickly to snatch the hatpin from his grasp before brandishing it in line with his right eye. David was still holding him immobile.

"An eye for an eye," she hissed above his screams, as if she really could carry out the gruesome threat.

"Stop the bitch! David, she's mad!" Laurence shrieked, twisting his head from side to side while he tried to release himself from his cousins's grip. "She has a needle pointing at my eye!"

With shaking hands, Grace held the needle steady. Never had she felt so fuelled by venom. This man deserved everything he had coming to him. He'd destroyed her life. She drew in a breath and forced herself to speak evenly. "Tell David what you did to me. Tell him what you did and why you did it."

Infuriatingly, the corners of Laurence's mouth turned up. He'd stopped his shrieking. He drew out the pause while Grace's trembling increased.

Mary, Mother of God, please make him admit the truth.

She'd believed herself forsaken years ago but if someone would just hear her prayer she'd never ask for anything again.

Laurence gave a little laugh and swivelled his eyes in David's direction. "Would you believe what a whore will extract under duress?" he drawled. "David, I suggest it's time to summon the full force of the law before your afternoon's dalliance gets even more expensive and there's blood everywhere."

Tensely, Grace watched the play of emotions cross David's face. To her relief there was no uncertainty.

David shifted position, as if to anchor his cousin more securely beneath him. "Answer her, Laurence." There was a curious note to his voice.

Grace flicked her tongue over dry lips. "Tell David about the letter." Her whisper was barely audible. "About where you found it."

She registered David's new awareness in the level, warning tone he used to repeat, quietly, "Yes, Laurence, tell me about the letter. Where did you find it?"

His request was greeted by silence. Grace lowered the needle menacingly, aware Laurence had the power to knock her off balance again, and to burst from David's choke-hold but that he knew the risks he took to do so.

The silence lengthened. Grace made a small movement he was obviously unwilling to see translated into action, for finally he muttered, "I found it in Grace's room."

"*Grace's* room?" repeated David.

Clearly David had been expecting some momentous disclosure yet his tone registered shocked disbelief. "In the attic? What were you doing there?"

After a reluctant pause Laurence muttered, "Waiting for her. I had a proposition to make. While I was waiting I went through her drawers."

"How dare you?" David's voice dripped disgust. He gripped a handful of his cousin's hair and yanked.

Laurence howled and jerked his head. Not too vigorously, though, for Grace kept the needle positioned within a few inches of his eye. His tone was whining, self justifying as he replied, "Your mother was concerned at the inappropriate friendship between the two of you. She sanctioned me."

Grace drew in a shuddering breath then whispered, "She didn't sanction you to do what you did two days later." Hatred filled her, making her voice hoarse and unsteady as she demanded, "Tell David what your proposition was!"

Laurence twisted his head away from the point of the needle and Grace moved accordingly. He muttered, "I wanted Grace to be my photographic model. She was so willing to give you hours of her time to paint her I assumed she'd be just as happy to oblige me with a few moments to photograph her."

Grace lowered the needle a fraction. "Yes, but what did you propose … exactly?"

Silence.

Furiously, Grace stabbed the needle into his shoulder, raising it above his eye once again as he yelled with pain.

"All right, I threatened I'd show your mother the letter I'd found in Grace's drawer."

"Which letter?"

"The letter about going to Florence."

Grace saw cognition register in David's unseeing gaze as he asked, slowly, "So Grace agreed to let you photograph her provided you kept my secret?"

Laurence nodded but David couldn't see. "Answer me!" he said harshly and Laurence burst out angrily, "Grace came to my studio and I arranged her as I would any other model."

David obviously saw where this was going. Angrily he said, "Only you coerced her to remove her clothes." The bitterness in his tone grew. "And she did because she thought it was the only way to keep my letter … my secret … my hopes safe from my mother."

Laurence's silence was answer enough.

Holding her breath, Grace watched David battle the silent fury within before he screamed, "And then you raped her!" Seizing his cousin by the shoulders he raised him with unnatural force and slammed his head into the floor.

Grace watched the violence with grim satisfaction, Laurence crying out with pain as David continued to shout, "You raped her and made her pregnant! Mama dismissed her. She had nowhere to go. Her life was destroyed because of you! All our plans were destroyed because of you!"

"David, stop!" Suddenly Grace was frightened by the extent of his rage as he continued to pound Laurence's head upon the floor. His strength was being channelled from forces greater than any of them could control and Laurence's life was in danger unless David could be calmed.

The sound of the door grinding open and Mrs Willowbank's shocked cry made David drop his hands.

"My God, what is happening?" Mrs Willowbank rushed forward as David rose from Laurence's chest. With a cursory glance at Grace she spat, "And you ... Miss Fortune or whoever you are, get out! You're the cause of this, aren't you? I paid for a high-class prostitute, not a common whore."

"How dare you, mother?" David warned in a low voice.

Mrs Willowbank spun round. "I want the slut out of here."

"She's not going anywhere." David had risen. He stood, tall and straight. Confident. He took a challenging step forward and reached out for Grace, who stepped forward, relief making her shoulders sag as she felt his protective arm go round her. "This is not Miss Fortune and you will treat her with respect." A flicker of emotion crossed his face. There was a fraction of a second's uncertainty as he glanced across at Grace, almost as if she might object, before he pushed back his shoulders and said, "Miss Fortune is going to be my wife."

"Your wife?" Mrs Willowbank gave a shout of hysterical laughter. "Have you taken leave of your senses? She's addled your brain. Why, this creature has walked off the streets—"

"Where you and Laurence condemned her." David's voice shook but there was a hard, threatening edge that made even his mother flinch. "Laurence forced himself on her then you dismissed her. I hope you're ashamed. Yes, this is Grace who used to work at Barton Manor and as today I came into my majority and can do what I like, I *am* going to marry her. Just like I promised all those years ago."

CHAPTER 7

Six weeks later

Standing behind Grace as she leaned back against him, David smiled as his seeking fingers traced the delicate pattern around her eyes. A gentle breeze stirred the open shutters as they gazed out over the city.

"The sun is making you squint. I can feel its warmth on my skin," he murmured.

Grace shivered with pleasure. She felt lazy and peaceful. A little over a month ago she and David had sought comfort in each other's arms in David's London bedchamber just after Laurence and Mrs Willowbank had tried to direct their lives once more. They'd both been shivering, on that occasion, too. From fear.

The silence that had followed his mother's departure after David had again declared his intention to marry Grace had been a welcome contrast to the earlier shouting and shrieking, but it had been ominous, too. Grace already knew to her cost how unyielding—and unforgiving—Mrs Willowbank could be.

But David had held her close and reassured her—of his feelings and his unwavering devotion and honourable intentions. "There was something about you that felt so right from the moment I touched your hair," he'd whispered, nuzzling her neck. "I'd dreamed about you so often, I just thought it was me imagining you in a different guise."

Not for one moment had Grace imagined they were to enjoy a happy-ever-after. Men like David did not marry girls like her.

But David had refused to let her leave him, declaring she'd slink back into the underworld where he'd be unable to find her—which was just what Grace had intended.

Instead, David had helped to lace Grace back into her corset and put on her clothes so that by the time Mrs Willowbank had returned with a barrage of uncles and others she'd brought along to shore up her arguments, she could face her detractors with dignity.

She'd not even blushed when she'd recognised the family lawyer as a client who regularly enjoyed the offerings of Madame Chambon's salon though he'd turned crimson when she'd sent him a knowing smile. With her perfectly modulated vowels, her gracious bearing and her cool self possession, Grace could have passed for any of the fine ladies Mrs Willowbank might have introduced to her son, so David told her.

He'd told everyone else that Grace was infinitely more *preferable* to him than any of the fine ladies Mrs Willowbank had ever introduced to him. Not that he needed his mother's help to choose himself a wife—or her approval—he'd added. He'd done that for himself and as he was twenty-one with an independent fortune, he could do what he liked.

He'd made the most of his authority.

As the fine linen curtains of their honeymoon villa billowed about them, Grace exhaled gently, twining her hand up behind her to cup David's beautiful cheek. "In the distance I can see the Basilica di San Miniato al Monte. There are rolling hills—"

David stopped her words with a gentle finger upon her lips. "A mountain behind, and the red roofs of the village in front. You don't need to tell me, Grace, for I carried this scene in my heart and my head every day I was in Cambridge and dreaming of when you and I would come to Florence to take up Señor Borteli's offer."

"And now we are here." She twisted in his embrace to rest her head upon his chest. A strong, muscled and comfort-inducing chest that belonged to a young man who knew his mind. He'd made that clear before Mrs Willowbank had departed with the uncles and lawyers and goodness knew who else.

And he'd made Grace his wife.

"Come in," Grace now called out in reply to the soft rap upon the door.

"Señor Borteli is here to see you and he's brought a friend...a sculptor." The little maid curtsied. "Shall I send them up?"

Grace drew in her breath and squeezed David's arm. "A sculptor? Is there something you've neglected to tell me, David?" She felt ridiculously gratified to see the light dancing in David's sightless eyes as he enveloped her in a hug. It was so easy to read him. He'd been keeping this secret until he knew he'd not disappoint her.

David nodded slightly as he turned towards the maid who was awaiting orders. "I think your mistress needs just a moment to prepare herself, Maisy," he said. "You've always known just what she needs for every occasion so why don't you fetch the jewels you think she should wear when she sits for the portrait that will make her the toast of Florence."

"Yes, sir."

Grace smiled. Maisy had been invaluable in assisting them in their flight from England. While Madame Chambon's exorbitant fee had been settled by Mrs Willowbank in advance, Grace knew her employer would not release her without a battle, so Maisy had bundled up Grace's most valuable belongings and met the eloping couple secretly at the docks. Naturally Grace had been in need of a lady's maid and the girl had been overjoyed to step into the role.

"So, not only is my portrait to be painted by Italy's most famous portraitist?"—Grace cupped David's face and touched her lips gently to his—"I am to be modelled in clay by the city's most eminent sculptor?"

David gripped her wrists lightly, his lips parting in a smile, his eyes alive with warmth and love. "That's what I hope to become by the time I've been properly instructed. And you, my darling, will forever more be—as you were in the old days—my muse."

The End

FORSAKING HOPE

CHAPTER 1

W*ilfred Hunt*

If there was a name to tip Hope into the abyss of despair, she was hearing it spill from Madame Chambon's lips now as the older woman directed Hope to take a seat in the reception room, presumably so Madame could loom oppressively over her.

With her hands on her ample, expensively padded hips, Hope's benefactress—procuress, employer, and gaoler were other monikers—sent Hope a beetling look that needed no interpreting. Regardless of Hope's true feelings, Hope must project the required show of warmth and delight at being the *chosen one*.

Madame patted the side of her faux curls. Years of hot irons had reduced her hair to the texture of wool, but her crowning glory these days was supplemented by the lustrous locks of those girls who dared cross her—before they were thrown back into the street from where most had come.

Nevertheless, Hope had to make her resistance clear. Surely Madame, who knew her history, would understand her loathing for *this* man, above all others. "I shan't do it," she whispered. There was little evidence of the wilful child and wild adolescent who'd been the despair of her family. "I won't—"

Outside, the noise of the traffic rumbling over the cobbles and the shrill calls of competing vendors settled upon the tense silence. Madame Chambon's other girls, ranged around the sumptuously appointed room on red velvet upholstered banquettes, watched the exchange with prurient fascination. Hope knew it had been a calculated ploy of Madame's to conduct her interview in public so that Hope would serve as an example to them.

No one crossed Madame Chambon.

The shrill cry of a fishmonger caused Madame to look pointedly out of the window. With something between a smile and a sneer, she smoothed a tangerine Marcel wave. "Is that where you plan to return, Hope? The gutter?" Her nose twitched, and in the sunlight that filtered into the room, the grooves chiselled between mouth and chin were thrown into harsh relief, highlighted rather than hidden by the thick powder she used to conceal her age.

Madame Chambon's comfort, now and into retirement, depended on obedient girls. Hope knew that as well as anyone. She'd had to bury her rebellious streak just to ensure food in her belly.

The Frenchwoman raised a chiselled brow and began to pace slowly in front of her girls. A painter with an eye for beauty would have been ecstatic at capturing such a spectacle on canvas. The discerning young man-about-town who visited 56 Albemarle Street frequently admitted to being overwhelmed by the range of delights Madame Chambon's girls offered in addition to the visual.

"You forget yourself, Hope. I put a roof over your head and deck you out as handsomely as Mr Charles Worth ever did for his most discriminating customer." There was acid in Madame Chambon's tone. "But for me, you'd be starving and glad of the pennies you could trade for a grubby stand-up encounter in a dark alley." Madame Chambon thrust out her bosom and breathed through her nose, her response a calculated warning to the other girls, arranged in various languid poses about the ornately decorated reception room, that intransigence would not be tolerated.

"Mr Hunt has requested *you*." She paused, and when Hope

remained silent, though her stance and expression left no one in any doubt as to her horror regarding this enforced assignation, went on. "Remember what I told you—what I tell all my girls when they first come here? The past must be forgotten the moment you step over my threshold. You are reborn, remodelled, refashioned into the most exquisite delectation of womanhood. A marquess, a prince, is well recompensed for the tidy sum he hands over in order to enjoy your sparkling wit, to converse with you in French, or if he chooses, on philosophy...to enjoy your charms...and," she added significantly, "your gracious hospitality and tender ministrations to his needs. That is our agreement, and you are no different. If Mr Hunt wishes *you*, Hope, to attend him at his residence, then you will go."

Faith, one of the kinder girls, patted Hope's arm in silent solidarity. Hope didn't expect any of them to speak up in her defence. Not when they all relied on Madame Chambon as much as she did to provide them with the necessities of life. Anything more than that was part of a strict contract that indentured a girl for life, unless she was able to secure a generous benefactor to settle Madame's severance bill. The fine clothes were part of the charade, necessary to entice a more elite clientele. Hope's exquisite wardrobe did not belong to her, though she'd have forsaken all the Spitalfields silk and Valenciennes lace for the freedom of the gutter and to be mistress of her own destiny—and her body—if she could only be sure of a plate of gravy and potatoes every second day.

Closing her eyes, she hung her head, the carefully coiffed curls that fell forwards brushing against her tear-streaked cheeks. It was as well that they not be in evidence. Tears, weakness, vulnerability were like a red rag to a bull where Madame Chambon was concerned.

"How long...do I have to prepare myself?" She was not so stupid she couldn't admit defeat when there was no alternative. Obduracy was beaten out of one, but tears ensured a girl got the very worst next assignment. Their clients weren't *all* marquesses and princes, though they did require a very fat pocketbook.

"Tomorrow."

"Tomorrow." Hope repeated it in a leaden tone, and stared at her hands clasped in her lap; white-knuckled. As white as the rabbit-fur that edged her fashionable black-and-white striped satin cuirass. Hope had the tall, slim figure suited to the scandalously tight tie-back skirts that were all the rage, the back flowing into a train adorned with elaborate swags and trimmed with bows. She'd turned heads the length of Oxford Street as she'd promenaded along the pavement following a walk through Hyde Park earlier that afternoon. In fact, for the first time in two years, she'd almost felt happy as she'd pretended a sense of freedom in the afternoon sun, blocking her mind to the prison to which she was returning.

She drew in her breath and forced herself to be brave, knowing the punishment she'd invite for daring to speak her mind. "Please tell Mr Hunt I will see him again *under sufferance*."

Madame Chambon's voice was surprisingly caramel. "Well then, now that you have made your objection clear, Hope, you will be pleased to hear that Mr Hunt's desires are not only motivated by fond memories of your no-doubt mutually satisfying congress. I believe he wishes to acquaint you with news of your family."

Hope hid her shock. "I have no family." With care, she modified her tone so it was as leaden as before though emotion roiled close to the surface.

"Not even a sister?"

Hope raised her chin. Here was the chink and Madame knew it. The woman did her research.

Aware that the other girls who surrounded her were tense with anticipation, Hope struggled not to respond. Camaraderie existed at surface level, but one never knew when it might profit one to have the dirt on a fellow prostitute. It was, clearly, another reason Madame Chambon had chosen to make this conversation public.

"Mr Hunt will see you at nine tomorrow evening," said the so-called Frenchwoman who, it was whispered, was from the gutters of Lambeth, not Paris. "At his apartments in Duke Street. Now go and prepare yourself for Lord Farrow who is pacing the drawing room in anticipation of how you might entertain him this evening. Married to a monolith like the venerable Lady Farrow, he likes his girls vivacious and free-spirited. There'll be less coin in your pocket if you sully the transaction with that long face, Hope."

CHAPTER 2

Hope was received in the drawing room of his lodgings.

He was as handsome as she remembered, though it was a dispassionate observation. Wilfred Hunt's striking Adonis looks were not all that distinguished him, Hope knew.

"You look well, Hope. The new style suits you." He indicated the princess-line bodice of blue velvet over the striped blue and white bustle hobble skirt. Hope had been aware of his undisguised appreciation as his gaze followed her progress from the doorway after she'd been announced, to the Chippendale chair upon which he'd invited her to sit.

She inclined her head and he lowered himself onto a delicate chair opposite her, resting one elbow on the writing desk beside him as he leaned forward, his expression searching. They might have been two old friends and he was favouring her with a confidence.

"But not in a talkative mood, it would appear, so I will get to the point."

Hope steeled herself not to blink. She'd not give him the satisfaction of showing she cared anything for what he might have to say; much less that she was afraid.

"You are acquainted, of course, with our old friend, Felix Durham."

She stared. *Why state the obvious?*

"He's in London."

That was hardly surprising.

"I thought he'd like to see you." Wilfred's tone was falsely conversational.

"Why do you suppose that?" With an effort, Hope kept her voice neutral. She was giving nothing away.

Wilfred studied the half-moons of his fingernails as he shrugged. *He was testing her. Trying to needle her.* "You're right, of course. You were on good terms with his sister, though, were you not? Letitia?"

"Our paths crossed."

"She's dead now."

Hope clenched her teeth. "I'm sorry." She wouldn't ask how. The less questions she asked of Wilfred, the better. He'd told her in such a cold way as to disarm her. That was the way Wilfred operated. Always going for the weak spot. Hope had liked Letitia on the few occasions they'd found themselves together.

"Typhoid. She and her brother were infected, he worse than she, so her death was a shock. Poor Felix has been inconsolable. That's why his friends thought they needed a novel idea to cheer him up."

Hope could see where this was going now. Though not why. She gripped her reticule more tightly, if only for something to occupy her hands, and stared stonily at him.

Wilfred sighed, shifted in his chair, then said with sudden irritation, "Despite what you think, I've asked you here because I want to *help* you." He paused. "If you'll help me."

A small laugh escaped Hope before she could catch it. "You want to help *me*? Frankly, I find that very hard to believe." She cleared her throat. "Naturally, though, if there's anything you want, you don't even have to ask me. You never did—before."

"No need for the snide tone. You were foolish, Hope. You put me in an impossible situation! What was I supposed to do?"

Hope rose. She'd not expected to upset him so easily though Wilfred had never found it easy to control his temper. She glanced at the door, glad it was the middle of the day with a house full of servants scurrying about the back corridors. "I certainly will not help you if it has anything to do with Mr Durham."

He glowered, not rising, his fingers tapping the tabletop. "Sit down, Hope. I'm surprised at your attitude. I thought you rather liked Mr Durham. Or is it on principle you intend to refuse any request I make of you, Hope?" His nostrils flared. "Your sister is in London, rubbing shoulders with high society. She's a lovely, sweet little thing. So blonde and delicate and obedient. So different from you, Hope. Not surprisingly, there are high hopes she'll make a fine match, though, of course, there's little enough with which to launch her. You don't want to be the one to stand in the way of Charlotte's happiness, do you?"

Hope was already halfway to the door, but she stopped, calculating whether it was foolish to make any kind of response.

"I thought that might make you see sense." Satisfaction dripped from his tone. If Hope could have scooped it up and thrown it back in his face, she would have.

"Don't think you can blackmail me, Mr Hunt."

"Mr Hunt, is it now, when we were on such familiar terms?" He was gloating, now that he saw he had the advantage as she turned. "Come, Hope, don't be churlish. Come back to the table so you may hear what I have to say. It's hardly onerous, and you'll earn yourself a pretty penny into the bargain."

"I don't want to involve myself in any bargains with you, Mr Hunt. I've been burned once before, in case you've forgotten."

"Through your own carelessness, as I said. Now." He reached across to pull a piece of parchment from the escritoire, dipped his nib into the inkwell and began to write. "You won't be doing anything you haven't done a thousand times before," he muttered, not looking up as his pen ran across the page. "And you'll be making an old acquaintance very happy, not to mention ensuring your sister has as successful a debut as such a lively, enchanting beauty could wish for. Indeed, that is how your dear Charlotte is these days. Lively and enchanting. The belle of London Town." He sent her a beatific smile. "You might say, she's the *real* hope of the family."

When he'd finished writing, he snatched up the paper, waved it in the air a few times, then folded it and placed it in an envelope.

"There you are, Hope. Your instructions," he told her when she reluctantly returned. "It'll hardly be a chore considering Mr Durham is such a handsome, personable gentleman. At least, my sister thinks so, though the noble, honourable type tends to stick in my craw, to tell the truth." He leaned across and forced her fingers over the parchment. "Come on; smile, for God's sake. There's always something for you to complain about, isn't there? And now I've given you an assignment you *should* enjoy since Annabelle recounted to me the look she intercepted that made her cry into her pillow so many nights since."

Hope turned her head away. How well she remembered the look that Annabelle Hunt had intercepted.

Madame Chambon had failed to unleash the sobs of despair that had been so close to the surface yesterday, but they were perilously close to being unleashed now.

CHAPTER 3

The noise from 23 Half Moon Street could be heard from the pavement as Hope stepped out of the hackney into the yellow glow of a gas lamp. She paid the jarvey, took a few steps towards the wrought iron gates that surrounded the elegant town-house, then paused.

This was the moment of truth. She could carry on boldly, right up to that front door and confront the 'what might have been', effectively ending all those beautiful daydreams with the truth of what she'd irrevocably become.

Or she could turn around now and effectively tell Madame Chambon to go to hell. And Wilfred, too. Yes, there'd be a glorious split second of satisfaction before she'd be cast out in the three-seasons-old dress she'd been wearing when Wilfred had delivered her to Madame Chambon's exclusive Soho brothel.

Daydreams. That's all her thoughts of rebellion were.

Just like her fond imaginings of what might have developed between Mr Durham and herself if things had been different.

Even with all the spirit in the world, Hope had long ago accepted that only Madame Chambon stood between her and starvation.

"Good evening, Madam, please come in. We've been expecting you."

She supposed it was hardly surprising it wasn't the butler who opened the door and invited her in with an extravagant flourish that almost caused the young man before her to lose his balance. The no doubt disapproving family retainer would have been dismissed for the evening, as suggested by the sounds of revelry within. Hope was surprised. Had Mr Durham changed so much or was he nothing like the rather serious gentleman she'd thought him? She'd been attracted by his earnestness tinged with a suggestion of suppressed passion—his character had seemed in direct contrast to her own wild, rebellious spirit—so that when he'd taken her hand at the Hunt Ball and drawn her into the shadows *that last night,* she thought wistfully, the greatest excitement had rippled through her.

His gaze had been intense and filled with longing. As if he were yearning for something he feared he could never have. That's what it had felt like to Hope, tremulous and aching with the knowledge they could never bridge the divide that separated them. She, the penniless vicar's daughter, revelling in her special evening before she was shipped off to her governess position, and he, the son of the great Durham family of Foxley Hall, the venerable manor that had looked down upon the rest of them for the past four hundred years.

But that was all in the past, and there was no look in the eye of the clearly bosky young man currently leering at her that suggested a longing for what he could never have. More like a brash assessing as to whether he might sample the wares before Hope was led like a lamb to the slaughter—the surprise cheering-up gift for Mr Durham, as she'd been informed.

Bile stung the back of her throat. What would Mr Durham think?

And did she have the courage to do what she wanted, which was to turn tail and run?

Instead, Hope clasped her reticule to stop her hands from trembling and adopted her most dignified manner as she inclined her head. She'd honed deference to a fine art at the risk of a backhander from Wilfred, and as the price for survival working for Madame Chambon.

"Well, well, I was told Madame Chambon's girls rivalled the Goddess Aphrodite for beauty and pleasure-giving," the young man went on, standing aside to admit her. "You certainly do not disappoint."

Hope stepped into the passage, trying to put dull resignation ahead of pure panic. Her palms were slick with dread, and she hoped she was successful in concealing the rapid, shallow breathing that might make her more of a victim. Evil relished vulnerability.

The young man closed the door and cast a look of appreciation the length of her stylish scarlet velvet bustle skirt, following the line of her wasp-waisted cuirass to where it lingered on the swell of her breasts above the tightly fitted bodice.

"You are not the gentleman I'm here to see," she said in quelling tones. "My time is precious. Thank you, sir."

He blinked rapidly a few times, seemed to gather his wits, then preceded her up the passage, saying over his shoulder, "Now don't go speaking so harshly to Felix, will you? That's why you're here. To cheer him up. I'm Ralph Millament, by the way."

Cheer him up. She swallowed painfully.

"I say, are you coming?"

Mr Millament blinked owlishly through the three yards of gloom that separated them, for Hope had dug in her heels. She couldn't do this. Not for all the tea in China, all the fashionable gowns from Madame Soulent's, and three years worth of good food and reliable shelter. It was too much. How could she even trust Wilfred to keep his word when he'd proven himself such a cad?

A door just behind her was thrust open, filling the corridor with noise as two gentlemen nearly barrelled into her in pursuit of a young lady who disappeared, giggling and shrieking, into another room.

Somehow, in the process, Hope was knocked like a skittle towards Mr Millament who'd started towards her. He caged her hand on his arm and marched her quickly up the stairs saying, "Poor fellow's been in a blue funk since he lost his sister, though he's always been the serious type. Not quite like this, though. No; nothing like this. My friend Beavis and the other chaps wanted to find a lovely lady such as yourself the last time he was under the great black cloud of despair, but Felix would hear none of it, so this time we thought we'd take it upon ourselves. We'd hold a great party and invite a girl just for him." He sent Hope an appreciative look. "My, I would say you are his idea of perfection."

Hope was about to ask why he thought that having a prostitute brought in would cheer up his friend if he'd previously rejected the idea, only Mr Millament had just thrown open the door to a scene of such total disarray that at first Hope thought the room was unoccupied.

It was a man's bedchamber. Hope had seen enough of those to recognise one when she saw one. The large four-poster looked as if it had seen a great deal of action lately, the counterpane half on the floor; the sheets twisted.

A chair near the washstand was upturned.

Hope turned to look at Mr Millament, who patted her on the shoulder. "Bit of a ruckus earlier. Nothing to worry about, my dear. Just go in and see what you can do to bring a bit of comfort to that poor lost soul over there." He sent her a wry smile. "The old fellow had a run of bad luck last night, and now his bride-to-be is in high dudgeon. Saw it all at Lady Mildew's rout last night and it was not a pretty sight. He's definitely in need of something to lift his spirits."

He'd started to go on but Hope raised her hand for silence, saying, "If he's about to be married, I'm not going in."

"Lord, come back. I'd have thought morality was the last of your considerations. Besides, it was a figure of speech."

Hope was surprised to see real concern in his eyes.

He shook his head vigorously. "All right, he hasn't asked her yet, though she's been in the wings for as long as I can remember. Don't know if he can bring himself to take the final plunge, for all she's not going to give up. Poor Felix. He's in dreadful shape. You really are our last hope."

He pointed to the bed, and Hope saw what she had not before.

There was a man, prone, lying face down upon the mattress, half under the covers. How she could have missed that was impossible to speculate for the man was quite naked. His long, muscular legs, lightly dusted with dark hair, ended in a very manly pair of buttocks.

Mesmerised, Hope's gaze travelled from his buttocks—where her eyes lingered—up the length of his spine. There was just the right amount of flesh covering his bones. He looked like a man in the prime of good health, though she could not see his face. His ears were instantly recognisable though. There was the slightest point to the tips. Perhaps a characteristic that would go unremarked by anyone who hadn't gazed from the back pews each Sunday at the neighbourhood's most eligible bachelor; first with interest, then with growing appreciation, and finally with excitement at the fact he seemed conscious of her.

He'd confirmed this the fateful night of the Hunt Ball, telling her he'd been awaiting the right opportunity to approach her, which seemed ludicrous since he was the catch of the neighbourhood and she just the vicar's daughter. A penniless one, at that.

She turned back to Mr Millament but he had gone, closing the door softly behind him, and Hope's fond memories of the past were exorcised by the shocking reality.

And of what she had to do.

She stared at the figure on the bed. She sniffed. An unfamiliar, not unpleasant aroma tinged the air. No, she had smelt this before. Once she'd been amongst a party of Madame Chambon's girls invited to a Soho den of iniquity where a strange substance had been smoked through a water pipe in one of the rooms she had mercifully been spared from having to enter. Grace, who'd accompanied her, had been required to dance an exotic dance with veils, to recreate a dream that had visited one of the men smoking this drug. Opium.

She put her hand to her throat. Mr Durham was an opium eater? Isn't that what dangerous Lord Byron had called them in his poem a generation earlier?

Her horror turned to tentative relief. If he believed himself in the grip of an hallucination, surely he'd believe her appearance was just a dream? When their encounter was over and he had no memory of it—she hoped!— she could live with her pride intact, and her heart not quite so eviscerated.

The man groaned. She supposed it *was* Mr Durham. She only had his naked back, buttocks, and pointed ears on which to make a judgement for he still lay face downwards on the pillow.

Hope took a step forwards, and was visited by an excitement so out of character, she thought *she* must be the one hallucinating on just the smell of the drug.

Why, if Mr Durham thought all this just a dream, she could indulge her own wildest fantasies. Ones she'd never had when she'd last seen him, for, as a young girl just out of the schoolroom, her wildest fantasies had gone no further than what might happen in a less-populated corner of the local Assembly hall.

Of what might happen during that fateful assignation he'd organised in a hurried whisper the night of the Hunt Ball. The assignation at which she'd failed to appear.

Now that Hope had become acquainted with the desires of London's Upper Ten Thousand—well, it felt like it, though it was really only a handful of the gentlemen who fell into that category—she'd learnt what men enjoyed. Mr Durham, as a pink of the ton, would no doubt have followed the conventional model of masculinity: taken a wife based on financial and family considerations whom he'd consider it only right to revere for her virtue, and a mistress to pleasure him in bed. Hope must have no illusions that the gallant gentleman who'd laughed away her embarrassment at losing her slipper during the waltz, who'd *nearly* kissed her, would have been any different.

So, if Hope was going to save Mr Durham from his demons as Mr Millament had exhorted her to do, she supposed her erstwhile admirer would enjoy imagining a dream along the lines of doing more than just kissing the debutante who'd failed to meet him at his proposed secret rendezvous.

She took a tentative step forwards, and craned her head as far over the bed as she could to ascertain the intensity of Mr Durham's slumber.

He did not move.

She sat down on the mattress, felt it dip beneath her weight while she eyed the prone gentleman for any sign of movement.

There was none.

Now that she was this close, it was very tempting to stretch out a hand and stroke his dark brown hair back from his face. Was he as handsome as she remembered? Or had the demons wrought a dissipation she'd see written in bloodshot eyes and a ruined constitution? Hope had observed that happen often enough to the privileged gentlemen who bought her time and her body.

When there was no response, only his soft, steady breathing, Hope stood up and went to the writing desk that was littered with a dozen drafts of a letter he'd not finished beyond, "My dearest Annabelle…" "Annabelle, my dear, I'm sorry…." "Forgive me, Annabelle, but…" "Lovely Annabelle, I'm afraid that…" Hope didn't have to do more than glance across the surface of his desk to see these, but other crumpled letters written on his signature pale blue writing paper littered the floor.

A niggling worm of disquiet unsettled her even more. *Annabelle*? Of course, there was more than one woman named Annabelle whom Mr Durham would know.

Was *this* lovely Annabelle the cause of his demons? She wondered what Mr Durham had done that he would wish to beg Annabelle's forgiveness. Was he desperately in love with this woman he'd wronged?

Who was Annabelle?

A freshly minted debutante or was she, in fact, Annabelle, the squire's daughter and if not Hope's nemesis, then certainly a determined and competitive miss who'd had no fondness for the vicar's daughter during their years growing up. More to the point, was this Annabelle to whom these pleas for forgiveness being directed, in fact Wilfred's sister?

A soft groan from the bed made her whip around. She mustn't be caught snooping. There were dire consequences for the girls about whom such complaints were made by their gentlemen customers.

Nervously, she ran her hands down the figure-hugging lines of her polonaise, toying with the dozen tiny buttons and wondering if she had the courage to undress.

Of course, she'd undressed a hundred times before. Or rather, she'd mostly *been* undressed. It's what the gentlemen liked, though clearly, Mr Durham was not in a position to do anything.

She worried at her lower lip as the fingers of her right hand toyed with the tiny top button of her cuirass. Right now, only Mr Millament knew she was in the house. She could leave and no one would be the wiser, including Mr Durham. This was business after all—and not a business she'd chosen. Mr Durham would have absolutely no idea if he had or hadn't performed. Or, if she'd serviced him as required. Dear Lord, this could be Hope's lucky day. The easiest money she'd ever made while enabling her to retain her pride.

But she couldn't bring herself to retreat. The impulse to touch him was too great, and she put out her hand.

Then hesitated, horrified at her brazenness. Disgusted to realise that *she,* in fact, was the one dissipated by loose living. For didn't she want to climb into that bed beside him and slide her naked body the length of his lean flanks as a tribute to all the 'what might have beens'? She was past the frailty of falling in love, but that didn't mean her body didn't crave connection with the one human being who had made her heart beat a little faster and a little more raggedly during her brief girlhood. What a naïve innocent she'd been in those days.

Those were the days when Hope had…well, hope. She could truly believe only good things would happen as she'd closed her eyes, half swooning in the arms of the dashing, handsome man who'd held her on the dance floor with such restraint; and who was now sleeping within inches of her seeking, tentative hand.

A snatch of music drifted through the open window, a breeze stirring the papers on the escritoire beneath. Hope remembered that she had more than just the usual job she performed as one of Madame's girls.

Wilfred's job. He'd made it clear what was at stake if she didn't carry out his instructions.

She tossed back her hair and grimly set to work undoing the tiny buttons that extended from just above her décolletage to her waist. If the paperwork was at Wilfred's behest and the payment for sexual favours at Madame's, then Hope was going to have something for herself.

While she set to work divesting herself of her clothes, she did not drag her eyes from Mr Durham's shapely buttocks, flanks, or handsomely constructed shoulders. He was as finely put together as any man she'd seen.

When she'd wriggled out of her cuirass, unbuttoned her skirt, and slithered out of the heavily upholstered bustle cage, she stopped to consider her options.

Could she *really* desire this? The feel of skin against skin?

Every day of her life was a constant battle to retain what barriers she could between what she was forced to do and her inner self.

Sighing gently, she sat on the bed, half undressed, and placed her hand on the mattress within a hair's breadth of touching him. This couldn't be more different. This was the man who'd once represented hope in her otherwise joyless life. Without her darling sister, Charlotte, to protect, and the gentleman of the manor about whom she could daydream, there'd been precious little else to get excited about. Nothing Hope did could satisfy Mama who never stopped harping on about the sacrifices she'd made to rear and nurture a child as ungrateful as Hope.

The night of the Hunt Ball had represented a turning point. First, the Hunt itself, when she'd fallen and Mr Durham had galloped to her aid, and then the ball that followed in the evening, when the light in Mr Durham's eyes, the pressure of his fingertips against her cheek, had seemed to promise so much.

Even now, the memory was fresh of how her skin had tingled all over, and how her nipples had hardened. She'd felt embarrassed at the time. Such bodily sensations were alien to her, but the fact that Mr Durham had whispered a final urgent request to meet him in private at the church before she went to Germany was—then and still—the most thrilling thing that had ever happened to her.

It seemed extraordinary that after that fateful carriage ride that would take her from her home forever, she'd ever see Mr Durham again. In truth, Hope never *had* wanted to see him again. She simply couldn't bear to witness his disgust.

But here she was now with that very same lovely man—only he was fast asleep and in the grips of an opium dream if she was right about the water pipe by his bed, and the lingering aroma.

She trembled. Did her desire make her weak? Or was weak with want a power in itself, now that she had the choice to use it as she chose?

Here was her chance to feel what this man had silently promised through the mere pressure on her fingertips and the look in his eyes. His desire had pierced her as he'd asked her to meet him on the way to catch her train. The intensity in his gaze had left her in no doubt as to his feelings.

Hope closed her eyes as grief welled in her breast. One lingering kiss would have been enough to have sustained her through what awaited her in a cheerless chateau in Germany, far from friends and home.

Hope had long before accepted her fate. She was not wanted at home, but nor had she wanted much. She'd lost her heart, and any indication that one desirable man felt something for her that went beyond simple regard was to be nurtured.

She'd nurtured it alright. Through that shameful year with Wilfred and all the men since, she'd nurtured that precious, pristine, innocent joy of a future that was different from the one that had been thrust upon her.

She wore only her corset now. The intricacies of the unlacing required help, and usually the gentleman enjoying her charms for that evening was only too happy to oblige.

With trembling fingers, Hope untied the laces of the final petticoat and let it slither to the floor. Now, she was naked from the waist down, two creamy mounds swelling from the top of her corset. This was not how Mr Durham would expect to see her, but then he'd never know it was her.

And that was how it should be.

All Hope wanted was to enjoy one physical encounter in her life that created in truth the sensations she had to simulate in order to leave a client satisfied: the show of desire, lust, craving for whoever was paying her. And, for the aftermath, just the right degree of admiration, appearance of being sated, a hint of wanting more though not to the extent he'd propose another round. Lord, not that. No adoring prince of the realm, or noble, however handsome, apparently besotted, had been worth that.

But this man, with his kind, earnest, blue-grey eyes, his reputation for proving himself so much more worthy than his father to run an estate so important to the livelihoods of the local district, was different.

Flicking back the dark ringlets that fell over her right shoulder, Hope put one knee on the bed and leaned over. He stirred a little as the pressure of her weight caused the mattress to dip.

Her heart ratcheted up a notch. Would he turn and open his eyes, registering horror as he realised what she'd become?

It was a very real possibility, so she must prepare herself. She hesitated. There was still time to retreat with her dignity—and her money, she mustn't forget. Her eyes strayed to the writing desk. Could she bring herself to do as Wilfred demanded?

Shame scalded her as she considered the ramifications. If Hope carried through with her desires—her own bodily desires—then Mr Durham would realise what she'd done, albeit at Wilfred's behest. He'd know *she* had betrayed him.

Yes, he'd add betrayal to her list of sins on top of his scorn and disgust.

A sliver of hope drifted through that train of thought. He would *if* he was in a state to register what was going on around him.

He was murmuring now. Unintelligible words. That woman's name amongst them. Annabelle. The woman to whom he was writing. His lost love? The Annabelle Hope knew?

She leant forwards and put out her hand. He could dream he was having intimate relations with someone he'd once admired even if it was just a little for a short while—and he could attribute it to a dream, never knowing it was Hope in the flesh—or that she had taken something from his pocketbook. The note Wilfred wanted as proof that she'd discharged his mission.

Hope glanced towards the table where she'd seen a carelessly discarded leather pouch, out of which spilled a few loose coins, suggesting there was more where that came from.

But Hope was not a thief, and Wilfred could not force her to become one, for all his threats.

She hung her head. She did have some dignity. Enough, at least, to gracefully withdraw before she ran the risk of shredding her soul.

With a sigh, she rose. She couldn't do this. One more lingering glance and she'd quietly dress herself and leave.

Carefully she extended her body across the mattress and ran her hand through the air, just an inch above the back of his head, closing her eyes as she imagined what it would feel like to touch him.

It was far too dangerous to get any closer, and she should have realised this before.

But she could dream.

Just as he could.

With an unexpected stirring to life, he rolled onto his back, his arm arcing through the air, collecting Hope's hand along the way. It was as if he expected a woman to be there, for his beautiful mouth stretched into a smile and, although his eyes were still closed, he reached for her, gripping her hand more tightly as he drew her across the bed; tugging, sighing contentedly as he settled her on top of him. He chuckled as he skimmed his fingers down her contours, lingering over her breasts which surged out of her corset.

Hope caught her breath, suspended between the thrill of what might happen next and pure terror.

"Beautiful!" he declared, opening one eye as his hands cupped her bottom, and his mouth latched onto one of her breasts. "Delectable!"

he declared, his eyes closed again as he teased out a nipple and rolled it over his tongue.

Hope could not have torn herself away if she'd tried. Since she'd met this man, she'd wanted to feel his hands gently stroking her face, his lips touching hers. She'd hoped so much, as she was taking the carriage to meet him, that this might happen.

It hadn't, of course. And that was the reason she was here. A pragmatic bitterness encased her heart—necessary if she were to survive her calling—but there was still enough feeling there to register the deep and painful ache of loss and regret.

It was gloomy, but light enough for Hope to study the face she remembered so well as her flesh tingled at his touch. She felt him harden beneath her as he continued to knead her buttocks, and although she straddled him, she was careful to keep her distance. She did not intend this to be a grubby encounter that was finished before it was begun.

She should not let it proceed, either, but while he was enjoying himself in such blissful ignorance, she could continue a little longer.

He brought his hands up to cup her face.

And then he opened both eyes and Hope waited.

Waited for his shock, his disgust, his utter repulsion.

But after a flare of confused surprise, he simply stared at her with the most beatific smile and murmured, "I knew you'd come one day." He sighed, a gentle shudder of pure happiness. "Now, kiss me, so that I know you're real."

Hope avoided kissing the men who paid for her, but she needed no urging now.

She smiled down at him, wildness at the possibilities presenting themselves surging through her. And then, with exquisite slowness, as she savoured what was about to come, she lowered her face to touch her lips to his.

He moaned softly, tightening his arms about her while his manhood strained against her belly. Yet, he made no movement to enter her. Like her, he seemed to want to prolong the exquisite prelude to the inevitable coupling.

Without warning, he flipped her over, caging her with his body, holding the side of her face with one hand as if to protect her, while the other rubbed gentle circular movements over her highly sensitised skin of her inner thighs.

The touch was like a promise met; the sensations he evoked all she'd dreamed of while his eyes bored into her. As if he couldn't believe what he was seeing.

She arched into him, using her fingertips to contour his high, noble forehead, his fine aristocratic nose, the smoothness of his cleanly shaven jaw, before she trailed her hands downwards to explore the contours of the body she'd seen only in well-cut hunting or evening clothes.

And then, in the greatest of daring movements, she reached out to explore his maleness, that which was so terrifyingly out of bounds during the brief time they'd known each other.

Her nipples were so hard they were positively painful, but all the better. She wanted to feel everything. She wanted this to remember. Her always. The culmination of her girlish hopes and dreams.

Closing her eyes, she tasted the saltiness of tears unshed in the back of her throat. This was exquisite. She wanted the moment to last forever.

He shuddered as she gripped him, then rolled her onto her side so he could pull her against him, at the same time feeling for the moistness that would leave him in no doubt as to her desire.

A great contentment edged with excitement found itself in a soft exhalation as he found just the right spot. He was perceptive enough to her needs to register it, and with a short laugh of satisfaction, he set himself to toying with that most sensitive, most private part of her.

Hope gave herself up to the growing intensity of excitement within. It was clear he was as invested in pleasuring her as he had clearly desired a woman to give him pleasure. It accorded with the man she knew. The handsome, kindly, and honourable man who'd captured her heart. A man who needed a woman right now. Her heart hitched as she thought of Annabelle. Was he thinking of her? Imagining her in Hope's place?

It was her job, she accepted, to be proxy for all the erotic fantasies of unfulfilled reality, but if this were the only way to enjoy Mr Durham's attention—his kisses, caresses, and pleasuring—she'd happily submit.

As she felt the pressure within her build, she gripped him harder with one hand while she clenched her other in a fist and tensed her body to maximise the wave of pleasure that would be the culmination.

"Come, my darling girl," he whispered, increasing the speed and pressure within the moist, swollen folds between her legs. "My beautiful girl, come."

Her breath came in short, sharp bursts. She felt the sweat break out on her forehead, and her body moved in concert with his.

"I want you…" she ground out, rolling onto her back and gripping his buttocks, exerting all her strength to bring him to her, "…inside me."

He didn't need much coaxing, breaching her entrance with an ecstatic cry as he began to pound his enthusiasm.

And she matched him, movement for movement, trading on his excitement to reach her own climax in a simultaneous outpouring of mutual abandonment.

Except it was more than that. Their bodies were as one. He'd worked to ensure her pleasure matched his, and now he was holding her tight, stroking her face, her back, murmuring to her.

As if he knew her intimately in mind as well as body.

As if he loved her.

When she was certain he was sleeping, Hope quietly rose and dressed. Her body pulsed with life and her mind felt reinvigorated. Mr Durham had loved her, believing her a figment of his dream, believing her to be Annabelle. And she'd been happy to be his fantasy. Until tonight, she'd never experienced sexual pleasure. Who'd have imagined it could be so satisfying?

She ran her hands down the side of her modish ensemble, pulling down the little veil of her neat, pert hat as she took a step backwards, still studying the beautiful man on the bed.

He looked peaceful, a gentle contentment replacing the tortured expression he'd worn in his sleep, before he'd opened his eyes and seen her.

The power of love, she thought as she plucked at her skirt to make the swathes and bows sit just as they ought. Perhaps he'd trade on what he'd gained from his lovemaking with Hope to make the necessary overtures to Annabelle. Maybe, on the strength of what he'd enjoyed just now with Hope he'd ask Annabelle to...what? Marry him? Forgive him?

Regardless, Hope's job was done. She turned and put her hand on the doorknob before she remembered. But as she glanced across at the escritoire, encountering Mr Durham's beautiful naked body along the way, she knew she had not the heart to do as Wilfred had demanded.

He'd exerted as much power over her as she ever intended he would again.

CHAPTER 4

Hope didn't expect to wake the following morning feeling so renewed. It was nearly noon which was early, for most of Madame Chambon's girls would have been up all night, including Hope. She'd climbed sleepily into bed at dawn, her body still alive to the touch of the man she loved.

Yes, loved. She realised that now that she'd had so much experience of the male sex. He'd changed something within her.

She could never have him, of course. She fully understood that. But there was a strange glee to the thought that she'd tasted him. Lain with the man of her choice, and that he'd touched her as if he truly cherished her.

But as she stared at the dancing beams of morning light playing over the walls, her glee slowly turned sour. Tears stung the back of her eyes as she acknowledged that last night's brief moments of pleasure would likely be the only pleasure she'd ever enjoy. She was destined to live out her few remaining years of youthful promise within these walls, unless she was lucky enough to find a more accommodating benefactor than Madame Chambon.

Loneliness, ugliness, penury. These were what awaited her.

She rolled onto her stomach and buried her face in the pillow as there came a rapping on the door before it was opened by Minette bringing her the usual morning croissant and hot chocolate.

"An' there's a letter fer ya, too, miss," the girl said, placing the tray on the side table. "Mayhaps it's good news like the letter I brought Miss Marguerite from the fella proposin' to set 'er up in 'er own 'stablishment. Ain't that what ya girls all dream of?" She handed Hope the cream envelope as she turned her attention to the grate, picking up a small black brush to begin the routine brushing and polishing.

"We have lots of dreams here, Minette." Hope dragged herself up against the pillows and turned over the letter, trying not to feel excited for she knew the letter could not be from the only person she wished to hear from.

A newspaper clipping dropped onto her lap, and she stared at it, a clutching fear in the pit of her stomach as her sister's name caught her eye.

Who had sent this? And why?

Her fingers were trembling so much she had to rest the clipping on the counterpane so she could read the announcement of Charlotte's engagement to Lord Hartley, heir to a vast family coal empire. A gala ball was to be held the following Saturday, hosted by his *Lordship's* family.

Heavens, this was a love match?

Hope's heart began to skitter. Their father had been a poor clergyman. Hope had left the vicarage to become a governess. At the time, Charlotte had been only fourteen. A schoolgirl with long flaxen plaits and a sweet disposition. She was to follow in Hope's footsteps. Lord! Not the one Hope had ultimately taken, but as a governess, for there would be no money to launch Charlotte with the wardrobe she'd require as a debutante.

That is unless Great Aunt Catherine had done for Charlotte what she had not for Hope. Relaxed her purse strings just a little and funded a small opportunity for the child of her long-dead brother's daughter. It didn't sound likely but what other explanation could there be?

But what did the whys and wherefores matter if Charlotte had found a man who loved her sufficiently to ignore her lack of position and dowry.

For the third time, Hope read the clipping, desperately trying to understand more than the words would divulge.

But as much as she exulted in this great opportunity for her sister, a dull sense of inevitability was gnawing away at her core.

Who other than Wilfred would have sent her this? He was the only person who knew Hope's whereabouts. The clipping had been unaccompanied, but it wouldn't be long before he would send a repeat of his menacing threats in a different form.

Hope clenched her fists as the old rebellion rose up within her. She would resist. She would *not* be Wilfred's emissary of evil if it meant harm to either her sister or the man she loved. Mr Durham was an innocent. Uncorrupted and pure—unlike her. If he was tormented by his feelings for another woman, taking relief from opium was no worse than blanking out the nightmares with a few drops of laudanum. Laudanum had been Hope's undoing but it had been a long time before she'd been able to cure her addiction. Initially, she'd used it to block out the disgust she felt at herself until she'd started hallucinating and then lost her vigour. Laudanum was most definitely not the cure-all it purported to be.

Carefully, Hope tucked the letter into its envelope and slipped it under her pillow. She had no illusions that something terrible would follow such good news.

THE DEMAND CAME THE NEXT DAY. HOPE TOOK THE LETTER FROM Madame, who'd summoned Hope to her private sitting room in order to ensure the communication contained no money.

As expected, it was a threat from Wilfred which only hardened Hope's determination that she would never be Wilfred's plaything ever again.

When Minette entered Hope's room at four o' clock that afternoon to help her with her evening's toilette, Hope was in tears.

The young servant was used to finding Madame Chambon's girls in tears, so she just sighed and asked Hope if she'd like to lie down and she'd get her a few drops of 'tincture'.

Hope, dressed in an apricot and cream silk dressing gown edged with lace, continued to pace between the iron bed with its elegant rose satin bedspread and the window and shook her head. "I need to think clearly; I need my wits about me." She waved the note in her hand, not looking at Minette. "I must make an important decision."

"Yer overset, miss. A little laudanum never did no one any 'arm."

But although the girl loyally unstoppered the little glass vial on Hope's dressing table and poured a few drops into a glass of water, Hope knew the danger the innocent-looking tincture of opium represented. Tempting though it was, she needed to be sharp-witted. Sharp enough to outwit Wilfred.

Yet how was she to manage this when she'd thought Wilfred had already done his worst?

With another sob, she smoothed the crumpled cream missive on which Wilfred had penned his evil demands, and her vision blurred by tears, read it for the hundredth time.

It began as if he and Hope were old friends. Couldn't she just imagine his delight at Charlotte's engagement, and that he'd been invited to attend the grand event at Lord Hartley's family home the following Saturday. What a sad thing it was that Hope could not go, despite the bonds that bound the younger sister to Hope who adored her so.

Wouldn't Charlotte be devastated to learn to what depths of vice and depravity Hope had sunk? But not to fear, Wilfred would never hint at Hope's whereabouts much less her employment.

Indeed, Wilfred would be assiduous in ensuring no taint of scandal attached to Charlotte that would blight her extraordinary matrimonial conquest.

All Hope had to do in order to rest easy on that score was whatever Wilfred told her to.

And so, outlined in Wilfred's letter, was another demand that she return to Mr Durham's lodgings and, by whatever means available to her, secure what she'd failed to do the first time.

"Mr Durham's pleasure was purchased at great expense, but you failed to deliver upon your obligations, other than be the whore to surprise and delight him," Wilfred had written. "From what I hear, Mr Durham's addled wits at the time rendered him insensible to your true identity. This time, your visit will be at your expense for I have not the ready to outlay such an exorbitant sum for your dubious charms. But service him, you will. Otherwise, all of London society will be speaking in hushed and horrified tones about sweet, innocent Miss Charlotte Merriweather, tainted forever by the sister who can be bought by anyone with a fat enough pocketbook."

THERE WAS NO ALTERNATIVE, OF COURSE. HOPE HAD EXPLORED EVERY avenue, including disappearing into the night, but without friends and family she had no one to aid her, and the inevitability of living in the gutter before too long prevented her from leaving her current employment.

As for any possessions for which she might redeem a few coins, Madame had covered this too. The girls' wardrobes were kept under lock and key, while payment was dealt with by the proprietress. Even when girls returned from a job, Madame took measures to ensure they secreted no tips upon their person by having them searched by her assistant, a bony, elderly woman called Mrs Whippet who looked like a dirge-singer and carried out her duties as her name suggested.

Therefore, it was with weary resignation that Hope presented herself upon the doorstep of Mr Durham's lodgings the following afternoon, her heart hammering as she contemplated in what state she'd find Mr Durham. Though more to the point, how he'd find her.

"Miss Moore, what a pleasant surprise." Mr Millament, charming and dapper and not two sheets to the wind as on the previous occasion, raised his eyebrows in enquiry as he invited her in, using her assumed name. "Felix is a changed man. He's seen the brightness of the future beckoning him when the past threatened to weigh him down forever." He led Hope up the now-familiar corridor of a much quieter house. At Mr Durham's door, he stopped and turned. "He'll be delighted to see you again. Felix spoke as if you were too good to be real, but obviously, he must have been convinced you were not a figment of his imagination. Nevertheless, it is a surprise to see you at this time of day since he said nothing of it to me, but I am his friend, and I do not judge."

If this were meant to be reassuring it had the opposite effect. Yet there was no other time Hope could have come. She had a client that evening and now was supposed to be her rest time. But Wilfred had given her no option to resist his strictures if she were to save Charlotte from her shame by association.

Unable to answer with more than a wan smile and brief nod, Hope put out her hand to balance herself against the flock wallpaper. The silence was oppressive and her knees were shaking, but she hoped her fear was not branded on her face. She'd perfected the art of looking impassive. In fact, her ability to show no emotion had driven Wilfred to violent fury on more than one occasion.

"Thank you, Mr Millament."

"Not at all! I'm just glad you're here for I know you'll do my friend the world of good."

Nervously, Hope worried her lower lip as a sluggish dread enveloped her. What else could she do but follow through? She was imprisoned by what Wilfred had turned her into. And that was compounded by the need to prevent a great tragedy befalling the one person in the world Hope would sacrifice her life to protect.

Hope was about to stay the dreadful inevitable with a question, but before she had a chance to even open her mouth, Mr Millament had thrust open the door declaring, "Felix! Your angel has returned," before closing it abruptly, plunging Hope into gloom.

CHAPTER 5

Only the light from outside penetrated the window, below which she could barely discern the figure of Mr Durham seated at a writing desk.

Hope felt for the support of a nearby table, afraid her legs would give way before she was able to hold herself tall and erect.

Meanwhile, straightening at the intrusion, the handsome profile had transformed into a fully rendered man, the brooding dark eyes and sensitive mouth of a poet providing a fascinating contrast to the strong jaw and broad shoulders of a pugilist. Still half in shadow in the recess of the window embrasure, he regarded her with a puzzled frown. She could see by the creases in his forehead and the tilt of his head that he hadn't recognised her.

Yet.

Hope half turned. There was still time. She could leave now and he'd be none the wiser. She'd been too weak to do so the last time, but she'd survived, unrecognised and with her dignity intact.

She'd not succeed this time. Mr Durham was fully in charge of his wits today. He looked as if he'd been intent upon some business, his demeanour alert, his movements charged with purpose as he'd folded the page upon which he'd been writing as he turned.

Hope wasn't sure what to do. Surely there was some other way to discharge Wilfred's demands without exposing herself and destroying what little pride she had left?

Awkwardly, she stood near the end of the bed, a few feet into the room. It was late afternoon. Perhaps, in the poor light, he'd not recognise her. After all, it had been so many years. More than two, for the other night didn't count when he'd thought her a figment of his dreams. A ghost blazing through his imagination.

"Miss Merriweather!"

His exhalation of astonishment made her freeze in shock. He *couldn't* have recognised her from afar. From such a distance?

He rose, his expression one of the greatest shining pleasure, as if she truly were the incarnation of his dreams, his wildest hopes. "Good Lord, is it really you? After all this time?"

He took a step towards her, his smile tentative, hopeful, while he extended his hands. "Is it *really* you? Why…you are as lovely as the day I last saw you."

Hope didn't know what to say. The truth would extinguish the light in his eyes, and at the same time obliterate the least bit of pleasure she was about to derive from this exercise. Yes, most definitely it was better to retreat now. She could just pull down her veil and hurry out of the room and up the passage, letting him believe he'd imagined her all over again.

Before she could decide upon an action, he was striding across the room, one hand outstretched as if he feared she was about to do just that, and he was determined to stay her at any cost.

"Who brought you here? Surely not my friend Millament who obviously thought you…someone else." With a look of horror, he glanced over his shoulder at the bed behind him, muttering, "Dear Lord, forgive the error! Please, let me usher you to the drawing room. I can't believe I'm seeing you in person when I've searched for you for so long." There was both unutterable relief as well as uncertainty in his expression. And his concern for her reputation was as keen as if…

She was still the innocent governess he remembered.

Hope stood her ground, calmly putting her hand on his wrist

when he would be too forceful in implementing genteel manners as she prepared to utter the most difficult words of her life.

"I was here the other night, if you recall, Mr Durham." Her shoulders dropped an inch, but she didn't drop her gaze from his face. He needed to know the truth. The truth of what she really was. And that she wasn't the incarnation of all his fanciful day dreamings in which she was the angelic creature he'd set upon a pedestal. That's certainly how it looked as if he'd interpreted it, and it was not an easy image to destroy.

He paused, seemingly suspended between the greatest excitement and a slowly dawning reality of what she was trying to tell him. Very slowly dawning, she could see.

She clenched her gloved hands, concealing them in the folds of her skirts. Better get it over with. After all, she'd come here to destroy his illusions.

Taking a deep breath and pushing back her shoulders, Hope put both her hands upon his forearms and looked up into his eyes. It was an strangely intimate gesture given that the only physical intimacy they'd shared was when he'd held her on the dance floor following their almost kiss after she'd been thrown from her horse. Yes, that had been a day of intimacy she'd remember forever; two images of sweetness and purity that had sustained her through the many tawdry episodes since. For wasn't sleeping with a prince tawdry if she didn't love him—even if she'd lined her pockets—or rather, Madame Chambon's—with five hundred pounds to give him the pleasure?

"Miss Merriweather?" It was a question. She'd not given him much to go on, and he'd not wish to draw the association.

Lord, but it was hard to wipe the smile—uncertain thought it was now—from his handsome face. However, she had no choice.

"Yes, Mr Durham. It *is* me."

It was time to redraw the lines of their relationship. If he were a man who enjoyed transient pleasures like most of her clients, then he'd be in heaven very shortly.

The trouble was, she knew he wasn't—unless he'd changed.

The shadows had deepened in the few minutes she'd remained

standing near the door. Mr Durham continued to gaze at her, his rapture tinged with increasing puzzlement.

Hope knew she was at the peak of her beauty and powers in what she could offer a man. Madame Chambon had turned her into a rare prize who could entertain the most discerning client as much with her wit, her scintillating conversation, and her sharp mind as with her body. She'd had to pass many a test before she'd been accepted into the inner sanctum. Half of Europe's royalty had been her reward and, before her retirement in a few years, she could hope for a handsome annuity as the favourite courtesan of one of those who'd formed a special fondness for her. It was the way it worked for the lucky girls at Madame Chambon's, and the best Hope could aspire to.

Did Mr Durham know how it worked? The rules?

She forced herself to remain strong while she awaited the moment of revelation.

He shook his head. "You say you came here…before?"

Was he pretending he didn't remember their night of madness? Of impassioned lovemaking?

Of course he was. He simply couldn't reconcile it with the Miss Hope Merriweather he'd daydreamed of kissing in the shadows outside the ballroom where they'd hurried to be alone for a few moments.

Fate hadn't favoured them, for Annabelle Hunt had issued from the brightly lit ballroom and, like a homing pigeon, discovered them making plans. *In the church vestry. Tomorrow. Before you catch your train.* He'd gripped her hand and whispered the suggestions, though Hope had not had the opportunity to confirm anything before Annabelle had insinuated herself between them.

Shortly afterwards, Mrs Merriweather had bundled up her daughter into a warm cape and hurried her to their carriage. Why could she not be happy for Hope? Mr Durham was the finest catch in the neighbourhood and exactly what Hope imagined she'd want for her girls. Why would her mother object to Hope establishing something more than polite friendship between herself and Mr Durham, the future lord of Foxley Manor, before he returned to Cambridge while Hope was to begin her working life as a governess?

Hope put her hand up to her hair and twisted a ringlet around her forefinger. Her curls were natural, her hair a glossy dark mahogany; a fine contrast to her unnaturally pale skin and sparkling blue eyes. Men loved the combination. She could tell Mr Durham did too, but then, he'd loved her when she'd been simple Miss Hope, the penniless vicar's daughter.

How innocent they'd both been in those days.

Clearly, Mr Durham had changed a great deal since then. She could see it in the shadows of weariness beneath his eyes, the pallor of his skin, the nervous tic that worked at the corner of his mouth. This was not the carefree young man she remembered. This was a man who had endured much.

Very softly, he asked, "What are you trying to tell me, Miss Merriweather?"

And very softly, she replied, "That I am no longer the innocent Miss Merriweather you once knew."

The inference was implicit, but she realised she needed to spell it out otherwise he'd continue to hold out hope that she couldn't really be the fallen creature she so brazenly presented. Why did men have to make goddesses out of earthly creatures who were every bit as susceptible as they were to life's dangers and temptations?

"Nor am I an innocent governess who has lost her way." She gave a soft laugh, adding, "Though I daresay it could be argued that indeed I have lost my way." She shrugged. "No, Mr Durham, I did not leave you to follow a path of virtue, and I do not stand before you as the woman you remember."

"Then...why are you here?" He looked desperate. "I don't understand."

She pitied them both in that moment. "You've been very low, I believe, and some friends of yours who had only your best interests at heart were worried about you." Nervously she plucked at her glove, glancing away and finding her eyes trained on the large bed upon which they'd enjoyed such sport so recently. Was she imagining it, or did he in fact blush as he followed her gaze? Was the truth finally hitting home?

"They sent me to visit you a few days ago, and...they've funded this visit to you now." She swallowed before meeting his eyes, adding with difficulty, "Because they saw how improved you were after the last time."

"The last time?" He looked as if he'd received a blow to the solar plexus. "Dear God, it truly wasn't a dream? It *was* you?"

Hope nodded, unsure whether to take a step towards him or to begin her retreat now. Mr Durham was not the kind of man to indulge in prostitutes, and this encounter was clearly as distressing to him as it was to her.

"I'm sorry if I disappoint you, Mr Durham." She truly was sorry, but warring in her breast was how to expedite matters so she could protect her sister *and* the man before her. Both were innocents—unlike her. But both stood to be destroyed by what she did or didn't do in the next few minutes. Her burden was a great one. "I think I should leave now."

There, she'd voiced it—the turning point that meant she had to find some other means of safeguarding Charlotte's future. She could disappear into the sewers so no one could find her and hold her up as a shameful contamination of the hopeful bride-to-be.

"Wait!"

Oh, there was so much hope in that word that was followed by so much disappointment when common sense filled the vacuum left by extinguished optimism.

"I don't understand any of this! I thought you'd gone to the Continent to work for a family in Leipzig." His anguish at discovering how deeply wrong was his belief was hard to witness. He ran his hands through his hair. "I gave a letter to your mother to forward to you—two, in fact. But you never replied." His eyes widened at the broader ramifications. "Your family *know*...what you do?"

Hope shook her head. Woodenly, she said, "I'm dead to them, and that's the only way it can be. Dead to my whole family." She drew in a breath. "You know my sister is to marry?"

"Everyone knows it. The match of the decade. You'll not be there, of course." There was a harsh edge to his voice that shouldn't have distressed her so much. Of course, he was putting up the barriers around his heart to protect it from an unwelcome and undesirable reality.

She shook her head. "But you will, naturally. And I'm sure I needn't ask you to withhold my personal congratulations. Charlotte doesn't need to know I'm not where she believes me to be." Hope sighed. "I have no idea what story they've concocted, but she needs to be protected. Do I have your assurance you'll keep my…secret?"

"Secret? And how did this become your…secret, Miss Merriweather?" His nostrils flared as he took a step towards her. "What changed that you did not make our assignation two years ago?" He ran the back of his hand across his face. "Do you know how often I've thought of you? Dreamed of you?"

"You *have?*"

Ridiculous that the sentiment in his tone should touch a weakness she didn't know existed within her. The fact she had ever meant more to him than a brief encounter was both joyous and tragic.

"Of course I have!" He seemed to have trouble controlling his breathing. "You must have known that for years I watched you in church, on horseback, hoping for the opportunity to speak to you. And then suddenly you were riding with us during the Hunt. I don't need to tell you what nearly happened after you fell. When I rushed to your side…before we were interrupted."

Hope brushed away a tear she did not let him see. She was glad of her choice of the midnight-blue velvet rather than the dark brown satin which would have revealed the droplet like a badge of shame. Fallen women were not allowed to cry for the sins of their own making.

She let him go on. He seemed to want to tell her everything as, agitated, he began to pace. "And that night, at the Hunt Ball, we danced. I thought there was…something…" he choked on the word "…something special between us. I spoke of us meeting at the church the next day, and although you didn't agree, I believed you wanted to make that assignation as much as I did. Now I see there was obviously someone else. Someone who led you down the path of ruin. Was it a man? Money? A lust for something beyond what your virtuous existence could offer you? Why did you run away, Miss Merriweather?"

Hope should have been more immune to the accusations into which he channeled his disappointment. She'd clearly been his angel on a pedestal, and now that he'd discovered her so weakly human, susceptible to human vices, his lovely dream had been obliterated.

"It was a man." She drew in a shaking breath. Would she tell him what Wilfred had done? Or did that no longer matter? All that was important to Felix Durham was that she was no longer the paragon of virtue he needed her to be. She'd disappointed him. Let him down. Whatever she said in her defence would sound like a weak excuse for her own susceptibility.

Hope touched his arm, not expecting him to flinch as he did.

"You wish for a return of my former regard?" He shook his head. "What do you want from me?"

"I enjoyed what we shared three nights ago." She was back in character, her voice husky and suggestive as she slowly stroked his cheek. It was her best defence. Let him sate his disappointment through the pleasures of the flesh. She'd loved him but he was just a man, after all. Like all the others, he saw her only as a conduit for *his* dreams of what a good woman should be.

His sharp intake of breath was proof that he was not immune. He might like to pretend his disgust of a woman *like her*, but the kind of woman she'd become offered him delights more compelling than his reluctance to engage.

Facing him squarely, she ran her fingertips lightly up his flanks to cup his cheek.

He remained rigid. "Is this what you do to all the men who…pay you?" He shuddered slightly. "Who *is* paying you now? Millament? It doesn't sound like him."

Hope pretended she neither knew nor cared. "Those friends who are concerned about your state of mind. They paid Madame Chambon in the hope of restoring to you your former spirits, and now here I am again." She pushed back her right shoulder just a fraction. "I'm the remedy for a great many sorrows and disappointments." She licked her lips. It was part of the act. Not that it was usual that she had to resort to any measures to entice a man before. "So you may as well enjoy me while I'm here."

Strangely, she'd never found herself so desirous of wanting to make a man bend to her. Of his own free will. She'd excited his desires when he was responding only to bodily cravings. But his moral objections were a barrier she needed to breach. Not just because she wanted to, but because of what she needed to do for Wilfred. For Charlotte.

He straightened and moved back slightly, watching her with horrified fascination. "You're trying to break me, aren't you?" He spoke through clenched teeth. "You want to destroy my dreams. Otherwise, you'd just leave. Why torment me? I'm tormented enough already."

Squeezing his eyes shut, he sank suddenly onto his bed and hunched his shoulders, his breathing fast, but controlled as he half turned away.

Hope thought he'd have taken her in his arms by now. Most men would have, especially one who admitted to loving her. Well, to *having* loved her.

She glanced at the door. If she left now, she'd still have the memory of their lust-crazed lovemaking. Two days ago, he'd been insensible to the fact she was reality, and therefore free to love her without censure. He'd indulged himself like a man in love. Truly in love, so she'd felt at the time.

Now, the circumstances were very different. Excruciatingly so.

"I'll leave." She said it decisively, and she meant it. "I didn't come here to torment you. Go back to Annabelle. That's her name, isn't it? She's pure and untainted, and you can love *her* without guilt." Hope was pretty certain she'd summed up the situation correctly when she saw the rigid awareness transmitted through his suddenly stiffened shoulders, though he didn't speak. Gaining courage, she went on, "Whatever you do with me—or feel about me—will cause you only more torment, and ruin whatever little we shared once. I don't want that to happen."

How noble she could sound when she fell so very far short of it. She started walking to the door, the decisive click of her neat kid boots giving substance to her intentions.

"Annabelle?"

She stopped when he spoke the name, but she didn't turn. "She's the woman you intend to wed, isn't she?" Just speaking of it made her heart convulse.

"What do you know of Annabelle?" His voice was barely above a whisper. Hope looked over her shoulder, but he remained hunched over the bed, his face in his hands.

She sounded as guilty as she felt. "I saw you'd made several written attempts to apologise to Annabelle. Several of the letters had fallen to the floor."

"Did you find anything else of interest when you went through my correspondence?"

"As I told you, I picked the letters up from where they'd fallen beneath your escritoire." She changed the subject. "Are you in the habit of apologising to Annabelle for consorting with women like me?"

She deserved it when he swung around, fury in his eyes. "I have *never* consorted with women like you."

"You've never been with a prostitute?"

"I was initiated at the urging of my father and I'm not proud of it. I do not choose to take my pleasure with a prostitute over a virtuous woman, if that's what you're implying."

"But you did," Hope interrupted, speaking slowly. "You had me not three days ago. And you enjoyed me very much." She smiled, pushing aside a loose ringlet that fell across her face as she met his stare. His eyes flared with frustrated desire as again she turned and began to walk towards him, using her body like the instrument of pleasure Madame Chambon insisted her girls must regard it. Not for themselves, of course. But for men like Mr Durham.

The rustle of her skirts across the floor was loud in the sudden quiet. He seemed to be mesmerised. The longing in his eyes made clear she'd won.

Until he whispered, "Miss Hunt is my likely intended. It's all but agreed."

"So, it really is Miss Annabelle Hunt?" Hope blinked rapidly and put her hand on the high mattress to keep her balance. "Annabelle Hunt?" She couldn't help but say it again.

He was angled to look at her, sitting on the other side of the mattress, and when she repeated the name he said, "You and she were rivals, were you not? Though I'd have chosen you over Annabelle any day had circumstances not put you out of my reach." He finished on a bitter note though his feelings could not have been as bitter as Hope's.

In a flash, she understood the reasons behind Wilfred's game of revenge and wondered why she had not before.

"You wrote your apology to Annabelle because you wanted to avoid marriage to her?"

Felix rose slowly from the bed. "I was on the point of proposing. In fact, she was expecting it, when I received a note from your sister six months ago saying she believed she knew where you were."

Hope put her hand to her mouth, but he gave a harsh laugh. "Oh, she was clearly wrong. However, she believed you'd been unable to communicate from your position in Leipzig. It went without saying you were in a *respectable* position, Miss Merriweather; however, she feared you'd been detained against your will. After all, what else could account for your silence?" He looked accusingly at Hope. "When your sister contacted me, I told Miss Hunt that this new information changed everything. That I had to find you. At all costs. I was quite honest with her. I told her that you and your well-being would always be my first priority. I thought you needed rescuing. That I could be your saviour..."

He let the sentence trail away in the heavy silence so Hope could assimilate his meaning. He'd kept a flame burning for her all this time. Since their separation.

But Hope knew what Felix did not. And could not, now. Not if she were to protect her sister's future.

So *Annabelle* was the reason Wilfred had sent Hope on this mission to reveal herself as being far from the gilded object of Felix's dreams. Wilfred wanted Felix to resume his courtship of his sister, and the only way to do that was to destroy his regard for Hope.

Felix treasured purity. He'd held Hope up on a pedestal.

Well, look at her now. A degraded creature destined for hell.

Hope took in the hurt in his eyes and knew what she had to do—what Wilfred intended for her to do. Tonight was her last chance to exorcise herself from Felix's romantic daydreams so he'd pledge himself to Wilfred's sister, Annabelle—heart, body, and soul. Little matter that it was Annabelle who was as complicit in Hope's fall from grace as her brother.

So, as Hope revealed herself as the rotting corpse of noble, high-minded Mr Durham's dreams, the young heir to a viscountcy would be free to pledge himself to Wilfred's sister, so that pretty Miss Annabelle Hunt, the squire's daughter, could look forward to a title and a life of leisure in the house on top of the hill.

Hope forced her tone to sound light. Madame Chambon was an exacting teacher. Her standards were high and her tolerance for failure as low as Wilfred's. Between them, Hope stood no chance.

Unless she resigned herself to the gutter.

"And now I am here. It's true I stand before you in a guise that sits uncomfortably with you, but you'd be far from alone if you took your pleasure with me, Mr Durham, when I am already paid for."

Even though her heart was close to breaking, she must shore up her remaining reserves and follow through with this hateful charade. For Charlotte.

When he didn't respond, she gave a light shrug of her shoulders and went round the bed to stand just in front of him. "What will you do, Mr Durham?" She put her hands on his shoulders and smiled, as if she cared nothing for the parody role she played. The angel had fallen. She offered what he'd always wanted—but she was a poisoned chalice.

He stiffened and turned his head away, but she felt what it cost him to deny himself.

It both angered her and ripped at her heartstrings.

A moment went by. She couldn't believe it. He wasn't going to succumb when *she* felt scorched by the heat of attraction. Yet he truly was going to turn away from her.

And deny her the only pleasure she was likely to ever enjoy on this earth again?

Not only that, he'd prove how truly abhorrent he found her. And yet, he'd enjoyed her body but a few days beforehand with complete abandon.

No, she would not allow him to do this to her. To make her feel so worthless, when she relied on him to nourish her if she were to make anything of her future.

Carefully, she lowered herself onto his lap and draped her arms around his neck.

He didn't respond other than to stiffen slightly. He didn't move his own arms.

With a soft sigh, she pressed her cheek against his.

Although he still didn't move, she heard him catch his breath. And she felt the effort it cost him to hold himself deathly still. He was on a knife edge. He couldn't bring himself to push her away, which must mean he was dangerously close to caving in.

Using her eyelashes to trail a sensuous journey from the sharp delineation of his cheekbones to the corner of his lips, she felt the straining of his thigh muscles and tautness of his chest.

When she lightly ran the tip of her tongue across the seam of his lips, she knew she had won.

With a terrible cry of agony, he clasped her tightly against his chest and pressed his hungry mouth to hers. Hope had never embraced a kiss more. Or rather, the hope in that kiss. Pushing him onto his back on the mattress, she straddled him, securing each of his wrists above his head in a light clasp he could break as easily as a fly's if he chose.

But he did not. He was her willing slave for the moment, taking every drop of love she spilled from her lips until she rose to alter her position, and he reached up to pull her down, flipping her onto her back and caging her body beneath his.

They were both fully clothed but now began the torturous, exciting, and desperate race to divest themselves and each other of trousers, coat, and shirt in Felix's case, and Hope's elaborate bustle skirt. It unclasped at the waist, and she was skilled at wriggling her hips so that it shimmied down past her ankles and she could kick it gracefully free. Beneath it, she wore nothing but her stockings.

His eyes were closed, their mouths fused, when his seeking hands registered this. She felt his shocked awareness and the swelling of his member against her belly. Arching her back, she quickly worked the fastenings of her cuirass, wriggling expertly out of it so that the only garment she wore was her corset.

It nipped in her waist to a tiny twenty inches, but it would take too long to unlace. Besides, she knew he enjoyed the sensation of entering her when she was so confined. He had before, anyway.

And right now, Hope was determined Felix was going to enjoy her —*consciously*—even more than he had last time.

She had to prove she had some semblance of power over him. Even if it was only for the twenty minutes they were destined to spend together. What happened after that, she would not dwell on for there would be only these few moments to enjoy what she once might have forever, had her future not been swept away from her by Wilfred Hunt.

What a cruel irony, that Wilfred was both facilitating and destroying these final few moments of pleasure—these *only* few moments of pleasure—Hope would ever have to call her own.

Felix Durham's eyes blinked open a moment and caught her in the blaze of his despair. She might have lost him then had she not gripped his manhood and again covered his mouth with hers. Oh, she'd have let him go if he truly found her abhorrent. If he had no feeling for her. If there was no desire beyond lust.

But he had carried a candle for her; raised it to her memory. Admitted he desired to be her champion. Every tortured admission of what he'd been prepared to do to discover her whereabouts, reclaim her, was an admission of that love.

But how quickly love is disappointed, made a mockery.

With renewed determination, Hope pleasured him with all the

considerable skill she'd learned over the two years of her dreadful calling. If he had loved her, she would not let that love fizzle out for lack of being well met. No, she'd see it go up in flames, incinerating them both.

Withdrawing her lips from his, she pushed him onto his back and wriggled down so she could take him in her mouth.

He gasped, moaned—though it sounded more like defeat or surrender than ecstasy. Still, he did not push her away. He did not choose to end the encounter. He was entranced. His hand cupped the top of her head as his body notched up his growing desire in each slight jerk of taut sensory pleasure.

To pleasure a man to climax in these circumstances was Hope's preferred method of ending the encounter.

Tonight, she was desperate to have him inside her. She'd carried the feeling of their last encounter like a slow-burning flame within her heart, and the anticipation of knowing that tonight he was a willing participant—yes, willing, albeit reluctant—might go some way to dispelling the grief that was a foregone conclusion of tonight's encounter.

When he was near the edge, she wriggled up the bed and cupped his face. "I want to feel you," she whispered, arching her back and making her invitation implicit. "I've only ever wanted you."

She closed her eyes and gripped his buttocks as she opened her legs to him, awaiting the sensation with heart-pounding anticipation, whimpering as she felt the tip of his manhood breach her entrance.

He'd not hesitated. She understood he was now pledged to end this. Finish this and end this. With her.

It was a relief. His reluctance had frightened her from the moment she'd seen the dismay in his face. She'd not wanted to believe she might not be able to repeat their first time together.

With a cry, he plunged into her, his hands pinioning her wrists as he thrust into her, and she whimpered in pleasure. Let him take that away. The fact he'd brought a jade to the pinnacle.

He would exorcise her through this act of lust and passion; he would remind himself that the sexual act was base, and that tenderness played no role for he had been badly hurt.

Just as she had.

With a cry of rapture and despair, he came, his face buried in the pillow beside her as he continued to breathe heavily, not moving.

Nor did Hope move. She wanted to feel the weight of him, bearing down on her, depending on her, loving her, hating her. She wanted him close.

Too soon, he rolled off her. Wearily, he sat on the edge of the mattress and put his head in his hands.

Hope hadn't expected this. The silence was terrible.

She'd wanted this so much, but now she wondered if this act of what was for her pure love would come at the cost of her soul.

When he didn't move, didn't speak, she crawled over the mattress on the other side and slipped to the floor. She dressed quietly. Only the soft rustle of her blue velvet skirts across the floorboards indicated what she was doing.

It was an ensemble that she could get in and out of without help, but if the circumstances were right, she could claim helplessness for the man who enjoyed participating in disrobing; or she could cater to the chivalry or pretended tenderness of the man who wished to assist the woman he'd just ravished.

When she'd smoothed her ringlets and arranged her pert confectionery of exquisite millinery upon her head, she regarded Mr Durham uncertainly.

It seemed he really had managed to exorcise her from his heart through their base actions for he neither moved nor looked at her.

Her throat was dry. She blinked away her tears. On the far side of the room was his escritoire where he wrote his letters and where she could see he kept his pocketbook.

What could she do? Wilfred wanted her to steal from him. Prove that she was a worthless jade.

Well, she didn't need to steal from him to prove that. His immobility and patent disgust proved she was no longer a threat to Annabelle.

CHAPTER 6

"Stay." Her hand was already on the doorknob when the reluctant directive issued from him. Reluctant it clearly was. Hope was practiced at distinguishing between the tones that indicated desperate want and weary resignation.

She didn't want to stay. To stay threatened the strength she'd built up in that agonising transition from her naked vulnerability on the mattress to being mistress of her own destiny. To stay put her back in his power. He was the man she wanted, desired. She'd not wanted or desired any other man, and to be in thrall courted her own death. Death of her tenuous inner being.

Hope stopped, but she did not turn. She didn't remove her hand from the doorknob. She didn't want to hear what he had to say. Perhaps he didn't know either. A great wall of disappointment welled between them. He wanted her as he remembered her: pure and unsullied. But now that she was the opposite of that to all men, and for the taking, available to anyone prepared to pay for her, he'd still wanted her. No doubt he already despised himself for his weakness, hating her all the more for what she'd had no choice in becoming.

Silence stretched between them. Finally, she turned.

"Will you come back?"

She gave a light shrug. "If somebody pays me." There. She'd be on her way soon enough after that, and he'd never know how much it cost her to sever ties. Self-preservation. That was worth anything. Madame Chambon had instilled that into her girls.

"All right."

Puzzled, she watched him reach forward to open the drawer of his escritoire. He pulled out a roll of banknotes.

"How much do you want?"

"I told you. This afternoon…now…is already paid for." Shame burned her cheeks. Paid for, in effect, by the man who would ensure that their connection did not continue.

He nodded, slowly, though he still held the banknotes in a tight ball. "But you'll come back if I pay you?"

"If that is what you want."

"Is it what *you* want?"

"It's of no concern what I want."

"I was afraid you'd say that." He straightened and looked out of the window. "So…I could be any man, and you'd do what was asked of you…as long as you were paid."

"It's how I keep from starving."

"Dear God," he muttered, turning, his eyes boring into hers. "What happened to you?"

She couldn't help herself. She moved slowly forward for the connection was too strong to ignore. He wanted her back. For another precious half an hour she could drown in his arms and imagine the life she might have had.

"I made a miscalculation." She stood only a couple of feet from him now. "But that's not a conversation I want to pursue. I am here for your pleasure now."

He raised his eyebrows with faint scepticism. "Certainly not for yours. Pleasure is the preserve of the man willing to pay for it. Not for the woman?"

"I don't think that's quite accurate." She smiled as she put her hand on his cheek, for she could when she was playing a role. The coquette. That's what he'd enjoy for it was safely removed from earnest, innocent Miss Merriweather. "I think gentlemen like to use that as their excuse for variety after they've wed."

"You don't think a wife would prefer to be spared the excessive attentions of her husband?"

"Only a husband who does not share a mutual love with his wife would believe that." He moved his cheek into her hand, and she raised her other hand to gently ruffle his hair. Just as she'd always dreamed of doing. "You must feel something for Miss Hunt to have gone so far as to contemplate marriage. Tenderness, perhaps? A desire to do with her what we've done today? Why would she not feel the same?"

He closed his eyes and gently gripped her wrist. "When I kissed her, I hoped I'd feel more."

Hope experienced a sense of grim satisfaction at the admission. She also knew that Wilfred's promise not to sully Charlotte's wedding aspirations hinged on Hope doing all in her power to promote the shaky union between Felix and his sister.

"Sometimes it's better not to hurl oneself into a union in a surfeit of desire only to be disappointed. Love grows."

"And a harlot would know? Have you ever been in love?"

Hope was glad he couldn't see her expression. "I've felt desire, contrary to what you apparently believe. And I'm not an aberration. Every woman wants to feel desired by the man she loves. Every woman wishes for love when she must take a husband. Annabelle would be no different. She loves you, doesn't she?"

Hope lowered herself onto his lap and put her head on his shoulder. It was nice to feel him like this. Yes, he was angry but in a more contained, contemplative way. Passion spent, they could, perhaps, go some way towards being honest with one another. Honest in voicing their disappointment. And Hope could persuade him that Annabelle was the woman for him. If she could manage just that without having to damn herself in his eyes at the same time—with the thoroughness Wilfred wanted—it would be some small victory. Satisfying Wilfred was all that mattered.

"Yes." He began to stroke her hair, moving his hand to her cheek which he caressed gently.

"And she would make a good wife." Hope squeezed shut her eyes as she remembered the malice in Annabelle's when the girl had raised her gaze from Hope and Felix's clasped hands after she'd come upon them in the shadows after the Hunt Ball.

"She would." He cupped her chin and moved his face closer. "She would make an excellent wife." He touched his lips to hers, and Hope felt the familiar need and want within her flower as it took on a life of its own. A deep throbbing sensation began at her core and made her tremble as he increased the pressure of his lips. She felt she was breathing him in. It was a powerful aphrodisiac. Until he murmured, "And you could be my mistress."

She drew back, rising rapidly to her feet. She should have expected it, she berated herself silently. She should have been prepared for the lash that followed the loving. It was not good form to show her emotions like this.

"You don't like the idea?" he asked. There was a strange insolence in the tone of the question. Or was she just imagining it?

Hope raised one shoulder slightly as she affected a amusement. It was hard to pretend the heartless jade when she threatened to combust with feeling. "You'd not be able to afford me." She tried for a trill, or at least a lighthearted tinkle of a laugh, but it sounded hard and mercenary. Just as he believed her to be.

He rolled onto his side, full length on the bed, and regarded her from this semi-recumbent position, naked on the vast expanse of white linen. What an exquisite vision he was. She turned her head to look through the window, blinking away the scalding tears she must save until later.

"A man of my means and station is almost expected to take a woman to please his carnal needs. I'm confident we could negotiate a price."

This was not the Felix she knew. There was a brittle edge to his words she'd not heard before. Had she truly not known him? Was her love based on a false effigy? It would be easier if she *did* believe that.

She glanced at him, trying to read him, and found she could not.

Flailing in uncharted waters, she was unsure how to respond. "I don't think Annabelle would like that."

"We are talking about what I want, not Annabelle."

"Would you be so cruel that you'd do that to her within…within a month of marriage?"

"I was thinking now might be a good time." He smiled at her. "A good time to take a mistress, that is. If Annabelle learned of it and wished to seek a husband elsewhere, then I would not try to persuade her otherwise."

Hope almost felt sorry for Annabelle. But then, it would be rough justice.

"I've been under pressure to take a wife," Felix went on. "I've been contemplating the prospect of Annabelle with no real joy." He regarded her stonily. "Now that you've reentered my life in the guise of a woman of pleasure, I like the idea of taking you as my mistress and marrying Annabelle."

She had no response. Was he really so base and shallow that it made no difference she was a whore just so long as his desires were fulfilled? But she knew he wasn't like that. He was testing her.

He cleared his throat. "Or do you have objections?"

Hope turned away. She could be his mistress. The idea was agonisingly appealing. She could never be his wife, after all. And she'd be the exclusive property of the man she loved. Not shared around by those who could pay for her.

"Or would you miss the variety?"

Stung, she turned on her heel. How could she agree? Wilfred would never sanction it. It would demean his sister and, in turn, himself.

"I don't know how to answer you," she whispered.

"Come closer." His command was uttered in little more than a whisper, but she was like a toy in his hands, unable to deny him.

Except where her sister's future happiness lie.

She approached him warily.

"Sit on the bed."

She sat and he came up behind her, kneeling to twine his arms about her neck, dipping his hands into her bodice and kneading her nipples. She breathed in deeply. Was he going to punish her now?

She still couldn't read him.

His mouth was hot on her neck. "Do you want to be my mistress?"

She exhaled on a sob, inclining her head the slightest fraction as she whispered tearfully, "I never thought you the kind of man to take a mistress."

"I never thought myself the kind of man to take a mistress until I realised it was the only way to have you."

The harshness in his tone was at odds with the gentleness of his loving for his hands were roaming beneath the bodice of her cuirass as he nipped her earlobe. "How do I take this off?"

She guided his hands to the fastenings, and he unclasped her skirt, taking obvious pleasure in following its progress to the ground, kissing his way down the length of her thigh then removing her bodice and, finally, her corset, before he lay her on the bed.

When he leant over her, looking into her eyes, he murmured, "You know nothing of me. Do you expect I'll be generous?"

"If you're a generous lover you'll be generous in other ways." She tried not to cry. His tenderness hurt, his harshness was as painful. She suspected revenge might be his motive, but she could not be sure. She'd not thought Felix to have a vengeful nature. But then, what did she really know of men? Or women?

"And *would* you call me a generous lover?' His breath was hot on her neck as he curled his body round hers. She was naked now except for her stockings and corset.

"You'll have to remind me." She injected salaciousness into her tone and he responded as she'd hoped he would. No more of this dancing around the edges of what they were both about. It was too exhausting, too disorientating.

With a growl that suggested he was actually enjoying himself, he rolled on top of her and latched onto her nipple, filling her with a pleasure so exquisite she gasped aloud. She ruffled his hair, the smooth brown waves caressing her skin as he kissed her breasts, her throat, her mouth, before working his way down her belly.

A deep throbbing at her core filled her with a cocktail of the most intense ecstasy.

Skitters of desire made her tremble in his arms.

This time he held her tenderly and made love to her generously.

And Hope thought it was how she would like to die.

CHAPTER 7

Their lovemaking had been slow, intense, and deeply satisfying. Until this man, Hope had never enjoyed the act before. Now, as she stared at Felix's rested, angelic face while he slept, she supposed she never would again.

She glanced between the bed, the writing desk, and the door. Wilfred's promissory note was in Felix's wallet, which was in the drawer. She'd caught a glimpse earlier of what she believed was the document Wilfred demanded she retrieve. Once she'd seized that, together with whatever money she could find, her job would be done.

She stopped. No, she'd not take the money. She was not a grubby thief. Wilfred would get the promissory note for five hundred pounds that he'd signed over to Felix when he'd lost at the gaming tables ten days previously but that would be all. Just possibly, he'd not find the opportunity to hand it over to Felix before Charlotte's wedding in which case, Hope's reputation in Felix's eyes mightn't be completely shredded. Just possibly, there might be some kind of future for Hope and Felix.

But her first duty was safeguarding her sister's happiness.

As for Hope, she'd be no different than she had been three days before: a sinful, shameless, harlot destined for hell.

Only now, she'd be one who'd discovered that the scar tissue surrounding her heart was less impermeable than she'd feared.

FELIX AWOKE, CONSCIOUS OF A GREAT EMPTINESS. IT WAS USUALLY SO, but this time, in addition to the emptiness in his heart, was his consciousness of the emptiness of his bed.

As if something had been actively taken away from him.

For two years, he'd felt a sense of loss, but during the last six months that feeling had been augmented by a sense of utter devastation. There was nothing, he felt, that could cut through the despair and blame he felt at his sister's death. He'd been spared when everyone had thought he'd die.

His mother couldn't hide her devastation at the loss of her only daughter, and at each tortured look she directed at her son, Felix felt the guilt all over again.

Rolling onto his stomach, Felix put his face into the pillow where Hope's head had rested and breathed in her scent. It was a bolder scent than he remembered. The innocent Miss Merriweather of two years ago had smelled of something light and floral. The sensual and experienced Miss Merriweather who had come to him last night had smelled of something more exotic, but that had not lessened his desire.

He kept his eyes closed while he continued to breathe in the lingering traces of her.

A deep and strange out-of-body lethargy had overcome him, yet the feeling was more healing than the lethargy that had sapped him of his desire to live for the past few months.

Now, a life-affirming conviction stole through him, like a thread of something giving him strength. The circumstances were not ideal, but Hope would be his.

He shifted position and stared at the ceiling. Thinking.

For two years, he'd dreamed of making Hope his wife. After receiving no response to the three letters Felix had written to the address Mrs Merriweather had given him, Felix accepted that her daughter had become swallowed up by the Continent and her new life there and, understanding she wanted to sever her past ties, he'd resumed his desultory courtship of Annabelle; mostly because Lady Durham seemed always to be inviting the girl to the house and planning social events which Annabelle invariably attended.

When Miss Charlotte Merriweather had said she had news that suggested her sister was in some kind of danger or difficulty, hence her lack of communication, Felix had been spurred on by the greatest sense of at last having a quest to fulfill. He'd told Annabelle, kindly, that she must lay to rest her dreams of a shared future now that Miss Merriweather was again within reach.

Yet even the discovery of learning what Miss Merriweather had had not exorcised the tenderness and passion he felt for her. She was, he believed, evading the truth when she'd hinted at how she'd come to follow her degraded path. She'd not denied it when he suggested another man.

Was it someone with whom she had a pre-existing affection and Felix had misinterpreted Miss Merriweather's interest in him at the Hunt Ball?

Whatever had happened, Hope had apparently been abandoned and resorted to the only employment open to women in her situation, it would seem.

He drew in a deep breath. If he could just rise above his repugnance and set aside his pique, anguish and all the other emotions he felt, Miss Merriweather was willing to be his.

His.

That, in truth, was what he wanted above all else, and it wasn't just about the sex.

As he continued to stare at the plaster cherubs adorning the ceiling, Felix contemplated the road ahead—marriage to Annabelle and nights in the arms of the woman he loved. Hope. He could reconcile the double life because each woman would know what he offered beforehand.

He would not lie to them or pretend it could be otherwise.

The ornate collection of plasterwork winged creatures that frolicked with bucolic abandon around the ceiling edges seemed to smile down at him. Since he'd inherited his grandfather's townhouse, he'd been in the habit of seeing Hope's features in their innocent gazes. Of course, they were not representations of innocence. They were from another age. A more ribald age that celebrated the pleasures of the flesh.

Felix had not thought himself a sensuous man, but by God he'd taken his fill of it this afternoon and been left wanting.

In typical fashion, his father had taken him to visit a prostitute on his twenty-first birthday. The experience had left him cold although he'd returned recently on a couple of violently ribald occasions instigated by his friends who were determined to cheer him.

While he'd have been unable to name the house or location to save his life, he wondered if it might have been the residence to which Miss Merriweather was attached. Thank God he'd not encountered her within its precincts. It was bad enough that she'd come from there, but that was the reality he'd have to get used to. The virtuous creature he'd put on a pedestal had lost her wings and taken on an earthly guise, but she was just as desirable.

Hope had mentioned the name Madame Chambon. Her brothel madam.

His nostrils flared as he breathed through his disappointment. For two years, he'd dreamed of discovering her, saving her...she was too late for saving now.

But he could still have her. The thought was accompanied by a surge of bile. He would still have her, but he would not punish her for disappointing him like he might have, once.

Like he might have as a callow youth whose notions of womanly virtue were so at odds with who and what a woman really was.

A LOUD KNOCKING DISTURBED THESE REVERIES THAT MIGHT HAVE GONE on for hours, and if he'd been sucking on the pipe again, might have put him out of contention for the evening Millament obviously desired for him.

"Gad's teeth but you look like the cat that's swallowed the cream and is contemplating a second foray with much wickeder consequences," his friend declared as he strode through the door.

Millament was dressed for the theatre, looking the debonair man of fashion as he glanced at the rumpled sheets and his friend's disarray.

"Not like you at all, Felix." He shook his head, his expression bemused and interested. "But a little light entertainment seems to have done you the world of good. What a shining star she was. A magical, mystical creature of the night. I wonder where the boys found her?"

Felix raised himself on his elbows. "What do you mean, the boys?" The thought she might have given herself to a number of his friends presented itself as a sudden, shocking possibility.

Millament shrugged. "After that disastrous game of poker the other night when you were so very far from yourself, someone proposed—I forget who—that he procure you a creature who would take your mind off your earthly woes. You've been a monk, Felix, and that damned pipe is making you no fun to be around." He glanced at the smoking apparatus by the bed and his smile brightened. "But a glorious woman has brought you back to life. She came to you three nights ago when your senses were addled and she clearly was prepared to come again, which augurs well for you, judging by the egg-like look on your face." He walked to the wardrobe and pulled out a coat, anxious clearly to get his friend ready for the evening. "Remind me of where this divine creature can be found."

"She's mine." Felix sat up. The energy fuelling him now was unlike anything he'd experienced for as long as he could remember.

"Calm down. I'm not about to steal her from you, though I'd hurry and stake your dibs before someone else lays claim."

"What have you heard? What do you know about her?" Felix flung his feet over the side of the bed.

"Steady, old chap. Of course I know where she's from. A bower where the princes of the realm are ready to bankrupt themselves for a night of her charms. I hope you know that pocketbook might take a beating if you fancy exclusive rights."

Felix reached for his silk dressing gown and encased himself in its cool and sensuous folds. "Give me ten minutes and I'll be downstairs," he said, conscious it sounded more like a snarl although Millament, with his perpetual good humour would in all likelihood forgive him.

But his friend's words had opened a chasm of fear that worried at the wound that had blighted him these past six months. It had begun to close over these last few hours as he learned, finally, what he needed to set his life to rights.

Felix had just tasted the closest to contentment and ecstasy, and it was even more addictive than the opium.

Even if the cost to his well-being might be greater.

CHAPTER 8

The Red Door was a favourite haunt of the young bloods. Felix hadn't rubbed shoulders with his friends in such a den of debauchery since the tragedy over his sister. Now, however, a sense that normalcy might again reign—despite Millament's unsettling words earlier—bolstered him to match the revelry displayed by Millament and the others whose company he'd eschewed for so long.

"Bold move," mocked Ravensby, an old Cambridge colleague as Felix threw down what was in his pockets.

Felix grinned. He'd never been a big gamester like so many of his friends. Still, he was in an impulsive mood tonight. He'd just sated himself with the woman he adored and he was addicted.

Yes, she'd been gone by the time he'd woken, but she'd given herself to him a second time in a manner that could leave him in no doubt that she'd agree to his proposal. She'd agreed to be his mistress. He didn't want to remember that she'd also agreed to his proposal to meet him at the church two years ago, and then failed to appear.

No, *this* was different. Miss Merriweather returned the feelings he had for her, he was sure of it.

"I say, Felix, what's the matter old chap?"

It was Millament returning to his side, his dear concerned friend, always on the lookout for him since he'd moved into his townhouse after Felix's spectacular disintegration six months before. Felix sometimes wondered if his mother were paying his friend to attend him so closely, or whether Millament truly was one of those friends in a million.

Felix shook his head and put up his hand to allay the concern directed his way, but the truth was, the familiar fog of despair had descended without warning.

He'd set out for an evening as if the answers to his problems were all but neatly solved but now suddenly he was flailing in a morass of uncertainty.

The acrid cigar smoke that swirled about him did not have the soothing effects the opium pipe delivered, and he coughed, gripping the arm Millament put out to steady him.

Blindly, Felix allowed his friend to steer him towards a large wing-back chair near the window.

"Please tell me I didn't imagine the woman who came to me this afternoon—"

"You've not taken leave of your senses," Millament soothed. "And I won't go after her. On my oath."

"Then she was real. I didn't imagine it." Felix blinked open his eyes and saw Millament staring at him with a look of sympathetic understanding.

"She's the kind of woman a man dreams about, to be sure, but she certainly was real." He patted Felix's arm in a brotherly fashion. "And she liked you, Felix, my friend. That was very clear. You go and find her again if that's what you want. I'm glad to see you lusting after a woman, truly. She'll be good for you. Banish these black moods, once and for all."

Felix nodded. "I will find her. I made her a proposition and I must find her and make it binding." He took a deep breath. "I *need* her." Saying it made him feel better, even if the mire of unpleasantness he'd have to pass through was equally on his mind. A vision of her black-eyed gaze, her skin so pale framed by ebony tresses, drifted tantalizingly through his mind.

Yes, he would find her, and he'd make her his, regardless of what it cost him.

An owl perched on the drainpipe of Wilfred's lodgings. In the dead of night, it seemed a portent of doom, a symbol of unearthliness. Yet it was Wilfred's malevolence Hope feared more. Nothing good would come out of this forthcoming interview, but she was duty-bound, for her sister's sake, to follow through.

"Madam." The butler inclined his head, eyeing her with scorn as he opened the door for her. A young, single, unaccompanied woman calling on a gentleman was beyond the pale in his eyes. In the eyes of anyone respectable, in fact. Especially so late at night.

She was used to it. In two years, she'd developed a thick skin to the mixed responses she'd received from members of the public who regarded her enviously for her beauty and boldness, at the same time as reviling her for daring to brazen it out in public on whatever mission she might be on.

"I'm here to see Mr Hunt." She barely glanced at the disapproving retainer. He was beneath her, and he'd despise her even more for her autocratic tone that suggested she was on par with a duchess and that he was beneath notice. He'd loathe that, but then she loathed the way the servant class took the moral high ground. They, of all people, must know how hard it was not to starve without a benefactor. But then, had her scope of the world been no broader than that of a governess out of the schoolroom, what would she think of a woman of suspect morals? A woman like her?

"Miss Merriweather, what a delightful surprise." Wilfred greeted her with a cool smile as the butler bowed himself out of the library to which he'd just led her. "Refreshment?" He waved her to a seat and went to the sideboard, raising the brandy decanter with an enquiring look.

Hope shook her head. "I shan't stay. I came here only to give you what you requested."

"You don't wish to linger over past reminiscences?" He feigned disappointment.

"I've spent enough time in your company to last me a lifetime, Wilfred." She shouldn't have said it, and not in that cool detached manner that suggested she believed she was better than he. Wilfred was a man, which gave him so much more power, and he was a petty one at that. "You brought me into your orbit against my will, but it was you who thrust me into my current profession. I have no recourse to change the past or to change people's perceptions of me, but I would ask one concession." Her fingers tightened over the clasp of her reticule with its contents she was so loath to surrender.

The ormolu clock on the mantelpiece sounded loud in the silence as he took his time responding. His lips thinned. It was clear he did not like her attitude, and Hope wished she'd employed some of the tact Madame Chambon had drilled into all her girls when there'd be many an unsavoury assignation they must pretend to enjoy.

"Concession? Here, drink this." Ignoring her refusal of brandy, he thrust a cut-glass tumbler into her hand. She glanced at it suspiciously and remained standing.

"I haven't laced it with poison," he snarled.

"Or laudanum? That's what you put into my drink when you took me to London. When you had your way with me. When you defiled me. That's why I'm what I am today." She sent him a twisted smile. "Let's talk about that, shall we, Wilfred? I have no memory of my first time. I only knew I was ruined, and I could never return to my parents. You told me I had to rely on you." She shrugged. "What choice did I have but to stay with you. That is, until you'd had enough of me."

His eyes flickered and he glanced away, but that was the only indication of any acknowledgement that he may have behaved in a manner to invite censure. Before a second more had passed he'd closed the distance between them.

Hope stepped back as he gripped her shoulders and glared.

"I looked after you, didn't I? I bought you pretty things and took you dancing. I spent a fortune trying to please you."

Hope felt his hand tremble despite his efforts to make his point in as passionless a manner as he could. Wilfred did not enjoy passion except when his needs were being gratified.

She tossed her head. "And then you sold me to the highest bidder."

"Quite simply, I couldn't afford you, my dear." His hands fell away, and his hooded eyes blazed beneath their reptilian lids though his words were measured.

"Why, Wilfred?" Hope asked the question that had puzzled her for so long. For the moment, she was more perplexed than angered. "I'd been your mistress for eight months when you simply abandoned me. I had no friends. You made sure of that. There was no one who could help me. You took me unwillingly from my family, my home, and you made me dependent on you. *Why*? Only so you could dispose of me with as little compunction as you would an old coat. Did you despise me so much?"

"It was clear the feeling was mutual."

Hope shook her head. "Did you really expect me to love you?"

Wilfred made a noise of irritation as he flung around and took a few steps towards the window, turning to rest his hand on the back of the green velvet sofa and shaking his head at her. "Lord, Hope. We were both scorched that day. It was not my intention to take you with me. Heavens, you'd go so far as to say I kidnapped you when nothing could have been further from my mind. You know you were as much to blame as I. Everything that happened that day was unfortunate. An accident." He sighed. "I've told you a thousand times how much I regret it, but it doesn't matter now. What's done is done."

"*You* ruined me, Wilfred!"

"Only because you were too stupid to seek the other avenues I offered you."

"I tried." Hope said it under her breath. Bitterly. "Papa died that very night. I was supposed to be on a boat heading for the Continent. I received no answer to my letters, my pleas."

"Precisely. Which is why the responsibility of looking after you when I had not a feather to fly with landed on my shoulders." He looked outraged at her suggestion that he was culpable. But then,

Wilfred had a knack for turning the blame back on the other person. "You could have continued to Leipzig."

"How? The boat had gone. I had no ticket, and you had no money, you said, to pay my fare. I wrote. I tried everything to get out of the situation you placed me in. *Nothing* you say excuses drugging me, kidnapping me, making me your mistress, and then selling me to a brothel madam!"

Wilfred put up his hands. "I had no intention of doing any of those things! You drank from the flask Annabelle offered you. I didn't realise it was all but undiluted laudanum. Before I knew it, you were fast asleep. I tried to remove you, in as gentlemanly a manner as I could. I had the door half open, and I was contemplating where I could leave you."

"It was freezing. The snow was three feet high. I'd have died. You could have made some excuse."

"I could have," he conceded. Then his tone changed, and he looked like a petulant schoolboy with a perpetual sneer at being the butt of life's misfortunes. "If you want to blame anyone, blame your high-and-mighty Mr Durham. Just as I was about to carry you out of the carriage and leave you by the church door, there he was, coming towards me, passing the vestry where I'd hoped to be rid of you. I knew he'd jump to conclusions; he was always so protective of you."

Hope gasped, her hands jerking at the shock of this surprise revelation, causing her drink to splash over her skirts. "If you'd been a gentleman you'd have thought fast enough to say whatever necessary to protect my honour which was *not* besmirched at that point, Wilfred."

His mouth twitched and not with humour. "I might have had he not incited me."

"Incited you?"

Wilfred nodded. "He was ten feet away, striding towards me through the snow. He shouted something."

"What?"

Wilfred shrugged. "He was threatening me."

"Threatening you? How?"

"He was walking towards me in a very menacing manner. He's never liked me. I knew the moment he saw me with you unconscious in my arms he'd orchestrate some smear campaign. So, I leapt back into the carriage and ordered the coachman to continue. "

"The train station was only ten minutes away. That's where I was destined. You promised my parents you and Annabelle would take me there after the snowstorm blocked the drive. Mama believed I had only to travel as far as the train station in order to catch the boat."

"And you were in the deepest stupor. Believe me; I *went* to the station. I *tried* to rouse you."

Hope gasped. "You were afraid! Too afraid to take me back to my home because I was alone, drugged in your carriage."

He looked through the window. "By God, I cursed you at that moment. I drove around for hours until finally I was in London. I arrived at my lodgings and you were *still* asleep. By that stage, I feared you were dead. So, I carried you inside but there was only one bed made up." He shrugged again. "There was nowhere else to put you and nowhere for me to sleep, and you were so damned enticing, I'll admit." A slow smile curled his lip. "What choice did I have? I didn't want to be saddled with a penniless governess for a wife, but you have no idea how much I'd wanted you, Hope. And for how long. And now you were in my care." He shrugged as if he truly did not see himself as an opportunistic predator. "I looked after you when you needed a protector. Wasn't it more fun dancing until the small hours than improving the minds of a pair of German infants? I saved you from all that. There's no changing the past. I refuse to have my future, or that of my sister, blighted by your stupidity and the threats of Felix Durham."

Hope's first instinct was to throw herself at him and rip her fingernails down his cheek. But she held her head steady, and even though her vision blackened with emotion, she retained her dignity, just as Madame Chambon had taught her girls. Hope had more self-possession than the man before her would ever have.

"So, you admit you ruined me, Wilfred. Then, you can do just one thing for me. One thing so you can rest easy with your conscience."

She tried not to show how much it meant to her. Wilfred thrived on vulnerability. So she added, perhaps unwisely, "Or fear retribution from my hand."

"A fearful threat, I must say." He tossed back his drink then cocked his head.

Hope opened her reticule and held out the promissory note he'd requested. As he went to take it, she withdrew her hand. "This is to show you that I have done what you asked. I slept with Felix, as you would have me do." She was tempted to tell him more. Of what a superior lover he was compared with Wilfred, but she was not that stupid. "I stole from him, just as you requested." She licked dry lips and steadied her voice.

Wilfred tried once more to snatch the note, but Hope pulled back her hand again.

He glowered. "You came here to give me what I directed you to if you were to spare poor Charlotte the scandal and ignominy of knowing what her sister does for a living. That was our agreement."

Hope sent him a level look. "If your intention in blackening my name in his eyes was so that he'd ask for Annabelle's hand in marriage, then that is achieved. You needn't brand me a thief into the bargain."

"I like to hedge my bets, Hope. What does it matter? Felix won't run you to ground and have you arrested if that's what you're worried about. He'll just be very disappointed."

"He intends to ask Annabelle to marry him. He told me. Now that he knows what I am, and that he can never have me for his wife, he's accepted that Annabelle is the perfect candidate." Hope heard her voice break and cursed herself for her weakness.

Wilfred looked at her suspiciously. "Then he still has feelings for you? Annabelle won't like that. She needs to be sure you are absolutely no threat."

"Felix is going to ask Annabelle to marry him," Hope repeated firmly. "Quite likely he will do that in the next day or two. That's what you wanted. That is what both you and Annabelle want. Please, Wilfred. If Felix asks for Annabelle's hand before Charlotte is married in two days' time, then you'll have achieved your aim. Felix marrying Annabelle is what's important to you. Not blackening my name."

He looked at her and the silence drew out.

"Why should you wish for the vestiges of his minimal regard if there is nothing between you and Mr Durham?"

Hope closed her eyes and heard the chink of glass as he poured himself another drink. When she looked up, he'd already tossed the contents down his throat. It seemed to give him renewed confidence.

"Think of it as the tiniest bit of atonement towards me," she said in a voice that sounded small and puling. Hope was stronger than this. She'd had to become so over the past two, terrible years so why was she parading her weakness like this in front of Wilfred?

"Atonement suggests culpability, and I'll not admit that!" The drink had fired him up. He strode across the floor and put his hands on her shoulders, staring into her eyes. They flashed fire and hatred. Hatred for what she'd made him feel. Less than a man. She'd made clear her contempt for him through their tortuous months together, but it was only at the end he'd hurt her. She flinched. Once was enough, though it was more than that.

"You set your sights too high, Miss Merriweather. Two years ago, my sister was all but betrothed to Felix Durham, and then you broke her heart at that damned Hunt Ball. I had her honour to protect."

"So you destroyed mine." Hope raised her chin. "*And* yours. You can never call yourself an honourable man again after what you did to me."

Casting aspersions upon Wilfred's honour was a big mistake. Hope saw that instantly.

But it was too late.

CHAPTER 9

Felix had drunk more than he usually did, but he had his faculties about him. Millament had spoken sense, soothing him and he was glad to closet himself in a dim corner for a while, going over in his mind everything that had happened that day.

Was he adopting the right course? He'd never considered a mistress, and he'd never in a thousand years dreamt of making the incomparable Miss Hope Merriweather anything other than his wife.

But, he could not marry her. He simply could not.

Unfortunately, inconvenient though it was, he simply could not live without her.

He was about to finish his brandy after reclaiming his winnings when he caught sight of Annabelle's brother following in Millament's wake. Felix had little affection for the man he'd known since he was a puling youth. Annabelle's fragility was to be expected in a female, but there was no excuse for Wilfred. The boy had never played fair, always finding someone else to blame if something didn't go his way during the occasions they were thrown together as children, for their mothers had been friends from their own schoolroom days. It was one of the reasons Annabelle had been dangled before him since before he'd grown chest hair.

Fortunately, the boys' education had taken them in different directions, and while Felix had suffered through a spartan education at Eton, Wilfred had been tutored at home, indulged and cosseted as ever.

Felix glanced at the clock. He'd spent all evening weighing up various approaches, and the wisdom of his choice.

Yes, he'd be laying his heart on the line, putting to Hope a prospect she might not find as enticing as one she might have received from a Prussian nobleman or an English marquess—Millament had elaborated on the rigorous training Madame Chambon's girls were put through—but she had genuine feelings for him. She might not have said it in so many words, but their encounter had revealed enough of her susceptibility towards him that he was confident that when he turned up at Madame Chambon's ready to negotiate, Hope would come away from that house with only Felix to call her protector.

The reasons as to why Miss Merriweather had fallen so far were not important for now. Rescuing her before she succumbed to another lure certainly was.

Felix was aware that the girl's wildness had been the despair of her parents. Daring and careless of her neck, she'd ridden the jumps and hedges during the Hunt like the best of the men that fateful day.

Felix had admired her from afar for years before he'd spoken to her.

Why had he waited so long? She was penniless while he was the catch of the neighbourhood. Perhaps it had been due to her manner; the way she'd treated all young men. As if they were nothing to her. And Felix's pride as an untested youth was too fragile to bear rejection.

"Haven't seen you gracing a den of vice like this in a while." Wilfred Hunt's face was flushed, and he slurred his words slightly. He clapped a hand on Felix's shoulder in a gesture that was too familiar. Felix stepped away but he didn't seem to notice.

"I've had the devil's own luck, I tell you." Wilfred's mouth turned down. "Still, although I could do with the blunt, it'd be dishonourable if I didn't give this back to you." He reached into an inner pocket of his coat and drew out a paper that looked familiar to Felix before it took on a whole other dimension.

"Your promissory note, I believe. From me." Even as Wilfred said the words Felix was feeling for his own pocketbook, rifling through the notes inside while his gut churned in confusion. "I don't understand. How did you get it?"

Hunt cleared his throat. "Sorry, old chap. Very embarrassing to admit, but I thought if I returned it to you in good time you'd not have had the matter investigated by the authorities."

"The authorities? What are you talking about? Who took it?" He swung around as if he might see the guilty party in this very room.

"I'd rather not say." Hunt looked sheepish. "Protective instincts and all that."

"Annabelle?"

Hunt snorted. "Lord, do you think Annabelle would steal from you? Besides, when did you last see her? No, it wasn't Annabelle, but as I'm a gentleman I'd rather not say. Suffice to admit it was a young lady who committed the bold felony out of a sense of misguided loyalty. Lord knows if it's the full reason, but she said she was worried that my not being so plump in the pocket might mean I'd not favour her with a visit as I regularly do on a Thursday."

He sniggered, and Felix drew himself up. No, Wilfred was lying. Miss Merriweather would never. He realised he was clenching his fists.

"Apparently, this last week she's been lining her pretty little palms with ill-gotten gains from clients who for the most part wouldn't notice the theft of a few guineas here or there." A look of sorrow marred Wilfred's soft features even more. "She visited me this afternoon at about six o'clock and handed it over. When I saw that the promissory note was the very one I'd made out to you last week, I knew here was at least one fleeced recipient to whom I could make amends." He glanced at his shoes then up at Felix's face. "Very embarrassing and all that, but now you've got back what you lost, I hope you'll let the matter rest and say no more about it."

Felix thrust out his hand and drew Hunt back roughly. "You are, of course, referring to Miss Merriweather. You know her as well as I. How can you pretend this is nothing?"

Hunt looked surprised. "Miss Merriweather? Surely not! I thought no one knew the sorry history of what she's become." He sent a furtive look over his shoulder. "Her sister is to wed Lord Hartley. You won't say anything that would imperil Miss Charlotte's future, would you?" He put his hand on Felix's coat sleeve. "The girl is an innocent. She knows nothing of the vice into which her sister has fallen. Though couldn't we all see—even before she was ten years old—that wild Miss Hope was destined for a fall."

Wilfred looked deeply concerned now. "Miss Charlotte could not be more different from her sister. I beg of you, do not enlighten her. Miss Hope sent her father to an early grave by running off with one of the footmen, of all things, the night of the Hunt Ball. I happened upon her a year ago." He dropped his voice which held a salacious edge as he murmured, "Her circumstances were…rather unexpected circumstances, I must say, and she appreciated the comfort of an old friend. But pray, have some concern for her mother and sister who know nothing of what she's become."

Felix stared with disgust at the hand still gripping the cloth of his coat.

The other young man, noticing, uncurled his fingers and rolled his shoulders. He smiled almost in sympathy. "And have some concern for Hope, I beg you. Despite her wild nature, she was deeply upset, her loyalties divided, she told me, when she realised that it was *you* for whom her services had been procured."

"She told you this, did she?" Felix sounded sceptical but the truth was, he didn't know what to think.

"Indeed. She told me she was in despair as to what to do, in view of the childhood friendship between you, but when she saw that the promissory note was from me and would leave me five hundred pounds further out of pocket, her loyalties came out on the side of the man who's been a constant for the past year." He looked smug. "You might say we've formed an intimacy that goes beyond the pleasures of the flesh." Wilfred put out his hand and said as if suddenly wishing to reassure Felix, "Please don't imagine I'm jealous. I don't have exclusive rights. Miss Merriweather has hundreds of admirers, though, like all of her kind, she'd like to be set up with some exclusivity. Apparently, she's hoping Lord Westfall will make such an offer."

Felix found he was breathing very heavily through his nose. Around him, the room was a blur of excited activity, some fellows playing billiards, others cards, others smoking and drinking in small groups.

He'd never felt more alone as he became conscious of Wilfred's promissory note in his palm while he watched the other man melt into the throng.

CHAPTER 10

Hope ran a trembling hand across her forehead as she made her way along the passage towards her room. Her gown of pink satin, trimmed with lace and ribbons, ordered by Madame Chambon but chosen by Hope, reminded her of the gown she'd worn at the Hunt Ball. The virginal debutante she'd been then had turned many heads wearing the pretty dress Mama had reluctantly sanctioned.

Everything good about her life was concentrated upon that evening when she'd been a girl full of hope. Wearing pink.

Nevertheless, there were other details about that day and evening that were confusing and unsettling. Annabelle's obvious dismay at seeing Felix go to Hope when she'd fallen from her horse was understandable. But why was it that Hope's mama had not seemed happy that Hope was garnering so much attention? When Hope had danced with Mr Felix Durham for the second time, Mama had been waiting for her on the edge of the dance floor and had led Hope away before Felix could say even two words in parting. At the end of the evening, she'd bundled Hope into the family carriage so Hope couldn't say a proper goodbye to Mr Durham or even tell him in so many words she longed to meet him at the church the following day. That, indeed, she *would*. He must have known her true feelings, surely?

Hope had always known Charlotte was the favourite, but Charlotte was only fourteen—far too young to look for a husband—so surely Mama should have been delighted to get Hope off her hands?

But that was all in the past. For a short while today, hope and happiness had lodged in Hope's heart. Lying with Felix, the love in his eyes and the words he'd used to build up a shared future, had allowed her to believe there might be something more for her than the shell of existence offered by Madame Chambon.

But Wilfred was determined to destroy what little there was left of her dignity.

And what recourse was there? Alone in a world where a woman's chastity counted for everything, Hope was irredeemable.

"Hope? Are you…well?" The timid question came from Madame Chambon's most perplexing recruit, Faith. Perplexing because of the fact that she'd lived for more than a year under Madame Chambon's roof yet never had to service a single gentleman. There'd been a time when Hope had felt for every newcomer, understanding how events beyond a girl's control could so quickly force them into such an avenue of no return.

Faith, however, had a mysterious benefactor who paid for her to attend a tutor in philosophy and art three times a week. She also attended demonstrations with the other girls in how to stoke the fires of desire of even the most reluctant gentlemen.

Hope wasn't surprised that Faith kept to herself as much as she did. The girl wasn't like the others. She'd obviously been chosen for a very special mission and, while she might have retained her virginity thus far, her fate nevertheless, was like that of the other girls': to be a prostitute.

And who would choose to be a prostitute if there were even the faintest possibility of a life of moral rectitude as an alternative?

Hope had seen how the girls became hardened, she no less than any of them. Some were role models in the cunning they displayed when reeling a man in, fleecing him in some instances cleverly, though. Madame Chambon didn't mind provided no crime was ever laid at her door. Some had indeed made fine alliances and set themselves up with a generous, even doting benefactor. Some had invested wisely. A king's ransom for the ripe years of a young woman's life enabled her to retire and live as she chose. Few, though, emerged from their life of sin unscathed and most, to tell the truth, died young and in penury.

Hope wondered what the future held for Faith. She knew Lord Harkom was interested; a terrifying proposition given his disposition for putting young women in their places if he felt he'd not been given the servicing or respect that was his due.

Another possibility was Lord Westfall. He was personable enough. Early-forties with an ailing wife. Madam Chambon was encouraging it as it meant a fat severance bonus for her, even though Hope had overheard the brothel madam saying she believed Faith could become one of her most popular girls. A bird in the hand was worth two in the bush though, for who knew if Faith might suddenly lose her lustre, or her health, or even her looks.

"Am I well?" She repeated the question Faith had asked her, closing her eyes as she leant against a Corinthian pillar in the dim passageway between the receiving room and the stairs to the upstairs bedrooms. She almost dismissed Faith's concern with a trite or flippant response that helped keep her distance. It did not do to form confidences. No girl here was entirely trustworthy for survival often depended upon sacrificing someone else. Madame Chambon had spies everywhere, and every potential escapee or undeclared guinea resulted in serious consequences.

In the gloom, Faith's eyes were luminous. Hope wondered suddenly how she'd come to be here. It was not something she generally asked. The answer was usually a lie anyway.

"I have been better." She drew out the sentence as if it cost her a great deal; which it did, for her heart was so heavy she wanted to sink to the ground and put her head on the wooden floor and simply dream herself somewhere else.

"You're not…hurt?"

Very occasionally a girl was physically abused, though not often. In this respect, at least, Madame Chambon was a good protector, though of course she was protecting her assets. An abuser might find himself suffering a range of humiliations the reason for which he'd be left in no doubt. After that, he'd be blackballed.

Hope smiled wanly and put her hand to her heart and the other girl nodded, her expression one of surprising empathy.

"I hoped one's heart might have hardened so this didn't happen," she admitted in little more than a whisper. She couldn't risk being overheard.

Faith ran her hands the length of her long-line princess dress. She looked very beautiful, her pale skin a striking contrast with her thick golden hair that was arranged in a complicated series of braids coiled around her head. "You've been here a little more than a year?"

"Longer."

"You count the days?"

"I do." Hope made an effort to breathe properly as she drew herself up. "No point in dwelling on what can't be changed though. If we can't choose our destiny, we must make the best of it."

"But *is* this the best?" Faith clasped her hands in front of her. "Surely...?"

"No fallen woman is ever granted a second chance." Hope spoke the truth harshly. "I'd take a job as a servant if I could get a character, but my past will always catch up with me, and I wouldn't know the first thing about blacking a grate. I'd be found out because word travels." She never poured out what was in her heart, but something in Faith's sympathetic look of enquiry invited confidences. Now that she'd started, she seemed unable to stop. Bitterly, she went on, "No, there's nowhere to go and nothing I can do. My name will always be as black as my heart supposedly is. But I had hoped today to be granted a little dignity."

"Dignity?"

Hope laughed harshly. "Dignity in not being forced to thieve, if only to protect someone I love dearly. There! I've just confessed to being a thief. Do you think regret ameliorates the crime? It never did in any court so I don't expect lenient treatment. Oh God!" She clutched her side and closed her eyes as she sagged against the pillar. Speaking the words made it worse, not better.

"Oh, Hope, you are not in love?" Faith said it as if it were the most dire of circumstances, which of course it was. "You've not done this because someone you love asked you to?"

"I don't love this man!" Hope spoke scornfully. "He's made me do something against my will in order to protect someone close to me. A family member but..." She thought about it truthfully and then admitted as if only acknowledging it for the first time, "Yes, I am in love with the man I visited this afternoon, and he's the one I was forced to steal from. If he doesn't already know, he soon will, and then he'll feel none of the love he professed for me today." She stopped suddenly and gave a wan smile. "Too much information, Faith. You should not have asked."

The other girl gripped Hope's hand in a quick squeeze and said in a rush, "You don't know how much it means to me that you make a confidante of me. I have no friends. No one here I trust. I trust you, though. You do not speak behind one's back; you keep to yourself. I know you didn't choose to be here. I won't ask why you are. But you're the only one who's been kind to me. Even just a little. If I can ever do anything to help you, I would."

She said it with such fervour Hope was touched.

But what help could Faith offer her? Hope was doomed. She forced herself to open her eyes if only to offer the other girl a little of what she clearly craved: understanding, if not gratitude.

"You are kind," she said, her heart so heavy it physically weighed her down. "But now I must rest. And for once...I think I might take something. Madame wanted me to engage with the gentlemen in the drawing room before Lord Westfall visits, but I really think I cannot."

"It must be hard to see...a gentleman when you've just come from the man you love." Faith spoke urgently, following Hope a little way along the passage. "Please, Hope..."

Hope turned, staying her words with a gentle finger upon her lips. "Ah, Faith, I hope you get out of this line of work before it's too late."

She didn't want to hear any more. Shaking her head to deter the girl from continuing after her, Hope picked up her skirts and made for the sanctuary of her room.

Lord Westfall would visit her in two hours after he'd been to his club and before he hit the gaming tables. She suspected it was likely he would make her some kind of offer. If she'd not seen Felix again, she'd have accepted. One man was better than many, and it would give her a measure of security she'd never enjoyed.

But Felix was imprinted on her mind, just as the essence of him permeated her body. Even though she knew he'd not repeat the offer he'd made when under the influence of love and lust and fired up by their lovemaking, Hope didn't think she had the heart to even contemplate accepting a similar offer from another man.

When she reached her room she sank onto the bed and put her head in her hands. Felix had been animated when he'd last gazed at her. What did he think of her now? If he'd not yet discovered evidence of her betrayal, it wouldn't be long before Wilfred made sure he was under no illusions as to the truth of Hope's blackened soul.

With a whimper, she curled herself into a ball and huddled on the bed, though it was difficult to breathe due to the restraints of her clothing.

Again, her mind drifted back to the day of the Hunt. She remembered the freedom she'd enjoyed when she'd donned her riding habit and joined the other riders. Secretly. Oh, but her mother had been furious, though her father had applauded her when he'd heard of it. *What an ally he'd been,* she thought with a pang. The only positive side to the fact he was no longer alive was that there'd be no risk of him learning of her sinful life.

Outside, the bell tolled midnight.

In another hour, Lord Westfall would arrive. Perhaps she could sleep a little. She was bone-weary. She sat up and consulted her appearance in the mirror. Madame Chambon would have noted with disapproval her failure to present herself earlier for general conversation with the gentlemen who crossed their threshold. However, if Hope's presence had been essential she'd have received a summons, but Madame Chambon knew Hope had entertained a gentleman in the afternoon and would again just after midnight. A girl needed her rest, and Hope would not be disturbed while she prepared herself for Lord Westfall. Vivacity and a sharp mind were requirements of the job.

Sitting in front of the mirror, she tidied her hair, the ringlets not quite as perfectly formed on account of her afternoon exploits. Her body sang at the memory.

But she'd be lanced by Felix's scorn next time she saw him.

She began to remove the pins that secured her elaborate confection of ringlets until her hair hung loose past her waist. Dear Lord, she needed to breathe, too. She undid the fastenings of her cuirass and skirt then unlaced her corset.

She'd only just slipped on a silk dressing gown when there came a sharp rapping at the door and a muffled voice amid feminine protests was heard just outside.

Hope turned the doorknob, and to her amazement, Felix burst in. His eyes were bright with a fervour very different from their mutually satisfying lovemaking of a few hours earlier.

"It's all right, Faith," Hope said over his shoulder, as calmly as she could. "I will see him. He's the gentleman I spoke of. In the meantime, please don't let anyone come in." When Faith had disappeared, closing the door, Hope retreated into the centre of the room, meeting his passion with cool dignity. "So, what can I do for you, Mr Durham?"

Broad shoulders and injured masculinity seemed to dominate the room. While he glared at her, Hope shored up her defences. She was in vulnerable territory here. Charlotte was to be married in less than three days, and Hope dared not test Wilfred's threats. So, she raised a faintly supercilious eyebrow and put her hands on her hips, wishing with all her heart she could wipe the glower from his face with the words he wanted to hear.

He did not advance. He did not cast his gaze over her modest room or the bed, merely glared at her from the doorway. "I cannot conceive of your motives in doing what you did this afternoon, Miss Merriweather, so I decided I had to hear what you thought you were about from your own lips." He was breathing heavily; his hands fisted at his sides.

"What exactly are you referring to?" She made sure there was no chink in her tone that would give him reason to suspect she was playing games. No, she was Hope Merriweather, hard-hearted prostitute, and he was nothing but her last assignation.

"Making me fall in love with you all over again. Stealing from me." His nostrils flared. "Mocking my manhood."

"I am guilty of just one of those things you listed."

He shook his head and lowered his voice as he advanced a step. "Hope?" His voice cracked just a little and she turned her head away. She couldn't go through with this if he persisted in this manner. But… she had no choice.

"I thought you cared for me." He looked truly as if his heart were about to break. "No, I shan't hurt you. I'd never do that. But you stole from me to give to Wilfred Hunt. What is he to you?" He cleared his throat and gathered his defences, it seemed. "That is the question I am here to ask."

"What is Wilfred Hunt to me?" Hope repeated the question musingly as she traced a pink goose-down-filled swirl upon her eiderdown with her forefinger. Oh, he was so many things. Seducer. Or was that putting too fine a point on it. Rapist? Yes, but men in his position didn't go to court for doing what he'd done to women like her. With her father dead, Wilfred—rapist, seducer—had become, ironically, her protector. And now he was protector of her sister's happiness. Or rather, he'd forced that role upon an unwilling Hope.

And by God, it was unwillingly that she said, "He is the man to whom I offered my allegiance. Long before you reentered my life, Felix. I did what he asked in this instance because of what I owe him, and therefore, I did it simply *because* he asked it of me."

His expression was steely. She wondered if he'd taken opium though she thought not.

"I've come from the gaming tables. I was at my club before then, and I've had some to drink, but by God, this comes straight from the heart." Taking two steps towards her, he seized her waist and drew her against him, pushing his face close so that she could feel his breath on her lips. His closeness made her feel faint with longing, but his anger would always now be between them.

Because of what she had done.

Because of what he believed was her duplicity, a falsehood she must perpetuate if she were to live with herself. For her sister's sake. Hope had lost all hope that something good might come out of the life to which she'd been reduced, but Charlotte balanced on the cusp of a future that was bright and full of…hope.

For a split second, she wondered if he'd strike her, out of character though that would have been. She'd have expected it from Wilfred.

Instead, Felix put his hands on her cheeks and, suddenly and with no warning, his lips to hers.

The sensation sucked all resistance from her. She felt her nipples puckering and that strange, desperate need in the pit of her stomach that made her cleave to him.

There was no resistance between their embrace before the fire and his lifting her onto the bed. No dialogue, no protests, nor words of love even. Their actions came from base desire, on her part as much as his, despite his anger, despite her grief over what might have been and what was forever destroyed by Wilfred.

For Felix now was taking his pound of flesh. He felt betrayed and now he was making her atone. She should have felt diminished, resisted.

But she wanted what he did as much as he did.

She rolled on top of him, her mouth fused to his as she worked the buttons of his trousers while her silk dressing gown fell away, exposing her breasts.

Heat speared her as he latched onto her right nipple, suckling, as she shimmied his breeches down past his knees until he was almost as naked as she was.

Just as she wanted him.

She had the power. On top, caging his body with hers as he laved at her breasts with his tongue, she wriggled into position, grasping, pumping his member while their breaths intertwined, mingling with increasing excitement.

Their bodies were attuned, their desires on par.

But their minds were so very much at odds.

He thrust into her when she was more than ready, her womb quivering with need, her entrance slick with want. And when he climaxed, she came too; her cries and gasps triggered by the sensation of being wanted by the only man for whom she'd felt desire, even if his lovemaking was driven by something so far from what she'd have wished.

"And this is what you enjoy with Wilfred Hunt?" he demanded, rolling onto his side when his panting had subsided sufficiently to speak, and his anger was finely tuned enough to turn its blaze upon her.

Enjoyed? That's hardly how she would have put it, but she had to maintain sufficient barrier between them until Felix had asked Annabelle for her hand in marriage. Every word she said now, every action, risked her sister's future happiness, but if somehow she could successfully navigate a tenuous path towards a future rapprochement between her and Felix, she would try.

"I am not in the habit of comparing lovers," she said, sitting up and encircling her knees with her arms as she tilted her head to look at him. Hurt and anger blazed from his entire body, so she turned away. It would take so little to sink into his embrace and cling. He mustn't know how much she wished only for him.

He put his hands behind his head as he contemplated the ceiling, the covers twisted about his shapely flanks. "You are the only woman I ever wanted." He spoke softly, his voice heavy with hurt and recrimination. "That night, at the Hunt Ball, I realised my obsession with you was not going away."

"Obsession?" He'd not used the word before though it was what he'd insinuated, and it's what she'd felt for her own part. A deep, abiding obsession that simply grew more acute with every encounter.

"Whenever I came down from school, then later, university, I always hoped I might see you. It's the only reason I attended church so meekly and obediently in accordance with my mother's wish every Sunday. And you smiled at me, Hope." He cleared his voice. "You gave me hope that you returned my feelings for you. The look on your face when you gazed up at me from the ground where you'd fallen from your horse. Do you remember?"

She smiled. The memory of every second of that day had sustained her through many a terrible ordeal—the handsome viscount's son, galloping after her, separating from the rest of the party, their shared laughter as they dared each other to more dangerous jumps over fallen tree trunks and hedges, until Hope's mount had balked at a jump, and she'd flown through the air and landed on her back on a soft, grassy knoll.

The horror and concern upon his face as he loomed above her, the distance between their mouths lessening until it was inevitable they'd kiss. And the rude interruption of Annabelle's cries.

Annabelle had galloped over, enquiring with false solicitude if Hope was uninjured but her interest—no, longing—for Felix was unmistakable while her suspicions had clearly been aroused.

Not that there'd been anything to be suspicious about until that moment. And even that had not, in fact, amounted to anything.

"It's true; I wanted you, but I also knew there could be nothing between us," Hope said slowly. "It had long been assumed that you and Annabelle would make a match, so I was not about to go breaking my heart." She swallowed, painfully, but said brightly, "And now you and Annabelle *will* make the match that will please your mamas. *I* am quite clearly ruined for you, but I was always warned by my mother to be careful around you for she feared I might be preyed upon for something other than marriage. It's the danger facing every penniless young woman with any claim to beauty."

"And you assumed I'd behave like any young man trading on his privilege to get what he wanted, even dishonourably." He didn't look at her as he rose from the bed and began to dress. His tone now matched hers: cool and detached. "You never took the trouble to know me, Hope, but if that's how you believe my character was formed, I suppose it would only ever have been about the sex. You enjoy that part, at least, it seems. Nothing more." He spoke through his teeth as he shrugged on his jacket, then did up his collar before reaching into his pocket and withdrawing a roll of banknotes. "How much do you charge for fifteen minutes of sex? I'm not in the habit of these kinds of transactions. One hundred?"

"That's more than generous."

"I'll make it two. It will probably be the last time."

"*Probably*? I thought you enjoyed it." With an effort, Hope kept her voice light as she leaned across the bed that separated them to reach for the money.

"I believe you're weighing up an offer from Lord Westfall. I heard it at my club." He closed his eyes briefly as if in pain. "He's a great deal richer than I am."

"But not as handsome as you, Felix. Or as satisfying a lover." Hope plucked her dressing gown from the end of the bed and shrugged into it, careful to appear heedless of his feelings. "He's due here shortly, so I must prepare myself. You realise what Madame Chambon would do if she caught you trespassing? I don't know how you slipped past her guard, but let me reassure you that I enjoyed our little session very much. I'm sorry I stole Wilfred's promissory note from you. That was naughty of me but I'm glad you're not too angry. I'm glad you came back for more of what we enjoyed this afternoon." She tucked a curl behind one ear and gave him a meaningful smile. "And I hope that when you've fulfilled your matrimonial obligations and given Annabelle the husbandly attention every new wife deserves, you will call on me again."

Hope had no concern whatsoever for Annabelle. Charlotte was a different matter. Until her sister was safely married, she wasn't about to put a foot wrong.

"I suppose if I'm in the market for sex with no strings attached and no danger of my heart becoming engaged, then a heartless jade like you would suit my purposes." He finished buttoning his jacket at the door then bowed his head. "It was, perhaps, a good thing we've had this conversation. It's brought me clarity, for I'd always believed you felt...*something*...for me." He touched his heart. "Something that might have grown into what I felt for you. Now I realise you always were the hardened little trollop my mother called you and, certainly, this way of life has hardly softened you."

CHAPTER 11

Hope threw herself face down on the bed and held her breath as she listened to his footsteps pounding down the passage. She was unprepared when the door was pushed open and Faith's voice floated tentatively through her distress.

"I…I'm sorry to interrupt."

The soft hand of sympathy that the girl laid on Hope's bare shoulder was too much. For so long, Hope had bottled up her emotions so that even she might have believed Felix's assessment that she had no heart. Until the storm of emotion hit.

"Hush!" Faith climbed onto Hope's bed and wound her arms about Hope's shoulders. "Hush, you don't want Madame Chambon to hear you." She sounded frightened. "I shouldn't have let him in, but when he said you'd visited him earlier this afternoon and hinted at what you felt about him, I'd hoped he might …" Her voice trailed away.

Hope tried to bring her sobs under control. If the other girls heard, Madame would be here in a flash demanding to know every last detail, and declaring roundly her disgust that Hope had failed in one of her primary duties: to be impervious to all feeling when it came to the gentlemen. Hope had never received one of her famous lectures, though girls who'd been so foolish as to have fallen in love had.

Hope rubbed her eyes. "Hoped he might what? Ask me to marry him? That doesn't happen at Madame Chambon's." She gave a bitter laugh.

"But if he was here, why didn't you tell him what you really felt? He might have set you up. Isn't that what all you girls want? A steady gentleman who is kind, and for whom you might feel a little tenderness."

Hope shook her head. "I couldn't tell him, though how I longed to."

"Why not?"

"Because unless he marries a certain young lady, I've been assured by someone that my sister will learn the truth of what I am, which will threaten her magnificent marriage which is to take place on Saturday."

"Oh. Blackmail." Faith nodded slowly. "That's a difficult one. Still, there's always later." She brightened. "Once you see your sister safely married, you can approach your young man and tell him the truth. Even if he is married, to someone else, he'll be glad to know what you really feel for him. And *then* he might offer to set you up."

Hope shook her head. "I don't believe I'll ever have an opportunity to tell him how I feel. Not when there is a malevolent gentleman who is determined to kill all feeling between Mr Durham and myself. And so, I must get used to the fact that the one man I've ever had feelings for is lost to me." She drew in a shuddering breath and apologised. "I don't know why I'm allowing myself to behave so foolishly when I knew long ago our love was doomed. Why, at fifteen, when I used to steal glances at him in church, my mother would kick my ankle and whisper that a future viscount, Mr Durham, would never look at a penniless female like me. A governess was what I was destined to become, and she always said I must remember my place."

She saw Faith was dressed for entertaining. Her hair was curled and elaborately pinned, and she wore a silk princess-line gown in palest blue with an elaborately looped bustle skirt and train.

Hope laughed, her look admiring, as she attempted to steer the conversation from her own distress. She sat up, settling herself against the bed end. "You'd turn every head in the room if you were being presented at court."

"My father is a silk weaver. Who knows but he wove this." Faith touched the fabric reverently.

Hope put out her hand and touched the girl's silk-clad shoulder. "And so you must look like a duchess to entertain the gentlemen. How long have you been here?"

"Eight months and I've never been with a gentleman."

Shocked, Hope looked from Faith's exquisite ensemble to the girl's beautiful face. "But Madame Chambon teaches you the graces with everyone else. She teaches you how to entice the gentlemen with gestures and wit. She pays for your clothes"

Faith shrugged. "My benefactress pays for my clothes and for my lessons."

"Your *benefactress*? She pays for you to live *here*?" Hope wasn't sure how to go on. "What do your parents think about that?"

"Of course they don't know. I was dismissed from my position as a housemaid one night after the young gentleman of the house took liberties. And Miss Gedge, an elderly lady staying at the house rescued me and, true to what she told my parents, has been responsible for turning me into a lady."

Hope couldn't fathom it. "A lady? Here? At Madame Chambon's? Who is this Miss Gedge? Have I seen her?"

"She'd never come to this house. She's a *real* lady. But I meet her for tea at Fortnum & Mason's once a month where she 'puts me through my paces' as she calls it."

"And is she satisfied with your...progress?"

"When I saw her yesterday she seemed satisfied." The girl pressed her lips together. "Mrs Gedge smiled—which is rare—and touched my cheek. She called me her 'beautiful weapon'."

"Hope!"

The two girls drew apart guiltily as Madame Chambon threw open the door and beheld the miscreants with a fiendish glare.

"Faith! Get out of this room. And Hope, Lord Westfall is downstairs waiting for you, and do you look like you're ready for him? He's early but that's no excuse. Good Lord! You'll pay for this, believe me! Now, get dressed while I ply him with drink, and make sure this is the last time you ever disappoint me or a gentleman caller again."

CHAPTER 12

"Darling, you look like you've seen a ghost." Felix's mother intruded into his orbit in a waft of lavender-scented water. The Ball at which his engagement would be announced later that night was the last place he wanted to be. It seemed surreal to be here after all that had happened since Hope had reentered his life two days before.

"Is it the lovely music that brings back memories, or the sight of your lovely betrothed?" she went on. Felix hadn't seen his mother this happy in years.

Strangely, it was his mother who echoed his thought, but with respect to the woman he was to marry. "I haven't seen Annabelle look this happy in years." Lady Durham tapped him playfully on the chest with her fan. "You certainly took your time about it, my boy. Annabelle's been expecting you to offer for her since she was presented, and that's more than two years ago." She gave him an incisive look. "For a while, I thought you must have lost your heart to someone else."

Obviously noticing the grim set of Felix's mouth, she added, "Please look happy about this, Felix. You know that I'd never force any marriage upon you if you were not fully committed, but nor have you been happy for a long time. You've known Annabelle her whole life and she'd do anything for you. I also happen to believe she will be good for you."

Felix nodded, eyeing the golden-haired girl as she was led off the dance floor by another escort. "I'm sure she will."

"As long as your heart is in this marriage, Felix." Lady Durham sounded concerned. She sent another glance in Annabelle's direction. "As long as you are not in love with someone else, Felix, for that would not be fair."

Felix shook his head, turning suddenly, his voice full of the scorn he felt. "No need to fear on that score, Mother."

Lady Durham put her hand on his coat sleeve as he turned to leave. "You will be kind to her, won't you? You know she's only ever loved you."

"Lord, Mother, you speak as if you fear I was Bluebeard himself." Despite himself, his mouth quirked. "I like to pride myself on being a cut above the usual reprobate."

"Yes, and I've always been proud of you for being a young man true to the highest ideals."

She hesitated, and he raised his eyes enquiringly. "Why do I think that was not all you were going to say?"

Lady Durham's troubled frown was swept away by her expansive greeting of an approaching couple, although the gentleman peeled away as he was detained by a knot of chattering women. "Why, here comes Miss Charlotte Merriweather. My dear Charlotte, you are blooming! Most brides would look considerably more nervous than you at the prospect of your marriage tomorrow."

"I have nothing to be nervous about," said the young woman with a quick smile at Felix, whom she'd come to know better during the past year since she'd graduated from the schoolroom. "I could think of no greater happiness than being Lord Hartley's wife."

Felix felt a tremor of emotion quite literally shake him to his foundations at the sight of the lovely, smiling, golden-haired creature, so different from her sister but clearly so at ease in her world. And so soon to marry a peer of the realm. *There really could be no greater contrast between Hope and Charlotte.* A spasm of rage and despair nearly choked him, though he managed with appropriate cordiality, "I don't think I've seen you in six months, Miss Charlotte." He kissed the back of her hand. "My mother is right. You look blooming."

"I have been fortunate, Mr Durham." She inclined her head with a smile at Lady Durham who now made her excuses to leave them. Lowering her voice when the older woman had gone, she added, "Unlike my sister."

"What do you know of your sister?" He regretted speaking so sharply though she did not appear to notice.

"I wish I did know something, Mr Durham."

"Please. Call me Felix as you did when you were a child. We've been neighbours our whole lives, and you are, after all, about to marry a friend of mine. We shall see each other often, no doubt." The thought brought a pang so acute he had to close his eyes briefly. Around him, the sound of chattering and the music of the orchestra that had just tuned up for a polka seemed overwhelming.

"Are you all right, Felix?" she asked anxiously.

"Heart pain. It happens. Please go on. What do you mean, you wish you knew something?" He tried not to let suspicion temper his words.

Charlotte frowned. "You recall the last time we met, when I chanced upon you in the village and we had only a moment to speak. I said I'd had a letter from Hope from her position in Germany, and that I'd thought the wording was odd and wondered if she was being kept against her will."

"How could I forget?" Felix had always seen himself as her knight in shining armour and had his studies and his mother not prevented him, would have searched for her himself.

Bitterness swept over him. But, he reminded himself, he had Annabelle now, and though she did nothing to set his pulses racing, he'd always liked her well enough. For a short while, after the shock of his mother's pronouncement that Hope appeared set to marry her employer's nephew in Prussia, he'd finally reconciled himself to the idea of marrying Annabelle. The two families had, after all, long been pushing for a union.

And that's what he'd do. Please them all. Hope Merriweather did not want him. She'd been playing with him from the start.

Charlotte's voice intruded, returning him to the noisy, heated throng with its brittle gaiety that sat so ill with his current mood. "Well, a strange thing happened last week, Felix, and I just can't stop thinking about it."

She looked troubled as he nodded for her to go on.

"I was looking through Mama's writing desk, which is usually kept locked, when I came upon a letter." She glanced quickly behind her as if afraid of being overheard.

Felix gave her a smile that was more indulgent than encouraging. Young ladies, he'd discovered, liked making secretive discoveries. "I hope you weren't prying where you ought not."

"Not intentionally, of course." Miss Charlotte looked concerned rather than embarrassed or chastened. She frowned even harder as she studied the ivory carving of her fan. "The letter was from Hope, and when I saw the postmark, I realised it had been sent from London two weeks after she was supposed to have boarded the packet to the Continent."

"Why is that so strange?" Felix asked. "She probably gave it to someone to post who delayed doing so."

Charlotte slid her eyes across the room to where her mama was in conversation with Lady Hunt. "I assumed the same but, you see, the letter was half out of the envelope, and when I pushed it back in I saw that she'd addressed it to Papa, not knowing that he'd died suddenly just after she'd left here."

"You read it?"

"Well, it was addressed to Papa, and he's dead, but Mama had obviously opened it, and I wondered if it would cast some light on where Hope might have gone," Charlotte said, a trifle defensively. She looked at him imploringly. "Oh, Felix, I've been tormented by what she wrote but I can't speak of it to Mama."

A chill of foreboding settled upon Felix. "Why not?"

"In the letter, Hope tells Papa she's in a terrible situation, and she begs him to go to London. She says she'll wait for him at a particular address if he will only meet her there. She literally begs him. And there are what look like teardrops, and her handwriting is all shaky. I've never seen her write like that. She says in the letter she'll promise to live quietly at home for the rest of her life and not to be the wild girl who Mama so deplores if he'll only forgive her and let her come home. But, of course, Papa died, only Mama said nothing at all about this letter, even though she must have read it *before* she told everyone about Hope writing to say she'd arrived safely in Leipzig."

Felix stared. He did not interrupt. He didn't, in fact, know what to say. When Charlotte continued to look at him, perplexed, he said quietly, "Go on."

"Well, Mama kept pretending that Hope *had* gone to Germany. Why, she was the one who passed on to me the letter that Lady Hunt said came from Hope in Germany, which is when I spoke to you."

Felix chewed his lip, his thoughts running all over the place. "Lady Hunt?" he muttered. "Why would she receive a letter and pass it on? What interest does Lady Hunt have in all this?"

"Surely you knew it was Lady Hunt who organised for Hope to go away?"

He shook his head.

Charlotte sighed. "Poor Mama was at the end of her tether with Hope. She said she was a hoyden and unmanageable, and I remember hearing Mama and Papa arguing about what to do with her. This was a little over two years ago. Then, Lady Hunt told Mama that she had the perfect position for Hope, as a governess to two children in Germany. Friends of Lady Hunt, in fact. So Mama told Hope that's where she was sending her, as they didn't have the money to launch Hope, and she might as well be a governess in Germany as here, for her prospects would be better, considering these friends of Lady Hunt were such an important family in their country."

"Go on," Felix prompted. "I presume Hope didn't want to go."

"She certainly didn't. In fact, she refused, and there was the most terrific fight between Hope and Mama and Papa. Then I overheard Mama telling Papa that it was beyond anything, and the most marvellous opportunity, that Lady Hunt should position Hope so well *and* that she'd offered to sponsor me for my coming-out when the time came." Charlotte worried at her lower lip, her expression troubled. "I was too young to realise that the two went hand in hand: that Hope's marvellous opportunity relied on her being sent away, and that I, by contrast, was to be given a new wardrobe and invitations to most of London when I was of age to make my debut."

The churning in Felix's breast increased. "I'd say so," he muttered. "But more to the point, what happened regarding Hope's request for aid?"

Charlotte shook her head. "Mama has been silent on the topic, and, of course, I didn't even know Hope requested help until I saw the letter last week which was dated after she was supposed to have boarded her boat for Germany." She fanned herself rapidly as if to channel her nervous energy into some occupation, for her distress was obviously increasing through the telling of her story. "I've not known where to turn. When I asked Mama if she'd had news of Hope, she said Hope was doing marvellously in Germany and was likely to soon receive a very fine marriage offer. This was only last week!"

"So *nothing* was ever said by either of you about Hope's letter?" A sudden thought occurred to Felix as he took in the lovely young woman before him, her looks so like her mother who'd been an acclaimed beauty in her day. "Has your mother tended to favour you over your sister?"

"I never thought of it when I was younger. Hope was always so fiery, and Mama was always slapping her, while I was always told I was the good girl, which made me rather smug." She looked rueful. "But I do remember one day when I was alone with Papa in the drawing room after Mama had gone to lock Hope up in her bedroom again, that I asked why Hope and Mama were always fighting. I'll never forget his answer. He looked at me sadly and said, more to himself, really, that it was hard for a beautiful woman to see the child she rears grow more beautiful as she herself ages, but intolerable for her to accept that her stepdaughter is garnering more interest than she."

"Good Lord, I didn't know your mother wasn't Hope's natural mother."

"Hope's mama died when she was born, and Papa married Mama when I was a year old. Hope's always called her Mama, and although I know she must have been told that Mama wasn't her real mother, I can't ever remember any mention in the house of Hope's real mama. I suppose that's because Mama tends to be a little jealous."

Felix nodded. "So your mama and Hope had their differences."

"I'd never have said it was something I noticed, especially, but after I came upon Hope's letter, I began to remember so many things that Hope had said were unfair when we were younger, though she seemed to have become resigned to it, later. Papa used to defend Hope when Mama flew into one of her furies and that used to make Mama even more furious." Charlotte sighed. "Since reading that letter I've been so worried about Hope. I just wish I knew where she was and that I could be assured she was all right. And as happy as I am." Her face brightened as Lord Hartley joined them, flanked by Lady Hunt and Annabelle.

Felix nodded at the easy-natured fellow whom he'd known since childhood. He was a decent chap, and he had no qualms he would treat Charlotte well. He also bore all the signs of a man in love which was good to see.

So did Annabelle, which gave him dreadful qualms of anxiety, for his mind was deeply troubled by the ramifications of what Charlotte had just told him. Gazing at Annabelle's luminous face framed by golden hair, he knew he'd have to work hard to make himself love the girl within, though her temper was equable and she'd always appeared to him pleasant enough.

She'd had no shortage of admirers, either, and seemed the kind of social butterfly who knew just what to say. Annabelle had set her sights on him from early on; he knew that.

And the previous afternoon, furious after his midnight encounter with Hope, he'd attended Lady Hunt's afternoon garden party, as arranged, and surprising no one more so than himself, agreed with Annabelle's father, Sir Reginald, when the fellow had said that the time really had come to put the girl out of her misery, and that Felix should get over his foolish objections to becoming leg-shackled and marry his daughter. For the next half an hour, Felix had had to put up with Annabelle's gushing as to how he'd made her the happiest bride-to-be in all England, and even before she'd stopped her prattling, he'd felt like the most trapped man in all England.

Still, he knew what was required of him, so when she clasped his forearm fondly, now, he returned the look as best he could before saying, as Mrs Merriweather joined their circle, "What a joyful occasion this is for everyone. My condolences, Mrs Merriweather, that your husband will not be around to witness Miss Charlotte's happy day, but I wonder if Miss Hope will attend the wedding."

Mrs Merriweather, a handsome woman of middle age, had been all amiable smiles. Now she looked momentarily discomposed before she glanced at Lady Hunt, who said smoothly, "Alas, Hope is unable to make the long journey from her situation in Leipzig. However, the news you clearly haven't heard is that she, too, is in receipt of an offer that will make her just as happy as her sister."

"Mama, you never told me!" gasped Charlotte, while Felix went suddenly cold.

Mrs Merriweather nodded. "I'd been meaning to, my dear, but the last few days have been all about you and your wonderful plans."

"Mama, she's my sister! Of course I'd want to know." Charlotte looked distressed, and Felix asked, "Who is the gentleman in question?"

Mrs Merriweather, at whom he'd directed his query, glanced at Lady Hunt who said, "The nephew of the family to whom she went as governess two years ago." Smiling at her companion, she added, "I told Margaret it was a wonderful opportunity for Hope, and so it has proven to be."

Felix glanced at Charlotte, who looked nonplussed but said nothing, and then Lord Hartley turned the subject by inviting her onto the dance floor, and the party broke up.

Felix felt it was appropriate to invite his betrothed onto the dance floor also, as he needed the exertion of some energetic waltzing if only to give his mind free rein. Making small talk with Annabelle would be excruciating, but fortunately the fast pace of this waltz would preclude that.

He needed to sort through his head all the conflicting information he'd learnt in such a short time. Not that he'd learnt much. He'd only been presented with unexplained anomalies.

Miss Charlotte had had only questions that he could not answer and which, indirectly, he'd asked Mrs Merriweather, who'd, in turn, directed them to Lady Hunt.

Felix had a dozen more questions though clearly he was going to get only lies if he asked directly.

He wondered what Annabelle knew of the clandestine affair between Hope and her brother. And how long had it been going on? Had Hope eloped with Wilfred before she was due to meet Felix at the church and then discovered she'd not chosen the better man, hence her letter begging for rescue and forgiveness?

"My, Felix, but you're a superb dancer," Annabelle told him, laughing at the pleasurable exertion as he led her off the dance floor a few minutes later. Her face was flushed and her eyes sparkled as she squeezed his arm. "I know you must be bored hearing it, but you truly have made me the happiest girl in all the land."

He had to go carefully. It would not do to burst her excited bubble. Annabelle, for all her generally equable nature, could sulk and rage, he knew from having known her since she was in the cradle. Not that they'd had very much to do with one another until she was a young woman assessing the local talent in the district before being prepared for her London debut. He wondered why she hadn't made more of her opportunities for snaring any number of the eligible and far more illustrious catches she could have made.

Felix forced a smile as he made an expansive gesture with one arm. The other was being tightly clung to by Annabelle.

"And you are a butterfly amidst the throng. Young and beautiful. Why choose me?"

She looked coy. "Why, you chose me, Felix."

"But you could have made any number of wonderful matches

during the last two years." He plucked two glasses of champagne from a passing waiter and handed her one. "I often wondered why you didn't marry in your first season out. Or your second."

Annabelle took a sip, staring at him over the rim. "I was waiting for you," she said softly.

He gave a nervous laugh. "Me? Why, I'm hardly the greatest catch in this room. Granted, there are many mamas who would have welcomed me as a suitor in the local district but you, Annabelle, could have done so much better."

"I knew from the moment I turned twelve years old that I wanted only you, Felix. And now my patience has paid off."

He repressed a shudder as she went on, "I remember the first local ball I attended. I hadn't come out yet, but Mama let me go so I could get my feet wet, as they say." She smiled. "You were the very first gentleman who asked me to dance, and when you put your hands on my waist and twirled me round the room, I knew I need look no further for my husband. I'd known you since I was a little girl, Felix, but here you were, a handsome, grown-up gentleman, down from Cambridge, and my Prince Charming. You danced with me three times that night, and when I got home, I told Mama I would save them the expense of a London season because the husband I wanted lived in the large house on top the hill."

"Waiting patiently for me to settle down, eh, and realise at last that I needed a wife?"

She put her head on one side, paused, then said under her breath, "Yes, once you'd got over your obsession with Hope Merriweather."

He felt her words like a knife and winced.

Perhaps she didn't notice for she went on, "That wild girl was the despair of her mama and papa. Her behaviour was scandalous—"

"Was it? I don't recall that." Nor did he. Yes, Hope was spirited and loved to ride fast and to run about the neighbourhood without restraint, but was that really wild? He'd done the same when he was a lad.

Annabelle's nostrils flared. She glanced about the room then back at Felix. "I know the local ladies decided she should not be invited to the local entertainments because she was a corrupting influence on the rest of us."

"Poor Miss Merriweather. That must have been hard."

"And wasn't that confirmed when she rode so boldly right into the Hunt! The ladies were scandalised. Her mama was mortified, but Hope wouldn't listen to anyone, and she rode with the rest of them as if she were...one of the men!"

Felix stared through the girl speaking as he remembered his impressions of Hope joining them so confidently, horses and hounds making way for the fine figure she cut. So young. So defiant. The gentlemen hadn't seemed to mind. In fact, some of them had applauded her for her spirit.

And she certainly hadn't seemed like one of the men when she'd fallen from her horse, and he'd nearly kissed her. But Annabelle would remember that.

"You rode too, Annabelle, if you recall. You joined us just after Hope fell from her horse."

Annabelle sent him a suspicious glance. "I went for a gentle canter. I did not join the Hunt, but I came upon the two of you, as you no doubt recall."

Felix nodded. "You seemed very concerned about Hope's well-being. I remember being a little surprised when you dismounted and rushed towards us, crying out to know if she were hurt."

Annabelle nodded. "Of course. We might not have been bosom friends, but Mama was on friendly terms with Hope's mama, or should I say stepmama, so we were together a bit."

"I hadn't known Mrs Merriweather was not her real mother. Hope must have been distraught when her father died so suddenly, just after she'd left for Germany."

Annabelle gave a somewhat frustrated sigh. "And now she's to marry the nephew of Mama's friend in Leipzig. She has been away a long time, Felix, and she's not once written to ask after any of us." She paused, adding firmly, "Hope's never coming back to England."

Felix nodded slowly. "Never coming back to England," he repeated softly, frowning as he asked, "I believe you farewelled her at the station on the day she left. Was she sad to leave? She'd promised to say goodbye to me but she didn't."

He saw her guarded look. "There wasn't time. You remember the snowfall we'd had the night before. Mr Merriweather couldn't get his carriage out from his stable, so he sent a message round and Wilfred and I picked Hope up on the road. But that's a long time ago. Hope's gone to another country now and you are marrying me. Please let's not talk about her. I've waited so long to be reassured that your heart belongs only to me. Perhaps you loved Hope once, but she didn't return your feelings otherwise she'd have waited. Or come home. Or sent you a message."

But Felix's thoughts were stuck in the past. Though no words of commitment had been spoken, he'd have staked his life on the fact Hope wanted to meet him at the church before she left for Germany.

"Did Hope ask you to stop at the church when she got into the carriage?"

Annabelle's expression was combative as she shook her head. "She was just worried she'd miss her train."

Felix couldn't bear the subterfuge. He gripped Annabelle's gloved forearm and put his head close to hers, hoping the gesture would be interpreted as loving by onlookers. Really, he'd never felt more angry and hunted in his life. "Tell me what happened inside the carriage, Annabelle," he muttered. "Something happened. Did she get on that train? Did you see her get on that train?"

Annabelle swivelled her gaze as she instinctively moved away from Felix's uncomfortable interrogation. "What an odd question. Well, of course she got on that train. Wilfred took her there. He told me so."

"He *told* you so? Then *you* didn't see her actually board."

"I was dropped off at my friend's house in the village," Annabelle said defensively. "But Wilfred was going directly to the station. Yes."

"So, if Hope was full of enthusiasm for her new adventure as you say, what aspect was she particularly excited about? Charlotte tells me she didn't want to go."

"Really, Felix, is this necessary when we are just betrothed? It's hardly nice to talk about Hope Merriweather to the girl you're going to marry."

"No, but I need to be reassured that Miss Merriweather said nothing about me before she left." Felix called on all the creative logic at his fingertips, knowing that his response was lame. Nevertheless, he needed something from Annabelle. Something to start working with to put the pieces of the puzzle together. "Please, Annabelle. Think. That'll help me put the past behind me, once and for all."

Annabelle gave a huffy sigh. "She was sleeping. She didn't say a word."

"*Sleeping?*"

Felix's shocked tones took Annabelle by surprise. Colour stole into her cheeks, and she looked like she was giving herself a mental shake as she replied, cagily, "She'd had something to drink which I think might have made her sleep. By accident, though."

"By accident? What do you mean?" Alarm was weaving through Felix now at a rapid pace.

Annabelle frowned as she apparently tried to recall. She seemed uncomfortable in the face of Felix's intense stare and tossed her head, giving a false little trill for the benefit of the others in the room, though her expression was concerned. "Hope had been waiting at the end of the driveway in the cold for us to arrive, for of course we couldn't venture to the house in the carriage with the fallen tree blocking the way. After Wilfred helped her into the carriage, I offered her what I thought was the flask containing warm honey and lemon that Mama had sent with us."

"What do you mean 'you thought'." Felix didn't care how menacing he sounded even if the consequence was that Annabelle looked frightened.

In a softer voice, the girl replied, "I accidentally offered her the wrong flask. It was Mama's, and Hope drank long and deep much more than she should have—and suddenly she was sleeping."

"Good Lord, Annabelle! What are you saying?"

Annabelle looked distressed. "Oh, Felix, if you must know, Hope was a complete fool for drinking so much from Mama's flask, though

I tried to pull it away from her after I realised it was the flask into which I'd added the contents of the laudanum vial I'd purchased earlier from the apothecary. One should only take a couple of drops in liquid at a time."

"I know," said Felix, heavily. "So you're telling me you drugged Hope."

"I didn't *drug* her," Annabelle bristled. "Not intentionally, and of course it was hardly going to kill her. Mama takes laudanum all the time. Papa worries, but Mama says she only takes a few drops and her mood is so much sweeter when she does."

"So you just left Hope sleeping?" Felix asked.

"Well, we'd arrived at my friend Jenny's house, and Jenny was waving to me from the window. Wilfred said he'd ensure Hope was awake to get on the train and that's how we parted." Annabelle shot Felix a suspicious glance. "*Of course* Wilfred would have waited until Hope was well enough to get onto the train. My brother is a gentleman."

She said it indignantly as if it were likely that Felix would refute the truth of her statement.

But Felix wasn't focused on Annabelle. Rather, he was assimilating how this new evidence from Annabelle accorded with what Charlotte had told him.

"Felix! Where are you going?"

But Felix ignored her.

CHAPTER 13

With a final flourish, Hope arranged the feather in her elaborate coiffure and stepped back to admire the finished ensemble. Madame Chambon had been disappointed Hope's wealthy admirer had not offered the lavish terms expected during his last visit and Hope was feeling the pressure.

Daisy, her dresser, clapped her hands. "I reckon Lord Westfall will throw a pearl choker inta the bargain when 'e sees ya, miss." She knelt to arrange Hope's train. "Will ya be sad to leave this place, then, if Lord Westfall makes ya the offa ya's bin expectin'?"

"It'll be nice to have to please only one gentleman," Hope said, thinking to the future and trying *not* to think of Felix whose marriage to Miss Annabelle had just been printed in the newspapers.

"Ya gotta twist him round yer little finger early, miss. When 'e wants ya real bad. That's when the gennulmen are most generous." Daisy fussed about Hope, dishing out advice like a seasoned professional. "An' ya gotta put some unda a stone fer a rainy day. That's what me gran always told me. Not that it's likely I'll eva 'ave any spare ta put unda a stone. But ya will, miss. Yer a sharp one. That's why Lord Westfall likes ya. 'E likes 'em with wit ta go with beauty an' all them other things gennulmen can't live wivvout. If ya play yer cards right, 'e might even make ya 'is wife one day."

Hope raised one eyebrow. "Women like me don't become wives, Daisy."

"Jess did."

"She married the blacksmith because she was so desperate to be respectably married, and his was the best offer that came her way." She gave a half smile as she thought of the lengths to which she'd go to be respectably married. Soon, she'd become Lord Westfall's mistress, she supposed, since there were precious other options that would not see her into an early pauper's grave.

As for Felix, she'd heard nothing from him since their tense, impassioned coupling of several days ago. Wilfred would be very careful to ensure Hope posed no danger to his sister's happiness and position as Felix's new wife—both before *and* after Charlotte's marriage—and Hope could only assume he'd done his worst.

Whatever Felix's feelings for her, there'd been no time to explore the intimacy sufficiently for Hope to take the risks she might have done had she known Felix deeper, for longer.

Adopting a falsely light tone, she said, "No, Daisy, I am irrevocably of the demimondaine class, and the demimondaine exist purely to *amuse* gentlemen like Lord Westfall. Neither he nor any of his friends would dare upset the natural order of things and outrage society by considering marriage to a woman like me."

Daisy sighed. "But them's the ones what put ya where ya are. It ain't right an' it ain't fair."

"Life isn't fair but we all have to make the most of it. Now, am I ready?" Hope asked, turning the subject briskly. "Lord Westfall has been kept waiting long enough."

Madame Chambon's curved staircase was designed for theatrical entrances, and Hope had perfected sweeping down it to a fine art.

The response from his besotted lordship was predictable and gratifying.

"Exquisite! You are a diamond of the first water, Miss Hope," he declared, holding out his hand to assist her from the bottom step. "You do me proud. Are you ready for a night of entertainment?"

Hope smiled. The idea of being escorted straight to Lord Westfall's townhouse for an orgy of sex was not appealing, but if she could become mindless after a few champagnes and some exuberant dancing, it would go some way towards dulling the pain that throbbed behind her eyes. Whatever bedroom delights Lord Westfall had in store could then be dealt with more tolerably.

She gazed at him over the top of her fan, employing the artful trick Madame Chambon taught her girls that suggested barely contained excitement at whatever delights the gentleman at hand might have in store.

"It sounds too wonderful," she murmured. "Where are we going?"

Lord Westfall then proceeded to list an evening beginning with a play in Covent Garden followed by some gambling, and finally dancing at the premises of a popular London demimondaine.

"It sounds exhausting," Hope commented, as Lord Westfall helped her into his carriage.

"Ah, *amusement*. You've proven yourself a young woman of stamina on many an occasion. I'm sure you won't be too exhausted for the culmination of our evening."

"I await it with pleasure." Hope fanned herself vigorously, careful to ensure her eyes sparkled at him from above the ivory points. Fortunately, Lord Westfall would be easy to manage and was among the more desirable of protectors, given that she needed to look to the future.

The future. She tried not to allow herself to be cast down by despair as the image flashed into her mind once more of the printed notice in The Times announcing Felix and Annabelle's betrothal.

Tomorrow, Hope's own sister would be making a match to a man every bit Lord Westfall's equal. Their mama had done well to pay for the accoutrements that would be required to fit Charlotte out as a contender for a gentleman of such address. Perhaps she'd remarried. Hope had heard nothing in two years about her family other than the news of Charlotte's impending nuptials. She'd only learnt of the death of her father from Wilfred two weeks after the event which, perhaps, explained why the two letters she'd sent had gone astray or been ignored. Either was possible, though she presumed the latter to be the case. After Papa had died, Mama must have washed her hands of Hope.

Hope had never known another mother—her own mama's name had never been mentioned—and she'd been eight when she'd deduced through something a visitor had said that Mama was not in fact her real mother. When she'd questioned her father, he'd said the matter was not to be spoken of again. Hope and Charlotte were equal in both their parents' eyes.

But that had not been the case. Hope knew that.

THE PLAY WAS ENTERTAINING, THE GAMBLING NOT SO MUCH. LORD Westfall drank too much, and persisted at the gaming table long after his luck had run out. Until, seizing Hope by the waist, he insisted she throw the dice, after which he was on a winning streak, and his jovial spirits had returned.

At last, Hope persuaded him it was time to move onto Skittles Parlour and was glad at the opportunity to converse with some of her friends there. Several of the lavishly bejewelled courtesans clinging to the arms of their respective aristocrats were graduates of Madame Chambon's.

When a lively waltz began to play, Lord Westfall took Hope onto the dance floor where he proceeded to display his expertise as a dancer.

Hope was sorry when the polka that followed it sapped his lordship of his remaining energy, and she was suddenly alert with fear and acute feeling when his place was taken by a newcomer desiring to partner Hope.

The two men greeted each other affably, Lord Westfall surrendering his soon-to-be mistress saying, "Be my guest. Hope has more stamina than I do. I'm sure she'll lead you a lively dance." He thought he was being funny with the double entendre which Hope ignored, but which caused Wilfred to laugh more loudly than was warranted. He, too, looked as if he'd had too much to drink.

"You're looking as beautiful as ever, my lovely Hope," Wilfred remarked, as he twirled her into the centre of the dance floor. It was a slower waltz, to Hope's annoyance, so conversation was possible. The last man she wished to converse with was Wilfred Hunt.

She stared stonily over his shoulder. "I saw your sister's engagement notice in *The Times*. You must be pleased."

"I am pleased that my sister is happy. And my parents. It's a fine match." Wilfred's smile was as artless as if he were discussing the marriage of a couple of acquaintances.

"So, you have achieved your aim." Hope was silent as she went through the elaborate lengths to which Wilfred was determined to damn her in Felix's eyes.

Wilfred merely inclined his head.

"Then perhaps, since you *had* already achieved your aim, you then felt it was *not* necessary to give Felix the promissory note I took from him?" She smiled sweetly as she caught his eye, and pushed her point in case he'd been too obtuse to understand to what she was alluding. "In view of the fact that it would be a small kindness to atone, in part, for what you have done to me."

Wilfred's mouth turned up at the corners. It was one of those small, self-satisfied, gloating smiles that made her vision go black, for that's how he'd always smiled at her when he knew he had the upper hand. How he did love to trade on his superior position. He had Hope exactly where he wanted her.

"Of course I gave it to him. And of course he was distraught. Understandably so."

The music trailed off, and Wilfred led her off the dance floor. Seeing Lord Westfall occupied, he caged her hand on his arm and continued walking her through the merry throng.

A large withdrawing room just beyond where the dancing was

taking place was empty. Leisurely, Wilfred closed the door behind them, muting the noise as they gazed down onto the gaslit street.

"Why do you hate me so much?" Hope asked, turning, resting her elbows on the window ledge. It was colder here. The fire was not burning as brightly as it was in the makeshift ballroom.

"On the contrary, I desire you more than I desire any other woman alive," Wilfred replied conversationally. "The fact that I can't afford you is what eats away at me. You can't imagine my regret at having to pension you off to Madame Chambon."

"Really." Hope's tone dripped scepticism. "I had very little say in the matter, as you recall."

Wilfred shrugged. "As I've told you before, you were costing me a fortune, yet you showed no gratitude after your mother disowned you, leaving me the only person in the world concerned for your welfare. You were hardly a pleasure to come home to, and I was the one person standing between you and the gutter."

"And what else might you have to say to me, Wilfred, when you know I am to become Lord Westfall's mistress?" she asked. "What might he think if he came upon us speaking so intimately now?"

Wilfred shrugged. "You're not his mistress yet, which means you are anyone's—at the right price. Perhaps I'm negotiating. It might be in your interests if I raise your price."

"You really think you could tempt me back into your bed?" Hope resisted the temptation to be more cutting. Wilfred could be unpredictable when his manhood was at stake. Yet she couldn't help herself, saying under her breath, "Alas, you'll never be able to afford me now, Wilfred. I would not offer you what you want at *any* price."

He considered her a moment, his gaze speculative. "What about if I put in a good word for you to Felix? It might soften the rage and disappointment he showed when I revealed your touching loyalty towards me after I told him that our tender feelings for one another were the reason you stole the promissory note in order to return it to me? You could have us both. I don't mind sharing."

She stared him down. "I'd not trust you to follow through, even if you gave me your word."

"Hardly the kind of thing a man of honour wants to hear, Hope." Wilfred put his fingers around her wrist, but she tugged herself free and, in a fit of chagrin, swept over to the fireplace, glaring at him as she leant against the mantelpiece.

"Yours has never been a word of honour, Wilfred. Your word counts for nothing. And that doesn't come from me. There are plenty who say it."

The flare in his eyes revealed she'd touched a nerve, though he contained his anger as he walked slowly towards her. Hope wasn't frightened. She could hear the music and the hubbub of voices quite clearly on the other side of the door.

She stood her ground defiantly as he loomed over her. "Look at you, Hope," he sneered as he put his hand on her shoulders. She stiffened as he moved them lower, contouring her breasts, waist, and thighs in her clinging, ruched gown, so thoroughly upholstered yet so revealing. His nostrils flared. "Do you think you'd have been so expensively garbed if you'd remained at the vicarage? Your father was ever a disappointment to your mama. She complained endlessly to my own dear mater that she'd married a man of reasonable fortune who'd managed to see it all slip through his fingers."

Hope breathed through her clenched teeth as she stared up at Wilfred. "My Mama's love of adornment was a large reason for Papa's pecuniary difficulties. Papa could refuse her nothing. Yes, her complaints were as endless as her demands for fripperies. Until finally, there was nothing left with which to appease her. My father inherited a fortune and a harpy for a wife, and he was no financier, but *he* did not kidnap and keep captive unwilling females."

"Kidnap? Lord, Hope." His mouth quirked. "You stayed with me for more than a year, but you were not a prisoner. It's not as if I kept the door locked and you bolted within. You could have left at any time."

Hope shook her head. She'd been so proud of keeping her emotions in check, but revisiting the time when her life had changed so irrevocably was proving too much. "Where was there for me to go, Wilfred?" Her voice broke. She took a deep breath and managed to regain her composure. "After Papa died, when Mama wouldn't take me back, how could I even get respectable employment when I had no character? And now, having destroyed every hope I ever had for happiness, you want to rub my nose in the dirt?" It was as inexplicable now as it ever had been. And the pain was just as acute. "Somehow, you think it'll make you feel more of a man to have me agree to the grubby arrangement you just put to me—you *and* Felix. Yet all that business before regarding the promissory note and my character blackened in Felix's eyes was so your dear sister's happiness would not be imperilled?You're a liar, Wilfred. You will *never* let me near Felix." She heard the dangerous passion in her tone but couldn't help herself. "I'm too dangerous. I might take something away from your sister, and I might take something away from you. So, you want to crush me."

Unexpectedly, Wilfred gripped her shoulders, bringing her face close to his. His eyes were black with anger. "By God, Hope, but for someone drilled in the noble art of the courtesan, you do not know how to please a man when it is in your interests."

Hope shrugged herself out of his grip and took up her argument from further along the mantelpiece. "If you wanted my love and respect, you'd have had to have had a modicum of honour, Wilfred. You destroyed every claim to honour when you bundled me into your carriage, took me to your lodgings, and…*raped* me when I was unconscious. There's no coming back from that for me." She trembled with emotion. "Or for you."

His eyes darkened and his lips twitched. "Is that the story you put about? Do you cast aspersions upon my honour behind my back? Why would people believe a prostitute who's parted on acrimonious terms with her former lover?"

"You were never my lover, Wilfred. I despised you from when you were a whining child. Felix was the boy I loved, and he turned into the man I loved. But your jealousy got in the way of that. You were determined that if I wouldn't love you, then I would never have the man I really loved. Isn't that true?"

Advancing a few steps, he shook her roughly, and her jewelled comb fell out of her hair and skittered across the marble hearth.

"Ever the bully, Wilfred!" Hope whispered as she bent to retrieve it, not prepared for the stinging blow he dealt her on the side of her head. Her knees gave way and she sank to the floor, staring up at him with more fury than fear as she touched her throbbing temple. "And so you hit me where no one can see the evidence of your violence. How manly of you."

"Bitch!" He hissed, his hands flexing but Hope was ready, wresting herself out of his attempted embrace and landing awkwardly, though her voluminously swathed skirts broke her fall.

"Don't you touch me again!" she spat. "Ever!"

"Don't *you* tell me what I can and can't do when your wares are available to any man who has the right currency!" Grabbing a hank of her hair, Wilfred pulled her to her feet and dragged her through the withdrawing room towards a door at the far end.

Before Hope could scream, he'd clapped one large, sweating hand over her mouth. "You're about to realise there comes a point where even the most long-suffering man must defend his honour," he muttered as he manhandled her out of the room and along a passageway.

He was too strong for her. Hope's attempts to kick and bite her way to freedom were to no avail, and her first instinct after he thrust her through a door at the end of the passage was to take the deep, sustaining breath she so desperately needed.

Though there was a bed by the window, Wilfred pushed her down on the cold stone hearth, straddling her as he clamped his other hand over her mouth. "You're about to see how good you had it when you were first under my care." He sounded both aggrieved and threatening as he pushed his face into hers. "If you'd only known how to treat a man as he deserves, I wouldn't have to show you who's the superior being. You always thought it was you, didn't you, Hope, with your scorn and your ingratitude."

"The superior being?" Hope sneered on a lungful of air when he removed his hand in response to a sharp nip of her teeth. "Always the bully, Wilfred."

"It's a clever man who knows how to get what he wants, even if that means using his superior strength, Hope," he grunted, forcing her back to the floor when she struggled to rise, running his hands over her and groping her breasts before clamping her mouth again when she tried to scream.

Hope fought with everything she had, but he was too strong, hiking up her skirts while she lashed out at him, clawing at his face, whimpering for mercy, and then in rage though it was hard to breathe. She thought she'd pass out, and perhaps that was a preferable way to suffer the indignity he intended to inflict upon her.

But when his fingers parted momentarily and a sustaining draught of air filled her lungs, her seeking hands came upon something long, and hard on the ground behind her. Too starved of air to realise what it was, another gulp of oxygen made it clear it might be her only chance to gain the upper hand.

Drawing back her right arm, she brought the fire iron through the air with all of her might, landing a slicing blow against the side of Wilfred's head.

He released his grasp, yelping with pain, his fury prodded to a fine point before, almost instantly he was looming over her, his mouth a rictus of rage, eyes bloodshot with fury. His hand shot out to seize the poker from her but Hope was too quick. Rolling onto her side, she aimed the point for the region of his eyes, closed her own, and with all of the strength she had left, lunged forwards and upwards.

A moment of silence followed. The world swirled behind her closed eyes in terrible shades of black and red.

Then, upon a terrible cry of agony, Wilfred's heavy body came down on top of her.

CHAPTER 14

"I don't care if she's preparing to see the Prince of Wales, I just need to know where she is!" Still panting from the exertion of his strenuous walk due to a hackney carriage accident which had made the roads impassable, Felix stood on the front doorstep of Madame Chambon's Nunnery and stared down the broad-shouldered custodian who'd been brought in as a reinforcement by the young maidservant after she'd failed to send Felix on his way.

"Where Miss 'Ope 'appens to be right now is nobody's bizness 'cept her own an' the gennulman wot's payin' fer her." The beefy fellow wore no jacket, and his muscles bulged beneath his shirt sleeves. He flexed his meaty fists.

Frustrated, Felix raked his hand through his hair, replaced his top hat and turned on his heel. There'd be no satisfaction this night, it seemed.

After his illuminating discussions with Charlotte and Annabelle less than an hour earlier, he'd left for his club. It was pointless trying to distract himself there. The fact was, despite the late hour and the fact Hope may well be entertaining, he had to see her at the earliest.

The past was the past and what had happened to her couldn't be changed by what he did tonight or tomorrow, but the urgency to learn from her own lips the events that had taken place when she'd left the district threatened to send him mad.

He was a few steps along the pavement and about to hail a hackney when a tentative voice behind him made him turn.

"You're the gentleman who visited Hope the other day, aren't you?"

Felix was struck by the girl's angelic looks. Wearing a clinging long-line gown in white and silver and standing on the top step of Madame Chambon's, she looked like an angel in the gaslight.

"Where is she?" His urgency overrode good manners.

"Will she want to see you?"

"Perhaps you know the answer to that better than I." His heart skittered as she appraised him.

The girl squinted as if trying to decide whether to engage him further. "Are you the gentleman who knew her before she came to London?"

"It depends which one. There were two of us." Felix realised this only as he spoke the words. Wilfred had always wanted Hope. As much as Felix had.

"The gentleman with whom she only recently renewed her acquaintance?" The young woman put her head on one side. "The one for whom Hope was a special surprise. The only gentleman she said she's ever loved."

Felix did his best to resist any feeling that resulted from her words. "Then why did she steal from me? If she told you she loved me perhaps she told you the answer to that also."

"Blackmail." The girl said it matter-of-factly.

Felix's suspicions hardened into a kernel of vengeance. The pieces of the puzzle were all coming together, and he'd soon be searching for Wilfred as diligently as he was now searching for Hope.

But Hope was his first priority, and he needed to find her before another day dawned, though it didn't stop him asking, "She said she loved me?" It was a delight to hear it from anyone's lips though he'd rather have heard it from Hope's own.

The girl nodded. "You'll find Hope at Skittles, if she's still there.

Lord Westfall took her for a night out, though he might have taken her back to his lodgings. You know he's going to make her an offer tonight?"

"An offer?" For a ridiculous moment, Felix misinterpreted her until she said, laughing, "What kind of offer do you think? To set her up, of course. That's what all the girls here hope for. And Lord Westfall is smitten. He's a good catch."

The imperative for Felix to scupper Lord Westfall's offer and make good his own was suddenly too great for him to stand there talking any longer. Bowing his thanks, he hailed the next passing hackney carriage and was soon bowling through the cobbled streets towards the lively premises of one of London's most notorious courtesans. Felix knew Skittles' lodgings well.

The party was in full swing, as it usually was at three in the morning. Felix had been to Skittles before, with Millament and others. Good food, good conversation and lovely women were the order of the day. The drawing room was a long expanse from which the furniture had been cleared for dancing at the far end. Felix scanned the dozen or so couples who were taking up the available space in a fast Viennese waltz. He could not see Hope. At the rear of the room, a few tables were occupied by card players, while to the side a supper table laden with tiers of rich fare had attracted a small crowd.

Felix made his way through the throng, nodding at various people he knew until he was accosted by Millament.

"Back in the land of the living again, eh?" his friend greeted him. "I dropped into Lady Hunt's and congratulated your future wife, though she seemed surprisingly out of spirits. No doubt it was on account of you leaving before your engagement announcement to go gallivanting about at a renowned courtesan's lodgings—though I'm sure you didn't tell her that!"

"I told her I was going to my club." Felix continued to search the room, looking over Millament's shoulder.

"Jolly good! Great progress since last week. I thought you were going to retreat back into one of those blue funks of yours. Last thing we all expected was an engagement to Miss Annabelle Hunt! Sly old devil. And there I was, thinking you'd lost your heart to a prostitute, though she's more than that, eh? What a beauty! She could pass as a duchess, eh. She's here, actually. With Westfall."

Felix cut him off impatiently. "I see Westfall over there. And she's not with him."

Millament shrugged. "She's probably dancing. Oh, yes, now I recall. She went yonder with that fellow I don't care for who, regrettably, is brother to your betrothed so you're going to have to suffer his company, which means I no doubt will too."

Felix stared after his pointing finger and took a step towards a closed door at the far end of the room before Millament clapped him on the arm.

"I say, you're not going after her, old chap. Not good form, I must remind you. Not been yourself, have you, so I feel justified—"

Felix removed his friends hand and ignored his call for restraint as he parted the throng of merrymakers in his pursuit of what he'd find on the other side of the doorway he pushed through.

If Hope was alone with Hunt, it didn't augur well, whether or not she was there of her own choice. Not that Hunt would have tied her up at Skittles and whisked her into a back room, with so many people about to witness his crime, he reassured himself.

Nevertheless, something malevolent was at play. Hunt was blackmailing Hope. The girl in the diaphanous gown had said it. She'd implied it was Hunt, and Hope had told Felix she'd been Hunt's mistress before joining Madame Chambon's establishment. What she hadn't yet explained was how her fall from grace had come to pass.

The large room into which he stepped was empty. A few pieces of elegant furniture indicated it was a private sanctuary, but the half-open door beyond suggested Felix might find his quarry along the passage.

It was eerily silent as he made his way through the back of the house, opening doors but finding only neatly made beds and cold fireplaces.

Two more rooms until the last one. He stopped. He thought he'd heard a noise. It was muffled. A thud, a faint cry. The chink of something metallic landing on stone. He'd heard it often enough when the housemaid disturbed his morning slumber, dropping one of the fire irons upon the hearth.

Someone occupied the last room, and he didn't care that he showed no restraint in bursting in. He gripped the brass knob, surprised and relieved that the door was not locked, and pushed.

The door did not yield immediately. Something was blocking the entrance so that he had to put his shoulders into it and shove with all his might in order to slide through the opening.

He was not prepared for the sight that met his eyes. Bathed in gloom, he could make out the figure of a woman, kneeling at the side of a man. A tall, large man in evening dress who lay, unmoving, blocking the door.

Felix was more worried about Hope than the unconscious man whom he was recognised as a horribly marked Wilfred Hunt.

"Hope?" Felix crouched beside her, his insides recoiling at the damning sight.

"I've killed him." She didn't look up, but kept her gaze on the figure whose right eye was smashed in. "I've killed him," she said again, even more softly, as if she couldn't believe what she'd done.

Nor could Felix. He didn't think he'd seen a sight so gruesome and his stomach clenched, but overriding his revulsion was his terrible fear for the woman kneeling by Hunt's side.

"What did he do to you?" Gently he put an arm about her.

The distant strains of the orchestra could be heard from the makeshift ballroom while the night caller declared it to be four in the morning. All the sounds indicated it was an ordinary night but Felix knew nothing would ever be ordinary again.

"He tried to force himself on me. I know I should have submitted, but I just couldn't do it again." Her voice cracked. "I couldn't give him the very last of me…of my dignity."

She turned, her eyes luminous in the dark but she didn't seem to register Felix's identity. He was simply the man who'd stumbled upon her crime.

"Wilfred is dead, and I'll hang. It was always going to end in tragedy." She sounded resigned, but then her eyes widened as if at last she realised to whom she was speaking, and she reached out a hand, her voice urgent. "Felix, please, don't let them release my name until Charlotte is married! She needn't know the truth of what I've become. It needn't destroy her happiness. Don't let my notoriety be known before Charlotte is Lady Hartley." She withdrew her hands to cover her eyes, adding brokenly, "Otherwise everything will have been for nothing."

Felix couldn't help himself. He'd wanted to rescue Hope his whole life and now he finally had the chance. He took her in his arms. She didn't resist but nor did she cleave to him. It seemed her fear for her sister's happiness was more important than her own future; more important than anything else.

He kissed the top of her head. "Is that how Wilfred blackmailed you? By threatening to reveal the truth of your…profession…and thus shame and disgrace your sister, putting her marriage in peril?"

"He was blackmailing me over what *he* turned me into." Hope raised her stricken face to his, then looked down at herself, her expression one of contempt as she contoured her ruby-clad gown with both hands. "I am anyone's who can pay for me. Would *you* like me, Felix?" Her voice shook as she uttered the words that seemed to brand her as so much worse than she could ever be. "Before they take me away, I'll give you a good price because I've always liked you. Truly, I have. And I know you once liked me. The night of the Hunt Ball. I wanted you to kiss me then. I'd never been kissed before, and I wanted you to be the first." She ran the back of her hand across her face. "But, of course! That's why you're here. You were looking for me, weren't you? You wanted to make me another offer?" She gave a bitter laugh. "A counter offer to Lord Westfall's. Congratulations on your impending marriage, Felix. I'm sorry I just killed your future brother-in-law. I never meant to cause trouble. But please, try and keep my real identity secret, at least for as long as it takes for Charlotte to be married. That's all that matters."

"Hush!" He restrained her hands in his to stop their agitated plucking at her skirts then pulled her against his chest. "No one knows who you are, Hope," he soothed, "and no one will know you're associated with Charlotte. *Ever*. I'll make sure of it."

She sagged against him and began to weep. "I'm sorry, Felix. I must be filth in your eyes."

He shook his head and held her tighter, kissing the top of her dark glossy hair once more and revelling in her need for him. It fulfilled his own desire to be more to her than he ever felt he could be. "Never," he whispered.

Gently, he put her away from him and turned at the sound of a voice calling him from further down the corridor.

"I say, Felix! Where are you? Westy's on the warpath, so if you're up to something I give you fair warning. Good Lord!" Finding the door difficult to open, Millament had given it a good shove and now stood upon the threshold, staring at the grisly scene.

"Close it!" Felix barked, and open-mouthed, Millament obeyed.

Hope began to speak but Felix cut her off, rising, and taking her hand to draw Hope to her feet. "I found Hunt in the process of ravishing Miss Merriment, and I killed him," he told Millament matter-of-factly. "When he rushed at me with the fire iron, I seized the poker to defend myself."

"You *killed* him?" Millament's eyes bulged. "You killed Hunt…your future brother-in-law…for ravishing a woman who's paid by dozens of men to do exactly what Hunt was no doubt going to pay her for? And you *killed* him?"

"I was defending the woman I'm going to marry."

"Christ, Felix, have you taken leave of your senses? You're going to marry Miss Annabelle Hunt!" Millament looked bilious as he glanced at the man lying on the floor then added, "The woman whose brother you just killed defending a prostitute, in case I don't have to remind you again!"

Felix fixed the young man with a steely stare. "Just between you and me, my friend, I shall offer you the truth before I concoct the story the court needs to hear." He reached out one arm to draw Millament aside. "The truth is, I killed the man who kidnapped the woman I'd *always* intended marrying; the man who stole her virtue when he raped her, who then sold her to a brothel, and, because he was drunk on the power he had over her, proceeded to blackmail her so that not one shred of her dignity remained." Felix took Hope's wrist, but she resisted when he tried to put his arm about her.

"You can't do this, Felix," she whispered. "You can't destroy your life because of me. Mine is already worth nothing. Don't sacrifice yours for nothing."

"For *nothing*?" He'd never felt more convinced of the rightness of his actions.

"It's too big a gamble," she said urgently. "You may think you're being noble now, but you won't when your life is hanging in the balance. Please, Felix"

They heard more footsteps. Felix dipped his head to Hope's ear. "Don't refute what I say. I have a chance of being exonerated if I claim responsibility. *You* don't!"

"You can't, Felix!"

"Why did you not contact me when Wilfred held you against your will? Or when he came back to blackmail you? Why? Was it because you thought my sense of propriety would be offended? That I'd consider your actions so dishonourable? Well, I am that man of honour you believed me to be, and I will not see a travesty of justice condemn you to death." He turned to Millament, his heart racing, never more desirous of his friend's acquiescence. "Promise that you'll agree with everything I say! And promise me that you'll ensure that Hope is safe. She must leave this house *now*. I don't want there to be any association made between her and Hunt. Not ever, and certainly not until long after her sister weds Lord Hartley on Saturday."

"Hope's *sister* is to wed Lord Hartley?" Millament swayed with astonishment.

"Hope Merriweather left England for Germany to be a governess. At least, that's what everyone thought. However, before she even made it onto the train she was kidnapped by this man…" Felix indicated Wilfred with a scornful nod, "and sold to Madame Chambon. That is the truth. We will, however, adhere to the fiction that Hope has, in fact, spent the last two years in Leipzig, and that she was, only this afternoon, greeted off the boat by Hunt who took her here, to this house, against her will, where I found her and defended her honour. In no way must her good name be compromised."

"Impossible!" Millament shook his head, his horror having turned to measured concern. "Felix, I want to help you, but it's impossible. Why, half the men in this room have slept with the woman you claim is as pure as the driven snow. Beg pardon, Miss Merriweather, but we're speaking facts."

"It can be done," Felix insisted. He would not be dissuaded now. He pushed Hope towards his friend. "Take her away. Quickly! I'll deal with this. Our first task is to keep her name out of the newspapers until her sister is married tomorrow. No mention of her identity, and remember, I have spoken only to you about that because I trust you, and you are the *only* one who can help us now. I'll worry about the rest later."

CHAPTER 15

EIGHTEEN MONTHS LATER

"Goodness, darling! You'll never believe it!" Hope couldn't keep the shock from her tone as she stabbed her finger on the article in *The Times.*

Felix looked up enquiringly from where he was eating his breakfast at the table opposite.

"Miss Annabelle Hunt is to marry Lord Westfall."

Felix stood up and went round behind her, placing a hand on her shoulder as he read aloud the news. Hope twisted to look at him, smiling as she gazed out at the snow-capped mountains and the past flooded back.

"Well, provided nothing happened to prevent it, they're already happily wedded," Felix said, pointing to the date.

Two months prior. Although it took a long time for London newspapers to reach the Black Forest, this one must have been unusually delayed.

"Are you all right, my love?" Felix murmured, in that concerned, reassuring way of his that had been so hard to get used to. Not that he mollycoddled her. Hope had made sure he didn't do that. But, for as long as she could remember, no one had concerned themselves about Hope unless it was to further their own ends.

She nodded.

"And baby's doing well?" Gently he placed his hand upon her belly, not yet showing, but occupied by a growing little being that had, declared Felix, added a layer of joy to his life he could barely credit.

"Baby's doing very well. And so is its mother." Hope twined her hands behind Felix's neck and brought his face down for her kiss.

They were interrupted by the arrival of the parlourmaid carrying a silver salver with several letters bearing London postmarks. Hope straightened, thanking then dismissing the servant. She had taken well to being mistress of her own household and every day basked in the relief that her past was not about to destroy the happiness she'd found with her new husband.

"One for each of us, including news from Charlotte!" she cried happily, bending over Felix to reach for a knife to slit the envelope, then unfolding the parchment. "Oh, and she's having another baby!" she added when she'd scanned the page. "I wish I could see her children. *And* Charlotte. It's been nearly four years."

"Would you really?"

"Of course, I would!"

"I mean, would you really want to go back to England? With all its dangers?" Felix tapped the letter he'd just read. "It's an invitation from the London Literary Society to speak about *On Her Majesty's Service*."

Felix had not idled his time away in their mountain eyrie. In between loving Hope, he'd penned an exciting spy novel which had started life as a distraction when he refused to return to England without his darling wife.

Hope clapped her hands, excitedly. "What an honour! *You* want to go, don't you? Surely you need to, since you became Lord Lambton?"

"I won't go without you, and I don't think it's wise for you to return after so short a period of time."

Hope regarded him seriously. For some months, she'd been assessing the right time to broach the subject. She took his hands and began to chafe them lovingly. "You were the one who endured so much during the trial. My identity was protected. You arranged everything, Felix. And it's not as if you're proposing to live there. *I* have no fear in going back if you can contrive to keep my presence secret as you managed so assiduously before."

He looked troubled. "That's just it, Hope. I don't want to keep your presence secret. I want the world to know you as my wife. I want your stepmother to accord you the respect you deserve and which she withheld, and which makes her an accessory in the terrible crimes against you."

Hope shook her head. "You want a true justice, my sweetheart, but that's not possible. At least for another few years, it's wisest for me not to be introduced as your lawful wedded wife"

She was cut off by an announcement from the returning parlourmaid that they had an unexpected visitor who'd just arrived in the village and, learning that they were residents of the chateau on the hill, wished to pay his respects to Lord and Lady Lambton. "A gentleman by the name of Lord Farrow."

Hope gasped, and Felix looked discomposed before he said to the parlourmaid in German that he and his wife would be delighted to attend to Lord Farrow in the drawing room in five minutes.

"I can't possibly appear!" Hope whispered. Lord Farrow had been one of her greatest admirers when she'd worked at Madame Chambon's.

Felix only had to look at her panicked face to understand her. "If we're to visit England, then consider this your first test." He raised her hand and brought it to his lips. "Courage, darling. You're not the one who deserves opprobrium. I'm right here with you. And are you not the most consummate actress in the world when you need to be? Why, there was a time when I was certain you cared nothing for me!"

On Felix's arm, Hope swept into the elegant vault-ceilinged withdrawing room of the chateau they'd leased since they'd fled to the German dominion following the trial that had exonerated Felix who had been found to have acted purely in self defence after Wilfred Hunt, horribly drunk, had tried to murder him with a fire iron.

"Lord Farrow, I don't believe we've had the pleasure," Hope murmured after Felix had introduced her. Madame Chambon's training had been thorough, and there was no sign of the terror Hope felt at being recognised, even as his lordship sent her a long and scrutinising look after he'd failed to hide his surprise.

"Is anything the matter, my Lord?" Felix enquired as he led them to a cluster of seats arranged around the fireplace.

Lord Farrow appeared to collect himself. "No. Yes, that is, Mrs Durham—or should I say, Lady Lambton—looks familiar."

Hope feigned surprise as she exchanged looks with her husband. "Do you know, Felix, that's the second time someone's said that to me." She laughed. "Another friend who came to visit Felix said exactly the same thing: that I bear a striking similarity to someone who was well known to them in England. When I quizzed him on who it was, his memory failed him." She turned back to Lord Farrow. "Tell me, who is the lady you speak of whom I so closely resemble? It's rather amusing to be mistaken for someone else."

Lord Farrow flushed hotly and shook his head. "I can't quite recall and besides, you are far more beautiful than she, Lady Lambton, even if I can't remember her name." When it looked as if Hope might persist with her questioning, he went on in a rush, "And you're even more beautiful than your sister whom I met some months ago with her husband at the theatre. I believe you've spent the last five years in Germany."

Hope seated herself and inclined her head. "That's correct. Lord Lambton and I would very much like to return to England, though, if only to visit. Why, we were in fact discussing the possibility when you were announced." Hope smiled warmly at her husband, the glint in his eye telling her she was doing well.

Lord Farrow cleared his throat, dragging his admiring gaze from Hope's face to his host's. "In that case, perhaps you'd both be my guests for a little shooting party on my estate I'm organising next August—should you be there at that time. If you follow the Hunt, you'll be in excellent company."

Hope and Felix exchanged looks, and Hope nodded slowly. "I

believe that would fit in well with Felix's itinerary. He's been asked to address the London Literary Society," she added proudly.

"Splendid!" Lord Farrow clapped his hands together. "I'm so glad I looked in on you. You've garnered quite the notoriety, and I'll confess my curiosity got the better of me."

"Notoriety?" Hope asked, cautiously.

"Lord Lambton's runaway success. His book!" Lord Farrow explained. "Perhaps you don't know that everyone back home has been talking about it." A shadow crossed his face, and he lowered his voice. "I hope you didn't think I was referring to that...other matter."

Hope saw that Felix was looking warily at their visitor who went on, seemingly unaware of the sudden tension. "Hunt was despised, in the circles to which I belonged, at any rate. Although he was never called to account for it, he was a bounder. A thief and a liar. It came as little surprise to anyone that he could also be capable of violence and, my dear Lord Lambton, it was perfectly understandable in most people's eyes that you, being a man of honour, did the only thing you could under the circumstances."

When Lord Farrow had gone, Hope exhaled in relief as Felix took her into his arms.

"We've passed our first initiation," Felix murmured into her hair. "And you were marvellous."

"But will I be so marvellous if Lord Farrow *does* invite us to his estate and suddenly I'm faced with so many of the men I once knew under...circumstances I'd care not to remember." An unexpected sob rose in her throat. "Oh, Felix, surely an encounter like this—and every similar one to follow—will erode just that bit more of your respect for me?"

He put her away from him, shaking his head as he smiled.

"All that matters to me is what you are: a brave, clever woman whom I'm lucky enough to call my wife. And, if Lord Farrow invites us to his estate, and we join in the Hunt, it's my intention to do what I failed to do all those years ago and which might have inexorably changed the future had I not lost my nerve but rather just kissed you as you lay on the soft earth, in that secluded clearing."

"Oh, Felix, I would like that very much," Hope said upon a sigh, closing her eyes as she nestled against his chest, breathing in his wonderful, familiar, and comforting smell of fine wool and the sandalwood soap he used.

AND INDEED, AFTER LORD FARROW PROVED TRUE TO HIS WORD AND Felix, Hope and their first child—a lusty son they named Benedict—were ensconced at Farrow House the following August, Hope and Felix did find an opportunity to peel off from the pack and discover the perfect grassy glade for Felix's promised tryst.

Furthermore, with Hope's courage having been bolstered by Felix's reassurances that she was equal to anything, Hope was warmly received by the other guests, the gentlemen having been warned the evening prior that Lady Lambton bore a "startling resemblance to their favourite of all Madame Chambon's girls whose body had been tragically fished out of the Thames".

However, it was unanimously agreed that Lady Durham was even more lovely.

THE END

KEEPING FAITH

CHAPTER 1

"What did you learn last night?"

"A gentleman must always believe he knows best."

Confident that her answer was pleasing, Faith reached across the table to help herself to a macaroon, but a sharp slap across the back of the hand stopped her progress by the silver teapot.

Her smile of feigned contrition was rewarded with the briefest of nods from Madame Chambon. Not an invitation to partake of a macaroon though. The table laden with eclairs and petit fours in Madame's private sitting room was merely for show.

"Greedy girl, Faith! You can eat at Claridges Hotel tomorrow, and I daresay you won't even spare a thought for the other girls who are justified in being somewhat jealous of your cosseted life."

Madame sniffed as she patted one of the grizzled orange curls of her elaborate coiffure. Faith suspected a squirrel's pelt had made its contribution. "I'm sure they wonder every day why you never have to stir yourself, or anyone else for that matter, to get your fine clothes or a roof over your head." Madame Chambon piled three macaroons onto her already laden plate, before making a sweeping gesture that encompassed the furnishings of her surprisingly decorous private sitting room with its gold-tasselled, green-velvet curtains and flock wallpaper. "What have you told them, Faith? About why you are here, I mean."

Faith's stomach rumbled as she gazed from the prints of the famous artists that lined the walls to the fine fare in front of her, ordered from Fortnum and Mason. These monthly sessions in table manners were supposed to give Faith the practise she needed to deport herself like a lady when eating in public, though, under Madame's guardianship, Faith never actually got to try the specialties.

"Answer me, Faith. In all the three years that you've been here, you've had to do precisely nothing to justify your existence. Surely the girls have questioned you? I have my own version of the truth for them, as you know, but I'd be interested to hear what you have to say."

Faith didn't answer. She already knew how lucky she was, but Madame was not ready to drop the subject, despite having just crammed an entire chocolate éclair into her mouth. Faith just managed to make out the muffled words, "Every night you lie peacefully in your bed while the other girls have to earn their livings."

Lying *peacefully* in her bed was not how Faith would describe the restfulness of her slumber. She was kept awake every night by the grunts and cries of ecstasy that penetrated the thin walls of her attic chamber.

Still, she'd finally learned when it was wise to respond meekly, so she bowed her head and stared at her neat kid gloves while dreaming of the delicacies Mrs Gedge would order for them when Faith really was dining with her at Claridges Hotel the following afternoon. The Sacher-torte Mrs Gedge had *ummed* and *aahed* over before finally choosing the baked Alaska from the sweets trolley last month still haunted her. However, since part of Faith's tutoring included how to win over reluctant gentlemen 'and make them wild with wanting' which is how Madame phrased it, then surely Faith could persuade her American benefactress to order the Austrian chocolate specialty?

She was so busy rehearsing her words for tomorrow that she almost missed Madame's prophetic and appalling statement.

"Well, Faith, the time has come for you to start earning your way now."

It seemed the ground fell away from under her as Faith gripped the table edge. For so long, she'd known the reckoning would come. Yes, and with three years preparing for it, she'd believed she could meet it head-on with the necessary fortitude.

But there'd been no warning.

She began to shake, biting into her bottom lip and clasping her hands beneath the table to try and keep secret the manifestations of her terror from Madame, who'd only be spurred into gloating and make her suffer even more.

"Mrs Gedge reported last month that she wasn't entirely happy you were ready for what she has in store for you when she took you to tea, Faith." Madame chewed noisily, unperturbed, it seemed, by the crumbs that landed on her gaudy vermillion skirts.

Faith didn't suggest that Mrs Gedge's dissatisfaction was perhaps the fault of Faith's tutor, the one sitting in front of her, who knew nothing about deporting oneself as a lady.

With a dainty gesture using only her forefingers, Madame Chambon raised her plate and licked at the crumbs that had not been dislodged by her fat fingers before saying, "Fortunately, Lady Vernon is recovered at last from her long indisposition and has agreed to forget your rudeness to her from six months ago. In fact, she'll be here shortly. Yes, she'll soon have you passing the scrutiny of the most discerning duchess." Madame gobbled down another macaroon with as much finesse as the dogs Faith's father used to goad into fighting each other for the scraps from the scrubbed wooden table at the farm. Not that there'd been many scraps with ten children to feed.

"Should we not have waited for Lady Vernon?" Faith suggested, daringly. But she had to say *something* to stop herself from launching into a volley of querulous questions about exactly what form this 'having to earn her own way' might take.

Madame Chambon pushed aside an untouched plate of bread and butter to reach for another chocolate éclair and sighed. "There was just so much food on the table it seemed unnecessary to wait if her ladyship was going to be late. Ah! And here she is." Madame's orange-painted mouth turned up at a knock on the door. "Shoulders back, Faith! And make sure you don't talk with your mouth full."

Since this was not a danger, Faith supposed there might be some compensation in having to face her former nemesis, who surely must subscribe to the belief that learning table manners required one having to *eat*.

Madame threw her arms wide in a welcome as the door opened to admit the new arrival. "Good evening, Lady Vernon. We're so glad you've recovered from your chest ailment," she gushed. "A good rest has done you the world of good. Why, you look ten years younger. Just as you do every time I see you in fact. And we're indeed humbled that you've consented to return." Madame simpered at the elderly woman dressed all in black who looked, Faith thought, even more wraith-like than usual as she pinned up the veil of her bonnet and took the seat at the table proffered by Madame, who went on, "I'm sure you'll feel even better once you've heard Faith's heartfelt apology."

Faith blushed under the scrutiny of the two pairs of expectant, unforgiving eyes, and glanced longingly at the remaining macaroon.

Yes, there were times when it was worth being abject. She mightn't mean what she said, but if the last three years under Madame Chambon's roof had taught her one thing, it was how to sound heartfelt and sincere when she felt anything but.

"I'm sorry for my rude comments about..." Faith hesitated. Perhaps it was best not to stir up old memories. While it must be perfectly obvious to anyone who met Lady Vernon as to why an earl's daughter could remain a spinster into her sixtieth year, it hadn't been in anyone's interest—Faith's least of all, it turned out—for Faith to have gone into quite such specific and extensive detail regarding her thoughts on the likely reasons. "I behaved like a child, though it's such a long time ago now, I can barely remember what was going through my head at the time. I *was* only seventeen and, in those days, prone to losing my temper, but now I'm eighteen and thanks to all your efforts in teaching me how to act like a lady, Lady Vernon, I'm so far from the rude and impulsive young thing I was before, you'd not recognise me today. Thanks to your thorough tutelage, I am determined that I will never speak out of turn to you, or anyone. Indeed, I have changed! I truly believe that confronted by a table of delicacies like this, for example, I would certainly not embarrass you or Mrs Gedge or any lovely young man or his mother who might take me out to tea by any show of greediness or lack of restraint."

Lady Vernon's eyes remained fixed firmly on Faith for the duration of this speech with no indication of how forgiving, or otherwise, she might prove to be.

After a long silence, she spoke. "Restraint?" She sniffed. "Restraint is the most important requirement of any young lady, Faith. I've told you this many times, so I'm glad it's a lesson you claim to have finally learned."

Still with her eyes fixed on Faith, she reached towards the remaining macaroon that sat lonely on its plate just in front of them both, her long-fingered hand hovering just above. "Please pass that to me, Faith. I can't seem to reach it."

Wordlessly, Faith complied, schooling her features into impassivity while she railed inside, *I hate you! I hate you!* Outwardly, she gave nothing away as she watched Lady Vernon transport the coconut confection to her thin, bloodless lips.

"Delicious," murmured Lady Vernon. "In fact, I believe it is the best macaroon I have ever tasted. You must surely agree, Faith, since the plate is now empty."

She looked pointedly at the two remaining crumbs that clung to the edge, as if to imply that Faith had eaten the rest. Then she indicated the plate of bread and butter near Madame Chambon. "Please eat, Faith. Madame Chambon and I have a leisurely afternoon at our disposal. She and I will partake of the remaining chocolate eclairs..." Her pointed chin wobbled slightly, whether from the suppression of mirth, or the swallowing of bile, Faith could only guess, "while you make good work of the bread and butter with all the ladylike restraint you're so anxious to prove."

CHAPTER 2

Faith had learned to suffer in silence and to keep her thoughts to herself, long before she'd been brought to Madame Chambon's. Madame might have been gloating the day before over her silly little bit of power play but in a few hours Faith would be sitting at a proper grand table laden with even nicer delicacies. Ones she could eat.

Furthermore, she'd be free of Madame's cloying presence for an afternoon, admired in public by women who would sweep past in fashionable gowns adorned with cascades of bows and swathes of silk and satin who would see that she was every bit their equal.

Faith could barely suppress her excitement as Charity, from the room below hers, pinned up her hair the following afternoon.

"I'll bring a macaroon home for you, Charity," Faith promised, sitting as still as she could while Charity arranged a small jewelled comb amongst Faith's fair curls.

"I doubt your Mrs Gedge would take kindly to that. Wouldn't she call it stealing?"

Faith took a quick, surprised breath and glanced at Charity. Her best friend at Madame Chambon's had never before resorted to unkind digs. But perhaps Charity was simply reminding Faith of the very real dangers of taking what Faith honestly believed had been promised; only to have it called stealing. It's how Faith had found herself deposited at Madame Chambon's, instead of before a magistrate.

"You *will* get your macaroon, Charity. And it won't be stealing. I shall simply be practising what Mrs Gedge has instructed I be taught these past three years." Faith smiled sweetly. "Deception. Taking what I want without the other party realising they've surrendered what they had not intended giving. Inveigling my way into their good offices." Immediately, she felt overwhelmed by the unknown. "Do you think I'm up to the task, Charity?"

"Lord, Faith, I'm not used to hearing you talk like that, and it's unnerving." Charity stepped in front of Faith, her eyes skimming the length of her ensemble, from the demure neckline to the simple and depressingly plain skirt. Faith had expected to be dressed with all the flamboyance exhibited by Charity's black and scarlet polonaise with its daringly low neckline and whisper of a sleeve. "You always sound like you know exactly how to get what you want."

"It's what I pretend. To Madame and the other girls." Faith squeezed her eyes shut briefly and flicked away a tear. "Well, she might think I'm beholden to her because I have nowhere else to go and because Mrs Gedge pays her to keep me, but I swear to you that there are some things I won't stoop to, regardless of whether it's in Mrs Gedge's grand scheme for me."

Charity looked at her enquiringly.

It had seemed foolishly naïve to voice this determination in a bawdy house and to a friend who, every night, suffered what Faith was about to declare she'd never do.

"I will never go with a man I do not love. Yes! You might smile, Charity, but I have learning, and I have fine clothes, and I know how to behave like a lady. I'm cleverer than Madame Chambon thinks, and I am not afraid of Mrs Gedge anymore." Her bosom heaved. Now that she was voicing her most fervently held innermost thoughts, there was no turning back. "No Charity, I swear it! I will not be taken by a man I do not love."

"Ah Faith, now sit down again and let me repin that errant curl at the back." Charity's tone was as light as her hands were on Faith's shoulders as she resettled Faith upon the stool of her dressing table. "I believe that's what Anastasia said too, which got the fire up Madame's backside and all but condemned Anastasia to the very worst next gentleman. You be careful who you say such things to."

Faith glanced at the keyhole. They'd been foolish words and too loudly declared. What Charity said was true.

"How is Anastasia now?" she asked, biting her lip. "I haven't seen her for a few days."

"That's because she's not here anymore. Didn't you know?" Gently, Charity began to massage Faith's neck. "Once her bruises had faded, Madame said she couldn't risk Anastasia ruining the reputation of a house to which gentlemen came expecting the loving comfort for which Madame Chambon's is renowned. Now, you look beautiful, Faith. And I'm sure Mrs Gedge will think so too." She smiled and touched Faith's cheek, saying with genuine kindness, "And so too will the handsome gentleman Mrs Gedge has lined up for you. Indeed, I believe he'll be so kind and gallant that you'll fall instantly in love with him, and he with you, and soon you'll be galloping into the sunset together to some gilded castle where you'll enjoy a life of ease and domestic joy for the rest of your days." She sighed wistfully. "And I will never hear from you again, but I will go peacefully to my grave knowing that at least *you* found happiness, Faith."

CHAPTER 3

"A good thing you know how to balance your appetite for the good things in life without spoiling your pretty figure, Faith." Mrs Gedge's American accent seemed more pronounced when she was in fine spirits. She smiled at Faith across the damask-covered dining table, before taking a sip of Rhenish. Her violet ostrich feathers, coloured to match the silk polonaise she wore, reminded Faith of bowing acolytes. Like the other women in the room, she exuded wealth and privilege. Faith felt dowdy in comparison. She'd truly believed Mrs Gedge was going to dress her up to the nines to show off her protégé. "I was a beauty in my day," Mrs Gedge went on. "I worked hard at it, and I had many marriage offers."

A stroll through Hyde Park and an exhibition had followed their afternoon tea at Claridges, and now they were seated in a restaurant with hand-painted ceilings, attended by obsequious waiters while an orchestra played, partly visible through the sumptuous palm fronds that screened their table.

Mrs Gedge put down her knife and fork and sent a considered look about her. "The power and wealth of the gentlemen in this room could tilt the world's axis if they only knew how to work together." Her nostrils flared. "If they only harnessed it for good rather than expended their energies on satisfying their personal desires. I brought you here for a reason, you know. Because someone of interest was going to be dining here. Do you recognise anyone?"

Faith blinked at the abruptness of the question. She also put down her knife and fork and looked carefully at the faces of the dozen or so gentlemen dining with other men or, occasionally, a woman.

"Several," she said, returning to her food. The sole with chive sauce was delicious and not the kind of fare she generally enjoyed. The expense and effort to which Madame went to ensure the trappings of her sumptuous establishment and the outward appearance of the girls who represented it were only skin deep. Therefore, dining on something other than potatoes and gravy with the occasional piece of gristle made it worth pandering to Mrs Gedge.

"I trust you would not be recognised?" There was steel behind the question, but Faith knew that being kept hidden from the gentlemen who visited Madame Chambon's girls was an important clause in the contract Mrs Gedge had with the brothel keeper.

"Of course not." Faith dabbed delicately at her lips with her napkin and smiled again at her benefactress. "I recognise a great many people here in fact. That gentlemen dining with his mother over there is one of Charity's most regular clients—"

"How do you know she's his mother?"

"Because I used to clean the grate and make up the fire in her bedchamber when she was a guest at Wildwood Lodge. She's a friend of Lady Carmody's. That red hair is hard to miss." Faith hesitated. "Do you think she'll come over and say hello to you?"

Mrs Gedge shuddered. "Lord, I've worked too hard to ensure I'll not be recognised these past few years. Like you. No, I no longer care to recall those days at Wildwood Lodge." She picked at her food, sad and no longer the hard, determined woman Faith had always known. "Tell me, Faith, do you miss your friends from Wildwood Lodge?" Mrs Gedge's laboured breathing seemed due to more than just the stress put on her corset by the large quantity of food and wine she'd just consumed. Her mouth trembled. "Do you resent me for taking you away from there? I trust you've had no communication with anyone from your old life. If you have, now is the time to tell me."

"You know my only friends are the girls at Madame Chambon's." Faith resented the intrusion and the suspicion in her benefactress's voice, but she spoke the truth. "You made sure of that," she added, spearing a Brussels sprout.

"For your own good, Faith. I made you a lady. I think some sacrifices have been worth the position in which you now find yourself."

Faith offered the requisite smile, tilting her head to regard Mrs Gedge with a level stare and, in the process, intercepted the interested glance of a young man across the room through the fronds of the Kentish palm to her right. He was dining with an older gentleman and a woman. Parents, perhaps, in the way they communicated an expectation of filial obedience as they now rose, gathering gloves and cane.

The young gentleman got to his feet more slowly, his eyes lingering on Faith. Though surprised, and somewhat unnerved, she did not look away as he brushed back the heavy hair that flopped over his brow, all the while keeping his eyes firmly on her. His lips curved slightly as he made some signal to his companions that he was about to follow them.

Faith returned his level stare. *Give nothing away.* That's what she'd been taught. *Yet show that you have noticed him.*

She was brought back to the present by Mrs Gedge's thoughtful tone. "My, my, I did not expect *this*."

"I don't know what you mean." Faith clasped her hands in her lap and returned Mrs Gedge's look with unusual defiance across the table.

Surprise still lurked in the other woman's expression before Mrs Gedge laughed softly. "My dear Faith, you were magnificent." She sat back, her bosom heaving. "That young man…you don't know him surely?"

"I've never seen him in my life."

"Did you think him handsome?"

"Very."

"Why, pray?"

Faith shrugged. "I like an athletic physique. And he had nice eyes. He looked…kind."

"Kind?!" The word snapped like a whip across the table, and Faith felt her mouth drop open.

Before another beat had passed, Mrs Gedge had recovered herself. A slow smile curved her lips as she said slowly, "Why, Faith, this is a miracle. I cannot believe how easy this is going to be. You did not even try." She took another sip of wine, then announced, "Tomorrow night you are going to your first soiree."

Faith jerked her head up.

"I had not thought you ready, but it's important to strike while the iron is hot, as they say." Faith sent her a narrow look and wondered if Mrs Gedge had drunk too much. "I will not accompany you, Faith, of course. No, Lady Vernon will do that. A good thing she's recovered her health for it'll be a busy few weeks." Businesslike, Mrs Gedge went on, "She will accompany you to a great many functions: balls, soirees, picnics – and she will report back to me, you understand?"

Mrs Gedge finished her wine and put her knife and fork together. Faith waited. This was not some reward, she knew. She was expected to perform, though she wasn't sure, exactly, how. Surprisingly, tingles in the tips of her fingers were echoed by a prickling sensation on the backs of her legs, and her breath was suddenly shallow. Fear? Anticipation? Excitement?

Hope.

In the end, she had to ask. "Is this…to be my purpose, Mrs Gedge?"

A flash of triumph brightened the other woman's eye. "Yes, Faith. For three years, you've been trained to behave like a young lady, and I've asked nothing in return." Mrs Gedge had positioned herself so that she could not be observed by the company currently leaving; however, she could clearly see that the young man had stopped at the double doors for a final look over his shoulder at Faith.

Looking from the handsome young man with the athletic physique and the kind eyes to Faith, she said softly, "I have waited a long time for this but…tomorrow you will begin to repay me."

CHAPTER 4

A strong smell of boiled cabbage permeated Lady Vernon's musty lodgings.

The hackney carriage had dropped her off in the cobbled street in front of the narrow terrace house, and having been ushered into an unused bedchamber, Faith's earlier excitement was being sorely tested.

She stared with dismay at the simple gown Lady Vernon held up.

She was hardly going to make the grand entrance she'd envisaged in this plain, pale-cream silk ensemble trimmed with pink bows.

"Very virginal, isn't it, Faith? Not what you're used to regarding as up to the mark in the household you inhabit." Lady Vernon's fingers pinched Faith's flesh as she turned her around and, without ceremony, began to unbutton the back of her dress. "No, you fancy the tawdry, I daresay, because even if you've not yet had the pleasure of a man, you're still no better than those other girls you live with."

"Lady Vernon, don't you look just the thing!" Mrs Gedge, who'd just been admitted by the parlourmaid, interrupted the unwise response Faith was about to deliver. The American woman looked, in contrast to Lady Vernon, quite animated as she took in the gown that clothed the noblewoman's frail frame. Perhaps it had been up to the mark a decade previously, but it had been obviously refashioned into a poor copy of the day's fashions. The feathers in Lady Vernon's head-dress looked as tired as the grey-faced old woman who wore them.

"And Faith, you know what is expected of you, don't you?"

Faith nodded as Lady Vernon peeled her blue day dress over her shoulders and down her hips, then began to button up the cream silk once Faith had stepped into it. She was so disappointed she thought she might cry. The previous week, when the dressmaker had fitted her with the calico toile, Faith had been led to believe the figure-hugging ensemble was going to be in bold, eye-catching colours.

"And you, Lady Vernon?" Mrs Gedge began to circle.

"I know exactly what is expected, Madam." Lady Vernon's tone was grim. "I will not let Faith out of my sight."

"And she is to come back here tonight. I don't want to run the risk of her being followed. In fact…" Mrs Gedge sent them both a considering look. "Faith will stay here for the next few weeks. Lady Vernon, you will arrange for her belongings to be brought around and you, Faith, are to have nothing to do with any of the girls at Madame Chambon's from now on." She rubbed her hands as if in anticipation of something very pleasurable while Faith reassessed her idea of success. In the short term, success simply meant extricating herself from the smell of mould and boiled cabbage that pervaded Lady Vernon's premises. She didn't think she could bear it a moment longer.

"Whatever you wish, Mrs Gedge."

Meanwhile, Mrs Gedge was reaching forward to take a tendril of Faith's golden hair. "You were blessed, child," she murmured. "Blessed like few others of your squalid upbringing. I wish you to turn expectation on its head. That's what I wish for you tonight."

"And…who am I to play?"

The question lingered in the damp air, clearly a source of amusement to Mrs Gedge.

"Who are you to play?" Mrs Gedge laughed softly and turned to Lady Vernon. "Who is this shy beauty, Lady Vernon? Show me how well you know your part."

Lady Vernon inclined her head and intoned in a dry, unemotional voice, "I'd like to introduce my impoverished goddaughter rescued from an untenable situation in the north of the country. Well connected by birth but penniless." She looked at Faith almost with dislike. "A penniless beauty."

Faith ran her hands down the princess-line gown and glanced again at her reflection. She had to admit that there was an elegant simplicity to the unadorned cream silk. A tiny row of pink bows down the front of her gown and one large pink bow at the back of the swathed bustle would make her stand out from the crowd, she knew. A simple cross on a chain at her throat completed the ensemble.

It was the society event Faith had imagined but certainly not the grand debut.

She and Lady Vernon stood out for the very fact that they stepped across the threshold into the dazzling ballroom and richly garbed crowd as, clearly, the poor relations.

"Welcome, Lady Vernon. And who is the young lady?"

Their hostess for the evening, Lady Griffin, seemed pleasant and welcoming. Even sympathetic when Lady Vernon explained she was taking her goddaughter to a few places during her first visit to the metropolis.

"I agreed to sponsor the girl to the extent my limited resources will allow." Lady Vernon sighed as if Faith were the greatest cross to bear. But then Lady Vernon seemed to regard any effort on her part as an imposition. "She's the eldest of ten." She sniffed. "Daughters, mainly, so I'm doing what I can for the family. If Faith is not successful in the few weeks she has in the metropolis, I'll be sending her to Yorkshire where she's to take up a post as governess." She sniffed again. "It does seem a shame to see her wasted. Such a biddable girl, too." Her brow creased as she added, almost in wonder, "Not the slightest bit vain. She'd suit a young clerk with prospects, perhaps." Lady Vernon smiled hopefully at her hostess.

❄

On the other side of the room, Crispin Westaway was trying hard to attend to his aunt, who was waxing lyrical on the play she'd attended the previous night. However, his gaze kept straying to the unusual pair speaking to their hostess beneath the Goya painting. He'd barely been able to believe his eyes when they'd alighted on the vision from the restaurant the night before.

Now he couldn't wait for an opportunity to address her in person.

"The Prince of Wales is causing his poor mother headaches again," he heard his aunt confide in her nasal manner to her friend, Lady Braxsted. "Have you heard, Crispin? What a trial one's children can be."

Crispin didn't care what the Prince of Wales was up to, but he was happy to corroborate his aunt, Lady Pymble's mild outrage at the latest scandal while his gaze drifted to the humpbacked dowager in the far corner who seemed to be shielding her charge.

The girl's hair was like a halo of sensuous golden light, cascading down her back in fashionable ringlets, her small fringe highlighting her elfin face. He'd never seen anyone so lovely, and his fingers itched to grasp his paintbrush. It would be a challenge to capture the wistful half smile the girl directed at the woman when her companion made some remark.

"Excuse me, who is that young woman over there?" he interrupted, causing his gossiping aunt and her friend to stop midsentence and look at him in surprise. They squinted in the direction in which he pointed and shook their heads.

"Never seen her in my life," Lady Braxted said, "though it looks like Lady Vernon is sponsoring her tonight." She gave a snide laugh. "Probably did it for money."

Crispin narrowed his eyes. "Money? It doesn't look like the girl is blessed with a family who can expend much on the outward adornments."

His aunt made a tutting noise. "What a thing to say, Crispin. Most young men would not make observations about the plainness of her dress. They'd have eyes only for the beauty of the young woman. I have to say, she is rather exceptional. Shall I make some investigations on your behalf?" She sent Crispin a sly look.

He nodded. "I would appreciate that, Aunt."

His aunt looked on the point of happily announcing some scheme to facilitate Crispin's wishes, for she was a woman who adored schemes and plots, before she was nearly knocked over by an enthusiastic young lady cutting a swathe through the crowd.

"I am so sorry!" came the mortified, immediately identifiable mid-Atlantic tones of the young lady who'd inadvertently bumped into Lady Pymble. "I really have no idea how to behave, do I?" She put her hand to her mouth as she hiccupped. "Off the boat from New York last week and unleashed this evening for my first London soiree, and already I'm scandalising my English relatives. I'm Miss Amy Eaves, by the way. Pleased to meet you!"

Crispin smiled inwardly as he witnessed the aversion his aunt had in taking the hand thrust into her face. He wondered if she'd go so far as to tell Miss Eaves that young ladies did not introduce themselves in such a manner in *this* country.

To his surprise, she merely said, "You clearly have much to learn about English ways, Miss Eaves, but I daresay one has to start somewhere. I'm Lady Pymble, and this is my nephew, Mr Westaway."

"Oh, my! Lady Pymble, is it? My apologies again." Now Miss Eaves was curtseying. Crispin didn't know whether to be embarrassed or amused. He chose the latter.

"Welcome to London, Miss Eaves. And what are your plans while you are in our fair city?" Miss Eaves was not a beauty in any conventional sense, but there was an enthusiasm about her that set her apart from the coy, well-mannered debutantes of his acquaintance.

Miss Eaves replied with unsurprising directness, "Well, my father wants a title. That is, he wants *me* to snare one since he's got everything else. Including the world's biggest yacht which he's sailing around the world."

"Indeed." Lady Pymble seemed not to know what to say.

Miss Eaves rubbed her little snub nose and frowned. "So, why are you a lady and your nephew is only a Mr?"

Crispin and his aunt exchanged a glance. At least she looked more amused than scandalised now.

"My nephew is in line for a title. Once his father dies. But let's talk of other things, shall we?" She sent a searching look about the room and added, "I'm sure someone must be looking for you, Miss Eaves."

She took this for dismissal and nodded. "Well, I don't know how well you know my uncle, Sir Albion McKinley, but everyone here seems to know everyone else, and if you can persuade him to let me get a job, I'll be mighty grateful."

"A job."

Crispin wasn't surprised his aunt sounded so scandalised.

"Not for money, surely?" Lady Pymble went on.

Miss Eaves nodded again. "I've asked my uncle if I can write about the artists who exhibit for him, and he says I might dip my ink in the inkwell if I choose, but that he won't pay me a penny for my trouble and scandalise my father."

"I should think not," murmured Lady Pymble.

"Oh, I know ladies don't get paid, of course. But I don't want to be a lady." Miss Eaves sent Crispin a considered look. "So, you needn't worry you'll hear from me when you land that title. Anyway…" She took a step away. "If you hear of some newspaper job going, please keep me in mind, only don't get the message to me through my uncle."

"Your uncle is Sir Albion McKinley?" Crispin tried to see anything to connect the highly esteemed patron of the London Society of Artists with this brash young woman. "Not the greatest proponent of women's suffrage I would have thought." He envisioned the tight-lipped, balding and slightly stooped gentleman he'd met on the many occasions he'd ventured into the hallowed precincts of the Royal Society of Artists. Not that that had been for a while. Crispin's passion for art had been effectively strangled by his father's insistence he apply himself to following in the family tradition by entering the world of politics. It had been a long time since he'd picked up a paintbrush.

"No, he is not. I might have earned a way into his good books if I'd had an ounce of artistic talent in my little finger, but I do not." Miss Eaves shrugged. "No, I like to write, and I think I'm good at it. I also think it's a mighty fine way for a woman to earn a respectable income but…" she sighed. "There you go!"

"Yes, there you go," Crispin repeated, stepping aside in order to facilitate a satisfactory end to the conversation, for it appeared Miss Eaves was ready to settle in for the night, and he was growing increasingly impatient to meet the vision of loveliness still alone with her chaperone on the other side of the room.

With Miss Eaves finally despatched, Crispin was halfway towards Lady Vernon and her unknown charge when his father clapped him on the shoulder with a demand for an inventory on Crispin's activities for the past week.

Dutifully, Crispin outlined the tedium with which he'd occupied mind and body, surprised when Lord Maxwell remarked, "Your Aunt Alice thinks you look weary. Says she spied you across the street when she alighted from a hackney at Marble Arch, and she commented on your grey pallor and hunched shoulders, which she put down to the work in the satchel you carried." Lord Maxwell's craggy face grew more lined as he frowned, though Crispin recognised this as the ghost of a smile. "You'll be doing well if you've inherited half her persuasive talents, for by the end of the conversation, I'd promised that I'd give you a fortnight off. Yes, a week to amuse yourself before you return to the studies required by your new position."

Crispin couldn't have been more surprised.

"A fortnight, Father?"

"Possibly three, in fact, and funds enough to take yourself off to the South of France if you so wish." His brows knitted. "Just make sure you're ready to throw yourself back into work when you return and don't get enticed away by some Frenchie vixen, mind."

Crispin grinned, and content with this out of character interview, was about to buoyantly head off in Lady Vernon's direction when he saw that lady deep in conversation with Miss Eaves, who appeared to have wandered into their enclave with the same abandon she had when she'd met Crispin and his aunt.

Better to wait, he thought, so he could have the field uncluttered. Meanwhile, visions of his week of pure pleasure floated enticingly about his head. Where would he go? What would he do?

His friend Roger Jolimont had a boat. Perhaps they'd sail to the French Riviera. That could be jolly good fun at this time of year. If his father were in such an indulgent mood, perhaps he'd grant Crispin a month.

FAITH WAS BORED. TONIGHT WAS PROVING A DISMAL FAILURE. NO ONE had come up to speak to them except for a talkative American young woman whom Lady Vernon had collared, no doubt to extrapolate information about her earlier conversation with the young man she'd noticed glancing at Faith all evening.

Faith now knew exactly how things were to play out. First, Mrs Gedge had known the young man she'd seen at the restaurant would be there. And now he was here again. Clearly, he had been selected, for reasons that Faith would find out in due course. Faith's job, of course, would be to entice him, seduce him, make him fall in love with her, and then break his heart.

She was almost one hundred percent sure that this was Lady Gedge's plan. It seemed the obvious reason for calling Faith her 'beautiful revenge' for all these years.

And yet, *why?*

The young man chosen was certainly a very handsome specimen, so of course that made Faith's task so much easier. Her heart had even given a little jolt when she'd locked eyes with him through the Kentish palm at the restaurant the previous night. It was true that she'd declared she'd rather die than offer her body to a man she didn't love, but what if she simply found him attractive enough not to be repulsed by what Mrs Gedge wanted her to do? That would surely be within her code?

And she did need to eat. She had precious few alternatives other than the one Mrs Gedge intended for her.

Faith studied the young man closely through lowered eyelashes while she sipped from her champagne flute. He was tall, with dependable shoulders, and when he spoke, there was an animation about him absent from so many of the bored gentlemen about town who frequented Madame Chambon's.

That was certainly in his favour.

Faith decided she liked the way his mouth quirked when he was clearly amused, which, it seemed, he frequently was, and his quick, impatient gestures in raking his floppy fringe back from his face.

She couldn't decide whether he was of an artistic temperament or just filled with energy that needed to find an outlet. Part of her lessons at Madame's had been in how to read a man. Not only had Faith attended sessions where young men willingly revealed themselves to a dozen or so of Madame Chambon's girls for a practical demonstration of how easily they were aroused, and by what, but she'd had to listen endlessly to Madame discussing man's many temperaments and how to pander to them for the greatest return.

An artistic temperament required feeding a man's passion by suggesting that one, alone, had what was required to unleash his genius.

"There he is, Faith. What do you think?"

As Lady Vernon had asked the question, Faith was less inclined to answer truthfully. And yet there were benefits since it would be reported back to Mrs Gedge and, in truth, Faith had hoped very much that she'd be able to please her benefactress. It made life so much easier.

"He's very handsome," Faith conceded.

"And you'll be five hundred pounds richer once he seduces you."

Faith gasped and glanced about her, but they were within no one's hearing. Surprised at her reaction, when she'd lived so long in a house of ill repute, she said, staring stonily ahead, "That will be between the gentleman, whose name I don't even know, and myself." She offered

Lady Vernon her haughtiest expression. "I'll thank you to keep your nose out of my personal affairs."

"It's what I'm being paid for, and I am just as keen to earn *my* five hundred pounds and be rid of *you*, my girl." Lady Vernon stared down her thin nose at Faith. "The sooner you complete the business, the better." She hesitated. "Though there is a little more to the transaction."

"Yes, of course there is. Don't I have to make him fall in love with me, then break his heart?" Faith thought the acid in her tone was justified.

"Don't pride yourself on being too clever. That was plain for anyone in your position to know."

"And why does Mrs Gedge wish her revenge on this man, in particular?"

Lady Vernon shrugged, and the rise and fall of her bony shoulders accentuated her flat chest. Faith stared at the woman, unloved and bitter, but whose nature had perhaps never invited friendship, and decided she'd never be like Lady Vernon with a title and living a celibate life on a diet of boiled cabbage. No, Faith would make the most of her youth and beauty to find an escape from the evil house that confined her until she'd expedited Mrs Gedge's plans for revenge. She'd find a rich and handsome man who'd love her despite her secrets and sordid past, and who'd marry her and give her a life of comfort and security.

She sent her prospective gentleman another assessing glance. Perhaps he actually might be the one who would do all this for her.

"Mrs Gedge is a woman who jumps to conclusions. I think you know that, Faith. She also harbours grudges. Grudges that are never laid to rest until she's satisfied her requirements have been conquered." Lady Vernon rummaged in her reticule and produced a lace handkerchief. "That American woman has too much time on her hands to brood and too much money, but if she wants to throw it in our direction, I'm not going to stop her." She blew her nose. "Who knows why she wants revenge on him. Perhaps he's the sacrificial lamb substituting for someone else? His father, perhaps. I really don't care. I just want my five hundred pounds, as do you, I'm sure." She gave Faith a warning glance. "Just don't lose your own heart in all this."

"I'm surprised you care enough to warn me, Lady Vernon."

"Oh, I don't care a jot. I'm just stating the obvious to fill in a little time and to find something to say while this young man makes his leisurely way over here."

Faith now saw that Lady Vernon was using her handkerchief as cover for a very close scrutiny of the gentleman who was perhaps ten feet away, when the old woman took Faith by the elbow and started leading her towards the door, not pausing as they passed by him.

"Where are we going?" Faith asked. "It's so early and…he was just about to speak to us!" She felt ridiculously disappointed all of a sudden. Was Lady Vernon suddenly deciding she needed to protect Faith from herself, or the young man, or Mrs Gedge?

"Yes, I'm afraid we must go home now, Faith. My poor old back is hurting and I'm longing for my bed, but don't make the mistake of thinking Mrs Gedge will be displeased." Her lined face softened beneath a rare smile as they reached the double doors which were opened in unison by a pair of footmen. The cool night air hit them like a slap in Faith's face. "Tomorrow or the next your work will begin in earnest. Soon, Mrs Gedge will understand I'm worth so much more than the paltry allowance she pays me."

CHAPTER 5

Crispin opened the book that teetered near the top of the pile his father had given him, and tried to focus his attention on its account of British and Prussian diplomatic relations in the past decade.

An ornate gilt clock loudly proclaimed the passing of time, while the crackle of the small fire in the study grate on this unseasonably chilly day was even more distracting.

Last night had been a bore. And a sore disappointment. There'd been no lively conversation; no interesting revelations. And the young lady he'd wanted to speak to had simply disappeared in front of his nose.

He could picture her now, the golden hair that rippled down her back, the intricately coiffured curls complementing her fashionable hairstyle and contrasting with her spectacularly plain dress. Would she look more beautiful in bolder colours or did a more austere presentation highlight her beauty?

His father had promised him three weeks of freedom and, of course, Crispin was itching to be gone from his books and the stifling timetable his father demanded.

Yet, it would have been diverting to have made the girl's acquaintance. It had been such a long time since he'd confronted such a vision that made him so ready to whip out his paintbrush and paints and set to work.

After another half an hour of diligent study, Crispin was more than ready to entertain the interruption that came from one of the housemaids, who put her head around the door half an hour later to tell him he had visitors and should she show them in?

It was more shock than surprise that tore through him when they were announced.

"Lady Vernon?" he repeated. She was not someone with whom his parents were on any level of intimacy, though he knew of her. Her father had been a nobleman fallen from grace on account of some very shady dealings which his untimely death had fortunately meant were not fully investigated.

Not that that was of any interest when the lovely creature in her shadow was materialising upon the threshold.

Attempting to mask his delight, Crispin directed them to take a seat on the Chesterfield sofa positioned at right angles to the fire.

"To what do I owe the pleasure?" he asked, as he lowered himself into a leather wingback chair opposite.

Lady Vernon clasped her black-gloved hands in her lap with the look of someone who has something very particular to say.

Crispin glanced from her bony fingers to the interested expression on the face of the girl on the sofa beside her, and felt the heat rise in his cheeks and his body respond. He leaned forward and looked at the pair expectantly as Lady Vernon cleared her throat.

"My charge, Miss Montague, is well practised at achieving the utmost stillness required of an artist's model, though naturally I would be in attendance at all times, Mr Westaway." She cleared her throat again. "That is, if you believe she is suitable."

Crispin drew back in surprise, but even before Lady Vernon finished, he was conjuring up exactly what hue he would pick to achieve the soft peach colour of the girl's cheeks and the red of her Cupid's bow. Her hair was an altogether thrilling proposition.

Then common sense returned. In the next day or so he'd be

heading for the French Riviera. After that, he'd be heading for Germany where he'd take up the life of diplomacy just as his father had done and his grandfather before that.

Regretfully he said, "I believe there's been a misunderstanding, Lady Vernon. I no longer paint, and I don't know who gave you the impression that I would consider a painting commission."

The pucker between the old woman's grey, bristly eyebrows indicated the disappointment he was at pains to hide.

Crispin leaned back in his chair and steepled his fingers. "I am preparing to take up a posting as British Third Secretary to the British Ambassador to Germany. My intended departure is a little over a month from now."

"I saw the portrait of Madame Lascelles. A beautiful and faithful rendition so true to life, for I know the young lady. *You* painted that, Mr Westaway." There was the hint of aggression in her tone.

"I did, but that was two years ago, and my career was not decided then. I was following my inclinations only."

"You wanted to be a great artist, I heard, Mr Westaway, and there were many who believed you could be. Sir Albion considered you the finest talent of your generation."

The jolt Crispin felt was not altogether pleasant. Sir Albion had found plenty to criticise in Crispin's efforts. He was not a man to praise lightly. And yet he had always been encouraging. Crispin wondered with the vaguest tinge of regret, whether a more pointed word from the Patron of the Royal Society of Artists might have swayed him when his father was so intent that Crispin turn his back on his art in order to pursue a more serious path.

He was about to respond when Lady Vernon went on, "It is why I assumed you'd be looking for a model when I learned of this newly announced and extremely prestigious art prize under the auspices of the Society. I hoped, in turn, that a painting by you might improve the marital prospects of my goddaughter, Miss Montague."

Crispin directed a surprised stare at the young lady whose cheeks were a far rosier hue than they had been. She'd not said a word, but she clearly was invested in the conversation.

Lady Vernon's crisp tones reverberated through the silence. "I want Faith to be noticed, Mr Westaway, and I thought that through your talents, she would be."

Crispin refrained from saying that he thought she needed no one's talents to be noticed. Miss Montague was one of the most exquisite-looking young women he had ever encountered.

"Mr Westaway, I have taken it upon myself to do what I can for dear Faith. It may well be a futile and thankless task for she is the youngest of ten with nothing to offer anyone except a pliant nature."

"And her beauty." He swallowed. Had he actually said that?

"Precisely. Some gentlemen would overlook her lack of dowry because of her beauty, which is why I want you to paint her and show her to society. To the world. It is the only plan I have. Otherwise, she must return to her disappointed family in a few weeks, before taking up a position as governess to a family in Yorkshire that has evinced interest in Faith's keen grasp of politics and her interest in philosophy."

Crispin looked at the girl with even greater interest. "You have an interest in politics?"

She nodded as she dropped her gaze from his. She seemed nervous, and suddenly he wanted to reassure her. He smiled encouragingly, and she murmured, "The young boy whom I shall tutor has a desire to become a diplomat. It was after I was engaged in conversation with his father that I was provisionally employed…" She hesitated before saying with what Crispin perceived as a touch of embarrassment. "That is, if my London debut is not a success."

"How can it not be, Miss Montague?" Crispin smiled warmly at her and was delighted at the reappearance of the rosy hue in her cheeks. "I predict you will take society by storm entirely through your own talents. You need no help from me."

He offered them tea and carefully steered the talk to other matters after they declined and he led them to the door.

He said how deeply disappointed he was that he could not humour Lady Vernon, and refrained from saying that he was even more disappointed he'd see no more of Miss Montague.

But he knew that with his departure so imminent, he could afford no distractions. Succumbing to his desire to paint would be dangerous.

Succumbing to his desire to further his acquaintance with Miss Montague could prove fatal.

Faith stood on the doorstep of Mr Westaway's townhouse and plucked at the neckline of her blue cotton figure-hugging, but plainly adorned, polonaise, while she summoned the courage to do what Lady Vernon had insisted was their next step.

It was true that she was more than just a little excited to see Mr Westaway again, but she wished she could do so wearing a more lavishly embellished and modish gown. However, now that Mrs Gedge had endorsed Lady Vernon's plan of offering up Faith as a charity case, Faith had no choice but to adopt the role assigned to her.

In the hall, she heard muted footsteps before the door was opened and the butler stared at her with astonishment.

"I am so terribly sorry to disturb you, but my companion in the park just across the road has succumbed to a dizzy spell and begs for a glass of water," Faith preempted him to explain her unchaperoned state.

She was counting on the fact the butler would not leave her on the doorstep while he attended to her request so was relieved when he conducted her into the drawing room to wait.

Lady Vernon was indeed in the park, and Faith had a few moments to carry out the other woman's plan for Mr Westaway had been seen entering the house some minutes before. To Faith's intense relief, it was Mr Westaway who happened upon her before she'd been spurred into snooping about in the hopes of somehow stumbling upon him.

"Good heavens, Miss Montague!" he cried upon stepping into the drawing room, apparently deep in thought, before glancing up to see Faith gripping the back of the sofa.

Almost giddy with relief, she said, smiling, "You remembered my name, Mr Westaway. I am so very pleased, for you can't imagine how ashamed I was to enter your house unaccompanied by Lady Vernon. She's in the park and not well, and so I came here as I recognised the area we were in yesterday."

Mr Westaway's smile broadened before he quickly schooled his features into an expression more appropriate. "Your godmother is indisposed? I'm sorry to hear it. I passed my butler in the corridor who said he was fetching water for someone which I thought rather odd at the time. Now I understand. Please, take a seat while I go myself to ensure she's all right."

Faith moved forward as if to halt him then stopped. "There's really no need to do that. Lady Vernon regularly has dizzy spells. She'll be up to the mark as soon as she's rested a little and had some water." She heard the nervousness in her voice and counselled herself to be more contained. "The truth is, I wanted to speak to you, alone, Mr Westaway."

He stopped and waited. He certainly didn't seem as susceptible as she might have liked to the idea that she was alone in his home.

Yet.

Faith plucked at the fingers of one glove and avoided his eyes, before fixing him with a heartfelt look and launching into her hurried speech. "Please, Mr Westaway, are you certain you don't want to enter the art competition? The prize money is unprecedented, and Sir Albion has proclaimed it a call to arms for the country's greatest new generation of talents, of whom he numbers you amongst them. It's true." She tried for her most disarming smile, aware her mouth was trembling.

In the silence, she could hear the maids talking somewhere in the corridor and the ticking of the clock. Now she was truly nervous. So much hinged upon her success in making him yield. Mrs Gedge had thought it would be easy. Lady Vernon thought it was no contest at all, given that painting was all he'd ever wanted to do, apparently.

But now Faith's future hinged upon Mr Westaway reneging.

She gave a little sob as she sank against the heavy curtains in the window embrasure. "Please consider taking up the painting challenge, though I now beg you for purely selfish reasons." She put her hands to her eyes. "Everything Lady Vernon said yesterday is true. If I do not have a marriage offer by the end of July, I shall be sent to a remote household in Yorkshire against my will."

"A marriage offer?" He raised one eyebrow, smiling as he repeated the words. "I take it you mean a marriage offer from some *other* gentleman who might be made...aware of you through the interest a painting by me of you will inevitably garner when it's displayed amongst the competing entries at the Royal Society. An anonymously sponsored competition, which, I gather, has added to the sensation surrounding it."

She could see him wavering. Was it because of *her* or that the thought of wielding a paintbrush was so enticing?

Faith was silent as she waited. He would have to make some kind of response, even if it were to regretfully inform her that her request was, after all, out of the question. But his silence did not mean she missed the way his eyes roamed over her.

His awareness of her was thrilling. This was power. Yes, her first experience of holding the interest of a man. She was beautiful. She'd been told that, and although she hadn't actually met any of the clients of Madame Chambon, when she compared herself to the girls who were the paramours of dukes and princes, she knew she was every bit their equal.

What did it matter that Mrs Gedge was using her for some underhand purpose? That she called Faith her 'beautiful revenge'? Faith's greatest, perhaps only, power was in the allure she exerted over the male species, and now she was proving just how adept she was at her calling. Not her chosen calling but her calling by default. Succeeding in this arena was the only way she could survive, and the fact she liked this man gave her mission a life-and-death quality.

He gripped the back of the sofa too, his hands only inches from hers, his body angled half towards her. She could feel his tenseness; his desire. He was intrigued. Her beauty was a gift to the painter, her vulnerability hard to ignore. In a moment, he would waver. She could see it happening already. Mr Westaway would be all hers, and Faith would notch up her first conquest in the elaborate dance that would bind him to her and make him her slave, just as Mrs Gedge required.

"I believe my butler has taken your godmother a glass of water, Miss Montague." His voice broke the spell, his body relaxing, the tension dissipating. With a polite indication of the door he said with genuine regret, "I'm sorry to disappoint you, but the truth is that as much as I would love nothing more than to idle away many pleasant hours doing justice to your beauty and wielding a paintbrush, I will be leaving the country in a couple of short months to take up a position in Germany. I have too much to learn about my duties there to be able to accede to your request." His smile was kind. "As much as I would desire it."

Her mouth dropped open. She suddenly felt a fool. This was not how it was supposed to go. Failure? On her first attempt? Faith took a step towards the door and straightened her shoulders with as much dignity as she could manage.

"I am familiar with the political situation that exists between the two countries," she managed. "Great Britain and Germany. I could tell you about it while you painted me."

He laughed outright at that and Faith stepped across the threshold, defeated. "I did not mean to amuse you, sir," she said stiffly. "Thank you for considering it, nevertheless."

"Please, Miss Montague, it was not my intention to embarrass you." He extended his hand towards her, his kind eyes looking concerned, whereas she'd seen the amusement in his dismissiveness just before and it wounded her to the quick.

"Good day to you, Mr Westaway," she said, ignoring his overtures. "I wish you well for your new posting."

She avoided his attempt to stay her, gliding to the front door which the butler was holding open. Across the cobbled street, she could see the outline of Lady Vernon behind the railings of the park, no doubt congratulating herself prematurely on her success in sending Faith to personally petition for the dreams she was certain the young man would be unable to resist.

But Faith had failed.

CHAPTER 6

Faith was unused to the feelings that beset her as she sat alone in a small curtained alcove in one of the empty reception rooms at Madame Chambon's later that evening.

The velvet sofa was comfortable and the gold tasselled curtains opulent and concealing. She was very conscious of the heavy perfume that overlaid the air and looked down at her dress, so unusually plain in contrast.

Perhaps the Failure of Lady Vernon's latest gambit in thrusting Faith under Mr Westaway's nose would have Mrs Gedge adopting a new strategy that included dressing Faith a little more fashionably due to the failure of Lady Vernon's gambit. She'd changed out of her demure blue gown and was wearing one of the other girl's more tawdry cast-offs. The purple and gold striped dress with its tight skirt, heavily adorned bustle and low neckline would have been perfect had it been in more restrained colouring and made of a better fabric.

"What are you doing here, Faith?"

Faith glanced up as Charity stopped in passing. Her hair was uncoiled and hung in a thick dark curtain over one shoulder. In the dim light her cheeks were flushed and her gown was askew.

Embarrassed, suddenly, Charity straightened her dress. Faith knew Madame Chambon's ire was easily whipped up by untidiness. She would not house slatterns, Faith had heard her say on many an occasion.

"I fell asleep wearing this and then woke up and couldn't sleep again. It was too noisy to remain in my room," she said.

Faith nodded. Daisy who slept next door to Charity and below Faith had been entertaining a very noisy gentleman which was why Faith had retreated to the quietest part of the house.

Charity gave a snide laugh and ran her fingers through her hair. She didn't look as composed as she usually did. "You should have stayed out longer for I don't think there's a room unoccupied that isn't doing a roaring trade tonight. It must be the full moon." She closed her eyes and but her lip which Faith now saw was trembling. "Consider yourself lucky, Faith, if noise is the extent of your troubles. You're soon going to be leaving this place and it won't be a moment too soon."

Faith ran the tip of her tongue over her lips and hunched forward. "I shall be here longer than I'd hoped. Mr Westaway declined to paint me." With a few hours to think over the ramifications of her failure she'd become truly afraid. Her belief in her allure had been overblown. She'd misread Mr Westaway, for all he'd been apparently regretful, and now her future was a terrifying void.

"And I don't mind about the noise." She knew she was a source of conjecture amongst the other girls. Faith was so privileged, Faith never had to see customers. Faith was kept out of their sight, in fact. She never had to accede to the desire of anyone prepared to pay. Why? To attract a prince, perhaps?

Well, Mr Westaway was far from a prince. He was a privileged, handsome young man, in line for a title but far from the rich bounty that might have been imagined considering her three years of training.

"Charity! Come! Oh, and Faith, you too!" Red haired Mabel appeared in the entrance, her eyes bright with excitement – brandy, too, Faith thought – and beckoned to them, before darting forward to take their hands and pull them after her. "I've got something to show you. Well, Mr Schofield has and he's going to let me work the contraption."

Mabel was already hustling them towards a small group already positioned for what Faith saw was a posing for a photograph, the hooded camera unmanned before the young man who was apparently Mr Schofield, darted back to his place.

Three of Madame Chambon's girls giggled in a group while a single elderly gentleman stood just behind them, stroking the hair of a slim dark-haired girl in a green dress. Nell. Faith wondered if this was the gentleman Nell had been so excited might set her up. He looked much older than Faith had been led to believe.

Mr Schofield regarded the scene from his post, frowning, before clapping his hands suddenly and welcoming a new arrival who'd just stepped through the curtain as he pushed Mabel towards the camera.

"Aha, I think we have the numbers. Everybody, assume the waltz position!" He rushed forward, pushing Nell into the arms of the grey haired gentleman, Faith into the arms of the new arrival while he positioned himself with Charity.

"Now, remain very still until I tell you."

Obediently, Faith remained frozen like a statue while she thought of how Madame Chambon and Mrs Gedge were going to react to her failure.

Mr Westaway was not susceptible at all. Yes, he'd been interested. Clearly. But she'd failed to reel him in.

Why? After all her training.

Training. She shuddered at the term but it was true. She'd attended lessons and, in theory, she knew how to smile and simper at a gentleman. How to entrance them, make them a slave.

Well, this was how it had been described.

Yet, she'd never tried it in real life until now and she'd been patently lacklustre, apparently.

She forced herself back to the present as she became conscious of the light pressure on her waist and holding her hand, while in the background Mr Schofield exhorted them all, "Imagine you're on the dance floor. Look at your partner. Smile now and don't move until I give you leave."

Smile. Maybe Faith had been *too* restrained, thinking that her silent beauty and enigmatic presence would pique Mr Westaway's interest when in fact she'd simply failed to register in his consciousness sufficiently.

She blinked away the tears. Madame deplored weakness. She'd make Faith suffer even more if Faith displayed her fear and disappointment. Well, Faith knew how to shine. She tilted her chin, pursed her lips and unleashed her most devastating smile upon the gentleman with whom she was supposedly dancing while she heard Mr Schofield count down the seconds.

Staring at him was a novelty. She'd never stared at a gentleman in such a staged setting for so long and it was interesting to take account of the nuances of the face before her. He was tall and blonde and in his middle to late thirties, with a lean jaw and noticeably blue eyes which bored appreciatively into her.

More appreciatively than Mr Westaway's had, she thought resentfully. Yet the same speculative gleam had been in both gentlemen's eyes. Faith had just failed to lure Mr Westaway towards making the next step.

"Girls! Gentlemen! What a picture!" Madame Chambon's interruption broke the mood and as she pushed aside the curtain and entered the room, clapping her hands together, Faith, too, stepped back; but with a sudden sinking feeling, for she realised she'd made a grave miscalculation. She was not supposed to be seen with the other girls or by the gentlemen.

What had she been thinking? Well, she hadn't.

She felt Madame's eyes resting on her and felt ill before her shoulders slumped and she turned away from the gentleman who'd continued to gaze so appreciatively at her. Still, what did any of it matter? She'd leave this place. Perhaps she could go back to the country and beg her family to take her back until she found a position.

Any would do.

"Lord Harkom, I hope you've enjoyed yourself this evening."

Madame was addressing the blonde gentleman, her voice oozing obsequiousness but her hand was now resting heavily on Faith's shoulder. With ominous pressure.

"As always, Madame." He bowed deeply

"We are always honoured by your visits. Don't forget that there are always fresh girls to give satisfaction."

Faith exhaled in fright and pulled away but Madame held her so that she had to suffer the touch of Lord Harkom's hand upon her cheek as he said, "Indeed, and I see you have another one I've not laid eyes upon. What a beauty. Perhaps I won't leave so early, after all."

The air died in Faith's lungs. She thought she would faint upon the spot.

But then Madame was drawing her back from the brink, a protective arm about Faith's shoulders as she said, "Alas, this one is very new and quite untried. She needs more training."

"I am very good at that, you know." He was pawing her again, his fingertips brushing her face as he looked hungrily at her décolletage. "My, but she is strikingly lovely. Yes, I am definitely interested." His smile was for Madame Chambon, now, and Faith could see Madame yielding as he purred, "We've always come to an agreement, before, Madame. I'm sure this will be no exception."

"I'm not ready!" Faith pulled away, her bosom heaving, and felt the eyes of everyone in the room upon her.

She couldn't bear it a moment longer. Standing upon the threshold, she clutched at her neckline but found no comforting sheathing fabric, only bare skin. Bare skin that Lord Harkom, a stranger, soon would run his hands over as he sampled her wares at Madame Chambon's behest.

Had Madame given up on her so quickly?

"You can't make me, Madame!" she cried, her voice shaking. "I'm saving myself for Mr Westaway!"

"Mr Westaway doesn't want you, Faith." There was a low, warning note in Madame's tone which Faith knew she should heed. Madame would not thank her to make a scene in front of everyone but perhaps

Madame had drunk too much brandy and forgotten that Faith was 'special'.

"If Mr Westaway doesn't want you, Faith, then you're no longer any use to Mrs Gedge." Madame stepped close to Faith and gripped her chin as she said, lowering her voice "Which means you're mine now."

Faith wrenched herself backwards. She felt Charity's hands upon her shoulders to steady her. "I won't be sold like … an animal!" Her voice was shrill. She'd never heard the note before. For so long she'd taken for granted the fact that she did not have to sell her body like the other girls did. Seducing only one man would be her allotted task. A young, handsome man. A young man whom she thought she could like meaning she could fulfil her role with ease and no conscience.

But now her fate was like that of all the girls here.

"And where will you go, Faith?" There was a note of relish in Madame Chambon's. Perhaps she was now enjoying the fact that there were others to witness Faith being pulled down to their level. The fact that Madame Chambon did not distinguish, after all. A girl was only useful – and therefore would be housed and fed – if she brought gain to the ruthless brothel owner.

A terrible blackness consumed Faith's ability to think more than cursorily about the truth. There was nowhere else she could go. She was deluding herself to think there would be a welcome for her in the brutish household in which she'd grown up, the dilapidated cottage that housed her family in lieu of her father's obligation to the farmer for whom he worked.

She had no friends. No relatives. Well, none upon whose mercy she could throw herself.

"Perhaps I should hand you over to the magistrate or the police as Mrs Gedge wanted to do before she brought you here."

"I am *not* a thief." Faith enunciated the words carefully but with more bitterness than the fear with which she'd imbued the words when Mrs Gedge had found her in Miss Constancia's room admiring the young woman's bracelet the young woman had promised her.

She brought her hands up to cover her face, to block out the terrible images and whereas her fourteen-year-old self had wept piteously as she'd defended herself, Faith now intoned, bleakly, "I was given the bracelet, Madame."

"Well, that's not what Mrs Gedge told me and unless you want to go to the police or out onto the streets where it's dark and raining, I think Charity should take you upstairs to prepare yourself while Lord Harkom and I have a little chat."

Numb with shock, Faith allowed herself to be led to her bedchamber.

She'd assumed Charity would silently do Madame's bidding and find appropriate clothing, dress her hair, but once the door had closed behind them, Charity leaned against the edge of Faith's dressing table and just stared, white-faced, at Faith who sat on the bed.

"I don't know what you can do," she whispered.

Faith bowed her head and stared at her shoes that peeped from beneath the satin folds of her skirts. She felt dirty and shameful in her tawdry gown and wished she could be back in her simple, unadorned polonaise feeling special and full of hope and... *almost* free.

"I'll run away!" Faith raised her head and saw her hopelessness reflected in Charity's eyes. "What else can I do?"

"It's dark and dangerous out there, Faith." Charity pressed her lips together. "Where would you find shelter? I don't know anyone who could help you. No, stop!"

For Faith had risen as if about to carry out her determination.

"You don't know how vulnerable you are, alone on the streets. Someone will get to you and it'll be a lot worse than...staying here."

Faith sat down again. She saw the hopeless slump of Charity's shoulders in the looking glass and asked, "What can I expect?"

Charity was silent a moment, as if preparing her answer. "Like you, Faith, I was—until recently—a virgin though I did my apprenticeship. Just hope Lord Harkom will be gentle tonight. Knowing that you're a virgin, that is."

"So they're not all the same?"

Charity laughed. "Of course not! Lord, Faith, you really do know nothing! Some come here looking to cure their loneliness. They're the ones you want."

"And the others? What's the *worst* …so I'm prepared?"

"Those that come here are looking for someone to blame for their disappointments. They want to feel powerful and so they use us. A shadow crossed Charity's face. "But then there are the surprises." For a moment she was animated, and a look of such youthful hope crossed her face that Faith forgot her own terrors for a moment as she asked, "What are you saying, Charity?"

"Just that I've met a young man and…I'm in love." Her smile broadened. "*We're* in love."

"Faith! Are you ready?"

The girls jumped at the sound of Madame's voice from behind the door and leapt to their feet as she thrust herself unceremoniously into the room, furious when she saw that Faith was still in her old dress.

"Lord Harkom has agreed to far more than I'd expected and he'll not take kindly to being kept waiting!" she snarled, gripping Faith's shoulder and shaking her. "Get out of this room, Charity, and tend to your customers if you want a roof over your head and food in your belly."

For that's what have it boiled down to. Life's barest necessities in return for the only labour the girls at Madame Chambon's were trained in.

Lord Harkom was visibly impatient by the time Faith appeared.

Her hopes that he might deal more kindly to her on account of her inexperience were swept away when he began to circle her like a dog, sniffing out his next adventure, the moment she entered the room.

"Madame swears you're a virgin and I'll find out soon enough if she's lying." He put out one pale-fingered, long thin hand and toyed with the ringlet that lay upon Faith's shoulder. "Well, that's real enough," he commented when Faith gave a soft cry of pain and indignation after he tugged it. "It'll be interesting to see if all of you is real.

Madame knows I'm not one for artifice. It makes me very ill-tempered."

He had the petulant look of an indulged, overgrown schoolboy. His fair hair flopped over his forehead and he had a habit of tossing back his head as if he were a prime piece of horseflesh showing off his prowess amongst a herd of mares.

Faith could suffer this kind of pawing for only so long and when he cupped her face in his hands as if he might kiss her, she leapt backwards. "What are you doing, my lord?"

"I've bought you for the night. I can do whatever I want." His nostrils flared.

Faith's back was against the wall while the door was behind Lord Harkom. She was trapped. She shook her head. "No, my lord, you can *not*! You are rude and full of deceit if you think that!"

She got no further for suddenly his face was thrust towards her, mottled with anger, his hands on her shoulders. Her throat was dry and she suddenly felt entirely unable to move. Would anyone come if she screamed?

Not Madame, that was certain.

"No one speaks to me like that, you little strumpet! No one! Certainly not someone whom I'm paying for a night of pleasure." He fisted his hand as he insinuated it into her bodice, pummelling the tender flesh of her breasts pushed up above her corset.

Faith winced.

"Do you realise how fortunate you are that I of all people should have the breaking in of you?"

"I'd rather die!"

Her defiance seemed only to inflame him more. With a sharp tug, he ripped the silk of her cuirasse, pulling her towards him as he seized a hank of her hair.

Faith wept with pain as she lashed out with both hands, her fingernails scoring his stubble dusted cheeks.

"Harlot!" Whore!" His words blasted into her head as he threw himself on top of her, the bed behind her breaking her fall. A minor comfort she thought disjointedly as he hiked up her skirts.

CHAPTER 7

For so long had Crispin been staring at the open book in front of him, or rather, the honey bees hovering above the honeysuckle outside his study window, that he'd entered a different time zone. A more pleasant time zone. He'd swapped politics and diplomacy for a panorama featuring a beautiful sunset, which had him deliberating on the palette for the pale pinks that splashed through the darkening blue. Except that the blue kept metamorphosing into the blue of a neat, simple, figure-hugging dress worn by an exquisitely beautiful young girl with rippling golden hair.

A young woman bringing beauty to life in all its guises. A young woman he was itching to paint. That was, in truth, what was making him feel alive at this moment. Not two weeks on the French Riviera.

"I'm glad to see you applying yourself so diligently, Crispin."

He turned at the sound of his father's voice, gravelly and now, unusually, softened by approval. Crispin had long sought to win his pater's regard. Since Crispin had been appointed third secretary with his diplomatic prospects now all but assured, provided he didn't disgrace himself, the relationship between the two of them had greatly improved.

"With less than four weeks before I leave, I want to be as well versed in continental politics as possible." Crispin smiled, looking up from his books and gesturing for his father to take a seat upon the leather sofa at right angles to him. "I think I shall enjoy it though I'll miss you and Boxer, naturally."

"Is that all you'll miss? Your father and your dog? There's not a young lady who has captured your interest?" Without waiting for a reply, he went on, "I'm glad to hear it, Crispin, for you must focus your time and energies on your career for at least the next two years."

Crispin grimaced. "Is that a suggestion or a stricture, Papa? That I do not marry for two years?"

His father's expression softened to amusement as he idly picked up a book that was lying on the side table. "I'm not suggesting you deny yourself pleasure, my boy. Pleasure and marriage are not exclusive of each other." He tapped the book, which happened to be on portraiture. "Once you've established your career you can paint as much as you like. I'm only guiding you, my boy. I've trodden the path you're on now, and I have wisdom and experience which you do not have."

Crispin avoided his father's look to stare over the potted palms through the window. When his father insisted on continuing his monologue in the same vein, he groaned inwardly. "Designing females who throw themselves at you in the hopes of a title are a different kettle of fish to females who are in the market for pleasure; happy with a transaction that'll keep them in pretty clothes while you can let off some steam. It's the way of the world, my boy." He hesitated, caught Crispin's eye for but a moment, then stared out of the window. "Whatever happened in the past, Crispin…you were not to blame."

"Perhaps not entirely, Father."

Lord Maxwell swung round. "How quickly society would have judged had the wrong information been…reported."

Crispin was not about to be drawn. "You made sure of that, Papa," he muttered, rifling through the papers on his desk to distract himself and wishing his father would leave.

"Would you have expected me to do other than what I did?" his father returned sharply, his craggy face stern. "See my only son's name splashed across the newspapers together with whispers that you were a..." He shuddered, unable to say the word. "It would have ruined your career."

"I would have been cleared in an investigation, Father."

"Mud sticks, Crispin."

Crispin gave a taut smile. "But thanks to you, Father, my reputation remained pristine."

"By God, boy, I did what any father would do under the circumstances. A girl died. Tragic, of course. But the fault was hers. Alone!" His father made an effort to keep his anger in check. "So, tell me, Crispin, how will you spend the next three weeks preparing?"

"Preparing to leave my homeland? I shall do little different to what I have been doing. I shall study hard."

"You need diversion."

"Perhaps I should pick up my paintbrushes again."

Lord Maxwell sighed. "And get drawn into a world from which you can only extricate yourself with the utmost effort when time is of the essence?" He sighed. "No, Crispin. Establish your career and then you can dabble in your paints if that's what you wish. It's not for me to ban you forever from an artistic pursuit I'd happily condone if you could control it, but...it's an addiction with you, my boy. As dangerous as any bubble pipe, I fear."

"It's a diversion. One I find enormously fulfilling. Isn't that what you were advocating, Papa? A little diversion?"

"I was thinking along the lines of the female variety." Lord Maxwell cleared his throat. "A woman who can take away your cares for just a short while before you leave. If you need help in this area, I can recommend—"

Crispin cut him off curtly. "I don't need a woman, thank you." He might have added that the last thing he'd enjoy was a woman he suspected of being in any degree intimate with his father. Crispin respected his father in so many regards, just not when it came to the way he relegated women to varying degrees of usefulness; Crispin's late mother having been one of these: consort in public, mother of his children, and bearer of his heir. But when his father required pleasure, he consorted with an altogether different type of woman.

It was not the way Crispin intended to live his life.

With a sigh, Lord Maxwell made a move towards the door, his tone testy as if reading his son's thoughts, "If plans for the French Riviera came to nothing, I certainly don't advocate you mouldering here, in this musty townhouse, entirely alone with your books."

Crispin straightened, suddenly alive as a thread of possibility pierced his brain. "I don't intend to, Father. You're right. I've taken your words to heart, and I think I will head off to the country for a few days. Perhaps for some duck shooting. Perhaps to walk the peaks. Or, perhaps I'll visit Aunt Angela and Uncle Barnabus for the next ten days. They said I was always welcome."

"They are away, although the house is yours, if you wish it for a change of scene, of course. They've always said that. And, if you have a predilection for horsey women or career spinsters and country Assembly balls, for I'm sure nothing has changed in that part of the Cotswolds in fifty years, then I'm sure it'll do very nicely."

Crispin didn't care that his father considered the idea with as much enthusiasm as a plate of cold porridge. If there was little probability of being visited there by him, then all to the good.

His father farewelled him upon the threshold. "Not too much more studying tonight, Crispin. The light is poor and you need exercise. Perhaps a turn about Hyde Park would do you good."

Crispin shook his head. "No, there are a couple of other errands I need to do and the walk will do me good."

He joined his father on the front portico and stood for a moment upon the top step, staring at the setting sun. What palette could do justice to the pinks and golds that melded into each other? No longer did the French Riviera or a week of duck shooting hold any enticement for him.

As he watched his father's carriage disappear into the sunset, he frowned, wondering if his aunt who lived only two streets away, might know the address of Lady Vernon.

CHAPTER 8

How had it come to this?

Faith's terrified scream was muffled by Lord Harkom's cynical laughter as he straddled her, pinning her arms above her head with one strong hand while the other gripped her thigh.

He pinched her and she yelped; the wooden floor hard beneath her tailbone.

"You don't suppose your gracious madame is going to come to your aid when I've paid her such a hefty sum for the breaking in of you, do you?" He chuckled, clearly enjoying himself now that he had mastery over her.

His fingers crept higher up her thigh. Faith thought she was going to be ill. Was this what the sex act was all about? Mastery? Brutality? Power? The other girls were clear enough about their disdain for what was required of them. Some of them made a joke of the feigned pleasure gasps they'd perfected for earning themselves a tip.

Faith squeezed her eyes shut and forced her body to go slack. If a struggle was what he wanted, then she wasn't going to humour this man in any way. She opened her eyes, and it was the devil staring down at her.

It galvanised her to action. Meekly taking what was coming to her so as to lessen the pain was not how she'd play things. She'd not spent three years being turned into a lady only to be cast to the wolves and consumed like a sacrificial lamb the moment she fell short of Mrs Gedge's expectations of her.

She'd kill him. That's what she'd do. And then she'd run. She might have to jump out of the window first, but she'd not whore herself out to any man off the street willing to pay for her. She'd not whore herself for anyone except...

Yes, there was one exception. She could do it for Mr Westaway. *With* Mr Westaway. One man. Mrs Gedge's revenge. That was the mission for which Faith had been groomed, and she'd been prepared to compromise herself with *only* one man in order to earn her freedom.

"Lord Harkom!"

A furious pounding on the door was met by his lordship's horror.

"What is the meaning of this?" he shouted as Madame burst into the room.

"You've not spoiled her?" Madame demanded breathlessly. "Thank God!" she added as she ran her gaze across his still-buttoned breeches. With heaving bosom, and heels clicking across the floorboards, she arrived at Faith's side and, seizing her arm, yanked her to her feet. "Beg pardon but there's been a terrible mistake, my lord. Naturally, you'll be adequately compensated. I've any number..."

But Madame did not finish, for as Lord Harkom straightened his clothing as he stalked to the door, he was well into his threats against her house, issued from the threshold, that her business would suffer for the terrible insult he'd just endured.

Dazed, Faith stumbled into the passage as Madame led her past young women lounging with or without gentlemen consorts, who all eyed her curiously as she was pushed into Madame's private sitting room.

"You're to say nothing of this, do you hear?" Madame's voice was a low hiss, her body trembling with suppressed emotion as she pointed to the red-velvet upholstered sofa, indicating for Faith to sit.

To Faith's astonishment, a brandy was thrust into her hand with the order that she drink it all.

Madame sat down opposite her and fixed her with a beady stare.

"Nothing! Do you hear?"

Faith was trembling so much she could barely manage a reply. She nodded dumbly. What choice did she have but to agree? She'd been spared, and she had a roof over her head. She could count herself lucky.

Madame's fingers shook as she fixed the squirrel pelt with a pin to her coiffure. "Tomorrow, I'll see to your wardrobe, and the next day you'll be heading north to spend a week in a cottage in the country."

"With Lord Harkom?" It was all Faith could think to say.

"Don't be ridiculous. What do you suppose all that business just now was about? No, you're going to the Cotswolds."

TRUE TO HER WORD, IT WAS MADAME HERSELF WHO, THE NEXT DAY, personally oversaw the petticoats, stockings, shoes, bonnets, and gowns Faith would take with her to her unusual destination.

And, all brand new.

"Am I going to see Mr Westaway?" Faith asked. "Did *he* request that I come?"

"Mrs Gedge will tell you what you need to know."

Madame did not speak with her usual aplomb, and Faith suspected the previous evening's events had discomposed her, too.

Her friend Charity confirmed it as she took over the more menial task of folding ribbons and seeing that Faith's jewellery, simple pieces, were properly secured in their velvet boxes.

"Serves her ladyship right for selling you to the biggest brute that's ever crossed this threshold. And for your first time, too!" Her scorn was apparent, and when Faith stared, open-mouthed, she went on, "There's nothing that woman won't do if enough coin crosses her palm. It wasn't just Anastasia he hurt, though I couldn't say it to you last night. Lydia and Ruby had bruises for days after their sessions with the beast, and while Madame banned him for a month, I suppose she couldn't refuse him when he offered her such a bounty for supposedly the newest and loveliest virgin in town."

Faith sat heavily on the bed. "He must have come offering just moments after Mrs Gedge said she no longer wanted me."

"Oh, it was Lady Vernon who told Madame that you were no longer any use to Mrs Gedge. I think the old cat thought she could make a pretty penny on the side by selling you out."

"Lady Vernon?" Faith gasped, clenching her fists. "By God, I'll scratch her eyes out."

"It was Lady Vernon who came hurrying over just an hour later to say there'd been a new development, and that you were suddenly required by Mrs Gedge to go to the Cotswolds," Charity said. "Perhaps she only wanted to frighten you."

"How could Lady Vernon do such a thing? She's so...old and...poor."

"She needs money. Exactly. And she's ruthless, and you are nothing but a means of keeping food in that skinny belly of hers and a roof over her head. So, when you spend your enchanted week with Mr Westaway, I'd be far more distrustful of Lady Vernon than your young man who seems quite harmless." Charity folded another petticoat and dropped it on top of a pile of folded underwear lying in Faith's carpetbag. Seeing Faith's look of concern, she smiled. "Don't worry, Faith, Mr Westaway will think you're quite delightful; I'm sure of it. I've seen him, and he has a pleasant manner. He's not the kind who pushes his weight around to prove he's better than his peers and want to show the likes of us just how important he is. I think he'll be kind to you."

"He's been here?"

"Lord, no!" Charity laughed. "I've asked around and he doesn't frequent establishments such as ours. In fact, he's not been associated with any young woman whom anyone knows about so perhaps Mrs Gedge will be disappointed in her grand designs by finding his tastes run more to the Greek."

Faith put her hand to her mouth. "He doesn't fancy women?"

Charity shrugged. "I don't know. Perhaps he likes both. Perhaps he's a virgin, and you'll have to be the one to show him what to do."

Faith stared at her shoes. Her encounter with Lord Harkom, so fresh and horrifying, had made her feel vulnerable and powerless in a way that being Mrs Gedge's pawn never had. Ever since she'd come under Mrs Gedge's thumb, Faith had been quietly confident she would one day outwit the older woman. Yet in only a few minutes, Lord Harkom had used his brute strength to subdue her. Not only would he be able to subdue her, physically, any time he wanted, the frightening reality was that in the world in which Faith lived, his money sanctioned any amount of brutality.

"How will I do that when I don't know what to do?" she asked.

Charity laughed as she sat on the bed beside Faith and hugged her briefly. "What a question when you've lived in this place so long," she said. "You've seen the living displays. Besides, haven't you ever put your eye to a peephole in all these years?"

"Of course not! And I block my ears if I have to." Faith shuddered, and Charity put her hand to Faith's chin and turned her head so she could look into her eyes, saying quite seriously now, "Have you really been able to live at London's most notorious, high-class brothel for three years and block out everything that goes on here?"

"I know what happens...physically. But that's very different from everything else."

"Don't let your encounter with Lord Harkom colour your feelings." Charity was matter of fact now. "He's a well-known brute and granted, there are a few like him. But mostly, the men are respectful, even if they're self-absorbed and think only of their own pleasure." Her smile broadened. "Sometimes it's even possible to fall in love with a kind regular. That is, when he brings you gifts, and fills your ears with sweet ones, telling you you're the only one. Making you believe him when he says that one day he'll take you away to a new life."

"Do you really believe that, Charity?" Faith felt sad for her friend. Glad that she could enjoy the brief pleasure of being in love, but sad that her love was doomed.

"Of course, I know not to believe it," Charity added quickly. "It's words only. But it makes the act tolerable. No, it makes it a pleasure."

"A pleasure? For a woman? But what pleasure *is* there?" Faith was now more troubled by the possibility that she might have some feeling unleashed in her than by the mechanics of what she'd long resigned herself to. Tonight had made everything a sudden, horrible reality.

Charity rose. "You'll have to leave that to Mr Westaway. Make him desire you, encourage him with your shy but eager responses. You've learned how to do *that* during your apprenticeship here. And those other classes Lady Vernon took you off in your carriage to attend?"

"Philosophy, politics and art and classics with Professor Monk?"

"Professor Monk!" Charity let out a scream of laughter. "And was he? We girls used to speculate his reception of you was far from monkish."

"Professor Monk is at least sixty, no, seventy! With hair growing out of his ears and nose and, obviously, no interest in women at all." Faith considered the gentleman who'd opened her mind to the wonders of the wider world through the uncensored education he'd given her, teaching her the same curriculum he taught all the boys who came to him for similar instruction. "But he was always kind to me."

"So he taught you nothing about the workings of the body? How to prevent conception, how to feign pleasure?" Charity gave a sly smile. "How to give and receive pleasure?"

Faith imagined her wizened old tutor being involved in any such instruction and laughed for the first time.

"Oh Faith, you are so pretty when you're not so serious!" Charity exclaimed. "But, of course, Madame has taught you these things? She has, I know it, for all we girls must attend the instruction Madame conducts here."

"I know the basics," Faith admitted. "But for you girls, it's all so real and necessary because it's all about the things you do every day. For me, I never dreamed the day would come when I really had to…" she swallowed "…sell my body."

Charity rose with a shrug as she headed towards the door. She had to leave, Faith knew, as she had a customer waiting for her. Daisy, the tweeny, had just called through the keyhole to tell her.

"It's not so bad when you get used to it," Charity said bolsteringly, as she let herself into the passage. "As long as you have a plan to escape. Even if that plan is just in your head."

With quiet resolve, Faith said, "I plan to escape the moment I've done all the damage to Mr Westaway that Mrs Gedge wants me to. I've signed a contract giving me five hundred pounds if I can get from him an agreement to set me up as his mistress which I will decline. If he makes me an offer of marriage, then she'll double that."

"A marriage offer is worth a great deal more than a thousand pounds, Faith! What a strange contract. You surely didn't sign that, did you? I mean, sign to say you'd reject him and break his heart in order to get yourself a thousand pounds?"

"I did sign it, because when I first came here, the alternative was that or be handed over to the magistrate." Faith felt uncomfortable. "And then I just did my lessons, and I had a place to live, and I didn't give it much thought. Now, though…"

"Well, if you can make him fall in love with you, maybe you can fall in love with him, Faith. Maybe, out of all of us, you can be the one to get your marriage offer and live happily ever after."

Faith saw that although she smiled, she looked worried. "It's a legal contract," she said. "I know it is."

Charity sighed. "I just worry that if Mrs Gedge is anything like Madame, you'll never be free."

"But if I can truly make Mr Westaway fall in love with me, then maybe I can be."

CHAPTER 9

Faith hadn't left London since she'd arrived a little over three years before as an innocent country girl from Dorset. Now her transformation was complete, and no one from her village or perhaps even her family, would recognise the poised young woman who swayed from side to side in the train carriage beside her chaperone.

Not that she felt poised. Faith was a jumble of nerves inside.

She and Lady Vernon had not spoken in two hours since their initial brittle greeting before being transported to the station.

Lady Vernon had immediately opened a book once the conductor had led them to their seats and slammed the door on their compartment.

Faith had tried to read, but after an hour, the anger bubbling inside her could no longer be suppressed. Lady Vernon wasn't some brutal dominator who could reduce Faith to a quivering mass of tearful powerlessness, and yet that's what the frail old woman hunched in the corner had effectively done to the 'goddaughter' she was supposed to protect.

Finally, she could bear the silence no longer. "How much did Madame pay you to release me to the first high-paying customer who happened to fancy using strength and violence to break in a virgin?"

There! The words should have made the old woman turn from her usual grey parchment colour to a sickly off-white.

Lady Vernon put her book down. She swayed from side to side as the train rounded several bends. "Madame Chambon told me she arrived just in time." But there was fear in her tone. Obviously, she trusted Madame to tell her the truth as little as Faith did.

Faith stared at her. "How long does it take for a big, strong, arrogant man to rip the clothes off a lady and have his way with her? I don't suppose you know, Lady Vernon, though I see the thought is unpalatable to you. And yet you were willing for that to happen to me as long as you got enough gold coins in your pocket."

Lady Vernon's nostrils flared, and the lashes over her rheumy eyes fluttered. "You are…intact, Faith. Madame assured me you were."

Faith banged her hand onto her book in frustration. "Do you ask because you're filled with remorse and truly hope I am unscathed out of concern for me? Or because I'm worth more to you if I *am*… intact?"

"Regardless of what did or didn't happen, you'd do well to preserve the fiction you're a virgin if you wish to keep Mrs Gedge as a benefactress." Lady Vernon sounded bolder now. "If you're not, and word gets out, then you're no good to anyone. And if you're no good to anyone, you'll starve, my girl, so consider yourself lucky that you're here with me."

Faith looked out of the window at the passing countryside. It looked green and lovely, the air fresh and clean now they were out of London. "As if anyone would know or care to wonder if I was a virgin if they knew where I've spent the last three years," she muttered. Lady Vernon looked so harmless, so utterly inconsequential, sitting in the corner like a bundle of rags, except that the gown that covered her bones was silk. Very old silk, now dusty with age. But perhaps she was even more ruthless than Madame. Or Mrs Gedge? Faith would have to remember that as she embarked upon the next part of her journey.

"Now, I understand that you are aware of the requirement that you're to enslave this young man's heart, but don't be too eager," Lady Vernon said, changing the subject. As if she knew anything about enticing a young man—or any man.

Faith sent her the filthiest look she could but said nothing.

"We both know that your future, and mine, hinge upon your success."

"How do you know his heart isn't already engaged?" Faith asked. "How do you know he'll even like me?"

"His heart is not engaged, and you are just the kind of young lady to appeal to this young man. Appeal to his chivalrous nature; his protective instincts. Don't be too eager for intimacy or it won't ring true. Reel him in, slowly."

"Have you had much success using this strategy yourself, Lady Vernon?" Faith enquired politely and was rewarded with a bitter smile. Good, she'd touched a nerve.

"What if I feel sorry for him and don't wish to ruin him?" Faith added. "I'm not cruel by nature. Not like you and Mrs Gedge." She gave a short laugh. "If he falls in love with me, then I may think it more worthwhile to run away with him than accept Mrs Gedge's fee with my freedom."

"My dear girl, I certainly don't think you're quite so stupid." Lady Vernon pulled out her wire-rimmed spectacles to examine Faith as if she honestly believed the girl could be mentally deficient. "You surely must realise that Mrs Gedge will reveal everything about you to him if you were to do that. And then what future could there be for you? Do you think his father would allow him to marry a prostitute, even if you both were madly in love with one another? No, break the boy's heart, wait for further instructions, and when you've fulfilled your duty to Mrs Gedge's satisfaction, you will be given your freedom and assured that your prospects for making a respectable match with some other worthy gentleman will be fostered by the woman who has been so good to you all these years."

Faith sighed. The prospect of her journey into Mr Westaway's arms and into his bed didn't particularly move her, though she supposed anything was preferable to being pounded into submission like Lord Harkom had nearly done.

But at least Mr Westaway seemed pleasant enough.

Though falling in love was not something Faith intended doing for a long time.

CHAPTER 10

Crispin couldn't remember the last time he'd whiled away a few hours in a hammock. He should have done this a long time ago—had a few days' break from London and his father's scrutiny.

He raised the book resting over his face by a few inches and waved it in the air to shoo away the bee or fly that threatened to settle on his chin. For the moment, the enjoyment of simply doing nothing was almost more enticing than picking up a paintbrush. Perhaps his father's strictures that he give up his art until he was well entrenched in his new position was not such a bad one.

He wondered now at the wisdom of asking Miss Montague to be his model for the painting he intended entering into the prestigious art competition that had so stirred his blood a few short days ago.

For today, languid in the sun, he had no urge to do anything very much except rest completely. His brain was tired; his body was tired. In the three short weeks before he was due to board a packet to France and begin his journey to the country that would be his home for the next few years, perhaps he should simply rest.

He'd have to compensate Miss Montague for her time, of course.

He'd been fired up by the idea of furthering her acquaintance, but over the past few days, her image had dimmed. And over the past day and a half spent lazing in the lovely cottage garden of the small manor house that had been given over to his use by his aunt and uncle, all his desires and ambitions had quite drained away.

He was drifting off when he heard a clear voice say, "*The History of a Crime*. I enjoyed Victor Hugo's essay about Napoleon III's takeover of France, though I did find it heavy in parts."

He opened his eyes, astonished to find himself staring at Miss Montague, dressed simply in white and flanked by the funereal-looking Lady Vernon.

"When did you read that?" he was startled into asking, before good manners came to the fore, and he removed himself from the hammock and ushered the ladies to a garden bench nearby.

"As soon as it was published. I love anything by Victor Hugo though my papa feels he's unsuitable."

"Unsuitable?"

"Yes. Do you think it's unsuitable for a young lady to read Victor Hugo? And if so, why?"

He hadn't expected she'd be so direct when given the chance to converse with her beyond the confines of the ballroom.

"Unexpected, perhaps, is a better term. It was recommended reading by my papa in view of my imminent posting. I must admit I find it heavy going too. If you gleaned anything from it, you'll have to impart your insights when you pose for me." He studied her covertly while pretending to arrange the cushions in the chair upon which he sat opposite her. Her hair had the look of newly threshed corn. There was a golden glow about the rippling tresses that immediately had him envisioning his palette of oils.

"It would be a pleasure. I'm very good at keeping still, but the time passes more quickly if we're discussing something interesting. That's if your concentration is up to it."

Crispin smiled. Her transformation was astonishing. She looked much more at home in the colourful summer garden in the country discussing an intellectual topic than when she'd been so obviously on display in a public arena.

And, the more he thought about it, the way the sun glistened on her beautiful hair made him long to run his fingers through the ringlets that fell over her right shoulder in preference to painting it.

The thought startled him, and he made a mental note to beware of any similar urges.

Miss Montague was a penniless girl sent here to model for him, and he was off to the Continent in just under a month for a posting of many years. He had a career that couldn't include dowerless potential brides, no matter how entertaining and easy on the eye, while she was on the lookout for a husband. Her godmother had already admitted that Miss Montague could not afford to be discerning if she were to escape her fate as a governess.

No, Crispin was expected to do much better than Miss Montague when the time came.

Nevertheless, the interested way she was looking at him now was having a rather tumultuous effect on him.

"I'll enjoy testing your knowledge and reporting back to your tutor," Crispin said with a levity he did not feel for, in truth, his fingers were just itching to seize a paintbrush and stand in front of a canvas while his senses directed him from there.

That's what he loved so much about being a painter. The ability to let his mind wander at will. It was something his father had deplored in his dreamy young son, insisting that learning and application led to a future based on merit.

Lady Vernon cleared her throat. "We are putting up at the White Swan for this week. It's convenient as it's only a short walk, and the weather looks set to be good for the next few days. When will you want Faith for her first sitting? And what should she wear?"

Crispin laughed and immediately apologised. He was not used to being asked for his advice on a lady's attire. Suddenly, the situation in which he'd been thrust seemed ludicrous. And yes, as the sun fell across Miss Montague's sweet, smiling face, quite delicious.

At his hesitation, Lady Vernon went on, "The title of the work that is to be painted is *Lady at Sunset*, if you recall, Mr Westaway. How would you like to direct Faith? Do you have a location in mind? Or will you paint her in a studio and do the setting later?"

Good lord, this woman, oh yes, the girl's godmother, knew what she was about. Crispin hadn't given a proper thought to the requirements of the piece. He didn't expect to win. Perhaps he wouldn't even enter the work. However, as an opportunity for a week or two of idleness, or rather indulgence, doing what he loved most, he was not about to look a gift horse in the mouth. As long as his father had no idea what he was actually doing, Crispin could look upon this week as a necessary holiday before the hard work of his career began.

"Whatever Miss Montague wishes," he said, remembering she had little in the way of a wardrobe. And as Miss Montague would look lovely in whatever she chose, he didn't want to embarrass her over her impecuniousness.

"And when would you like us to return?"

Crispin felt like a ten-year-old, the way he was being spoken to. He hoped Lady Vernon didn't always insist on being present, though he supposed it was necessary. He certainly didn't want to be responsible for anyone casting aspersions on Miss Montague's good character. In fact, he rather liked the idea of aiding her in her quest to find herself a better match through his painting. A painting that would advertise her beauty to the world. A noble cause.

This would be a week of wicked indulgence for him when painting had been long forbidden. But it would be a means to elevate Miss Montague's chances in the world.

An image flashed through his mind of the dead girl. Miss Montague would be his chance to atone for the past. He could improve her future prospects, and hopefully, because of him, see her enjoy prosperity and happiness rather than a cruel and impoverished destiny.

"Tomorrow." He flexed his fingers, remembering how deft his hands were when he had a project that fired him up. "At noon." He closed his eyes briefly and imagined the leisurely morning he would have constructing the scene in his head that he would paint. "And bring something warm. It might be a long evening."

He would have to scout out a suitable spot by the lake in which to paint her. He'd have her in position when the sun went down, burnishing her hair with gold, while the long shadows turned her skin to toasted alabaster.

CHAPTER 11

The White Swan was a comfortable and respectable country inn. Fortunately Faith had her own bed chamber and had slept surprisingly well before she was disturbed by the knock on the door that heralded the start of her mission.

However, she was suitably docile as Lady Vernon selected her wardrobe. In fact, she barely troubled herself with any of the decisions associated with her sojourn as she sat up in bed reading the final of Victor Hugo's essays. She'd found them instructive, even compelling reading, and was rather looking forward to discussing them with Mr Westaway. That is, if he'd really read them. Many times she'd caught out a gentleman in a lie. In her younger days at Madame Chambon's when she'd served the girls refreshments as they'd entertained gentlemen in the drawing room, she'd overhear some pink of the ton boast of a literary accomplishment, only to discover, upon listening further, that it was likely he'd never truly read the book.

She tried to stifle her fears for the future. For any possibility of failure.

Now that she'd progressed to the stage where Mr Westaway wanted to paint her, and she'd be in his company for at least a week, she had to play her cards right.

Overcoming any physical barriers on her part would not be a problem. She was confident she liked him enough to do what she needed to.

Overcoming any gentlemanly restraint on his part would be the challenge.

Yes, she'd seen the admiration in his eyes that she was confident could be attributed to enthusiasm for his project on a number of fronts. But would he be easily persuaded to kiss her?

If she could manage just that, then she hoped matters would progress as Mrs Gedge required.

Her ugly encounter with Lord Harkom had put things into perspective. He was a violent brute.

Therefore losing her virginity to Mr Westaway didn't trouble Faith too much if it meant she gained her freedom.

Having heard the primal grunts and cries of release through the thin walls at Madame Chambon's for so many years, the sexual act held little interest and certainly no appeal. It was simply a means to an end.

A way for Faith to gain her independence and be free of Mrs Gedge and Madame Chambon.

And that detestable cockroach, Lady Vernon.

"The blue, I think."

She could hear Lady Vernon muttering under her breath as if the decision were of the utmost importance. "The colour of forget-me-nots. An innocent colour; a simple yet alluring gown. Ah, my dear, he won't be able to keep his hands off you."

This brought Faith's head up with a jerk. When Lady Vernon turned back to her, her minder was all innocence herself, as if she'd never spoken of Faith in such terms.

"Are you ready? No, ten minutes longer, I think. We need to keep him waiting. Increase his impatience because you need to trade on every advantage. You are the supplicant, after all. The penniless creature who needs his good offices, yet you need to shore up your power. Impatience is the way to play the game, my dear, though I've no doubt Madame Chambon has taught you all the tricks of the trade."

Faith stretched and put her feet on the floor but made no answer. The less she told Lady Vernon the better, and besides, she was hardly about to divulge such matters of a personal nature. That yes, for years Madame Chambon had included Faith in the regular sessions that acquainted her girls with a myriad of ways to whip up a man's desire. Innocent things like the feather-light touch of fingertips grazing exposed flesh, a flare of promise at odds with demurely lowered lashes.

Once, Faith had been required to sit in on a lecture-like session involving a handsome, well-built young man, who'd reclined on a bed and exhibited to the newest and most innocent of Madame Chambon's recruits the astonishing ways in which a man's body reacted to certain stimuli.

Intrigued and horrified in equal measure, Faith, fortunately, never had to return to a similar lesson after she'd communicated her disgust to Mrs Gedge one afternoon tea at Claridges. Clearly, Mrs Gedge considered she was behaving with proper moral rectitude by simply housing Faith without requiring her to be a participant in the less savoury dealings of the household.

Mrs Gedge was biding her time for when she needed Faith and Faith's pristine innocence to do her bidding.

Finally, it was time to go, Faith feeling like an obedient little lapdog, beautifully brushed and prepared for her afternoon encounter.

They found Mr Westaway in the garden, all impatience as he grasped his paintbrush and paced back and forth by the rhododendron bushes staring at the sky.

"Lady Vernon, Miss Montague." He swept them a bow and then led Faith to an arbour amidst the trees and bushes where he invited her to sit. She could sense his urgency for something which he believed was purer than it was. She saw, also, Lady Vernon's secret smile of satisfaction, but all Faith could recognise in Mr Westaway's manner was his desire to fulfil an artistic challenge. Nothing more.

Concerning. She'd have to use everything she had at her disposal to change that.

"I've laid out a blanket and a cushion for your comfort though I'll paint them out in the final rendition."

Faith shrugged. "I don't mind doing without such comforts if it'll make your life easier." Easy to please. She'd start with that.

"You may need to remain still for up to three hours." His brows arched as if surprised by a thought that hadn't occurred to him. "I've been told you're practised at keeping still for long periods of time, Miss Montague?"

"Three hours is a trifle," she assured him though secretly horrified at the prospect. But if this was necessary to please Mr Westaway, she'd gladly start with three hours of boredom.

Except that it wasn't the kind of boredom or discomfort she'd expected. Yes, bees buzzed a little too close sometimes, and the odd beetle crossed her flesh and made her cry out in surprise, but that just lightened the mood unexpectedly. And soon she and Mr Westaway were laughing companionably as Lady Vernon snored gently in a chair beneath the overhanging branches of an ancient elm tree.

"Stay! Just like that!" The sudden imperative was out of keeping with the earlier tone, but Faith recognised artistic passion when she heard it. She also proved adept at complying just as her benefactor had obviously wished judging by the gleam in his eye. Faith lay prone, relaxed upon the grass, her head resting on her arm and supported by her elbow, her expression enigmatic. Yes, enigmatic was what he wanted and apparently Faith did it well.

"Keep looking like that," he murmured, moving away from his easel and kneeling at her side to tweak a fold of her forget-me-not skirts that the breeze had moved slightly. His expression was intense, his frown of concentration when he got closer suggesting that what he was about to do was of the greatest import.

To touch a fold of forget-me-not cotton twill?

A surge of pique made her shift position though she hid her frown.

He was not looking at her. She was an object. Not an object of lustful desire as Mrs Gedge would have her but upholding the same degree of value to him as if she were inanimate. A Sèvres vase, perhaps?

She was more discomposed by the realisation than she'd expected. After all, it wasn't as if she desired to be desired. She didn't. Yet, nor could she fail at her task.

Her task to make him fall in love with her.

But there was *nothing* in his eyes to suggest she might even come close.

As his fingers smoothed a fold of her skirt, she gasped, as if stung, and rolled onto her back and away from his hand while he blinked in surprise and said, "I suppose I should have warned you I was going to touch you." He reddened. "I mean, touch your dress. Make it look exactly as it did before the breeze disturbed it. I beg your pardon, Miss Montague. I meant no disrespect."

"None taken," she murmured, reddening also. How interesting that she could simulate these innocent responses when she didn't feel embarrassed in the slightest. Merely a little frustrated that she was taking so long to elicit from him any kind of interest. She pressed her lips together. He was still on his knees beside her as he tried to explain. "I truly am sorry. Something happens to me when I paint. And it's been so long I'd forgotten how intense I can be."

His laugh sounded forced as he rose and returned to the easel where he spent a long time mixing paints and staring at the result, as if he couldn't bring himself to look at her. Finally, he glanced at her from around the canvas. "It's probably why my father detests my passion. He sees I can have no sensible thought in my mind when I am so preoccupied."

"What does he consider sensible?"

"The security of England. The possibility of a threat from Germany. Assessing that threat. Mitigating it. Diplomacy." Now his laugh was more genuine, though self-effacing. "None of the kinds of things a young lady like you would trouble herself about."

Faith closed her eyes and raised her face to the sun while all the book learning she'd acquired floated through her mind. She'd been surprised to discover how much she loved history. Her tutor had loved politics, and the result was that she was often engaged in a series of spirited discussions on various topics in the old man's musty little study in Maida Vale. Including the increasing threat posed by Germany.

"Your father was a diplomat, wasn't he?" Faith didn't want to look at Mr Westaway while she formulated her words. If she couldn't impress him with her beauty, Mrs Gedge's hope was that Faith would interest him with her mind.

"He was, and I am to follow in his footsteps."

"He wants you to be just like him?"

There was a silence, and Faith opened her eyes to see him looking intently at her. "Yes." He nodded slowly. "He does."

Clearly, Mr Westaway wasn't enamoured by the idea.

"I daresay you discuss these matters with him," Faith went on innocently. "France's shattering defeat by Prussia a few years ago, for example. Do *you* think that means that France has been supplanted as a threat by a new potential enemy? Should we be worried?" She gazed at Mr Westaway with her most disarming half smile. Some men couldn't resist the combination of a young girl's innocent desire to impress, at the same time as be educated, she had learned.

He opened his mouth to reply but she wanted to push her advantage while she had it, going on quickly, "Germany is efficient, militaristic, ruthless, and ambitious. Of course, we should be worried, shouldn't we, Mr Westaway? Your job is to reduce the risk to our country through gathering information, but of course you have to be discreet. Your father would want you to be as vigilant in your attention to detail as a diplomat as you clearly are as an artist."

Crispin nearly dropped his paintbrush. Was this the same young woman whose quiet, artistic posture had first attracted his interest? She'd stood out from the many other debutantes that night on account of the plainness of her attire, which contrasted with her beauty. She had been unleashed upon society in the hopes of finding a husband who might see her looks as compensating for her material deficiencies, and Crispin had taken pity on her for no other reason than that she made a good model when he suddenly had the opportunity to paint.

A clandestine activity because it bore no relation to his work. His all-important work for which he'd been groomed since childhood—to follow his father into the diplomatic service.

Yet in a few sentences, she'd succinctly summarised the situation with which he and his father had grappled during long dinner conversations these past months.

He wished his father could have heard Miss Montague speak just now.

And then remembered his father must never know of Miss Montague's existence or the fact that Crispin was painting.

"You have a remarkable grasp on the situation, Miss Montague," he allowed. "Where did you pick up such information?"

"I read a lot."

Her face was turned up to the sun, and her lids had drifted sleepily closed while a contented smile played about her lips. In her hands, she held a small posy of flowers he'd placed there for artistic value. Now, as he gazed at her, he was struck by a sensation he was completely unable to identify. He frowned as his eyes roamed the length of her. She was a beauty, and she seemed entirely unaware of the fact.

What else was in that mind of hers? He could wonder for it went without saying that any other part of her was out of bounds.

Into the lengthening silence, she volunteered on a small sigh, "There's not much a girl like me *can* do except read...and do other people's bidding." She blinked open her eyes suddenly and smiled. It was like a shadow giving way to the sun. Her eyes were pools of crystal water; her skin dew-brushed petals.

"Don't move!" he cried again, dipping his paintbrush into a blob of colour on the palette. "Keep smiling. You don't smile enough. Yes, that was the problem before."

Feverishly he returned to work. He'd thought a pensive creature suited the mood of what he sought to recreate. But that was before her lightness had transformed his work. His world. She was all vibrancy and life, not a half-dead creature lying languidly amongst the grass. Not a girl living a half life, burdened by a destiny that would not be of her choosing. He'd not thought any of this, but it flashed through his mind in a blinding maelstrom of insight—replacing in the vacuum left behind only the fear that he hadn't the talent to capture the exquisite purity, the joyful radiance of a young woman, in that moment, uninhibited and alive.

She gave him a few minutes to satisfy the call of genius and then said lightly, "Ah, but I thought the problem was that *you* were too serious, Mr Westaway. I was afraid I'd fall in your estimation if I allowed my frivolous nature to reveal itself."

She was teasing him. The chit of a girl so beneath him in age, station, and everything else was smiling her amusement with all the consummate confidence of a dowager holding forth in a salon.

And he was entranced.

He returned her smile, but beneath the veneer of a sudden shared camaraderie, lurked an uncomfortable realisation that she was becoming just a little too interesting.

He'd have to bring the session to an early finish.

"Thank you, Miss Montague."

Her mouth dropped open as he nodded, suddenly brisk as he began to clean his brushes. He was sorry his words sounded unaccountably clipped and tried to ameliorate with a smile any sense she might have that he was displeased with her.

"You have been a wonderful subject."

"Surely, you've not finished the painting, Mr Westaway? May I look?" Once she'd got over her surprise, her good nature seemed to have returned, and he was grateful. Relations between them must be utterly proper, verging on formal even—if he were to do what he had to do. Paint the picture that would satisfy his artistic urges, so he could do his father's bidding and concentrate on more important matters in the world.

"Of course, though it is very raw in its current form."

He was too conscious of her closeness when she came to stand beside him, pointing out various flourishes she liked, admiring the work that fed his desperate need to be recognised for what was most important to him in the world—his art.

He stepped away slightly and glanced from the beautiful, smiling girl whose head came up just above his shoulder, to the withered, sleeping woman in the wicker chair beneath the apple tree. The contrast between the two suddenly overwhelmed him with possibilities, and without thinking, he put his hands on her shoulders to move her into a position in the foreground where her youthful bloom would shine as the subject, and the old woman in the background, surrounded by fallen apples, would be the juxtaposition.

Fuelled by artistic excitement, he cupped her cheek. Smooth. The essence of eternal youth. Her halo of golden hair would complete the picture. It would be better than anything he'd done. His head throbbed with excitement, and unconsciously, he stroked the beautifully rendered contours of her brow, nose, and cheek. Her lips. Yes…this was the angle.

And then, as his fragmented vision for what could be coalesced into what *was*, he saw that she'd closed her eyes and raised her face to his.

She was anticipating a kiss? A plethora of emotions slammed through him. First and foremost was the desire to respond, but fast on its heels was the realisation that succumbing to such desire would doom them both. He swallowed, and she opened her eyes in time to catch his confusion.

Quickly, he said, "I want to paint you exactly as you are and in just that position…that alignment with your chaperone just behind, still sleeping, is perfect. Please indulge me a few minutes longer, Miss Montague?"

"Of course." She pressed her lips together, and as the hot blush spread from her bosom upwards, he cursed himself for putting either of them in such a position.

Channelling his frustrated desire into artistic energy he worked quickly, teasing out the expressions with a few accurate strokes, throwing the entire mood he'd wanted to create right onto the canvas.

It was done in a flash of time, a blur of colour, and he was breathing quickly when he put down his paintbrush and was ready to…

Dismiss her?

Yes, that's what he had to do if he was to get through this unscathed.

"You've been marvellous, Miss Montague," he declared with false bonhomie. "I've never had a better model. So still, so..."

"So obedient?" She was smiling that artless smile of hers, and he wondered if she had any inkling of the trauma he'd just been through.

But of course she would have no idea. She was very young but, yes, very obedient. Well trained would perhaps be apt, for once she'd recovered from the moment of awkwardness over the nearly kiss, she was as perfectly composed and well behaved as any demure debutante needed to be in order to prosper in society.

"Very obedient!" he said on a laugh which broke the ice and woke Lady Vernon, who now called out peevishly for her charge to fetch her sticks and help her to her feet.

"Will you require another sitting, Mr Westaway?" Lady Vernon asked as they prepared to leave. "I trust she was everything for which you'd hoped. She's not very experienced, but she wanted very much to please, didn't you, Faith?"

"With nine brothers and sisters, that's my primary duty, Lady Vernon. To please." She speared him with a look of amusement that insinuated itself more than it should. Was she sharing a secret joke with him? If she were older, more experienced in the ways of the world, he'd have *known* that's what she was doing.

"A great trial you obviously bear very well, Miss Montague," he managed as the safest response he could come up with. "And I'm delighted with today's progress. Thank you for your consummate professionalism for I have managed to get down everything I need and can work on the rest at my leisure. No, I won't require another sitting."

She nodded and gave a half curtsey. "Glad to have obliged, Mr Westaway. In that case, I daresay we shall return to London in the morning." She glanced at Lady Vernon for corroboration, but the old woman shook her head.

"We've booked the room for a few more days, and these weary old bones of mine aren't up to a return trip to the hustle and bustle of the city just yet. Where would you suggest we go for a short sightseeing trip, Mr Westaway? You know the area."

FAITH HAD GROWN UP A COUNTRY GIRL. UNTIL THE AGE OF TWELVE, THE cramped cottage she shared with her nine siblings and parents in the Welsh Borderlands had epitomised all she wanted to escape. At thirteen, she'd gone into service and learned the ways of the gentry. She'd learned how they spoke and watched how they behaved.

Now, the rolling countryside of the West-Midland Vales with its elm-fringed water meadows of the Severn and Avon, and orchards laden with damson, cherry, apple, and pear, represented freedom.

Even if just for a day or two.

That morning, they'd traipsed through the town of Stratford-Upon-Avon, imbibing the history of the Great Bard, William Shakespeare and, later, learned of efforts expended by the actor David Garrick whose Shakespeare Jubilee the previous century had contributed to turning it into a tourist town.

This was the kind of safe, prescribed sightseeing Lady Vernon preferred. Faith would have preferred to delay their journey amidst the lush green fields and go for a meandering walk in the woods. This, of course, was out of the question due to Lady Vernon's infirmity, though she'd proved nimble enough in town until clearly worn out in the Guild Chapel where she now sank into a pew to gaze at the medieval paintings in the nave.

"Five minutes, and no longer, and then we must have lunch at the teahouse at the end of the road," she announced between wheezes. The sunlight that streamed through the stained-glass windows was not kind to her, highlighting the sagging bags of wrinkles under her eyes and the energetic spouting of hairs from the fleshy mole on her chin.

"We can rest longer if you like," Faith said, determined to be amenable and charitable. She knew Lady Vernon would be reporting back to Mrs Gedge on Faith's success which, to date, had been negligible. Staring at the old woman, she wondered if Lady Vernon had ever had a modicum of good looks before her mouth had caved in and age had stuck its claws into her.

The reflection sent fear like a frisson of electricity up her spine, reminding her that she only had a handful of years, herself, in which to cement her own future. A future which, she'd assumed, would be assured by the conclusion of her visit to the Cotswolds. Mr Westaway should have been eating out of her hands by now.

"We need to be at Mrs Bromley's Corner Teahouse by one o' clock," Lady Vernon announced, consulting her watch, and the way she said it made it clear there was a very good reason for this. Something to do with Mr Westaway, Faith presumed.

Correctly, it transpired, when Lady Vernon fixed a pair of beetling eyes upon her and said, "You could at least pretend interest in the young man. I thought you were as anxious as your benefactress to expedite this little matter and claim your reward."

She made it sound so sordid.

Which, Faith supposed, it was.

"I like him very much, and I've hinted so, obliquely, which is all a well-brought-up girl like myself can do. With all due respect, you've been asleep most of the time, Lady Vernon."

"Well-brought-up..." Lady Vernon repeated on a decidedly ill-bred snort, thought Faith as she resisted the urge to offer a tart rejoinder. Too much hinged on Lady Vernon's good offices and while, before she'd sat for Mr Westaway, she could afford to talk back, her current failure could only be laid at her door. What was Mrs Gedge going to say?

Her earlier frisson of fear for her future paid a return visit and settled about her like a cloak 'which old men huddle about their love, as if to keep it warm.' Since they were in the town of the old bard, it seemed appropriate to borrow his quote for personal use. Faith had read much of Shakespeare and King Lear was her favourite.

"Yes, this old church is as cold as the grave and it's time we settled ourselves for lunch," Lady Vernon announced, mistaking Faith's shiver of fearful foreboding.

"So, Mr Westaway knows we'll be at Mrs Bromley's Teahouse then?"

Lady Vernon sent her an arch look over her shoulder as they trod the thin red carpet down the nave towards the open double doors. "Of course he does. Someone has to keep you on the right path if you're to succeed in this venture. I'd have hoped Mr Westaway would be eating out of your hands by now."

"There's not been much time." Faith gritted her teeth as she obediently followed Lady Vernon's wraith-like shadow down the nave. "I can't let him think I'm fast."

"No, a girl brought up in a brothel could hardly let a gentleman think that, could she?"

Faith wasn't sure she'd heard correctly for the muffled words were indistinct and partly swallowed up by the ringing of their shoes upon the stone steps.

Furious, she hurried to keep up. "I might wish my circumstances were different, and believe me, there's no love lost between Mrs Gedge and me, but I am better educated than any of the debutantes who have no doubt been paraded in front of Mr Westaway's nose *and* more beautiful, and regardless of where I rest my head at night, my virtue is unblemished. And will remain so!" Faith descended the steps beside her chaperone into the street. "So don't you make false aspersions about my good character." If ever there was proof that Lady Vernon cared little for Faith and had taken her on purely for the money, this was it.

"Ah, now, my dear, only a short walk and then we can rest our weary bones and see if Mr Westaway has taken the bait." Lady Vernon spoke as if she hadn't heard Faith, her smile cloying, her tone dripping with false pleasure at the journey ahead.

"You make me feel like a...dog or a...rat caught in a trap," Faith muttered. The more she spent time with this abominable woman the less able she was to hold her tongue. She and Lady Vernon were partners in a grubby intrigue of which no one else must be the wiser. Sadly, it meant Lady Vernon was the only person she could speak honestly to.

Lady Vernon swung around, and as her eyes met Faith's, her slack jaw snapped shut, giving her the look of a lazy bloodhound at rest transforming instantly into a pointer, alert and on the hunt.

"We are both rats caught in a trap, and you'd do well to remember that, young lady," she said, taking Faith's arm to lean on as if the pair were grandmother and granddaughter enjoying a gentle stroll. "That's what poverty does to a woman!" She sniffed. "At least I have good breeding as my insurance."

"And I have beauty as mine," Faith snapped back, tipping up her chin and wishing her searing gaze could reduce Lady Vernon to a pile of cinders.

Unscathed, and unconcerned, apparently, Lady Vernon cast Faith a dismissive look before her eyes settled for a second too long, lower down the girl's body. "Yes, it's *all* you have to trade on, girl, so don't make a mess out of this one opportunity to secure your future, and make mine more comfortable until my next call-out to chaperone some horsey-looking blue blood whose mama can't summon the energy." A look of triumph wiped away her peevishness, and the fingers of her left hand dug more deeply into Faith's arm as she raised her right to hail a gentleman hovering by the front entrance of Mrs Bromley's Corner Teahouse.

"Goodness, Mr Westaway! What a surprise to see you here!"

Suddenly, Lady Vernon looked like a sweet old lady with not a venomous thought in her age-ravaged, ugly old head, Faith thought as she was borne along upon a tide of hopefulness; the tide of hopefulness being on Lady Vernon's account that she would be paid for notching up a triumphant success.

As for Faith, she didn't know what she felt. There was so much riding on this next meeting with Mr Westaway. She didn't want to trade on her beauty and have to do things with a line-up of men that didn't involve her heart.

Yet, as Faith intercepted, then analysed, the look he sent in her direction, the foundation of the three women's collective plan suddenly seemed as rackety and shoddy as the multiple theatres they'd visited to honour the town's great bard that had either been swept away or dismantled to be utilised for something newer and better.

"Miss Montague." He rose from a gallant bow and there was genuine pleasure in his smile. Faith's earlier doubts dissipated. She had managed to conquer. Enough to get things underway, at any rate. Why else had he come in search of her after dismissing her the previous afternoon? "I hoped I'd find you in town."

"You did?" Faith tried to look coy, when in fact she was overcome by an unexpected wave of desperation. *Please, make him amenable and easy to manage from hereon in.*

"Yes, I did want to see you again because I…I can't do justice to your eyes, Miss Montague." He looked anxious as he tried to express himself. Right now, he was the artist, tortured by his creativity, not the diplomat. He tried again, using his hands as if that might make his meaning clearer. "The painting is so close to being finished. I'm nearly happy with it but—" He broke off and sent her a beseeching look. "Would you come back and sit for me one last time?"

Faith glanced at Lady Vernon then back at Mr Montague. He did look very appealing, hanging upon her acceptance.

With a slight shrug, she deferred to her chaperone. "I'm afraid that only Lady Vernon can make that decision. I know she's set on the idea of returning to London on tomorrow's early train, but if she can be persuaded, I don't mind."

I don't mind.

Was that the right thing to say? Would her lack of enthusiasm strike the right note with both Lady Vernon and Mr Westaway? She had to appear pliable; a girl who knew her place. Not too eager yet also hint at a flicker of interest. To bolster this last, she fluttered her eyelashes and looked demurely at her hands as if suddenly shy. That should be a nice finish to the whole charade before Lady Vernon fixed the time for tomorrow.

Yet her intake of satisfaction was expelled on resignation. She didn't feel true to herself to be taking manipulation to such extremes.

Still, she thought, the moment she had her cheque for five hundred pounds from Mrs Gedge she could do as she pleased. She'd never again have to worry about pretending or about what anyone else thought. How pleasing that would be.

"Tomorrow then. At ten o' clock?" He smiled, and Faith thought what pleasant grey eyes he had. "In the garden where the light is good. It'll be a fine day, I believe."

HE SHOULDN'T HAVE ASKED HER TO COME BACK. WITH SPARKLING morning light streaming from an azure blue sky imbuing the scene with a magical sense of hope and promise, it hadn't taken more than ten minutes with brush and paints and the girl lying amidst the daisy-strewn grass before Crispin knew this.

Still, what was the harm in the simple pleasure of transferring her exceptional beauty onto the canvas in front of him? He hadn't painted in two years, and there was fever in his fingers to create and do justice to his subject.

He felt alive.

That was all this feeling was. A desire to do his best work knowing that the girl in front of him offered him the means to do that.

"Would you put aside what you're holding please, Miss Montague?" She'd broken the ennui of her dull, wearying task to make a daisy chain. Now he needed her to be still. "Sorry to sound like the grim voice of authority." He tried to inject levity into his tone, though he was tense with the need to get his painting right. What *was* required to get the light in her eyes just so? He'd nearly had it yesterday. Now it eluded him. A pinprick of white, perhaps? "You'll be comparing me to your pater in his grumpiest frame of mind," he muttered, half attending to the need to put her at ease while he loaded his paintbrush.

"Oh, that tone is very mild compared with my father's temper." Obediently, she put down the daisy chain and stared up at the sky, and as he studied his work, pleased with the effect, he wondered for the first time about her large family.

"I'm sure he's only concerned for the happiness of you all. That's how my pater excuses his lapses of good humour." Crispin smiled across at her, but instead of meeting happy collusion or agreement, her expression was closed. And dark.

Of course, it was no business of his to pry, but he suddenly wanted to get a sense of Miss Montague's position in the world. Not that it would matter to him after today from a personal sense, but if he could aid her in any way in what he supposed was her primary duty, to succeed in the marital market, it would be helpful to know a little about her father.

"You have sisters, don't you, Miss Montague?"

"Six, Mr Westaway, and only one married. We are a great trial to our father."

"I'm sure if they're all as lovely as you, it won't be long before your father can bask in the collective success of his seven daughters who'll have made his family so well connected. I presume your married sister is older?"

"Twelve months older than me and married to a man who is to turn sixty in a few months. Not a love match."

That stopped him in his tracks. Crispin wasn't easily shocked, but this didn't reflect well on Mr Montague. He racked his brains to come up with what he knew of Miss Montague's family and realised he knew nothing.

"So, Mr Westaway, are you pleased with your painting?" She was turning the topic to lighten the mood, for now she was all smiles as she raised herself onto her elbows. "I hope I've been a good subject. Despite what Lady Vernon told you, I do find it hard to stay still unless there is a great deal at stake."

"My painting?" He felt ill at ease. Not only was there the self-imposed pressure of painting his best work, but that of producing a painting that promised this young woman a better future.

"Yes, I want you to recommend me to your artist friends as a model. My father knows nothing of what I'm doing here and would be shocked, but this is better than a great deal of other ways to save himself the expense of keeping me than the ones he has in mind." She rose and came over to stand at his shoulder, her admiring gasp sending desire washing over him like a hot wave. He stepped back quickly, masking his awkwardness with a smile as he said, "I could never do justice to your beauty, Miss Montague, but I believe it is a fair likeness."

Her surprise and admiration seemed genuine. "It's…it's truly brilliant! Oh, Mr Westaway, you'll win the competition; indeed, you will! And you'll show your father what talent you have, and he'll let you do what you want to be happy. I'm so proud of you."

"I only wish it were so simple." He thought of his father's fury should he learn that Crispin had been wasting his time on artistic pursuits, when he should be attending to the delicate strategic relations between England and her allies and potential enemies.

"But your talent is prodigious. It mustn't be wasted. You must tell him it's what you want." She took his hand and squeezed it, her eyes shining. "I knew you were good, but I didn't realise how good. You truly have made me the happiest girl."

"You enjoy admiration? Well, you shall have it in spade loads." *I just can't lavish it on you, personally, as I would wish.* Gently, he disengaged his hands and sent a glance up at the house. "Lady Vernon was hoping to catch the morning train to London, and there's still time, Miss Montague." He swallowed down his disappointment that he could not respond to her as he wished, and gave her what he hoped was a paternal pat on her shoulder. "Now, let me walk you to the house. I'll see you in London at the unveiling."

CHAPTER 12

"Why so glum, Faith? I think it was a poor plan of Mrs Gedge's to see you clothed like a parson's daughter when you're to be competing with duchesses." Charity was curled up on Faith's bed like a cat, her long hair undressed and pooling about her. She sent Faith a bolstering smile. "Don't be afraid. Tonight, it will all work out."

Faith nibbled her nail and nodded. She couldn't trust herself to answer.

Her vulnerability was like a gaping wound and the future like a black, angry, dangerous void waiting to hungrily devour her. She'd be like all the other girls at Madame Chambon's, with closed heart and open legs, submitting to a line-up of meaningless sexual encounters just so she could keep body and soul together. And then the moment she was no longer giving value, if she got sick or her looks were marred or faded, she'd be thrown into the gutter to fend for herself.

All because she'd not managed to do one simple thing—entice Mr Westaway enough to at least give the appearance to Mrs Gedge that he'd fallen in love with her.

She dusted her décolletage with a rabbit's foot loaded with fine powder while her brain whirled feverishly. Perhaps she could win him over using honesty. That would be novel?

"I know you're disappointed he didn't fall in love with you, Faith, but is he nice, this Mr Westaway?"

"He's lovely." Faith had no hesitation in answering. "I like him very much, and if it wasn't so vital to…everything…that I make him fall in love with me, I'd say I liked him too much to *want* to make him fall in love with me, if that makes sense."

"It doesn't make sense at all." Charity shook her head. "But then, nothing much makes sense."

With a sigh, Faith rose. "How do I look?"

"Like an angel, truly! You don't need bows and furbelows. In fact, you're more striking without, and I can now see exactly what was in Mrs Gedge's mind. Oh, but I do hope it works tonight. If Mr Westaway doesn't fall in love with you just by looking at you, he'll never fall in love with anyone!"

With this bolstering pronouncement ringing in her ears, Faith prepared to make her grand entrance at the Grand London Art Exhibition, arriving in Lady Vernon's hired carriage, which was waiting for her discreetly a little distance up the road.

SHE HADN'T THOUGHT SHE'D BE EXCITED AT THE OUTCOME. THERE WAS no outcome that promised what she needed without some compromise, and the fact she'd simply sat for a painting meant nothing when the real purpose behind the whole charade had come to naught.

Yet, as the double doors opened to the hallowed precincts of the Royal Society of Artists, a frisson of very real expectation skittered up the back of Faith's knees and lodged in her stomach. Mr Westaway's talent was undeniable. The painting had been exceptional. He deserved recognition.

And when across a crowded floor of patrons, mostly whiskered older men in sombre evening attire, Faith caught a glimpse of Mr Westaway, she was suddenly a jumble of nerves. He was in conversation with a lady and a gentleman, and he was laughing, a drink in his hand, and all eyes seemed to be on him. She noticed people around her indicating him with nods and veiled gestures, and her excitement grew.

People knew already that Mr Westaway was good. That they had a fine artist in their midst. She wasn't imagining all this.

While the crowd pulsed around her, she couldn't take her eyes off him. He looked so handsome, so self-assured. So right at home in his domain and Faith felt so proud of him.

As Lady Vernon gave her a little prod to keep her moving, she was addressed by a small, forceful young woman with a jaunty little feathered hat holding a notepad whom she recognised before the strong American accent gave her away.

"Miss Montague, I'm going to make you famous!" The confidence and enthusiasm in Miss Eaves's tone were in striking contrast to the way Faith felt.

"I don't want to be famous. I'm English," she said, making the young woman throw back her head and give an unladylike guffaw.

"Uncle, Miss Montague says she doesn't want to be famous. But I tell you, she's going to be after Mr Westaway wins this show hands down, and I write her story."

The gentleman with a long white beard and sombre, impressive bearing—which belied any relationship to the young lady who'd just addressed Faith—nodded at Faith as he introduced himself as Sir Albion, the patron of the Society. "Write your story, Amy, but don't tell anyone it's going to make them famous. It's a vulgar notion, I might add."

"Indeed, most vulgar," Lady Vernon muttered, her nose twitching as if she actually did have a barometer for what was morally acceptable. It was difficult for Faith to keep her own nostrils from flaring in disdain. Instead, she inclined her head and said with her most demure smile, "Notoriety is for those who seek it, and I certainly do not. If Mr Westaway is to be commended for his painting, I am simply happy that I assisted in some small way."

Sir Albion looked at her with approval. "I marked him out as a great talent many years ago, but I feared he'd lost his passion. Clearly you, Miss Montague, have reawakened it. Ah, here comes the gentleman in question now."

"My ears are burning." Mr Westaway looked a touch self-conscious as his gaze flickered from Faith's face to his esteemed patron as he acknowledged the ladies with a small bow. "But I'd not expected to have such strong competition when the time frame was so limited. Some of the finest are competing for the grand prize."

"The challenge of a time frame and the inducement of such a grand sum of money makes their enthusiasm not so surprising, for all that we like to think ourselves above such considerations."

"We all need to eat, Sir Albion."

"Indeed we do, Miss Montague," Sir Albion said, raising his eyes, before glancing at his niece. "Amy here thinks she owes it to herself to do that through her own merits. A very progressive thought indeed. Clearly, things are different in America."

"Things are changing, Uncle, both here and across the Atlantic where less and less is it considered vulgar for a woman to advance herself through honest toil and her own endeavours." Miss Eaves puffed out her chest importantly, and the little bird on top of her jaunty hat did a trembling dance of agreement. Faith stifled the urge to laugh, which was prompted more by her nervousness in being in such close proximity to such influential people. Influential because her fate lay in their hands more than they could know.

"There is no competition; we do know that, Mr Westaway," Miss Eaves said with conviction, and everyone looked at her in surprise causing the young lady to shake her head. "I don't know the outcome, if that's what you think, though my uncle does. The patron of the competition—who is anonymous, by the way, though word has it that she's an extremely wealthy American—has already judged the entries. In my opinion, though, there is no competition. Mr Westaway is going to become a famous artist, and Miss Montague is...." She looked enquiringly at Faith. "What do you hope to achieve out of all this?"

Sir Albion gave a gruff laugh. "Too direct by half, as you'd say yourself, Amy. One doesn't ask young ladies such things. Certainly not in company."

"Why, because their intentions can only be one thing? And it's vulgar to express that we all know what that is? Surely, we all want to succeed and profit, and get ahead. And what's the harm in that? It's human nature! So why should we not be allowed to voice such things aloud?" Undeterred by her uncle, she looked enquiringly at Faith, demanding it would seem, an answer.

Faith glanced at Lady Vernon for inspiration, but Lady Vernon appeared as caught off balance as she herself.

"Miss Montague is about to take London by storm." Faith was saved by Mr Westaway's gallant pronouncement. "When I am in Germany and reading the English newspapers, I shall no doubt come upon an announcement that she's either become the muse of a great painter or the wife of a great nobleman." He smiled at Faith. "I believe either would be the pinnacle of Miss Montague's ambitions."

Miss Eaves looked dubious but then conceded, "I suppose that would be a great advancement for a parson's daughter with nine brothers and sisters, I hope I have that number right, and yes, I have been doing my homework." She hadn't finished making her point though, and she strung out her response with a pointed look at everyone in turn. Faith wasn't sure if she liked the young woman or not. While she could concur with some of her sentiments, her manner was too brash and confronting for her comfort.

Miss Eaves sniffed. "Indeed, I look forward to the time when a woman is allowed to make her own way in the world without having to rely on any man; however, I will allow that Miss Montague has shown talent and strategy."

Sir Albion sent a pointed look in his niece's direction. "A demure, discreet demeanour will still get a young woman a great deal further than...otherwise," he finished with raised eyebrows. Miss Eaves was not put in her place. Faith decided she was not the kind who would ever be silenced by criticism.

However, she was glad when the collective attention of the crowd was stirred by something taking place at the far end of the room, and when Faith looked, it was to see that three paintings had been separated from the rest of the exhibits and were now lined up beside each other under lights upon the dais.

Miss Eaves gave a murmur of excitement; Lady Vernon gripped Faith's arm, and a great silence descended upon the room. The moment was nearly upon them.

Faith exchanged a quick, nervous look with Mr Westaway, her mouth dry.

He stepped close to her. "I don't know whether I'll be relieved or disappointed by the outcome," he admitted.

"You surely want to win, don't you, Mr Westaway?" Faith whispered. "Every great talent craves recognition, even if they are unwilling to admit as much." As a gentle hum went through the crowd, and as conversation resumed in the delay before an announcement, Faith told him, "My sister, the eldest and, seemingly, the most modest and retiring of all of us, worked twice as hard for the crumbs of praise that were few and far between in our household. But her zealousness, or martyrdom, came from the desire for recognition, purely, though she was the last to admit that she did what she did to be noticed. I know you love painting, but do you really do it only for the love of it?"

His surprise was obvious. After a moment, he confessed in a low voice, "I'll give you the truth, Miss Montague, and this is only between you and me because we have been part of something…more important than simply creating a painting. Yes, I crave to be recognised as a great talent. But I also crave the continued love and respect of my father. That, and my desire to be a great painter, are incompatible. And so, tonight I confess to secretly wishing I might be declared the winner to bolster my own vanity in my abilities. But perhaps more than that, I wish the prize might go to someone else as it would enable me to accept more easily that this is *not* my calling." He looked at her carefully, and Faith felt sure she read longing in the depths of his gaze. "You know I go to Germany before the end of the month, Miss Montague. Nothing will make my father prouder than to see me take up this important position. I've been groomed to follow in his footsteps for my whole life."

Faith felt a stab of something between pain and disappointment. Not for seeing her own dreams and ambitions go up in smoke, but for the bond between this man and his father. In all her young life, she'd never felt the kind of love and respect for anyone that would make her sacrifice her own ambitions. Granted, her scope had been limited, and she'd been at the mercy of those stronger than herself, but for these short moments talking to Mr Westaway, she wished she had an affiliation of the heart with someone that was greater than her own vanity, desires, and all those other foibles that made human beings so… fallible.

Mr Westaway's life was built on a foundation of love and filial duty, honour and nobility.

Faith's was built on a lie.

But if Faith only had the chance to prove to someone the inner core of nobility she was sure existed somewhere, she'd gladly make such a sacrifice for love.

She hadn't realised her feelings showed on her face and was surprised by his sudden concern. "Are you all right, Miss Montague?"

Faith took a sip of her champagne and tried to cleanse her smile of all bitterness and disappointment. "I was just thinking how nice it would be to love and respect one's father as you clearly do, Mr Westaway. Oh, my goodness!" She broke off suddenly as the first of the paintings on stage had its concealing sheet whipped away, and the audience gasped.

How strange it was to see herself lying in the grass amidst a field of daisies, her expression animated, her hair spread like a halo about her, the beautiful countryside as her backdrop. It was a picture of lovely innocence—even she could see that before the corroborating comment from a nearby dowager.

The next painting was good, also. A young woman was sitting on a swing holding a bouquet of flowers while a young fawn grazed nearby. It was a gladdening scene, but it had not quite the expertise as Mr Westaway's painting, of that Faith was certain.

When the three paintings were revealed, side by side, having been selected from a field of twenty-five, Faith had expected a clear winner was inevitable. But to her surprise, and obviously the surprise of everyone else, Sir Albion stood on stage and announced the unexpected news that these three painters would be pitted against each other in a run-off. A theme had been chosen; the deadline was tight, one week only, after which a clear winner would be announced and would receive an astonishing amount of prize money.

A great deal of murmuring and a few disgruntled mumblings followed this pronouncement. Mr Westaway looked distinctly discomposed.

Faith could only stare as she felt her heart pounding in her ears.

She'd been given a second chance. Mrs Gedge was the anonymous benefactor of this extremely handsome prize, and she'd manufactured a means by which Faith could spend another week in Mr Westaway's company.

That is, if Mr Westaway was prepared to risk the tenuous relationship of balancing his desire for recognition in the world of art with managing his father's respect and expectations.

She sent him a furtive glance beneath lowered lashes. He was not overjoyed at the prospect of having to produce another painting if he wanted to remain a contender. The tightly pressed lips highlighted the planes of his cheekbones. He looked like a handsome ascetic deliberating over a weighty matter that had repercussions for the world.

Before they were interrupted by the advancing well-wishers, Faith locked eyes with him, and it was as if the spear of his own agony communicated itself to her for the crucial second it needed for her to subsume her own desires for the justice of his.

"Don't accept on my account—if that has any bearing on your decision," she said quickly. "You have your father and your career to consider."

"Mr Westaway, you are a prodigious talent indeed! And this is the young lady? But of course, for you have indeed been faithful to the original, to such superlative beauty."

Two whiskered gentlemen and a lady bore down upon them. "The field is narrow, but you will outshine your competitors. I remember your first unveiling, why, five years ago it must have been. And then you disappeared?" It soon became clear to Faith that the lady, who was introduced as Mrs Cannington, the wife of the tallest of the whiskered gentlemen, was an authority and leading force in the organisation. It seemed she also was more than capable of achieving Faith's purpose, all on her own. "You are concerned you might discompose your father if you follow up on this incredible opportunity?" she paraphrased, or rather, interpreted from Mr Westaway's brief response. "Why, I understand that Lord Maxwell is not a great patron of the arts, but he is not a philistine. And only a philistine would place such an obstacle in the way of the nurturing of a truly great talent."

Faith was amused to see Mr Westaway blush. "Please, Mrs Cannington, don't blame my father. I'm about to realise his greatest ambition and take up a diplomatic post in Germany. In fact, I sail in less than three weeks, so you can understand the conflict."

"But part of the challenge is that the painting must be completed in one." She looked triumphant, as did the two gentlemen flanking her. As did Lady Vernon, who'd not had to utter one word to see the progression of Mrs Gedge's plan.

"It's not only that the prize itself is considerable, unusually and surprisingly so, but the recognition would be invaluable."

"Excuse me, but who is sponsoring the prize?"

Everyone turned, surprised, to Faith. "Are they known in art circles? A great artist, themselves, perhaps?" She needed to draw out what public knowledge there might be about Mrs Gedge, the kind of person she was and, perhaps even her motives.

"A wealthy American woman who wishes to remain anonymous," said Mr Cannington. "A woman who selected these three paintings herself," he indicated the three canvases with a flourish, "and who'd be exceedingly disappointed if one of her selections did not pursue the challenge into the final round. Now, please reconsider, Mr Westaway. All that's required is seven days in a pursuit that you have already admitted would give you great satisfaction. Surely there is no obstacle other than your reluctance to apprise your father that you are engaged in activities that do not actively further your imminent career posting." He checked himself. "I take it the young lady is available to sit for the painting? It is one of the stipulations that the original muse is to be featured in the second painting."

Faith nodded.

"Is it indeed, and is that the only stipulation?" Mr Westaway raised his eyebrows.

Mrs Cannington simpered. "Our American benefactress has a playful turn of mind. Indeed, at ten o'clock on the morning of the first day when painting is to begin, a messenger will arrive with the canvas, paints, and a bag of props, together with additional stipulations. Each of the three painters will receive exactly the same props and instructions and must complete the work by ten o'clock on the morning of the seventh day, at which time the messenger will arrive to collect the painting and take it back here for judging."

Her husband pulled at his whiskers and looked anxiously at Mr Westaway. "Seven days, Mr Westaway. What is seven days in a lifetime? Seven days which, in fact, may *change* your life infinitely for the better?"

CHAPTER 13

Change his life but *not* for the better. Faith was uncomfortably aware of this, sitting opposite Lady Vernon as the train pulled into the small country station and she saw Mr Westaway on the platform, scanning the opening carriage doors.

He'd invited them to be his guests and stay in his house rather than at the inn so that was some small victory.

When he recognised Faith he looked pleased, which gave her a small jolt of pleasure that was quickly replaced by dread. What must *she* do? Seven days in which to turn Mr Westaway into putty. Why should Mrs Gedge hate him so much she'd go to such lengths to play this game?

And why should it worry her? Faith had hardly been nurtured during *her* lifetime while Mr Westaway had been born with a silver spoon. The transaction between her and this man would be brief—not enough time to do too much damage, surely. Once she'd generated sufficient intensity in their dealings with one another to pass Lady Vernon's scrutiny, Faith could collect on her transaction, buy her little cottage in the country, and put all of this behind her.

Still, she couldn't help asking as the train slowed, "Does Mr Westaway genuinely deserve what we are going to do to him?"

Piously, Lady Vernon responded, "Mrs Gedge is a mother avenging her daughter who was led to believe by Mr Westaway that holy matrimony would be forthcoming."

"Then why didn't the girl simply sue him for breach of promise? That would have embarrassed the family."

Instead, it was Lady Vernon who looked embarrassed. "Matters didn't proceed down that avenue."

"He seduced her?" Faith shrugged. And if he had? But then, it seemed out of character for the man she'd come to know, unless he'd already learned his lesson, in which case, Faith was going to have to work extra hard.

She sighed and slumped back into her seat muttering, "I really don't want to do this."

Lady Vernon's tone was snide. "Madame Chambon *will* be pleased. I hear she is eager to continue to further your career with no return from you and to accommodate you in her comfortable Soho lodgings free of charge as she has done these past three years." She opened the reticule on her lap and pulled out a letter which she handed to Faith. "Mrs Gedge's contract, though if you'd rather we returned to London…"

Faith took the envelope, unsettled by Lady Vernon's words as a horrifying image of Lord Harkom seared her mind. The only person invested in Faith's future, and *safety,* was herself. She needed to play her cards right with Mr Westaway.

"Miss Montague, I do appreciate you coming back at such short notice."

Mr Westaway was standing before the open door, his hand extended to help her out of the carriage while someone else attended to her bags.

Faith smiled as she took his hand. It was large and firm and felt surprisingly dependable. Surprising because she hadn't considered that about him. He was an artist, and they were notoriously unreliable, weren't they? She also wasn't used to the feel of a man's hand—not since the clouts she used to receive when her father returned home, drunk and peevish.

"If I'm to be honest, this is quite an adventure for me," she told him as they started to walk towards his waiting carriage, Lady Vernon bringing up the rear. "My surroundings tend to lack variety, though it'll be an adventure going so far north when the season comes to an end."

"North?"

"Yorkshire. Remember I told you that I'm to take up a post as a governess there when the season comes to an end?"

He looked uncomfortable. "Yes, of course. But there are still some weeks until that time, and I feel sure that…other options may present themselves in the meantime."

"You mean because your painting will make me the toast of the town?" Faith shrugged. "I hope that will be the case. Sadly, I'm no different from most young women in London for these few months, though I suppose it's vulgar to say so." She laughed when she saw him colour up. "But it's true, Mr Westaway. Oh, don't worry, you've made your position very clear, and I hope that we can be good friends. But I won't deny that if a suitable match presents itself, possibly on account of your efforts with a paintbrush, I will consider my time these few weeks very well spent. There are better ways to while away a lifetime than teaching recalcitrant children or serving ungrateful relatives."

"You're a plain speaker sometimes, Miss Montague." He helped her into the carriage, smiling at her as he tucked her trailing skirts out of the way of the door. "I keep forgetting that."

"But we're friends now. I feel comfortable speaking plainly to you." She held herself primly as she clasped her hands together. "We both know where we stand with one another."

He laughed again as he leapt up front and took the reins, and Faith thought she could detect a note of friendly relief in his tone as he said over his shoulder, "Indeed we are, Miss Montague. I'd go so far as to say that we understand one another. In which case, the week ahead should progress swimmingly."

It was too late to begin painting that evening. Faith was tired after her long journey, and it was genuinely pleasant to relax on the terrace after dinner, enjoying the long daylight hours. The country certainly was a grand place to be compared with cramped and grimy Soho and, of course, the damp, leaky cottage she'd grown up in.

Both were a world away from where she was now. This lovely, yet extensive country house owned by Mr Westaway's absent aunt and uncle exuded a simple, relaxed charm. French doors from the drawing room opened onto a wide terrace, and the comfortable wicker chairs in which they sat were surrounded by urns and tubs of orange trees and quince bushes.

Lady Vernon, bundled up in a blanket, looked like a small, dissatisfied rodent, Faith thought, amused, as she enjoyed some desultory conversation with Mr Westaway. In the lengthening shadows, his pleasant smile appeared more readily during this conversation than previously. Yes, they were getting to know one another without the tension that must result from any possibility of a long-term future between them.

He was soon to leave on official business, and it was acknowledged by both of them that Faith was not a candidate for the role of anything other than an artist's muse.

But…

How was Faith to execute her duty if they were now to become simply friends? She was surprised to hear him laugh and realised she'd said something amusing. The anecdote about a lady in the street whose wig had been knocked off by a performing monkey had simply tripped off her tongue. As if she were enjoying playful banter with a trusted companion. When had she been relaxed enough to say words that weren't carefully calculated?

A whisper of ice through her veins made her shiver. A foreshadowing of something truly frightful held her in its grip for one terrible moment when the words died in her throat, and she must have looked as shocked as she felt, for instantly Mr Westaway was on his feet.

"I thought you were about to faint clean away," he told her after she'd regained her equilibrium and waved aside his offers of sending for a warm blanket, though he hovered by her side.

"I have a few years yet before I'll have need of such cosseting in weather like this." She tried to sound light as she indicated Lady Vernon, huddled into her blanket and fast asleep. Indeed, Lady Vernon was smiling as if in the middle of a very pleasing dream and Faith wished she could feel similar contentment for just a small part of her life. Then she remembered that soon, when she was her own mistress and living a life of blissful seclusion in her own little cottage in the country, she would always feel as contented as Lady Vernon looked.

But that relied on making Mr Westaway fall in love with her.

Mr Westaway had just begun to return to his chair. Perhaps he felt the evening was becoming too intimate.

Faith was about to announce her intention to retire to bed too, remembering from her lessons that it was important to foster a sense of loss if one was to keep a gentleman longing for more, when footsteps sounded upon the stone steps at the end of the terrace.

Sampson, Mr Westaway's faithful wolfhound, rose warily, tensed, then bounded forward, and Faith heard the bluff, welcoming tones of the elegant, white-haired gentleman emerging from the dusk and coming towards them with outstretched hand.

"You're back again, Crispin! I thought I saw evidence it was you and not your aunt and uncle. Sorry I missed you last week but good to see you now, my boy. And how did things go with your painting?"

It was as Lady Vernon stirred that Mr Westaway's friend and, apparently, neighbour, realised Crispin was not alone, for instantly he was all apologies as he rectified his omission and introductions were made.

"And tell me something of the composition of this painting?" asked their new arrival, Lord Delmore, relaxing into another wicker chair that was brought into the cosy grouping on the terrace while the fading light was supplemented by a bracket of candles. "I saw the first one Crispin painted, and I'm not surprised it garnered such acclaim. Though, of course, Crispin's talent is not alone responsible."

He smiled at Faith, but when she merely nodded her head, returned his attention to Crispin while Faith looked on. She was tired and wished she'd seized her opportunity to leave earlier. Still, it was pleasant to fade out of the conversation and observe the way Mr Westaway conducted himself when in the company of someone with whom he could obviously relax.

It was clear the two men had known each other a long time. Perhaps a little short of ten years, for she'd heard that was when Lord Delmore had bought the house next door. Yes, Lord Delmore knew Crispin's father from his London club and now made some comment about the man's ambitions for his only son.

"My week of painting here is perhaps a little more clandestine that I'd have liked, and I'm in two minds as to whether I want to win," Faith's host admitted.

Faith could tell he'd considered her to have dropped out of the conversation. She pretended to be as sleepy as Lady Vernon whose head had lolled to one side and who was gently snoring.

"Clandestine? To slip away and paint? You're in the wrong profession, Crispin. Foreign diplomacy is *all* cloak and dagger, and I know you hate subterfuge. Your father should have taken your character into consideration before he pushed you into following his footsteps."

"And yet, I can't think what else I would prefer. I have the necessary contacts, the enthusiastic backing of a father who's spent his life in the thick of it, and I won't deny there are aspects of what lies ahead that I relish." Crispin sighed. "Ah, to be of independent means but who am I to complain?" He grinned self-deprecatingly as he swept his surroundings with a languid arm.

After a few more minutes when Faith really was beginning to nod off and had decided there was nothing further to learn, she made a move to rise.

The two men stood and Lord Delmore, after acknowledging Lady Vernon, said indulgently, "I'm sure you'll be all the inspiration Mr Westaway needs under the circumstances. I admired the first picture he did last week, and as our esteemed painter says, the composition of the painting won't be known until ten o' clock tomorrow morning when the props are delivered, my curiosity is aroused. You'll not mind if I put my head in at some stage to see the work in progress? I know nothing of how art is made, but I'm a great admirer of it when it's good. What about you, Miss Montague?"

"All I know is that I must remain still and quiet, which is really my most important function, Lord Delmore."

He laughed. "How beautifully mannered you are. A credit to your parents with such sentiments tripping off your tongue, though I confess that I'm not averse to a lady speaking what is really on her mind. But you are young. That will come in time."

Faith liked his initial sentiments but felt a frisson of irritation at the paternalistic tone he adopted when referring to her suitably meek manner. Well, neither of them would ever know what went on in her mind, and what she did treat them to would be uttered with all the calculation of the most supreme diplomat.

But that was not for these men to know. Far better, right now, to simply blush prettily, bow her head, and say quietly, "I'm sure it will, Lord Delmore. Good night, gentlemen."

CRISPIN POURED LORD DELMORE AND HIMSELF A BRANDY WHEN THE ladies retired. There was something cathartic about a balmy evening with non-demanding company—namely not having his father present. Something that invited an ease of speech to which Crispin was unaccustomed.

Lord Delmore had been absent at his Scottish estate the last time Crispin had inhabited the cottage, and he was glad of the company now.

"I read a snippet in more than one newspaper that your painting was lauded a grand success. You're sure you won't mind if I wander over and see you at work in the morning? I shan't frighten the girl?"

"She's less of a shrinking violet than she looks. I think she was very tired tonight. Her conversation is usually more diverting." Crispin found himself defending Miss Montague even when he knew there was no need.

"She doesn't need to be capable of diverting conversation. She's an angel merely to feast one's eyes upon. Where did you find her? And how did you entice her up here when there's so much going on in London?"

Crispin shifted in his chair as he drained his glass. "Poor thing is penniless and jumped at the opportunity for a bit of publicity, to use the modern American jargon."

"Husband hunting. Naturally." Lord Delmore smiled. "She'll be snapped up before two months, I don't doubt. That's if *you* can resist her." He looked thoughtful. "Though I'd imagine you'd prefer your company a little livelier."

"Oh, she's sharp when she's well rested. Sadly, she's not in my scope. It'll be at least two years before I'm in the market for a wife. If I'm to be swept away by any romantic inclinations earlier than that, the young lady will need to bring a good deal more to the transaction than Miss Montague, I'm sorry to say." And he truly was sorry. Fortunately, matters had not yet got out of hand.

"Ah, the dictates of the pocketbook. Perhaps your father has someone in mind? An exacting man. Well, my advice would be to follow your own path, not the one laid out by your father if it's not what you want to do." He pursed his lips as if contemplating something unpleasant. "It can lead to a lifetime of unhappiness—for both of you."

Crispin was surprised by his candour.

At Crispin's look of enquiry, he went on, "Yes, I speak from experience because I was pressured into a path not of my choosing. Oh, it's not that I had great objections, but perhaps it was my passivity as a young man that caused a lifetime of regret. I agreed to my father's proposal when, had I been older and wiser and in control of my future path, I'd have steered well clear of it."

"You were pushed into a profession you disliked?" Crispin felt somewhat doltish saying the words, but the long silence unnerved him. Surely, Lord Delmore wasn't speaking of more intimate matters.

"My marriage, dear boy. No, I had no profession to speak of. Not a good state of affairs, either." Lord Delmore smiled ruefully. "I was pushed into a corner so that I had no choice but to make a declaration and then an offer that required me to follow through. It made neither of us happy. Poor Elsie has been gone many years, but it is to my eternal regret that I had not the strength of character to resist my father's pressure that I make her an offer when I was so inadequately equipped to make her happy. Neither of us brought the other happiness. And what sort of a marriage is that?"

"But you have two sons who have done you credit, and a daughter." Crispin spoke weakly.

"Indeed. A blessing and the greatest gift. Elsie said the same on her deathbed as she sought for something worthwhile to come out of being bound to someone so patently incompatible for nearly two decades. And two decades could be five in your case. Do not pledge your troth unless your heart is truly engaged. Don't let your father be the one to dictate what will or won't make you happy."

"Pleasing my father is satisfaction enough." Crispin was unable to meet Lord Delmore's eye. His father had always dominated him; he knew it. But now Crispin was leaving the country. In Germany, he could be his own man. He'd find fulfilment in his work and rise in the world through his own endeavours.

"Perhaps for now." Lord Delmore rose. "But your father won't be around forever and then who will you have to please? A wife whom you don't understand? Whom you don't love?" He touched his breast. "Painting is your passion; I know that. I'm glad you have a week to indulge it. I hope it'll be a reminder of how much else there is to indulge, and that indulgence is not a sin."

CHAPTER 14

Faith rose the next morning with a sense of excitement and expectation. It was so unusual to feel something that wasn't dull resignation, that she leapt out of bed and was smiling as she wrapped herself in her peignoir and threw open the casement window.

The fresh morning air was a welcome and exhilarating slap in the face. Today was the start of a new chapter in her life. Today, Mr Westaway would begin the painting that would be the catalyst for so much. It could make him famous. He would be venerated; his ambition cemented, and Faith could slip away into her new life with the funds to exist in the modest, quiet fashion she desired.

She went to her wardrobe and began to dress, pulling on the modest, swathed skirt that was fashionable but only just, due to the paucity of trimmings.

"What do you think you're doing?" Lady Vernon stood in the doorway, her gaze critical and her nostrils twitching.

"What does it look like?" Faith hadn't meant to sound impertinent, but honestly!

"The morning is fresh, and you want to pick some flowers in your nightdress. Put your peignoir back on and go outside. Mr Westaway will be watching from the casement; I assure you."

Faith rolled her eyes, but Lady Vernon was quick to snap. "You seem not to have the faintest idea as to how to wrap a gentleman around your little finger, girl! Do you want to succeed, or not?"

Sighing, Faith did as she was bid. As she tied the loose, flimsy garment about her, she muttered, "I can't imagine why you think you are better equipped to know how to entice a man. Have you ever received a letter purporting to a gentleman's passionately beating heart or, better still, a marriage proposal? That is what Mrs Gedge requires, and it's what I am *always* thinking of."

"I have received both, my girl, so I know very well how it is to be achieved. You have already thrown away your first opportunity, but you have been granted a reprieve. You have seven days. Seven days to achieve that letter or that marriage proposal. Otherwise, you are going back to Madame Chambon's and to many gentlemen far less tolerant and thoughtful than Lord Harkom if you're to continue to have a roof over your head. Where is your sense of urgency?"

Faith ignored her, of course.

A short while later, gathering a bunch of wildflowers that grew by the lake—in full view of Mr Westaway's bedchamber window—Faith reflected on her chaperone's chilling words. Seven days to achieve so much? Had she allowed herself to be carried away by confidence, again? Or was it fear, during the first week when she'd achieved precisely nothing?

She'd sensed she couldn't go too fast with Mr Westaway, but Mrs Gedge had always appeared so obliging during their afternoon tea sessions at Claridges, and Faith had been lulled into thinking she had all the time in the world to achieve what she had to. Not a paltry few days.

Lord Harkom had disabused her of that notion.

She rose slowly, enjoying the feel of the dew underfoot and the light breeze on her skin. As she turned back towards the house, a butterfly fluttered up from a nearby rose bush. She put her hand out and the delicate blue-winged insect hovered above it, finally landing on the flowers she held.

Suddenly, she was five years old again, enjoying a bank holiday with her parents in the days when her father still smiled and there were not so many mouths to feed. She and her two sisters had their parents' full attention as they picnicked with many other families enjoying a rare day off. The grass was soft and green; the sandwiches had never tasted so good, and nature was butterflies and blooming flowers—not vermin in the kitchen and mud underfoot picking stunted vegetables in the soggy garden.

She closed her eyes against the pain of memories unbidden. She didn't want to dredge up thoughts of her past. She had no past to call her own anymore. Her parents would have forgotten her long since. Perhaps the sisters closest in age, older and younger, would wonder what had happened to her, but it was best they never knew the truth—that Faith was a thief, according to her employer, who lived in a house of ill repute.

Her sadness was momentary. She was stronger than that. She had to be if she were to crawl out of the mire and be something more. Something more than what others would paint her—a thief and a prostitute.

But she *had* never been a thief, and she never *would* be a prostitute.

Forcing her thoughts to the painting she headed towards the house, glancing briefly at the casement windows and wondering how Lady Vernon could claim to know so much about the way gentlemen's minds worked.

CRISPIN STARED OUT THROUGH THE CASEMENT WINDOW TOWARDS THE small lake at the bottom of the field. A light mist rose above it, and wildflowers littered the soft green grass. The scene was enticing and even more so when a movement caught his eye.

His breath caught. Miss Montague was gathering flowers still wearing her nightclothes. At least, only a light peignoir covered her nightdress, a thought which made him unexpectedly aroused.

He quashed his feelings quickly. Inconvenient and impossible to act upon.

Yet that didn't mean he wouldn't enjoy her company in the spirit of accommodation they'd tacitly agreed upon.

In seven days, he would create a masterpiece, and he'd need her compliance. Nothing more than that. A pleasurable whiling away of the time could be anticipated. He knew already she was good company. Easy on the eye, as Lord Delmore had pointed out, but that didn't imply Crispin would be unable to rein in the rampant impulses of a young man who hadn't had a woman in his life for a very long time.

His future was in Germany, and while his artistic temperament might suggest a romantic and spontaneous nature, he intended to be exacting when it came to choosing the right woman to spend the rest of his life with. He'd need to spend a great deal of time with her to ensure their minds were of one accord.

He'd not act with reckless abandon and allow infatuation to have any bearing on his decision.

Indeed, as his father counselled, it was far better to consolidate his career. In another year, perhaps, he might be better placed to put the necessary search for a wife near the top of his agenda. Not that Miss Montague was a contender, as he'd made clear to both the young lady and to Lord Delmore.

So why did he have to keep reiterating it? He hesitated before he dragged his eyes away from the scene by the lake. She'd stopped as if a thought, compelling, but not pleasant judging by her stance, made her hesitate.

He quashed the desire to quiz her when she returned. It was unwise to invite confidences. The less they delved into anything of a personal nature the better.

But he must think like a painter, and a good painter had a sense of the essence of his subject matter.

No point in wondering how he would paint her. The delivery of the props in an hour or so would determine that. For a moment, he cast his mind over to the brief. An eccentric American was behind the competition. Rockefeller? Rosenstein?

Imagine painting a canvas that would hang upon one of the walls of their homes. The idea sent a thrill of excitement through him.

Just as the sight of Miss Montague turning her lovely face up to the sun, smiling for a moment, sent a spear of foreboding through him.

Her fate lay in his hands. He could craft a future for her that was more than being a wife to a no doubt appreciative, but almost assuredly impecunious, young clerk, or as an unpaid servant to aged parents or small children.

He was roused by the sounds of gasps and oohs and aahs downstairs. So, the delivery was early. Not that he minded being put out of his anticipation. His mind couldn't settle until he knew how he would stage the young woman.

He hurried into the drawing room where a canvas bag lay upon the table. Around it stood Miss Montague, Lady Vernon, and the parlourmaid; all three of whom looked expectantly at him as he entered the room.

So much for being the aloof master of this temporary household. But then, there had never been any secret that this moment was the beginning of everything.

"I suppose there's only one thing for me to do," he said with a resigned grin at the company before he began to undo the ties.

A piece of paper with neatly written instructions lay upon a set of paintbrushes he unwrapped from its canvas covering, and a bag of something whose contents he couldn't quite identify.

"Completely unnecessary. I have my own," he muttered, but Lady Vernon was holding up one of the sable brushes and saying, "Perhaps this mystery person is signifying their knowledge of what is considered good quality in the art world. Or is that not true, Mr Westaway?"

Crispin had to concede that the materials were of the finest quality and now that the entire set was laid out, his earlier scepticism had been replaced by a definite itching of the fingers to get started. As he bent to pick up a brush, he intercepted Miss Montague's smile. She looked as excited as he felt. Yes, as if she relished what lay ahead as much as he wished she would if it were to be good.

The painting. It was about the painting, of course, and she'd shown interest in art and culture, so they were on level ground in this instance.

"Roses?" He picked up a handful of crimson petals that must have been picked within the last twenty-four hours, then looked at Miss Montague. "You're more a wildflower girl, with your delicate colouring, I'd have said, but perhaps I'm mistaken and the richness of these deep-hued petals will bring out something I'd overlooked." He was considering her as the inanimate subject of his talent, not the vibrant flesh and blood creature who fed his inspiration, but Crispin needed some distance.

"And the title? What is the title of this painting?" Lady Vernon asked, picking up the paper with its instructions. *The Lady of the Lake?*" She looked from Faith to Mr Westaway. "I suppose you can interpret that any way you like, is that correct, Mr Westaway? Yet I am sure I've heard the title used before. However, you must use the props supplied, the instructions say. Water and red rose petals. It could be charming provided it doesn't resemble a scene of carnage."

"What do you mean?" Miss Montague frowned at her chaperone who gave a theatrical shiver, replying in a whisper, "Blood!"

Revulsion swept over Crispin, and he gripped the table edge to steady himself. These were not memories he could entertain if he were to do justice to the brief.

Miss Montague raised her brows before remarking, "I'm sure I've heard about a painting called *The Lady and the Lake*. Do you know it, Mr Westaway?"

The oil painting that featured a naked woman reclining on a rock had garnered a great deal of critical acclaim, and now Crispin found it was impossible not to look at Miss Montague and imagine what she looked like with no clothes on, reclining on a rock or, in this case, floating in a lake. He swallowed and stepped behind the table, saying, "Perhaps you're mistaking it for John Waterhouse's *The Lady of*

Shalott." Before she could contradict this with some incisive remark that she was sure she was *not* thinking about that painting, because Miss Montague's mind was as sharp as a needle, he found himself taking her by the wrist and pulling her into the light by the window saying, in a contemplative, artist's manner, "So many possibilities, but what would be best in this instance? A lake? I hadn't thought there might be logistical difficulties."

Lady Vernon's nose crinkled as she stared through the window at the body of water in the distance. "Not especially appropriate with the reeds and ducks and mud and approaching storm clouds. I hope you don't mean to drown poor Miss Montague for the sake of your art. Can she even swim?"

"I can't swim." Miss Montague shook her head. "But I can lie in a bath, and you could paint in a background afterwards."

Faith had been told by Lady Vernon that this is what she must suggest. She supposed Lady Vernon thought that having Faith wearing diaphanous wet clothing might somehow entice Mr Westaway more thoroughly than otherwise. An outside body of water would have done just as well, but it was true that the weather was deteriorating while a bath would be heated. Not that Lady Vernon would have been thinking of Faith's comfort.

Regardless of the motive, Faith was now experiencing her first pangs of self-doubt. Mr Westaway still didn't look at her as if he couldn't live without her. His scrutiny was decidedly painterly in an objective, distanced way. He had enough self-control that he'd buried his initial admiration beneath a veneer, possibly something much thicker than that even, of objectivity.

But he was a diplomat, after all. He needed to hide his emotions, so perhaps his real feelings were very different.

She continued to study him as he looked into her face, while she tried to read behind the mild interest in his expression. His interest seemed to be motivated by nothing more than where she should be posed and in what clothes.

"I daresay that would work," he said as the first raindrops hit the windows. He smiled. "No, this weather is hardly conducive to outdoors painting, after all."

"A bath," announced Lady Vernon. "A heated bath for we don't want Miss Montague to catch her death of cold." Faith could read very clearly the gleam in Lady Vernon's eye. No, her concern was far from Faith's comfort. She wanted to control the situation as best she could. She had something planned; Faith was sure of it. Especially when the old woman said, "I have an idea, if you'll permit me, Mr Westaway. May I be so bold as to prepare my young charge in what surely must be the only fashion that can be suggested by the props provided?"

What could Mr Westaway do? Faith smiled at the pained look that crossed his face. As she turned to follow in her chaperone's wake, she quirked her mouth in a rueful smile, whispering as she passed him, "See what I have to put up with every day, Mr Westaway! If you let her have her way today, you can paint me however you choose later."

When he winked at her, Faith felt a ridiculous jolt of pleasure. For a brief moment they were in collusion, and Lady Vernon was the common enemy.

Once inside the large bathroom, Lady Vernon closed the door and pointed to the clothing she'd laid out on the chair by the window. "Dress yourself in that while Kitty fetches the bathwater," she said, directing the young undermaid who had followed them in.

In the city, the modern plumbing that Lady Vernon decried was a luxury unknown in this part of the world so, a dozen pails later, Faith lay submerged in a warm bath, her white gown floating about her, a simple posy of white flowers in her hands.

"Close your eyes, Faith, while I call Mr Westaway. But first…we'll add the finishing touch."

CHAPTER 15

Crispin trod the steps with mixed feelings, though he had to admit he was more than intrigued by Miss Westaway's impish parting. She was not so pliable as she seemed. Previously, she'd been not as vacuous as she'd seemed. What would the next surprise be? The truth was, he knew he was going to enjoy the next few days more than he ought.

The next surprise, when he opened the bathroom door at Lady Vernon's command, was not something for which he was prepared.

With the pleasure and anticipation of his parting from Miss Montague still fresh in his mind, the last thing he expected to find was the manner in which she'd been...prepared.

Good God, but the grey drizzle outside the small bathroom window was a good deal more comforting and easy on the eye than the horror that met him in the bath.

A girl dressed in white; her reddish-gold hair spread about her, holding a posy of flowers. And the bathwater. Red. Only, of course, these were red rose petals. He had to remember that.

He had to remember that he must *never* revisit this part of his past if he were to stay sane. Turning away to look through the window, he tried to regain control of his emotions.

"Striking, don't you think, Mr Westaway?" Lady Vernon was smiling at him. "You can paint in the reeds and the river afterwards. Or had you thought to create an entirely different effect?"

He took a seat, pretending consideration while he attempted to push away the nightmare.

But would it be catharsis to face his memories head on and, in painting them, exorcise them from his mind?

Then again, was there something deeper at play? Why red rose petals? Why a girl in a white dress floating in water?

He had to rid his mind of what could only be ridiculous, unfounded conspiracies. Each of the other two painters would be doing the same painting, and they'd not be reacting as he was. Only if he could ground himself in common sense and allow his professionalism to dominate would he turn something good out of something bad.

"You've done well, Lady Vernon," he said. "And since Miss Westaway is already in position, I shall have my paints brought in and begin while there is still light."

A great weariness had cast its pall over the horror and fear. He was a survivor. At least, his reputation had survived, if not his soul.

"It's a strange question, I know, Miss Montague, but are you comfortable?"

She opened her eyes. "Unconventional, to say the least, but this seems innocuous compared to the stories I've heard from other artist's models."

"Who?"

"I spoke to several at the unveiling."

Of course, she would have. She was a young lady who didn't make up things. She liked to have her facts straight. Well, if he were going to be closeted with her in close confines for the next seven days, it would help to have some diverting conversation. Lady Vernon promised little enough of that.

He set up his easel and mixed his paints in the poor light, augmented by a sconce of candles and a lamp. For now, he was glad Lady Vernon stood stiffly by, or rather, had seated herself on a wooden chair at right angles to him. She'd better stay the entire time too, he thought, if he were not to be distracted.

Distracted? He had his work to keep him focused.

Time passed in a blur but he was jolted into the present by the sound of a loud clapping, and looked up to see Lady Vernon in the act of rising, her command accompanied by, "Mr Westaway, my charge might be in no danger of drowning in a bath, but she certainly is in danger of getting pneumonia."

"My apologies! Please, you must get dry." Without thinking, he put out his hand to help Miss Montague to rise, and she stood up, dripping before him, her gown clinging to her curves, entirely transparent though she appeared not to realise this as she asked with just a trace of coyness, "Wasn't I as still as the dead, Mr Westaway? That was what you wanted, wasn't it?"

Crispin wasn't sure what he wanted. He didn't want to paint her dead, and he certainly didn't want her standing in front of him now leaving so little to the imagination. Because the bath was elevated a foot or so off the ground, he found himself almost eye level with her breasts. And, of course, the effect of the cold was to highlight her nipples through the thin fabric.

Crispin didn't know where to look. Lady Vernon appeared to be occupied with arranging her bustle into the correct folds as she stood while Miss Montague was smiling happily at Crispin, taking the hand he offered her and leaning heavily on him to avoid slipping as she stepped over the side.

"You were perfect, Miss Montague," he managed, desperately conscious of the brief contact when one soft breast was slightly indented by his hand in the final movement.

Still, she did not seem to notice, chattering happily, though with chattering teeth, as the maid draped her in a towel and began to squeeze out the water from her skirts over the bath.

"The perfect drowned damsel, and now I no doubt resemble a water rat." She took a hank of her glorious hair and twisted it over her shoulder.

"You must sit in front of the fire and get yourself thoroughly dry." Lady Vernon managed to make a no doubt well-intentioned suggestion sound like a threat.

"I'll be down in a minute," said the young girl heading towards the door before she was halted by her chaperone's voice, "You'll dry your hair in your bedchamber and not disturb Mr Westaway with your foolish talk when now is the time for him to relax after his hard work."

Crispin hadn't realised he'd even said the words that encouraged them to join him in his drawing room before Lady Vernon was accepting and Miss Montague was clapping her hands and saying, "I've been dying to ask Mr Westaway his thoughts on Alsace-Lorraine. You will indulge me, won't you, Mr Westaway?"

What could he do except nod, even though Crispin knew that it was dangerous to exchange political views with anyone, and especially not a wide-eyed ingénue whom he'd now seen, firsthand, combined the most desirable curves with a mind like a whip and a face like an angel.

THE CRACKLING FIRE PROVIDED VERY WELCOME AND MUCH-NEEDED warmth, for the cold had seeped through Faith's bones. Lady Vernon's command had come in the nick of time, and now, to Faith's delight, Lady Vernon was rubbing her eyes and declaring she could not remain a moment longer in the heated drawing room without falling fast asleep.

"I should stay, of course, Faith, but your hair is not yet dry. Promise me you'll be up in the next five minutes."

Faith flashed a look at Mr Westaway and saw he looked uncertain in the wake of Lady Vernon's departure. Quickly, she said as the door closed behind the old lady, "I wonder if you wouldn't be so kind as to take over the brushing from Lady Vernon, otherwise my hair will be the most unmanageable tangle." She handed him the brush to detain him when she was certain he was about to excuse himself. "I'm sure you must be used to such requests from female cousins."

Mr Westaway shook his head but had no choice but to take the brush thrust into his hand. Obediently, he followed her to the chair vacated by Lady Vernon while Faith dropped down upon the footstool. "Lady Vernon doesn't like me," she confided on a sigh. "I fear that I am a sore trial to bear, and that she enjoyed wielding the brush like a prison warder. I trust you'll be gentler with me, Mr Westaway."

Faith had to force herself not to smile when she felt, rather than saw, the effect her words had on him. So, she *did* wield some power, after all. She was just congratulating herself on making if only marginal success when, without pausing in his steady, thorough, yet decidedly gentle brushing, he said in a low, deliberate tone, "Lady Vernon should be more vigilant in keeping watch over you. It would not do for word to get out that she'd been lax."

And, of course, that could mean only one thing—that he was keeping his distance from Faith and any possibility of entanglement as much as possible.

She twisted her head. "We've already discussed this, Mr Westaway. Of course you don't want to find yourself compromised with someone like me; I completely understand. And even if, despite the greatest care taken, it was suggested I was compromised, and it won't happen, I assure you, I would act with honour; you must know that."

"Those words sound so wrong coming from your pretty mouth." His tone was downcast. "Indeed, you do speak plainly." He spoke so softly she could barely hear.

"It was the only way in my household," Faith told him, trying to sound more cheerful. As if this wasn't the weighty conversation it was. "With so many of us, it was difficult to get our way at the best of times. So, I've grown accustomed to being grateful for whatever I can have."

"And what is it you want, Faith?"

She was surprised he asked the question but answered it with an admirable show of equanimity, adopting a more serious tone but, she hoped, with enough levity not to frighten him. "I want to be respectably married, have a husband who appreciates me and is kind to me, and I want children. I want what every woman wants. Surely you know it's the desire of each and every debutante in London with whom I'm competing."

He'd taken on the role of hair brusher with care and gentleness but he laughed, tugging a hank of hair which made her wince. Immediately he was full of apology, but Faith waved her hand in the air before resting it seemingly arbitrarily on…his hand.

She kept it there, saying, "I've borne a great deal worse pain than this. Please continue with the brushing, Mr Westaway. It's not often I get to enjoy such a gentle touch. Perhaps that's why I'm so competitive. Not very attractive in a woman which is why I try to keep quiet in company. Gentlemen much prefer a young woman to have no opinions."

She turned at the silence and the fact he'd stopped brushing and faced him. He looked nonplussed.

"I'm sorry if I've disappointed you with my revelations regarding my true character, Mr Westaway. I'm sure you'd have far preferred to uphold an image of me as mild-natured and demure. That's how Lady Vernon told me to behave when I first came to London. But as I've got to know you more, I can't hide my true nature. I'm so far from the perfect, demure debutante Lady Vernon thought she was going to be chaperoning about London."

"But your beauty makes up for that." He shook his head as if he'd not believed he'd said it. "I'm very sorry I said that. The sentiment was unseemly on both counts."

Faith swallowed. She was feeling her way in the dark, so to speak. Yes, part of her tutoring was to exchange banter with a range of gentlemen, and she'd enjoyed it. But one false step and she could lose everything for which she'd worked so hard.

She pushed to the back of her mind any thought that she might actually be wanting this for reasons to do with her own heart rather than as a means to an end. Faith had never had the luxury to think of anything other than survival. And her survival depended upon twisting this man around her little finger. Making him fall in love with her.

The way he was looking at her bolstered her confidence that she could do this.

"You think you shouldn't say I'm beautiful because it'll turn my head?" she asked softly. "Or you think that an independent mind should be irrelevant in the face of beauty." Faith shifted a little on her footstool but held herself back from contact. His lithe, strong body was within easy touching. She could have put her hand on his knee or risen slowly and cupped his face. How would he have reacted? Would he have sunk into a kiss...only to berate himself afterwards? Yes, she sensed a steeliness in him that would enable him to put reason above his emotions.

But what if she couched it as a business proposition? A ladylike proposition?

She cleared her throat and lowered her eyes, keeping herself firmly glued to the footstool.

"Mr Westaway..."

She wasn't sure if her approach was damning any chances she had, but she'd decided the logical path was best.

"Yes, Miss Montague." It looked like he'd managed, with an effort, to regain his composure, and that he was grateful to her for reining him back in, for there was a warmth in his expression that was far more friendly than incendiary.

"You know how I hope this painting is going to help win me suitors? I mean, I've made no secret of that, and it's ridiculous for any debutante to pretend otherwise."

"Yes, we both have high hopes for this painting. Though I don't know what I shall say if I do win and it comes to my father's ears."

"You'll be in Germany doing just as he wishes. And you'll have the accolades you desire. It's the perfect outcome." She sighed deeply. "As for me, I could be married in six weeks and, right at this very moment, not even know my husband—the man I'll spend the rest of my life with. Isn't that strange to think?"

"Very strange." He looked decidedly uncomfortable.

"Mr Westaway, I want you to kiss me. You see, I've never been kissed before, and I'm very curious and would like to have just a little practise for when I meet the man I will marry." She smiled at him. "A single kiss is all right, isn't it? I mean, it doesn't mean my reputation or yours is besmirched. I've read plenty of romances where it's quite normal for a man and a woman to kiss and nothing terribly awful happens afterwards."

She sat with her hands clasped in her lap and looked at him enquiringly.

He looked back at her and shook his head. "I'm sorry, Miss Montague. That's not how a kiss is conducted. And regardless of how it is or isn't conducted, I couldn't possibly kiss you."

She nodded, as if conceding a practical matter. "I understand. In the novels I've read there has to be a strong feeling happening here." She touched her heart. "I just thought that it would be interesting to experiment so I could see how my heart felt when you kissed me, which of course you're not going to do now. I thought it would be nice to have some level of comparison for when I'm kissed by a real suitor with whom I'd consider spending the rest of my life." She rolled her shoulders and turned away, offering him the back of her head, and within a few seconds was relieved to feel the steady tug of the hairbrush over her hair. "I hope I didn't embarrass you, Mr Westaway."

"Not at all. It's good to be able to speak frankly to one another. I like a young woman who doesn't resort to artifice and veiled lies to get what she wants."

A chill of foreboding rattled inside her and Mr Westaway asked with genuine concern, "Are you cold?"

"No, but I should go to bed soon, I think." She stretched her arms, yawning as she stood up. "Thank you for today." She smiled at him as he rose. "I can't tell you how much more enjoyable it is to be here and part of your artistic world; also talking to you about interesting topics than the usual deadly dull kind of day I generally endure."

"Miss Montague—"

She looked over her shoulder as she made for the door.

His expression was conflicted, his body tense as he rose and took a half step towards her. "Just one kiss. A quick one. So, you know what it feels like." He spoke rapidly. "And nothing other than that."

"All right," she said slowly. "Just tell me what to do."

He cleared his throat. "You just kiss me. That's all."

"And then it's done." She sighed, satisfied. Or at least sounding satisfied with the way it was presented as she returned to stand in front of him, twining her arms about his neck.

It was not the first time Faith had kissed a man. Her education had required this as a minimal point of contact and, thank God, she'd never found herself in the position of having to do more, as did all the other girls at Madame Chambon's. In fact, it was only when she had kissed men for whom she felt absolutely nothing did she realise how impossible it would be to have to give them her body too.

So, she twined her arms about his neck, tipped her head, and waited to feel nothing but the physical sensation of pressure applied upon her lips. A physical sensation with which she was reasonably familiar.

CRISPIN STOOD AND PREPARED HIMSELF. HE WAS DOING HER A FAVOUR. Lord, he was doing them both a favour by getting it over and done with, clearing the air, so to speak. It was reasonable that a curious mind and plain speaking would deem this no more than it would be. And Crispin had only gone along with the idea because he was confident she knew their respective positions. He liked to think he'd forged a friendship with the young woman. Friendship between the sexes was entirely possible, he already knew that. He had women friends who enjoyed probing him on matters political, and he gained great pleasure from their company.

Just as he did from Miss Montague's. Certainly, she was younger and prettier than his other friends but, by presenting herself as just as intelligent, and acute with respect to his need for no form of entanglement, he felt safe.

Yes, safe, was his last thought as he lowered his head and put his arms gently about her to seal the kiss. A chaste, brief kiss with a sweet but definite ending would be a fine way to show her his true feelings. He could imbue it with respect, the merest sensory illusion that there could be more, and as he withdrew with just the right expression, he'd leave her under no illusions that he was in any way affected by their connection.

Yet, as she moved closer, standing on tiptoe to twine her arms about his neck, he was taken aback by the rush of sensation that speared his body. Her mouth was still several inches away; her eyes were closed, and there was a smile of innocent expectation that was heartbreakingly endearing.

He felt trapped. It would be wrong to leave her with the sensation that a kiss couldn't be more. She was embarking on a big journey for an innocent debutante. She had no idea what to expect. Surely, he owed it to her to show her just what a real kiss could be like?

It was his last moment of rational thought before another rush of sensation speared his groin, pounded in his head, and turned his vision into a multifaceted plethora of pumping, pulsing need that sent him reeling as her mouth fused with his and her arms about him tightened.

His world seemed suddenly a different place. He'd not expected to be so affected. He'd not expected to feel such connection. He'd not expected to feel anything beyond the casual enjoyment he'd experienced with so many past kisses.

Yet he was conscious of every nuanced change as this one progressed from what was supposed to be fleeting—the softness of her lips pressed against his, tentative, then growing bolder, sending tendrils of fire right through his body. Her breasts pushing against his chest as she leaned into him. Enjoying herself. Throwing herself into this as if it were the greatest enjoyment to be savoured, losing herself just as he was losing himself.

He'd thought himself in love in the past. There had been moments of grand passion. Or so he'd thought. And yet...he couldn't remember them. His mind was cast into the void, for only the present existed. Only the here and now as he was swept into a maelstrom of intense, physically satisfying, and yet totally unsatisfied, desire.

And it was as this desire roared into the stratosphere, nearly out of control, that a single cognisant kernel of self-preservation brought him rapidly back to earth. His hand, unconsciously, had slid downward to cup her breast, and she seemed to be pressing against him, searching for satisfaction beyond what was being offered.

He registered the need to extricate it, yet it was squeezed fast, against the thin fabric between his chest and her heaving bosom. But as he removed it and his hand touched her heated skin, it took every ounce of willpower not to insinuate it beneath her bodice. With her encouragement.

Dear lord, she was losing control just as he was, and unless he brought this to an end, they'd both be engulfed by the fiery flames of hell.

Unless he took charge, Miss Montague was going to keep kissing him, and he *wanted* her to want it. Wanted her to continue.

And that could prove fatal.

Panting, breathless, he put his hands on her shoulders and stepped backwards. Out of danger.

With enormous effort he tried to maintain his composure, tried to be the bigger man, bigger than he was, by pretending it hadn't affected him as much as it had. Running one hand through his hair, he blinked and offered her what he hoped wasn't a totally sappish smile as he murmured, "My apologies, Miss Montague, if that wasn't what you were expecting." What else could he have said? The kiss certainly hadn't been what *he'd* been expecting. He could barely stand. His body was straining, still, to take this further, but she was as out of bounds as she'd ever be.

Miss Montague, he noticed, looked a little dazed. She wandered to the fireplace and put a supporting hand upon the mantelpiece. He'd thought she might look at him, dewy-eyed with affection, but she looked troubled as she raked her fingers through her own damp hair and said, "Oh, please don't apologise for you were very kind to indulge me. I'm sure it was...so much more than I was expecting, Mr Westaway."

FAITH MANAGED TO MAKE HER WAY BACK TO HER BEDCHAMBER. AS SHE lowered herself onto her bed, she wasn't sure how she'd got there, her mind was in such disarray. That kiss. No, it wasn't at all what she'd been expecting. The consequences were nothing like she'd intended. The kiss had been supposed to shore up her power, but with her knees still trembling, she felt entirely powerless.

A knock on the door was followed by the beady-eyed scrutiny of Lady Vernon, who lowered herself into a chair by the window and said, "I hope you used the time I allowed you wisely, my girl. He likes you, admires you, but you'll get nowhere with just that. Did you get him to kiss you?"

Faith objected to the question with an inner ball of such impotent fury she thought she might explode under the need to keep her response muted.

"That's between Mr Westaway and myself." She rose from the bed and went to sit at her dressing table where she began to plait her hair. "I am aware of what I must do. Please do me the courtesy of allowing me the freedom to do it at my own pace and using my own intuition."

Lady Vernon moved to stand behind her and began to undo the buttons on the back of her dress. "Please do me the courtesy of remembering your manners, and your gratitude. It was thanks to me you were given any opportunity to achieve anything at all, young lady."

"Yes, of course. But please let me go about this my own way. I assure you that you will get your money. That is, after all, what is important to you." She hoped the reflection of her gimlet eye in the looking glass was as piercing as the older woman's.

"I think you're in love with him." Lady Vernon's smile looked more like a grimace of satisfaction. "Don't think you'll marry him." Her eyes narrowed, and in the gloom, she looked like a witch or a goblin.

"You're cleverer than to daydream that, Faith. He won't marry you." After a pause, she added, "Everyone in Mr Westaway's orbit, and beyond, will ensure that he won't."

Faith's legs were still shaking after Lady Vernon had left and Faith was preparing for bed.

Of course, there were. Faith had a mission to fulfil and too many people stood to gain something as a result of Faith's success—herself included.

Though her success might just come at a cost she'd not factored into the equation.

She stepped out of her skirt and peeled off her cuirass-bodice. Why was she so affected by Lady Vernon's unkind truth? It defied logic. Mr Westaway was a man who could do as he pleased and that alone put him out of her orbit. Faith was inured, so she thought, to entitled, self-absorbed gentlemen who took what they wanted and bargained for the rest.

The trouble was, Mr Westaway wasn't like that. If he were, her job would be so much easier.

She touched her lips. They still tingled from the memory of Mr Westaway's mouth, tender upon hers at first, before his hunger became so pronounced for that brief moment before he broke away. There really shouldn't have been time to have decided anything much about the quality of it. And yet, it had lasted long enough for her to realise that she was changed. Affected.

And that he had been, too.

But he was a man. Rich, entitled. If he were affected, he'd have forgotten it by morning.

She sat on the bed and rested her head in her hands, the silence of the room seeming to break into her thoughts.

Who was she trying to fool? That was only if he were the kind of gentleman who frequented Madame Chambon's. The kind who thought nothing of paying for their transitory pleasures.

Mr Westaway was not like that.

And Faith had been trained to entrap men like him. Good, decent men who, when embarking upon something like tonight's kiss, thought they were attracted to a good, decent woman.

She was the honey trap. His disappointed hopes and dreams would be all the more bitter for having realised the extent of his being duped.

Except that Faith had no intention of it going so far, and nor did Madame Chambon. He would not know what Faith was because Faith came from Madame's establishment and Madame Chambon's was hallowed ground. Whatever devil's agreement made between Madame Chambon, Lady Vernon, and Mrs Gedge would protect the reputation of the highly lucrative Soho purveyor of beautiful and expensive women. Gentlemen of discernment and fat pocketbooks must always know they would be safe when selecting a girl from London's most highly regarded brothel.

Faith crawled into bed.

No, not a hint of scandal would link Faith with Madame Chambon's though Faith had no doubt Lady Vernon was as ruthless as her cohorts. She had no love of Faith, but as long as Faith delivered what was promised, Faith would be free to make her own way in the world.

Pulling the covers over her head, she thought of the days ahead—the escalation of searing passion, then a promise extracted from Mr Westaway so that the sting of rejection, timed just right, might be all the bitter.

It seemed too simple but, of course, there must be more at play than that for Mrs Gedge to have spent three years grooming Faith to be the means of breaking this young man's heart.

Perhaps there'd been a failed love affair between herself and Lord Maxwell, Mr Westaway's father?

Or was Mrs Gedge avenging the death of her daughter. Had the girl died of a broken heart after he'd spurned her?

Was money, not love, involved?

There was no point in quizzing Lady Vernon or even digging for the truth in her most artful and subtle manner. Lady Vernon conversed with Faith only upon her conduct.

And that conduct was required to become as scandalous as it was possible for a young, supposedly innocent virgin to be.

The night pressed in on her, her mind churning with questions but knowing only one thing— that tomorrow or the next, she must do whatever possible to compromise Mr Westaway in order to extract an offer of marriage, or at least an ardent declaration of love.

And, for the first time, the knowledge that this might mean sacrificing her virginity didn't trouble her in the least.

The fact that it might involve breaking hearts along the way, did.

CHAPTER 16

A beautiful, sunny day meant that the washroom wasn't the only alternative for creating a setting whereby Faith must recline amongst the water lilies.

At breakfast, when she went down and found Lady Vernon and Mr Westaway in the parlour, Faith was immediately besieged by conflicting suggestions. Lady Vernon thought the bath was the better alternative; Mr Westaway was keen on the lake.

Only the arrival of Lord Delmore stirred enough conviction one way or another.

"To the lake," he announced, and Faith wasn't unhappy about it. The surprisingly balmy feel in the air combined with her hopefulness was a good combination, so that she was unusually unconstrained and forthcoming as Lord Delmore quizzed her on her time in London during the walk through the gardens and along the lakeside, before they arrived at a small copse which Mr Westaway had spied out as a likely location.

The older gentleman seemed fascinated by Faith's impressions on the capital. He asked her about her family and her father, and she answered truthfully, for even though they were lost to her, she could imbue the reality of a poverty-stricken cottager with the high hopes of an equally poverty-stricken, though fictional, family intent on bettering their most promising progeny.

Surprisingly, Faith found she suffered no pangs of guilt for lying, or even sadness for letting her family believe her dead. There simply had been too many of them and her father too brutal and economical with words for her to have understood him. She genuinely had no desire to ever see him again. The others, too, were so different in the way they thought of life or conducted themselves that she'd have been happy to have called herself an only child.

Her future was here. In her hands. In Mr Westaway's hands. Meanwhile, Lord Delmore served a useful purpose in acting as a conduit for the questioning she'd have liked to have come from Mr Westaway, who appeared too absorbed in his painting to notice her or anyone else.

For the first half an hour, Mr Westaway occupied himself with setting up his easel, then sketching the backdrop so that Faith could enjoy being dry as she sat in one of the wicker chairs her host had a servant arrange for her, Lady Vernon, and Lord Delmore.

The last thing Faith felt like doing was going near water again but knew what was required. So, when Lord Delmore asked, "And does the idea of floating among the trailing water lilies horrify you, Miss Montague?" she just lifted one shoulder slightly and said, "This is a very pleasant country sojourn and being somewhat impecunious, which I've made no secret about, I shall pay my dues uncomplainingly when the time comes."

He seemed to like her answer enormously for he laughingly responded, "Not so demure, if you don't mind my saying so, Miss Montague. Most young ladies would not advertise such facts."

"I would rather no potential suitor was under any illusions, Lord Delmore." Faith decided she liked the candour in his twinkling blue eyes. He seemed far easier than the buttoned-up personages she was more likely to meet in London. And when he added, "I'll have to introduce you to my daughter-in-law. She could take a leaf out of your book when it comes to being candid and not putting herself above others," she decided he was quite fatherly in the kind of endearing way she liked to imagine her own father might have been had he not been cursed with ten children, no money, and a drinking problem. All of which, she supposed, meant that there could never be two men more different than Lord Delmore and her own father.

"It's time, I'm afraid." Mr Westaway cleared his throat, and they all turned. He'd not said a word in a good twenty minutes.

Faith was sure he'd even blushed when he'd nodded a greeting, earlier, before quite studiously avoiding any further direct contact.

Was he regretting last night? She certainly wasn't. An unbidden memory of the searing passion in that one short kiss sent the blood rushing to her cheeks. She was surprised that she'd blushed but also rather pleased that she'd managed it so artlessly. It served her purpose rather well.

Faith took a deep, audible breath, rose from her chair and glanced about at the company as she picked up her skirts and turned towards the water. Then she stopped and sat down again. "My shoes. I can't go in wearing these, naturally." She pressed her lips together and sent a rather imploring glance at Lady Vernon, who grunted as she moved forward in her chair before muttering, "I can't take them off for you, my girl. Not with my arthritis. Gentlemen, would it be so shocking if one of you were to do the honours." She put her nose in the air as if pretending great delicacy when Faith knew any pretence at anything remotely refined or delicate was a complete sham. "I'm sure you know that a lady is somewhat restricted when it comes to bending at the waist."

They'd know it, of course. Lord Delmore was a widower, and Mr Westaway must have had some experience with women, surely, to know that they always put on their footwear before donning their corset. And Faith was wearing a corset today, as directed by Lady Vernon for just this reason.

The two men exchanged long looks. Faith could tell they both wanted to offer but were reluctant to be the first. Finally, Lord Delmore conceded to the younger man, saying, "I'm not as agile as I once was, either, Crispin. Miss Montague, apologies for embarrassing you like this."

"I shall be more embarrassed when you see how poorly I manage in water. I presume you want me to float, but the truth is, I've never tried. I only know that if it can be learned, I'm sure I'll learn quickly. I don't want to delay you, Mr Westaway, when time is of the essence."

Faith stretched out her leg and pointed her foot while Mr Westaway went down on bended knee on the grass and rested it in the palm of his hand. She liked his touch. He seemed gentle and respectful, unlike many of the gentlemen who came to Madame Chambon's fuelled by rampant sexual desire.

But how surprising that she was enjoying her mission.

When Mr Westaway had removed her shoes, he took her hands and helped her to rise.

"Will you be all right getting to the water?"

"If I may lean upon your shoulder as I negotiate the mud. I'm not sure how deep it might be." She made the most of the contact, and when they were at the water's edge with the others a few yards behind them, he said, "I took unconscionable liberties, Miss Montague."

"And I do not hold you to account for any of them." She giggled happily. Silly, but it was no act. "It was too marvellously unexpected, Mr Westaway. And so comforting to know that I shall be able to enjoy these mysteries if I'm ever granted the opportunity." She patted his shoulder. "Don't trouble yourself anymore over it. It's in the past. Now I just have to lie amongst the water lilies and stare vacantly at the sky. I can do that. I can do whatever is required. Oooh!" She gave a squeal as the water reached mid-calf and then, because she knew when the dramatic would serve her well, plunged headlong into the depths with an even greater cry.

"I did it!" she squealed, emerging a second later. At home, the boys had sometimes bathed in the river, but Faith had never been tempted by the discoloured water from the tannery upstream. Her mother had always come down hard upon the girls for trying to emulate the boys who were so carefree in their nakedness.

Faith couldn't imagine what her mother would think of her daughter, now. But as Faith had never had the slightest respect for her mother, and truly felt her life was better for being free of her sanctimonious piety and propensity to lash out, like Faith's father, the reflection did not dampen this morning's proceedings.

All of which were progressing swimmingly if the admiration and mutual enjoyment on both Lord Delmore and Mr Westaway's faces were anything to go by.

"Just be careful amongst the reeds," Lord Delmore cautioned, "and keep well within your depth. This is a smart new set of clothes I'm wearing."

"You'd actually consider getting them wet and muddy on my account?" She sent him an impish smile. "I think that's the most gallant thing a gentleman has ever said to me." She could afford to feel lighthearted, for this morning was all about playacting, setting up the gentlemen to think of her as she wanted them to, not as she was.

"I think you'd inspire such chivalry from anyone who met you, Miss Montague."

Faith caught the surprised look Lord Delmore's words received from Mr Westaway and was emboldened. "What about you, Mr Westaway? I've heard that the focus of the true artist would not be torn away by anything."

"Except losing the very thing that keeps him focused." He grinned as he looked up from the canvas. "I suppose I'd have no choice but to rescue you if I wanted to finish my painting."

"Well, I prefer Lord Delmore's response, even though it's a relief to know I'd be saved in both instances. Am I floating artistically enough?"

Faith had adjusted to the water temperature and made sure her hair fanned out about her and the folds of her dress looked suitably artistic.

"It's perfect." Mr Westaway nodded.

"Will she have to go into the lake every day, Mr Westaway?" Lady Vernon asked. "There are logistical concerns with seeing her dress is dry when she puts it on each day only to then have to float in it for as long as it pleases you."

"Today will suffice, Lady Vernon." Mr Westaway barely looked at the old woman, but he smiled at Faith. "I promise not to sacrifice you,

Miss Montague, to my artistic pursuits. Today I only need to sketch in the background and get a general composition."

Faith, who'd been floating for as long as she could manage, stood up. The water reached mid-thigh, and as she glanced down, she could see the outline of her corset beneath the fabric of her gown. She decided to remain standing for a while and pretend to be unaware.

"Perhaps she'll need a new dress," Lady Vernon went on. "Faith, get back in the water this instant!"

"Only if Mr Westaway says I must," Faith countered. "He's the artist."

She saw the way his eyes lingered on her just a moment too long before he agreed with Lady Vernon, the pause and the obvious reluctance in his tone music to her ears.

Faith lay back down in the water, but after another few minutes, her task really was becoming difficult. The chill was starting to seep into her bones.

When she could take it no more, she rose suddenly, but her feet stuck fast in the mud and she stumbled and fell to her knees. Her hands went out in front of her, and now her knees were sinking in sludge while the water was too high for her head to remain above. Her corset cut into her, and she couldn't move properly. Panic was swift. She truly was trapped. With her clothing too constricting, she could neither rise to her feet, yet nor was she agile enough to roll onto her back so that she was again floating with her face to the sky.

By the time a pair of hands gripped her elbows and hauled her to her feet, she was choking on the water she'd taken in, shaking with nerves and on the edge of tears.

"I have you, Miss Montague. A nasty fright, that's all." Lord Delmore led her to his chair, his tone fatherly, his concern making her want to cry even more. There'd been precious few people in her world that had ever spoken to her like that. "There, there, Miss Montague," he soothed, patting her shoulder. "Open your eyes, here's my handkerchief."

Mr Westaway had barely registered until it was all over, it seemed, for he was blinking at her over the top of the easel, and she seethed inside at the injustice of losing such an opportunity to play to his concern.

"I won't cry," she said between gritted teeth, and it was as if she were six years old again and her father was berating her for letting the cow run away, bringing the willow switch across her shoulders in a series of violent outbursts. Little matter that *he* had left the gate unlatched plenty of times and that the cow had always either returned home for milking or been brought back by one of the neighbours. "I won't cry. I won't cry."

She'd said those words so often as a child and she never did cry. Nor did she cry, now, but clearly the combination of hunched shoulders, stiff jaw, and defiant mantra was not the usual reaction of damsels in distress.

"You're very brave." Mr Westaway was on one side and Lord Delmore, standing on her other, was wrapping a towel about her shoulders. Lady Vernon was blinking dispassionately at her, not having bothered to rise from her chair, but she didn't count. Faith could bask in the attention from two handsome men and believe for a few minutes they genuinely did care she'd been frightened.

She relaxed her shoulders and smiled suddenly. "I won't do that again." Mr Westaway's brow was creased as if he didn't know what to say, so she saved him the trouble. "I'm sorry I spoiled things, Mr Westaway. I hope I was there long enough for you to get the sketch you needed at least. But I'm ready to go back again, if you'd like."

"Of course not!" Lord Delmore was quite vocal in defence of Faith having a reprieve. "Ten minutes is more than enough time for a gently nurtured young lady to float in a swamp. I wouldn't hear of it, and I'm sure Mr Westaway wouldn't, either."

"Gad, but she's a rare jewel," Lord Delmore declared as he accepted the brandy Crispin handed him before taking a seat opposite him in the library. The long balmy evenings of sitting outside were gone since the summer days had given way to a dreary grey, with a decided chill in the air. "I wonder what her plans are when this is all over. Don't suppose she has her eye on you, do you think?"

"It's something that has already been aired between us," Crispin said, stretching his long legs towards the fire. She's very aware of my situation as I am of hers."

"And that is? Yes, yes, I know you told me she's penniless and looking to make a marriage." Lord Delmore seemed surprisingly agitated, which was uncharacteristic.

Crispin put down his empty glass and stared at the longtime friend of his aunt and uncle. A man of another generation. One he admired, certainly, but whose life and future seemed settled and predictable. "Are you suggesting you might make her an offer, Lord Delmore?"

Crispin had heard his uncle's old neighbour voice his disinclination to change his widowed status on many occasions.

So when Lord Delmore responded, "If you're not going to, I just might follow her to London and see how matters progress," Crispin couldn't have been more astonished. He was also astonished at the lurch of dismay that lodged in his chest cavity and hardened into a feeling he was quite loath to identify. For he really had been on his guard not to let the beautiful and engaging Miss Faith Montague get under his defences.

Perhaps Crispin's expression betrayed him for immediately Lord Delmore said, "Naturally, you have the superior suit, Crispin. You and Miss Montague make a good match, to my mind, and if I were standing here as your father, I'd be encouraging you to consider the merits of aligning yourself with a young woman with a lively intelligence and sharp wit, not to mention a good solid backbone. They're few and far between in my experience. Lord, don't I know it having been married so many years and rearing a daughter frighteningly similar to my wife, God rest her soul."

"You think I should make her an offer?" Crispin was incredulous.

"You won't, of course." Lord Delmore stared at the hearthrug, his expression wistful. "She'd make you a good wife, but if you loved her like she deserves, then you'd disregard your father's strictures entirely. But I know you, Crispin. Ever the dutiful son and you couldn't be happy if you'd displeased your pater, as I see it." He hesitated, raised his head and said very seriously, "Give it another few days, my boy, and if you haven't fallen head over heels, then I hope you'll agree that all's fair in love and all that. In which case, if Miss Montague is indeed prepared to marry without love on her side, then I'm sure I could make a good case for her considering me a good prospect."

Faith? Lady Delmore? Living as neighbour to Crispin's aunt and uncle? He tried not to grimace. To keep a cool head. What Lord Delmore said about Crispin's reverence for his father's word made him sound more like a kowtowing schoolboy than a young man of integrity who was of one mind when his pater spoke only common sense regarding Crispin's need to prioritise his career over his marital concerns.

"I'm sure she'd consider you very favourably, Lord Delmore," he said carefully, hating the way the words sounded yet knowing he could never make the young lady a similar offer. And wasn't it just as well he'd kept his distance and not allowed free rein to the feelings inside him that might have escalated beyond his control?

"You think so?" Now it was Lord Delmore who sounded like the schoolboy.

Crispin nodded and smiled weakly.

"Not so clever, Faith." Lady Vernon sucked on her gums as she took a turn about the gravel path that surrounded the house. Her head was lowered and her sharp nose, in silhouette, looked like a miniature scythe. Faith knew Lady Vernon would not hesitate to stab her in the back if it profited the old woman. In truth, her own desperation was rising for Lady Vernon was right. Yet again, Faith had failed to strike the right note.

Yesterday's episode by the lake had elicited Lord Delmore's chivalry, but left Mr Westaway unmoved. He'd barely registered what had occurred though he'd been all solicitude in the drawing room, later. However, he'd deferred all evening to Lord Delmore, who'd paid

Faith all manner of compliments and engaged her in light conversation. His attention had been enough to convince both Faith and Lady Vernon that the older man was interested.

"And don't think you can set yourself up with a peer and not have to account to the rest of us," Lady Vernon now muttered, echoing Faith's innermost thoughts. For what if Lord Delmore did surprisingly pursue her and offer her the respectability that would secure her future, and ensure she didn't ever land up in a gutter selling herself for a few pennies? She knew of enough girls who shared that fate, and she'd always considered she was clever enough for it not to happen to her.

No, Faith had believed she could secure her heart in a completely ironclad box so that the decisions she made to safeguard her future were entirely quarantined from any fanciful notions of romance. Love was not going to make a fool out of her.

So why was her disappointment that Mr Westaway seemed happy enough to let Lord Delmore pay court to her so acute? She was piqued from a distinctly personal point of view that had nothing to do with the greatest conundrum that must be faced—unless she carried out Mrs Gedge's orders she'd be out on her ear. Lady Vernon would see to that at the very least.

"I'm not going to encourage Lord Delmore, if that's what you're concerned about," she muttered, head bent against the brisk breeze, feeling on the back of her neck a spattering of raindrops from the branches of a monkey puzzle tree they passed under during their walk.

"Because you're in love with Mr Westaway?" the older woman asked. "It's been fascinating to watch, and I can't make up my mind whether you actually are a better actress than I'd given you credit for, or whether you've allowed yourself to be moonstruck by impossibilities."

"What does it matter?" Faith raised her head. "You'll get your cut, Lady Vernon."

"I will." There was a distinct smugness to her satisfaction, which made Faith wonder if Lady Vernon in fact had more belief in Faith's eventual success than Faith had. After a pause, the old woman said, "Tomorrow is the day you'll win him. I know what needs doing."

"Do you, Lady Vernon?"

She nodded.

Faith wasn't sure what to think. Lady Vernon had proved in the past that she could provide the impetus to get Mr Westaway to act in a more tender manner towards Faith. Even if he did withdraw immediately afterwards.

Lady Vernon had stopped and regarded Faith carefully.

"For such a well-tutored professional, you really don't know what to do when you're in love, do you?"

"I'm not in love."

"No?" Lady Vernon's look was ugly in its assessment. She shrugged. "Well, that's neither here nor there, is it, when you won't be able to claim him. But tomorrow he will realise he loves you and he has to have you. After that, there's no going back. Not for him, anyway. As for you, well, my girl, you have no choice but to do what you were engaged to do."

Faith turned towards the house and caught a glimpse of a face looking down at her from through the diamond-paned windows on the second story. Mr Westaway's bedchamber? Was that where she'd find herself tomorrow night?

She wanted to be there.

And because she wanted to be there, so much...with him...she realised that perhaps the only way to avoid disaster was to scupper Lady Vernon's plans.

Because, now she suspected there was more to this than simply making Mr Westaway fall in love with her only to break his heart.

No, there was something far deeper at play than she'd given credence to, and unless she ended this charade right now, she'd be the one paying the penalty for the rest of her life.

She was sure of it.

CHAPTER 17

Faith woke to the sound of rain beating against the windowpane. She opened one heavy eyelid and stared out into a grey sky. The tree branches scraped and scratched at the glass, and the wind sighed through the branches.

She sat up and reached for her poor, worse-for-wear cuirass-bodice and skirt that she'd worn the past two days for the painting and which Lady Vernon had arranged to be dried by morning.

But as her hands closed about the fabric, she encountered something light and unfamiliar.

These were not her clothes.

She put her feet to the floor and stood up, holding up the frothy, flimsy gown that was the right length for her but was not hers. She recognised it as something semifamiliar, an alternative fashion that eschewed the heavy corsetry, flounces, and swathing of the traditionally upholstered gowns of today's fashion.

As she held it up against her, a piece of paper fluttered to the floor.

Dear Miss Montague – she read – *Perhaps this will be easier to wear for the remaining days you are required to work for me. I certainly believe it will suit you, and so anticipate the pleasure I will have of brandishing my brushes to do justice to your beauty."*

Mr Westaway had bought her a dress. A light, flowing, delicious confection in white voile with flounces and furbelows that required no corsetry. A dress she could put on herself without the help of a dresser or lady's maid.

She stepped into it, wishing her heart did not beat so, and that her hands didn't tremble as she fastened the hooks and eyes.

Surveying herself in the mirror, she saw that the effect would be eminently desirable from a painterly point of view. She put her hands around her waist and smoothed the fabric over her hips. A perfect hourglass figure precluded the necessity of an undergarment that would impinge upon rapid undressing. She would be the creature in the medieval gown floating in the stream that was the stuff of Mr Westaway's imagination.

But she would not entice him.

No, her plans had changed. She would no longer play the temptress in the knowledge that her actions would lead an innocent man to his downfall.

Regardless of the contract she had with Mrs Gedge, she couldn't condemn the man she was afraid she'd grown too fond of to a future filled with dangers unknown.

"Miss Montague, you didn't sleep well?"

Faith shook her head and offered Mr Westaway a rueful smile while wishing Lord Delmore was on hand in the small bathing room. The piercing, soulful eyes of handsome Mr Westway plucked at her heartstrings in a way they had no right to.

He smiled sympathetically when she shook her head. "If it's any consolation, I didn't either."

He positioned himself behind the easel but put his head around to ask, "And what do you think of the gown? I know Lady Vernon's arthritic fingers make it difficult to help you with your ordinary dress. Besides which, this will create the effect I'm after." He seemed to falter. "I hope you don't consider me too forward in choosing your wardrobe."

"You're the artist, Mr Westaway. I would wear a hessian sack if you required it."

"You would?" He ducked back in front of his easel to grin at her. "I should like that."

"I shouldn't like it, though. However, you're paying me."

His smile vanished. The dampening effect of her response had created the desired effect, but it hadn't made Faith happy to see him so effectively checked.

With a sigh, she shrugged her shoulders. "Forgive my being so out of sorts, Mr Westaway. You're right; I had an abominable night's sleep, and I'm not an angel when I'm not well rested."

"Despite looking like one. I'm glad you're wearing the dress. I think it will free both of us."

He was back in professional mode, not thinking of the double meaning of his words. In the tiny bathroom, Lady Vernon sat on a chair by the window, silent like a bird of prey, the great tub of steaming water beckoning Faith to submerge herself. Such a contrast to the dreary outdoors. On the water's surface floated rose petals while beneath, the flame from a dozen candles kept the water at a pleasant temperature.

"This is somewhat more enticing than yesterday's escapade into the icy, murky depths of your local fishpond," she said, and he laughed.

"Yesterday, I sketched the reeds and the clouds above and the billowing folds of your gown, Miss Montague. It was the beautiful outdoors that will be writ large when the painting is exhibited and there was nothing wasted." He craned his head forward as if to study the planes and angles of her face.

"Now, I just need to render the perfection of my subject at close quarters," he seemed to stumble over his last few words, "so that the painting's viewers will appreciate the exquisite definition of my *Lady of the Lake*."

The air between them seemed thick with unspoken meaning. And promise. Faith swallowed and put her hand to her throat as if her lace collar were suddenly too tight.

His admiration was too much. But he'd not act on it. She strained to see the sincerity in his eyes and was rewarded with it a hundredfold. Why did he not see the need to hide his feelings as she did?

"I'm sorry, Miss Montague, but it's time to submerge yourself, once again."

Faith put her hand in his palm as he helped her into the bath. It was a curiously intimate gesture, and she imagined herself suddenly stepping into a bath as most ladies did, without clothing. Did he, also? Is that why he blushed?

She hadn't meant to immerse herself so quickly that her skirts skimmed up to her thighs before she was able to smooth them.

Lady Vernon would have been pleased to have caught the flare of desire in his bright, blue eyes, but it was not what Faith sought right now. Not now that she'd sworn off the plan.

The plan.

What should she do? What *could* she do? She caught Lady Vernon's eagle eyes upon her and said, "Is this the effect you were hoping to achieve, Mr Westaway? Will you want me to wear this dress tomorrow?" She smiled up at him. "Did *you* choose it?"

"There was a certain stiffness to your previous attire that did not accord with the vision I had in mind."

"So, you did choose it!" She sounded as delighted as she felt, even though she knew it was unwise.

"I went into the village and sought the offices of a dressmaker who knew exactly what I was talking about. She also happens to be a proponent of the Arts and Crafts movement, and she had a loose-flowing gown she'd made for herself that just fitted the bill. I'm delighted it suits you so well."

"And I'm delighted you have such a good eye, Mr Westaway."

He smiled warmly. "I've always spied out quality, Miss Montague."

"And where is Lord Delmore today?" she asked as Mr Westaway slid behind his easel and picked up his paintbrushes.

"Do you miss him?"

She gave an embarrassed laugh. "Should I? I thought he was being instructed by you in the art of painting; that he was thinking of dabbling in painting himself and that was why he was always with you."

"I think you misunderstand his motives, Miss Montague. Now, if you could stretch your neck a little. Yes, that's right, you have a very beautiful neck, and the dress shows that to perfection."

"Does that mean you'll have to start the painting again?"

"Only in the close-up of you and it won't take too long to alter. I'll be finished by the deadline in three days." He paused. "I will need you to suffer spending a little longer in the bath today, though. I hope you won't be too cramped. I promise I'll work as quickly as I can."

"Of course." Faith stretched her limbs and pointed her toes. The iron tub was enormous, and she could float freely. It was quite liberating, though she'd have enjoyed it more if the water were a little warmer.

"Lady Vernon, are the candles lit beneath? It's a little cold."

Lady Vernon did not seem impressed. "There are five candles burning, Faith. Please don't complain. Mr Westaway has work to do, and you mustn't keep interrupting." She rose. "This is no place for an old woman with arthritic limbs. I shall fetch Molly to sit in."

Mr Westaway didn't try to fill the silence when she'd gone. Nor did he seem to notice that Molly had not come to take Lady Vernon's place. He seemed intent on his painting, the brush moving rapidly now, his face with a mask of concentration.

The minutes ticked by leaden and slow for Faith, who was feeling the cold seep into her bones and feared asking Mr Westaway to relight the candles which had gone out some time ago.

She shivered, and her teeth chattered.

Surely, he'd notice and come to her rescue.

The light began to fade outside casting long, gloomy shadows across the room.

Still Mr Westaway worked, completely absorbed. In fact, never had Faith seen him so animated as his brush flew across the canvas. She dared not interrupt.

In the depths of the house, the grandfather clock struck seven o' clock. Faith had been in the bath for two hours. She tried to breathe, but was shivering too much.

She tried to speak, but the words wouldn't come.

If was as if her body were caving in on itself suddenly. It had happened so gradually, but now the impact was swift. She didn't know if she had the strength to ever move again. She was going to drown all over again but on the inside.

Perhaps she gave a soft moan for Mr Westaway looked up suddenly, and as his eyes locked with hers, it was as if he were only seeing her, the person, for the first time in all his frenzied painting, for he dropped his brush and strode forward, crouching by the side of the bath.

"Miss Montague?" He didn't wait for her to acknowledge him. Perhaps he saw that she was incapable. Certainly, the speed with which he rose and whisked her out of the bath and against him belonged to a man motivated by urgency.

She was shivering so hard now she couldn't speak. Her teeth chattered, and her body convulsed.

"Dear God, what have I done to you?" Seizing a towel, he wrapped her in it, squeezing the water out of her skirts so that it puddled on the floor and down his trouser legs. He paused, cradling her against him. She had her eyes shut, so she didn't see what expressions crossed his face, but the next moment, he'd hoisted her into his arms and was striding out of the bathroom and along the corridor to the servants' stairs, his footsteps echoing on the bare boards. This was not a part of the house frequented by the likes of Mr Westaway, yet it appeared they met no one. Not that Faith cared too much.

She was going to die of cold. Her bones ached to the very marrow, and her head ached. How had it happened so fast? Why had she let it happen? Her thoughts had wandered so very far away. Away to what freedom might feel like if she ever got out of the prison of her making. Of Mrs Gedge's making.

She felt his hand on her as he lay her on something that yielded slightly. A bed.

The ceiling was dark and unfamiliar. Not her room. Not a room a gentleman would inhabit, she realised vaguely. The servants' attics or a musty room somewhere else.

"It was the closest." She felt his warm breath against her forehead.

The bathroom was tacked onto a little-used part of the house; she knew that. Knew also that he was not going to strip her naked and have his way with her when she was vulnerable. Yes, cold she might be, but she was not insensible. A girl who traded on her wits and who didn't intend landing in the gutter couldn't afford not to have a semblance of consciousness of what was going on around her.

But she was so cold. The spasm that tore through her and his hesitancy following the light hand on her chest, not her breasts for he was a gentleman and would remain one, she was certain of that, banished his diffidence.

He began to work the row of tiny buttons at the front of her gown quickly, stripping her dress over her shoulders and down to her waist while she wriggled to help him. For the gown was like an icy mantle, and she was desperate to get warm. Desperate to feel warmth against her frozen skin.

His warmth.

Reaching out, she closed her hands about his wrists, and he stopped.

"Make me warm." Her hands found his thighs, the rough fabric of his trousers. Wet. Like the rest of him as he'd held her, dripping against him.

It was only reasonable he get warm and dry too. She didn't say it, but her seeking hands and the expression she levelled at him made her thoughts clear.

She reached out her arms for him, and one glance at her face was enough, for then he was tearing at his necktie, unbuttoning his jacket and waistcoat, stripping off his trousers.

All with the urgency and attention to what came next that she required.

The thought of skin to skin contact was like a burning obsession, although only conceived of in the minutes she'd spent conjuring them up while lying on the bed.

Before, it had been a necessary precursor to her freedom.

Now it was a raging want, and as he lowered himself into her arms and his hard, naked chest pressed against her breasts, she thought she would die of desire.

Warmth sizzled between them, his heated skin instantly communicating to her everything she needed, whipping up sensations she had no idea were possible in her carefully controlled human sphere.

"Hold me," she whispered, wrapping her arms and legs about him and pulling him tight. "Please."

He was as naked as she, and the searing contact lit a fire within her belly.

Desire? Is this what it felt like? She, who'd imagined she was immune was now as desperate as any common doxy to fuel the fires of the man in her embrace for her own ends. She wanted love; she wanted passion; she wanted human connection.

Sliding beneath the covers, they curled into each other, his warmth heating her all over, his erection pressing into her belly; strengthening her from within. Powerful. She felt it of her own accord and because of his worship, for that's what it felt like. As if he were imbuing her with a strength she could only experience through honouring this connection between them.

His lips found hers, lighting her up from inside, thrilling her with sensations she'd not thought possible.

She rolled on top of him, straddling him as she cupped his face, kissing him back with passion. What did it matter that the motion came naturally, observed during her time at Madame Chambon's though never acted upon until now. It gave her power and negated any gentlemanly requirement to question her desire to proceed.

She could no more have halted the escalation of raging need to take this to its culmination than tell him she never wanted to see him again.

For she wanted to see him...be with him...now...forever.

In all her life, Faith had never craved physical contact with another person for any length of time. Her body had never reacted to another human being as it did now. Conscious thought disappeared;

instinct took over, and it was the most fulfilling, liberating moment of her life when he rolled her beneath him, and his mouth found her breast.

"Oh!" she cried, desperate for what she did not know. Only that the suckling of her nipple was the most delicious torment she'd ever experienced. Meanwhile, her seeking hands liked what they found. His young body was strong, hard and...responsive.

She pushed back the hair that flopped over his forehead, and her eyes caught his as he positioned himself at her entrance.

Oh, she was more than ready. She was more than wanting.

She sucked in a breath, and a small smile was all he needed to continue with what could never have been stopped with all the will in the world.

He slid into her, eliciting a brief jerk of surprised pain that was quickly subsumed by all the delicious sensations that followed.

This was nothing like she'd expected. And so much more than she'd ever hoped for, when hope was something that seemed reserved for other people.

She clung to him and moved with him, loving the knowledge that he was in another sphere, and that she'd taken him to pleasures unknown. That's what it felt like, with his breathing fast and shallow and his sighs responsive to her slightest movement.

His body spoke to hers as if they were made for one another. Sweat slicked her once-icy skin. Sizzling sensation tore across her nerve endings. Inside, her body was experiencing a firestorm of its own; a raging conflagration divorced from the pleasure that flooded her mind.

With a cry, he thrust into her one final time, flinging his arm about her and pulling her tightly against his chest before, panting, he lay on his back, eyes closed, face raised to the ceiling.

Faith curled into him; her free hand stroking his chest, lingering over his nipples, making him jerk and smile as she toyed with him.

"My darling," he muttered, opening one eye and staring down at her.

She didn't pretend to be coy or shy away from him. She had bled, and thank God he need have no doubts that he had indeed taken a virgin.

But that was academic. Faith wasn't going to let him go.

Not now, not ever.

CRISPIN WAS INFUSED WITH NEW GENIUS. HIS PAINTBRUSH HAD acquired magical powers. A life of its own. In the early morning, with the light as sharp as could be achieved on another gloomy day, he painted the glorious creature who floated in the bath and who gazed up at him through lazy, half-lidded eyes.

The water was comfortably warm, and the candles would continue to be refreshed. He wasn't about to lose her to some foolish preoccupation with his art though, lord, he wasn't sorry by what had precipitated this descent into madness.

It was madness, but he wasn't about to call it out for what it was and deny the possibilities that lay before them.

Them. He was not a young man to downplay what was real. Denial had been hard won during the drawn-out process accepting her as the helpmate of his future.

She'd arrived too early in his life, but he recognised her for what she was—the wife he'd spend his life looking for if he didn't claim her now.

And he'd claimed her as surely and effectively as a man of his moral code could.

"Are you comfortable, Miss Montague?" he said above the clicking of Lady Vernon's knitting needles.

"Quite, thank you, Mr Westaway." She flicked a covert, meaning-laden smile at him, managed through half an open eye, and he was satisfied. Their communication was as subtle as needed to be with a chaperone on standby, and as satisfying as any lust-craven gentleman could want.

Having sinned once, there would be no impediments to strengthening the precious, fragile bond through further sinning.

He would wed her, there was no doubt of that, and in the process, restore her immortal soul.

The precious enigma that she was would be in no doubt that his intentions, when all was said and done, were honourable. And by making that clear, she'd dispense with the inhibitions that, extraordinarily, had not been in evidence when they'd sinned the first time.

No, she was pure, that was not in doubt, yet he'd unleashed in her a primal desire that surely every man would ache to have as the essential makeup of the woman to whom God had joined and no man must put asunder.

"The water is not too cool for you, Miss Montague?"

"Slightly, Mr Westaway, but your painting must come first before I warm myself."

And that, you will not do without my help, Miss Montague, he thought, though his glance made that clear enough for she slanted a secret smile at him, instantly regaining her former gravitas when Lady Vernon dropped her knitting and stared for a long moment between the two of them.

But the old woman did not suspect. How could she? She was a dried-up husk of a creature with no understanding of human passion.

Miss Montague reared up before him, water dripping from her hair and dress, spattering the floor as she reached for linen with which to dry herself.

"Forgive me, I suddenly couldn't stay there a moment longer."

"Faith, you were not given permission!" Her chaperone was angry, and Crispin enjoyed seeing the flint in his beloved's eye as she stood her ground, pretending she didn't care that her actions compromised Crispin's ability to paint the picture that would earn him his place in the world.

There was no doubt this was a masterpiece in the making. She was his inspiration, his muse, and another night in her arms would solidify the power of creation, of genius, that would elevate this painting above the rest.

"The cold has a habit of seizing one suddenly. Taking one captive, Lady Vernon," he soothed. "Let Faith leave now if she must."

The old lady was not pleased, it amused him to see. It amused him even more to see how well Faith played the pliant schoolgirl with the invisible armour that suddenly sprouted metal spikes when her ire was aroused. He wondered what words were exchanged when the two of them were alone and Miss Westaway was defending her need to break what Lady Vernon surmised was the contract between them.

The contract that had been rewritten.

CHAPTER 18

The words that were in fact exchanged between Faith and her chaperone of course bore no resemblance to any he might have surmised.

"You can't behave like a prima donna or you'll never get his measure."

"You think I haven't already?" Faith glared, wanting to taunt Lady Vernon and keep her wondering, yet wanting her to know that Faith had succeeded so beautifully already.

But caution and the long game stilled her tongue, so she merely looked enigmatic when Lady Vernon demanded to know what she meant.

"You have three days, Faith. Three days to enslave him, torture him." Lady Vernon's nostrils flared. "Ruin him." The old lady stared out of the window as she toyed with the brush she was about to use on Faith's tangled tresses. "And then it will be time to live your own dreams." She looked so enraptured by this thought that Faith could have imagined she was living Faith's life in her own mind.

Faith sat down on a wooden chair in the centre of the room and held her head erect, waiting for Lady Vernon to play servant. How she did enjoy that. The old woman was a parasite; a cosseted creature born to a life of leisure, but too unattractive to snare the attention of a protector, so that as she aged, she had nothing but her own resources to draw upon.

Faith didn't need a protector. She was too clever. And, unlike Lady Vernon, she had multiple resources to draw upon: youth, beauty, wit, intellect, education.

Mrs Gedge had equipped her with the tools to exact the other woman's evil revenge, but Faith would turn the tables with a pure heart.

It strengthened Faith to know that her vitriol had a pure edge. She wasn't truly bad, as she'd once believed. Love had freed her, cleansed her. Her words and actions towards Mr Westaway were motivated now by truth and honesty; honesty in that she feigned nothing of her feelings.

If that meant her dealings with Lady Vernon were tainted, so be it. If she needed to play a role in order to emerge like a chrysalis, reincarnated from evil into good, it was transitory, necessary. That was all.

Lady Vernon was out of sorts as she tugged the brush through Faith's hair. Faith was playing her cards close to her chest with nothing to support the old lady's suspicions one way or the other. And there was nothing Lady Vernon disliked more than not being in control.

Faith knew this, and it delighted her to keep her guessing while she dreamed away the moments before she could throw a cloak over her nightclothes and slip away up the back stairs to the room they'd occupied the night before.

He was waiting there for her as she knew he would be, his impatience clear, his delight at the fact she'd come as gratifying as anything could be when he strode across the floorboards to greet her.

The sun coming in through the window behind him highlighted his slender but athletic physique but it wasn't before she was in his arms that she could see how his eyes glowed with raw desire.

"My love, you've no idea how impatiently I've waited for this moment." He held her close, his breath hot against her ear as he murmured, "I painted you as you lay in the bath, with the sun burnishing your hair like a halo, dreaming of a time when I could see you just like that with no one but the two of us."

"And that moment has come." She twined her arms behind his neck and nuzzled him, breathing in the scent of him with rapture before he scooped her up and lay her on the bed. He joined her, holding her against his side while he kissed her eyes, her nose, her mouth, pausing to whisper, "You know what this means, don't you?"

She didn't, and her breath hitched, every sense suspended as she waited tensely. What would he say? He couldn't live without her and would she be his mistress? Or that she was the most intoxicating woman he knew, but this must be a secret between them? He loved her, but his father would never allow their union?

Silence stretched between them as a myriad of possibilities jostled for primacy. Faith couldn't be disappointed by what she knew was coming. She simply had to work with what she was offered.

"I want to marry you. I *will* marry you." He was above her now, his chest bare, his eyes boring into her with a fervour she could not believe was feigned.

Shocked, she couldn't answer but he went on, "You wouldn't be here if you didn't feel the same way about me. You're not one to give away your affections lightly, Faith. I've observed every nuance of you…the way your skin flushes when you're happy to see me, or irritated by your chaperone, or pleased with the way you see the painting taking shape. You're the perfect muse, but that's only part of why I need you." He was speaking faster now, the words tumbling out as if he had to persuade her to reciprocate his feelings. "Yes, I *need* you, Faith, because I think you are my perfect foil. My helpmate. We would be good together. A union in perfect symmetry. I am better with you by my side. Less selfish, more careful. I *need* to be careful with a painstaking eye to detail to be good at my job."

"Painting?"

"When I am a diplomat."

"But how can I be a diplomat's wife?" For the first time, she felt truly panicked. The thrill at hearing him put into words the depth of his feelings for her had given way to the practicalities. Little matter that she'd come to the country for the single purpose of receiving just such a declaration only to throw it back in his face, claim her reward from Mrs Gedge, and thus be free.

She would no more be free than a slave from Africa if she were forced to give up his love.

"I love you, Faith. My commitment is not in doubt." He stroked her cheek and gently kissed her mouth, his words more important than his desire, which was apparent as his body pressed against hers. "Is yours?"

She shook her head, and in a fresh burst of ardour pulled him down, her hands sliding to his trousers, indicating her impatience that he divest himself of all impediments to furthering the intimacy between them.

"I love *you*."

"Say my name."

"I love you, Crispin." The words came out on a sigh of happiness, made wonderful and magical…and pure...by the fact they were spoken in truth. And she was pure, wasn't she? Pure in the Biblical sense. She'd not lain with another; she'd given her virginity to this man, and she had every right to claim his love and whatever else he offered.

That she was a creature bred for revenge need not enter into it. Faith had lived by her wits, and the prize was freedom. Never had she doubted she'd get what she wanted for she was cleverer than Mrs Gedge, cleverer than Madame Chambon, and cleverer than Lady Vernon. If Mr Westaway…Crispin…wanted to marry her, she could make a plan that would enable it to happen.

"You are not the shy creature I thought you at first," he whispered, rising above her to unfasten the front of her dress and sliding his hands inside. "But you're a great deal more buttoned up than you were yesterday," he added, referring to the fact she wore a corset and underclothing beneath her ensemble.

"You'll have to make me less buttoned up," she giggled, rolling onto her side so he could slide off her skirt, then onto her back so he could unlace her corset, and finally, giving him unfettered access to her combinations. "If romance can survive all that, I am completely yours."

"My darling, I relish the challenge." He kissed her on the nose. "And your humour. Lady Vernon doesn't know the half of you, does she?"

"Lady Vernon thinks she does." Naked at last, Faith revelled in the way his eyes feasted on her breasts. She breathed deeply, causing them to rise and laughing when the invitation was so implicit, he lowered his head to take one nipple in his mouth.

"Too divine," she whispered as sensation snaked through her limbs and coalesced at the juncture of her legs. The weight of him on top of her was unbearably wonderful, and she felt all powerful at the feel of his erection pressing against her. She'd seen naked men aroused before and been disgusted. But Crispin was too beautiful for words. Tender and kindhearted, masculine but conscious of her needs, she was not going to let him go.

To be joined with him again was to reinforce their bond. Unbreakable. That's what it would be. Faith had never loved before this. It's how she knew what it was. She'd observed him with the same intensity he'd observed her. She knew his moods, understood what drove him, sympathised with the obstacles placed in his path.

Well, there would be obstacles they both must face, but face them they must. If this truly were love, as each believed, then they would overcome.

Arching her back, she guided his hand to her mound, as if by accident, gasping at the pressure so that he blinked in surprise for just a second before he did exactly as she'd hoped he would.

Dear lord, but he was good. Her legs went slack and she was aching for him before at last he was inside her. With a gentle sigh, she grasped his buttocks and moved with him in glorious harmony.

Until both could take it no more and came together in a shuddering climax.

"We shall marry as soon as possible." His voice was urgent as he held her close, both still breathless from their love-making. "I can't bear the thought of being parted from you a moment longer than necessary."

"Your father will object. We need to be careful." Except that it was Faith who needed to be careful. Mr Westaway's father was less of a danger than Mrs Gedge.

Crispin seemed reluctant to accept this, and Faith was relieved when he finally agreed not to make any immediate announcement.

She'd been about to slip to the floor and start dressing but she needed to secure his promise and a promise was more easily extracted with skin to skin contact.

Madame had taught her that.

"Promise me you won't say anything until I say tell you it's all right to do so, Crispin? *Please?*" Playing for time was of the essence. She needed a few days in which to plan, to set in motion a means by which Faith could extricate herself from the tentacles with which Mrs Gedge intended to bind her.

She did not feel she was abusing Crispin's faith in her. If he loved her and could be confident the girl he wanted to make his wife was a virgin when he first made love to her, and if he still wanted to marry her, knowing she was penniless, and despite his father's anticipated opposition, what did the rest matter?

She put her finger to his lips as she rolled on top of him, then stroked his face. "Let this be our secret, Crispin, until the painting is finished." She kissed his chest. "Don't signal to Lady Vernon your feelings just yet. Can you do that?" Playfully, she added, "Though if you want to write me love letters to make up for what you don't say to me in person, that would be very acceptable."

"MY MOST BELOVED FAITH,

You are the moon, the sun, and the stars. When I conjure up your image, it's imbued with a magical glow for you have lit up my life. In just a few days, I know that everything worth having is invested in you. I do not write these words lightly. I have lived, and I have loved, but I've never known what love was until I met you."

With hope and faith that you return the love I feel for you, and excitement for our future as husband and wife, I'll end with a reminder that surely must not be necessary—only two more hours until we can meet again...no one but the two of us."

FAITH KISSED THE ENVELOPE AND LEANED BACK ON HER WINDOW SEAT, gazing at the sky and the distant green verdant hills, bathed in evening light as if they were imbued with everything Crispin, she believed, seemed to feel right now—hope and…faith.

Yes, he had faith in her and in a shared future. And Faith had every expectation that her own cleverness would trump anything Mrs Gedge or Lady Vernon might conjure up to shackle her.

Life had never been so thrilling.

She closed her eyes and hugged the envelope to her chest. Crispin had written words that had found their way right to her heart. He loved her with the intensity she loved him. He'd put into words the very feelings she felt when she imagined him here with her and their life together.

She'd have to make a copy of his words to keep. The letter itself would be her ticket to freedom in the eyes of Mrs Gedge. This would be proof Mr Westaway had lost his heart to her, and all Faith had to do in return was pretend to break his heart. Having spent the last three years of her life living a lie, it would be easy to execute this final, simple task.

Yes, Faith was clever at the best of times. But when her heart was engaged, there was nothing she couldn't do.

LORD DELMORE CLEARLY COULD NOT KEEP AWAY AND HAD BEEN reluctant to discharge the previous day's business which had him visiting his solicitor rather than seated at Crispin's right elbow and watching proceedings.

A lot could happen in twenty-four hours, revealed his lordship a touch wistfully to Crispin, elaborating later that evening after Miss Montague had gone to her room to change into dry clothes.

"There's no point in my making a visit to the capital before the end of the season."

The two men sat in front of the fire with replenished brandy glasses as they waited for the return of the ladies and the edge in his friend's tone had Crispin pricking up his ears although he suspected what Lord Delmore was about to say.

"It's quite clear you're as smitten with the young lady as she is with you." Lord Delmore paused and looked long and hard into the fireplace, while Crispin waited for what would come next as clearly his lordship was pondering something deep and hard. Finally, he looked Crispin in the eye. "Your father won't like it."

Crispin wasn't sure how to take this. His friendship with Lord Delmore was not deep though it had grown over the years. The older man clearly lacked society since the loss of his wife after their two sons had gone to the colonies. Was Crispin being spoken to like an errant schoolboy for losing his heart unwisely?

Carefully he said, "I am twenty-six years old—"

"Oh, you have a wise head on young shoulders and I'm not about to persuade you out of your infatuation or your one true love. Just be sure you know what sacrifices you will have to make before you act too rashly."

Crispin was well aware of the obstacles ahead. His father would be intractable. In fact, he could possibly prove insurmountable, which was why Crispin had been toying with other measures to spirit Faith away—elopement being one.

"Lord Delmore, I am not a greenhorn, and I have known Miss Montague for some time now." He hoped he did not sound too defensive.

"Three weeks, I believe. I hope Miss Montague knows what she's taking on. It won't be easy for her, married to a man whose father exercises such fierce opposition as yours undoubtedly will."

Crispin felt the weight on his shoulders. If he'd had brothers, the burden of marrying well would have been shared. But Crispin was required to be everything to Lord Maxwell, and to fulfil his father's expectations both in the diplomatic arena as well as the marital.

"Initially, Miss Montague and I were very aware that a union between us would not be sanctioned by my father. We spoke about it openly at…the beginning." He hesitated over this. *The beginning* was only a few days ago, and yet a meteoric shift had occurred within him. And her? She seemed prosaic about a match between them. She was husband hunting; she'd made no secret of that. But her feelings had undergone the same metamorphosis his had done. They must have, otherwise she'd not have given herself to him with the intensity she had. No well-brought-up young lady would take such risks unless her hearts was inflamed. For her, this truly had to be love. Passion. Crispin was an artist. He knew what fire in the veins made one do.

"I cannot allow my father's disappointment to stand in the way of my future."

"Happiness?" Lord Delmore asked at his hesitation, and Crispin said quickly, "My happiness is not the only factor here. I believe that I will make the kind of impression on the world and progress as my father desires far more effectively if I have by my side the woman I believe will complement me and make me proud."

For a long time, Lord Delmore considered him. Then he sighed and returned his gaze to the fire. "How can I offer an opinion when I've never known what you describe?" His shoulders were slumped, and the sounds of crackling wood and the ticking clock were very loud. "My marriage was one of convenience. It brought me two fine, prosperous sons and a beautiful daughter, and I had every reason to admire my wife. I know nothing of the fires of which you speak." He touched his heart briefly. "Though having observed Miss Montague these past few days I can understand a little of what you mean. But you must do what you will, my boy, and accept the consequences."

"Do I have your support?"

Lord Delmore raised his eyebrows. "Of course! She is a fine young lady and you a fine young man. You are clearly an excellent pairing. Whatever support is required of me, I will offer it."

Crispin was relieved despite the faint acid in his lordship's tone. So, he truly had believed in a future with Miss Montague, for himself. Well, didn't that, in its own way, support the match? "Thank you, Lord Delmore. I'm much obliged. One request." Crispin smiled. "Please don't make this public before I do. Miss Montague is as aware as I am of the likely opposition. I will need to choose my moment carefully."

"Perhaps when you carry off the art prize of the decade. When the public sees for themselves the qualities, not least beauty, of your muse, it will be entirely understandable why you've let your impulses get the better of you."

"That is how it will be regarded? When the public cannot base their judgement on her fine intellect? Indeed, *that* is what swayed me. Her beauty attracted me, but her beauty alone was not, to my mind, sufficient for me to gainsay my father. I believe Miss Montague has a mind that will be an asset to both of us."

"I hope your father will be so forward thinking." Grudgingly, Lord Delmore added, "Though truth be told, it was the same with me. She does have a remarkable mind and a sharp wit. An intoxicating combination." He raised his glass. "I hear the ladies returning now. Good luck, old fellow. May you navigate the potential pitfalls ahead with the greatest of ease. She will win your father over; I have no doubt. And that's all you need to see this thing through as you would like."

CHAPTER 19

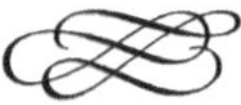

Only a day left before they were to return to London. For nearly one whole blissful week Faith and Crispin had spent almost all day together and, latterly, much of the night.

Her beloved worked at a feverish pace in front of his easel, sending her loving looks when he thought no one else was looking, and passing her notes and love gifts at every other opportunity. Faith had no shortage of tokens in both kind and in writing to attest to the intensity of Mr Westaway's love. It thrilled her, and it filled her with a deep and satisfied sense of completeness. No one had loved her before. Not her mother or her father or any of the gentlemen she had ever met.

Crispin had his own reasons for keeping their relationship secret, and it suited Faith just fine. As she lay on the small iron bed they shared in the servant's attic far from anyone else, she went over her best course of action. Crispin had briefly mentioned elopement. It was, in Faith's mind, the best way forward. To be married in secret would guarantee her a passport to a trouble-free future. That she loved him with equal intensity was irrelevant in one respect; yet it was only for this reason she wanted to be certain of spending the rest of her life with him.

Mrs Gedge wanted to ruin him. Wanted to see his heart broken. Well, what could she do after Faith and he were bound together in the eyes of god and the law?

If she worried that Mrs Gedge would be vindictive, she tried to put those fears aside. Mrs Gedge had supported Faith for three years. Their monthly tea meetings had suggested a woman who was interested in furthering the prospects of her little protegee. Faith need only persuade Mrs Gedge that vengeance would hurt Faith in this regard more than it would Mr Westaway. Mrs Gedge had been a mother. She was a woman who knew how to love.

She would understand.

And if she didn't, Faith would be in Germany before Mrs Gedge ever learned the truth.

Now, as Faith sat at the dinner table opposite Crispin, Lady Vernon at her side, she couldn't wait for the old woman to withdraw for the evening and so give the young people complete freedom. Faith didn't care that the servants could not be unaware of what was happening. But this was a borrowed cottage. These were not Crispin's servants.

"I expect you are anxious for the next few days to be over." Lady Vernon's nasal tones cut into the silence as the parlourmaid removed the main course and brought in dessert. "What will you do with your winnings if you are indeed the chosen one, Mr Westaway?"

"I dare not hope to think I will be."

"No need to be so modest. Everyone agreed that your skills were far superior to your two competitors. If you win, you will be a rich man." She looked meaningfully between Faith and Crispin. "You will be free to do as you choose, surely?"

Faith blushed at the lack of subtlety, and also the fact that Lady Vernon was fishing for words Faith did not wish Crispin to offer. The last person she wanted to know that she already had a marriage offer was Lady Vernon.

"My father is always my first consideration, Lady Vernon."

Faith let out a slow breath. That was the answer she'd hoped for.

And she told him so when they met each other in their attic room.

"We will get married in secret, darling," she whispered as she stepped into his arms. "Like you suggested. I don't want my parents knowing beforehand and coming to you for handouts. They will, you know. Far better that we slip away quietly to Germany with no one the wiser. We can tell them when…."

He tapped her on the nose, then kissed her on the lips as he tightened his hold on her in the centre of the small room.

"I want my father to be there to bless us and to congratulate us with true joy," said Crispin.

Faith stepped out of his embrace and looked at him, puzzled. "You've changed your mind? Why?"

The need for Crispin to proceed in secrecy struck her anew. She'd realised, with frightening clarity, that the love letters and the marriage proposal she had in writing must never fall into Mrs Gedge's hands. Faith must appear to her to have failed. Lady Vernon had no idea to what extent it had progressed. She'd witnessed the occasional longing look, that was all.

She tried not to appear as anxious as she was.

Faith's bargain was predicated on the exchange of such evidence for a fee of five hundred pounds. Well, she would forgo the money. Of course, she would have to if she were to gain the loving future that was more important now than anything.

Crispin stroked her cheek. "My father's approval is important to me. I want him to love you as I do."

Faith sent him a wry look and he smiled back, adding, "Perhaps not quite as I do, but I know he'll appreciate the qualities I've recognised in you. I do believe he would come to see that your intelligence is an attribute that trumps the fact you have no dowry."

"Or illustrious connections. Your father will not want you allying yourself with a nobody, no matter how quick-witted she might be, or indeed how independent you might become through winning an illustrious art prize. No Crispin, there's not enough time. Please, my darling. We must marry quickly. And in secret."

Still, he demurred. "Faith, sweeting, we can have it all—the society wedding that gives you the acceptance you need and deserve. I would far rather that than have us sneaking away with whispers and innuendo."

"Oh Crispin, we may *have* to get married in a hurry."

Faith put a hand to her belly, though she was reasonably confident the precautions she'd been taught precluded any possibility that she might have conceived during their week of passionate couplings. Ten times. And now she was about to initiate another. Her body was on fire, and although she was disquieted by his talk, she was also confident she could persuade him of what was required.

She rested her cheek against his chest and raised her hand upwards to cup his cheek. "Tomorrow your painting will be delivered, and the following night it will be judged. You will win, Crispin, for it is a rare show of true talent. It's not because I'm biased that I say it."

And it wasn't. She truly was proud of his talent. He was a gifted painter, and it was wrong that his father didn't recognise how far his son could go in this direction if he didn't force Crispin to follow the diplomatic path to the exclusion of his art.

But Crispin wasn't attending to any talk of talent. Understanding, and now full of remorse, he kissed her full on the mouth then regarded her with an intent look. "I'm a fool for not taking more account of the lack of time we may have," he murmured. "I thought of it at the beginning when I was determined to marry you, and any consequence was a boon. But since your acceptance of my proposal, I've thought only of how to make this marriage one in which you are given the respect and public acknowledgement you deserve. An elopement is a shabby, shameful thing, and I'd do anything to prevent you enduring the disgrace of it."

"And I would do anything to be married to you at the earliest possibility. There'll be a whole lifetime to prove the naysayers wrong."

Trailing a line of kisses across her brow, he murmured, "You want to make your family proud, I know you do, despite you warning me they'll be at the gates looking for handouts. I want my father to be proud. Let me look after this, Faith." He kissed her nose. "Trust me, Faith. I'll make sure our future is wonderful; gilded with hope and possibility."

His words filled her with foreboding as his lips found hers, and when she shivered at the dangers he knew nothing about, he thought she was angling for a closer connection.

So he whisked her into his arms and lay her on the bed, joining her there where they quickly divested each other of their clothes.

And Faith put all thoughts of what might go wrong out of her mind, because for too long she'd been weighed down by fears of the future, and for just for these wonderful few days, she wanted to believe that the man who returned her love would be able to navigate the terrain.

Of course, with the clear light of a new day, she was again mistress of her own destiny, and the only person who could possibly know the extent of the perils that lay ahead. Faith knew only one course was possible—elopement.

Crispin was nervous as he oversaw the loading of his painting paraphernalia in the trunk that was strapped to the back of the carriage that would take it to the train station. Faith wanted to squeeze his hand in comfort, but Lady Vernon's brooding presence precluded that. Faith was not relishing the thought of being confined with the old woman for the journey to London. Crispin would follow an hour later, as suggested by Faith, to preclude the possibility of their feelings for one another becoming too apparent.

Tonight, they'd see one another amidst the throng of artists and an eager and appreciative public. Faith hoped she'd be well received as the innocent muse, and to secure a modicum of respect and acceptance in advance of a marriage announcement.

So, Crispin accompanied them in the carriage only as far as the station for his intention was to proceed into town where he maintained he had business with a solicitor.

When they reached the station, Lady Vernon boarded first and found an empty carriage while the footman loaded their trunk. As Faith prepared to join her, the steam rising about her in such a fog tempted her to take the risk of a quick kiss, though of course such fancies were swept away by common sense. Faith had lost her heart, but she'd not lost the clear-sightedness that ensured her wits were undimmed by emotion when it was necessary.

"In a few hours, you may be declared the winner of a prestigious prize and find yourself in possession of a fortune, Crispin. Will you still want me?"

"All aboard!" The station porter walked down the platform, slamming doors. He'd reach Faith in a moment, and she hung on his answer.

"This is no infatuation, if that's what you fear," he told her. His eyes were warm. "I want to shout out to the world that I am so very proud to make you my wife. We *will* do this properly, Faith."

"I'm afraid," she said, admitting the truth. "I want us to be married soon and quietly. If you truly love me, you'll forget about the fanfare, Crispin."

The previous night she had tossed and turned fearing for the consequences of doing things the way Crispin would have them done.

"Please, Crispin. I love you; I adore you." Again, she touched her belly. "What if you are caught up by the consequences of tonight, and our wedding can only take place six weeks hence. Or, what if your father tells you he'll give us your blessing only if you wait six *months*. Yes, it may be with all the acceptance and pomp and ceremony *you* would like, but what about me? Think of the shame I would bear if I were to bear a child less than eight months after our wedding day?"

The guard was nearly upon them. She gripped his hand, her expression pleading.

Finally, he nodded. "All right, we will marry secretly, and we will plan a second ceremony as if we'd never contracted the first. Does that satisfy you?"

"Train's leaving, Miss. Please board now."

Faith smiled her relief at him. She'd not thought of such a possibility, but it was eminently pleasing—clearly, to both of them. She stepped inside the train, and Crispin gripped her hand briefly through the door that was about to be slammed shut. "I'll organise a special licence. We shall marry in secret tomorrow, or if it can't be managed, the day after. Does that satisfy you? We will marry at the earliest because I love you and I want to prove it."

Faith exhaled on a sigh of relief. "You've proved that a thousand-fold. Thank you, Crispin," she whispered, reaching forward to touch his shoulder before the conductor slammed the door. "I look forward to seeing you tonight. I think it will be a night to remember."

"LOVER'S PARTING?" LADY VERNON ASKED AS FAITH SEATED HERSELF.

Faith sent her an ingenuous look. "Mr Westaway and I have become friends, as is to be expected under such unusual circumstances. He cannot marry me, Lady Vernon; I explained that before."

"We all knew that from the beginning. Your job was to entice him into changing his mind. What progress on that front? Mrs Gedge will want to know. She's parting with a lot of money to ensure matters progress as she would have them."

"Mrs Gedge must have a very cold heart if she's spent three years plotting vengeance against the poor man." Faith couldn't help herself. "But *I've* not exactly been steeped in softness thanks to my less than tender upbringing. I want my freedom too. And I shall have it." She sent Lady Vernon a level look. "You are my minder, not my confessor. Nevertheless, you may rest assured we will all get what we want; you included."

A BEAUTIFUL GOWN BEYOND FAITH'S IMAGINATION LAY UPON HER BED when she returned to her lodgings at Lady Vernon's, for it had been deemed too risky to return to Madame Chambon's while she was in the public eye.

"Courtesy of Madame Gedge. She says it's her parting gift…on top of the five hundred pounds she anticipates handing over before too long."

Faith liked the fact Lady Vernon seemed uncertain about the

undercurrents between Faith and Mr Westaway. Well, she'd not enlighten her. The old cow could claim her reward, and Faith hoped never to hear from her again once she and Crispin had left the country.

All they needed to do was slip away to marry in secret, and then they'd be in Germany before anyone thought to look for them. There, Faith had no doubt she could cement her new husband's affections to make up for the untruths he believed about her.

"It's beautiful." And it was. Made of midnight-blue silk with a froth of a train decorated with pink bows and an abundance of velvet flowers, it showed off her hourglass figure to perfection. Once she'd bathed, Lady Vernon's personal dresser helped Faith step into the skirt that was held close to the front of her body by tapes, pushing the fullness all to the back. Low cut with a décolletage trimmed with tiny pink silk roses it was a fairytale dress.

Little wonder she garnered so much attention when she was admitted to the Royal Society of Artists' gala.

Her painting was already on display together with the others, but Crispin's superior talent was apparent. Faith could hear it in the whispers around her. Whispers that included reference to her bountiful assets, also. Tonight was the culmination, almost, of her greatest desires, and her heart felt very full. Crispin would be honoured, as was his due, but she, too, was worthy of honour in her own right. Even if it were only for her beauty, Faith was still proud to claim it. The penniless daughter of a violent, alcoholic farm worker had come far indeed.

But how much further she intended to go. She would extirpate her roots; her past. The time would come when Crispin would ask more about her family, but she would navigate that difficulty as she was navigating tonight. Nothing was insurmountable. If necessary, she could pretend a different family. She'd find the right help. She'd claim her parents wanted nothing to do with her. That she'd been unable to admit such a thing when she first met him, for how could any man marry a girl disowned by her parents?

"Miss Montague, Sir Albion is asking for you." There was Crispin, smiling, encircled by admirers, and now drawing her and Lady Vernon into a gathering that included the patron of the society and his wife. They welcomed her warmly, reiterating their earlier words.

"You have succeeded very nicely in unleashing brilliance from this gentleman's brush, Miss Montague," said Lady McKinley. "There is no doubt about tonight's winner." She waved her hand at the three paintings lined up side by side on the dais. "Perhaps you will not go to Germany after all, Mr Westaway."

Faith glanced at her husband-to-be. Much as she wanted him to have the opportunity to devote his career to his art, Germany factored importantly in her plans.

"A shame your father is not here to see this." Sir Albion's nod encompassed the gathering as a whole. "He would understand that the public admires an artist in the same way they appreciate their need for a clever diplomat."

"I hope my father will come to understand that, too. But alas, he is not here, and I have not yet won the prize."

It was only a matter of time, of course. Only a matter of time before a hush fell upon the crowd as Sir Albion ascended to the dais and made his pronouncement.

It was about to become real. All that Crispin had dreamed of would come to pass. All that Faith had ever dreamed of would come to pass also. She had to cling to that belief, or she'd have nothing. Crispin loved her, and she loved him. They were young, good for each other, and free to marry.

Her thoughts had been running over this like a mantra, when she became conscious of the buzz that swept through the room. She felt a surreptitious squeeze of her bare arm, above her long gloves and below the puff of her silk and chiffon sleeve as Crispin passed her, signalling his excitement, his connection with her before cutting a swathe through the room on his way towards the stage.

Dear lord, he'd been declared the winner.

People congratulated him, and Faith felt an empathetic surge of excitement to see him so recognised. As she stared at the scene from the centre of the room, amidst strangers and well-wishers, the lovers and scions of the art world, and society as a whole, a feeling of the most intense desire swept over her. She wanted to belong.

She wanted Crispin more, but to belong to Crispin, to have his heart truly and completely, she *needed* to belong and be accepted by this world.

Crispin addressed a hushed crowd. Proudly, Faith heard him convey his thanks for the support he'd received; his pleasure at the fact the crowd endorsed the judge's choice and finally, with the room erupting into polite but enthusiastic congratulations, she intercepted his look from over the top of the heads of the throng.

Brief, but intense. Yes, they would marry in secret tomorrow. Nothing could stand in the way of their love. And when he boarded the packet for the first leg of his journey to Germany, she would be there too. Unobtrusive and veiled, certainly, but discretion was essential if they were not to be hounded by those who believed a penniless debutante was not good enough for him. No, nothing would part her from his side.

"I couldn't have done it without you, Miss Montague." Once back at her side, he bowed over her gloved hand and kissed the back of it. Sensation speared her like a physical lance.

"I just did my job, Mr Westaway." She smiled and was about to say more when they were interrupted by a familiar American accent, mid-Atlantic, as Faith had heard it described. "Please tell me how you would define that, Miss Montague. Your job, I mean."

Miss Eaves arrived in their midst, her expression eager as she held a pencil poised above a notebook. Her gown was plain but expensive; however, she clearly had a penchant for incorporating birds in her headwear for tonight six ostrich plumes waved in her coiffure as she moved.

"I hope you don't mind my interrupting, but my uncle has tasked me with writing up the story of tonight's win for Artist's Magazine."

Faith glanced at Crispin who seemed unperturbed, still buoyed up by his success. "Of course not. It's a great honour and a great surprise, both to receive the prize and to be mentioned in such an illustrious publication. But your question was directed at Miss Montague."

Having been given licence to speak freely, Faith said, "I perfected the art of stillness sufficiently for Mr Westaway to recreate the fiction that I was floating, drowned, in a lake. Other than getting a little cold and bored at times, I really didn't do anything."

Miss Eaves scoffed at this. "No need to be so self-effacing, Miss Montague. I'm sure the physical trials caused more irritation than cold and boredom. I'm here to write the *real* story. Once I've heard from you exactly how cold and bored and filled with discomfort you were, and then added how elated, or otherwise, you must feel now, I shall turn my full attention to Mr Westaway."

The young woman rolled her shoulders as if she couldn't wait to start scribbling, and Faith and Crispin shared a smile over her bent head once she'd scratched a few notes.

"Is this your first piece, Miss Eaves?"

Miss Eaves shook her head. "I've found a variety of pieces with which to fill the magazine over the past three weeks. But this is my first important piece. The size of the prize and the secrecy surrounding its benefactor has had the art world agog. Is that a word you English use in polite society?" She looked unperturbed, rushing on without waiting for an answer. "My uncle calls me brash and likes to edit my stories himself, but I'm the reporter on the ground. There aren't too many of us. Women, I mean, doing this kind of work, but the world is changing, and whereas a few years ago I'd have been a curiosity, now that is not the case. At least, not where I come from."

"I think things are slower to change in England," Faith murmured. "Traditions are strongly adhered to, including a woman's place." She stared at her toes. "A woman's respectability counts for more than her intelligence," she added, more to herself, though Miss Eaves picked up on this immediately.

"Oh, in America too, but there is much greater license and freedom from where I hail." Her pencil paused, and two blackbird-like eyes regarded Faith. "I've been fascinated by the difference in the way people think here, how people get ahead, what is accepted. Lord, but I wouldn't like to live my whole life in this country as the unmarried woman I am, keeping my head down, not being allowed to work.

Anyway, I'm not here to talk about me. Mr Westaway, please tell me what inspired you to choose the type of painting you did? I believe you received a bag of props and had to create something from that. What did you have to incorporate? Each painting is significantly different though yours stands out, naturally."

"Rose petals, Miss Eaves."

Faith saw his clouded brow, and recalled his discomfort when he'd been confronted with the crimson flowers. His discomfort had clearly grown when Lady Vernon had made her suggestions, but with water as an essential medium, it was only natural that the petals had been arranged to float about Faith's prone form.

When they were alone together later tonight, if it could be managed in secret, she'd quiz him about it. There was so much they each had to learn about the other. But she'd observed a multitude of men during her years at Madame Chambon's, and there was a sincerity about Crispin that was lacking in the many braggarts and pumped-up blades who'd crossed that threshold.

Crispin's warm smile enforced every hope she had for the success of their marriage. When Miss Eaves departed having written her piece, and Lady Vernon was occupied in conversation with Sir Albion and his acolytes, he trailed her to the alcove where she'd sought a modicum of privacy.

"I hoped you'd not be waylaid," she said. "Or, at least, want to talk to me enough that you'd fob off everyone else."

"No one else is important right now." His eyes looked black and full of wanting. Turning, he plucked a full glass of champagne from a passing waiter and replaced Faith's empty one. "Only you, Faith darling." His low murmur was like melted chocolate, and it filled Faith with an inner glow.

"Tell me how important I am," she whispered, taking a small sip of her drink and fixing him with a sly, challenging look over the rim of her glass. She'd angled herself so that she faced the window and her flirtatious manner would not be observed. They'd not have long to be alone together.

"I need you like the earth needs the rain, like the birds need the nectar, like…a blank canvas needs a story. You're mine, Faith. My story, my sustenance, my inspiration."

"Inspiration?" She cocked her head, loving his willingness to elaborate, conscious that too much longer alone together might be dangerous. But then, she'd been crucial to him carrying off the prize. People would understand their solidarity for now. They were a team.

They'd always be a team.

"You are good and pure and honest. That's what inspires me. You're unlike any woman I've ever met."

"I'm sure you've met many women just as good and pure and honest." That was true enough.

He shook his head. "You're different. You are without guile. I love that about you. I look at you, and I see someone who would defend principle to the end."

Faith held up her hand, uncomfortable now. "Crispin, it's easy to believe the best when you're—"

"In love?" He took her hand and kissed the back of it before Faith pulled it back quickly. She tried to speak but he said, "You think I've had too much to drink perhaps? You're afraid that people will observe us? Why? Because you're afraid of the future? We are destined to be together, Faith. And we will be."

"You sound confident. I hope you're right." Her heart felt very full, but also very heavy suddenly.

"We shall be married as soon as I can organise a special licence." Now that she considered it, his eyes did seem unusually bright.

"A special licence is what's needed to elope?" she queried. Three weeks was the earliest they could be married in the usual way after having the banns put up in their respective parishes. For Faith, this was entirely impractical, so she was relieved Crispin had not even considered that idea.

"When I leave for Germany in two weeks, it will be with you as my wife."

"But it would still be a secret?"

"Are you certain you don't want your parents to attend? Not even one of your sisters?"

Faith shook her head. "They'll petition you for money. Oh Crispin, you don't know my family. They're impoverished, and the only reason I was given a few weeks in London was because Papa had ideas I could snare a duke."

"So, you think he'd be disappointed you snared only me?"

Faith coloured. "His excitement would be mortifying. If you love me, you won't bring my family into it. Please, Crispin."

"I do love you and I'm marrying you, not your family. You're right; it would be best if my father knew nothing of it until time had passed and I'd cemented my reputation doing what's required in Germany."

"Ah, Mr Westaway, there you are! Lord Athlone is anxious to meet you. Miss Montague." The new arrival offered Faith a cursory nod before drawing Crispin away, but not before Faith had recognised the curiosity and assessment in his eyes.

Of course, everyone would be wondering what Faith was to Crispin, and any more time spent alone in corners would have tongues wagging, which she could do without when it came to exciting the undesired curiosity of Crispin's father, should it get back to him.

But in terms of reinforcing to Lady Vernon that Faith was making inroads into her task of winning Crispin's heart for Mrs Gedge's evil plans, it was ideal.

"Mr Westaway seemed reluctant to relinquish you in order to meet Lord Athlone."

"He loves me." Faith paused in the midst of pulling the pins from her hair and viewed Lady Vernon with interest in the reflection of the looking glass. "Madly, deeply, unreasonably." She smiled. "I have him," she added slowly. "Are you pleased? After all, you'll get your money now."

"My loyalty is towards Mrs Gedge. I was more concerned that her three-year investment in you should be adequately repaid. Her desire to see justice done through you is more important to me than the pin money I shall receive to compensate me for the dreary time I've had chaperoning you about the place." Lady Vernon smoothed her black skirts over her knees. "You have to break his heart now, of course. That is, once you've proved beyond a doubt that you do have his heart."

"A pile of letters. You didn't guess, did you?" Faith hugged herself. She wanted to pretend ingenuousness. It would be her defence. Lady Vernon mustn't know that Faith was secretly plotting to forgo her own payment in order to disappear from the country without trace.

Lady Vernon sent her a glance laced with suspicion. "And how will you break his heart? You never actually discussed that part, did you?"

Faith shrugged. "He wants to run away with me. I shall disappear. With my money. With the money Mrs Gedge has promised me, and that is my payment for working for her for three years with the end agreement being all or nothing." Faith shook her hair free and wandered to the window. She stared out at the sun. "Mrs Gedge will have all the evidence she needs. Mr Westaway is a very passionate correspondent." She sighed. "And I shall have my freedom. At last."

"You speak as if you've been under ball and chain, when most girls in your position could only dream of what you've had: a roof over your head, an education, fine clothes, an introduction to society, all so that you might know how to behave."

"Oh yes, and I'm very grateful. I've made the most of all that she has insisted it suits her to bestow upon me...*as her slave*."

She took a few steps into the centre of the room and presented her back to Lady Vernon so that she could help unlace her. It was good to treat the old termagant like a servant; the way she looked upon Faith.

"So, you have no gratitude for Mrs Gedge? None for taking you out of poverty and giving you the tools to prosper?"

"I'm grateful that I now have manners and know how to use a knife and fork properly. But not for the years I languished in a brothel where I was surrounded by nothing but misery." She closed her eyes. "Each night it was like listening to my potential punishment. The moans of the gentlemen; the pretended cries of ecstasy of the girls—my friends—before they'd weep their eyes out and tell me everything the next morning. It was a constant reminder that that was my fate if I should fail at my task. And now I am about to fulfil it; fulfil my destiny. It is a joyous moment."

Lady Vernon stared at Faith as she moved around to help her remove her gown.

"And you have no regrets?"

Faith raised her eyebrows. "Regrets? For gaining my freedom? Why, I am fashioned in your own image, Lady Vernon. My heart is made of stone."

Lady Vernon turned her with a light hand on her shoulders and smiled her first real smile. At least, that's what Faith thought it was until the woman said, "And so tonight I shall help you disappear, Faith, for of course that is the only way to fulfil Mrs Gedge's decree, which is what you've just told me you're in the process of doing."

Faith managed to smile. With every ounce of willpower, she kept her mouth steady and her voice even as she replied, "You'd really do that? Help me? Though, of course, when I have the money I'm owed, I can get as far away as I want."

"But he would find you, and that would not be pleasant for you. It would not further Mrs Gedge's aims. No, have no fear, Mrs Gedge knew you would succeed, and she has everything in hand. You will be spirited away to a safe house, just for a short time because, as you say, you've earned your freedom. But it will be necessary; I'm sure you'll agree. For everyone concerned."

Faith blinked, smiled, and blinked again. She took a few steps to the bed and sat down with as much grace as she could before Lady Vernon said, "Now, where are those love letters you've received from Mr Westaway?" She held out her hand. "Mrs Gedge will naturally want to see evidence though I could vouch for the truth. You don't think I've been as blind as I've pretended, do you?"

"I have them in my escritoire. I'll...fetch them for you in the morning. I'm very tired, you know. It has been an awfully big day."

"I think we should well get it over and done with, Faith. Give them to me now so that you might sleep in longer without troubling yourself over it in the morning." Lady Vernon's bright tone was so false

Faith felt like calling her out on it, but she could not afford to unleash even a suggestion of anger; not even a hint that she was feeling suddenly beleaguered and frightened and as far from being in control as she ever had.

She knew when she was beaten, so she forced herself to rise and go to the small writing desk in the corner of the room. They were in a bundle, tied up with red ribbon, and the very sight of them made her heart sing before it dropped like a stone to the pit of her stomach.

What did Mrs Gedge intend doing with her? Where would she take her? No, Faith had to be prepared. She wasn't going to go with anyone, anywhere. Except Crispin. She'd pledged her love to him, and to him she would be faithful until the end.

When she turned, having picked up the bundle with all the reverence that such true and honest sentiment deserved, Lady Vernon was standing right behind her, hand outstretched, a speculative look in her eye.

"Ah, just imagine..." Her own attitude was reverential as she took possession of the only testament to loving feeling Faith had ever been shown. But Faith couldn't snatch them back. She had to be so very careful to hide her feelings. And she managed, for it's what she'd been trained to do her entire life.

Lady Vernon scanned the pages. She chuckled. "So, he really did fall hard for you, Faith. You were so sly I wasn't quite sure what was happening behind my back. And behind closed bedchamber doors. I'm sure you put into practice, admirably, everything you've learned from all the harlots with whom you've associated these past years." She fingered the letters, stroking them as she spoke, while Faith battled the urge to fly at her, whisk them from her and scrape her across the face with catlike claws, if only she had them. Instead, she whispered, "That was unnecessary, Lady Vernon. It makes me wonder who, here, is the real lady."

CHAPTER 20

"You've done well, Faith."

Mrs Gedge smiled at Faith from across the table. Pots overflowing with luxuriant foliage and crystal chandeliers endowed the room with an opulence Faith found slightly overwhelming, in much the same way she'd been overwhelmed the first time Mrs Gedge had brought her to Claridges a little more than three years before.

"Not only have you blossomed into the great beauty I suspected you would become, but you also had the intelligence and cunning I saw in you when we made our acquaintance."

Faith smiled dutifully.

"Furthermore, you have conducted yourself with the grace and sophistication of the most well-brought-up debutante. And yet you've not allowed your fancies to get the better of you. No, you have shown that you have a will and determination as rigid as mine, and a heart that is just as hard." She leaned back in her chair and put the tips of her gloved hands together as she contemplated Faith. "So, are you excited to receive your reward?"

A little part of Faith's heart leaped at the prospect of an independent fortune. Five hundred pounds was beyond imaginable. She could set herself up for life with careful maintenance of such a sum. And then she could find Crispin, and this would be her dowry.

But that would not work anymore.

She'd chosen love over independence, and for that, she could afford no delays.

"Men hold the purse strings, and despite modern advances, a woman is still beholden to the males in her life for everything. Yet you, Faith, will call the shots, as they say in my country. I don't wonder you're excited. So very ready to break this man's heart and claim your reward? I wonder how you plan to do that, Faith? Lady Vernon says you've been playing your cards very close to your chest. Well, we shall talk about it in the morning. It's late." She pushed back her chair, signifying that their tête-à-tête was at an end.

"And Lady Vernon is waiting for you. She has a special surprise, too. After all, tomorrow is the beginning of a new chapter in all our lives.

Faith had no choice but to rise when Mrs Gedge did. She was aware of the flickering interest of the other diners, for there was undeniably something arresting about the wealthy American woman that went beyond her sumptuous dress. Her auburn hair, streaked with grey, gleamed beneath the bright lights of the restaurant, like the diamonds of her choker. Her ageing skin was lustrous, and her teeth were small and sharp and very white for a woman in her fifth decade.

"Mr Westaway is basking in the glory of his sudden notoriety. He is being recognised for what he's always wanted—his talent. If only his father would appreciate him for it, too, the young man could be no happier. But you are his compensation for the lack of family support. In you, he has found something to love that loves him back. He thinks you are his rock; his salvation." Mrs Gedge chuckled as they wandered towards the double doors. "My Constancia could have been all that and more to him, if only he had let her. If only he'd been prepared to accept her as one of his set. But men like Mr Westaway are leery of outsiders, Faith. Outsiders like my Constancia. Outsiders like you, although he doesn't know it yet."

Faith glanced from a table of diners staring at them to Mrs Gedge's granite-like eyes. The pieces were starting to fall into place. "You sponsored the prize so he had a greater height from which to fall?"

Mrs Gedge looked satisfied. "I did indeed, Faith. But surely you guessed that long ago. Just as you guessed at my motive."

"To punish Mr Westaway for not falling in love with Miss Constancia? Your daughter..." She remembered the headstrong, beautiful, often rude and thoughtless young woman she'd been employed to serve three years ago.

"I did, Faith. Mr Westaway and Constancia were the perfect couple. But he spurned her, you know. Belittled her because she was not of his set. Oh, on first appearances he's every young woman's dream: handsome and charming, in line for a title and a fortune, earnest and ardent, intelligent and artistic. But at heart, he's like all the young men of his kind—completely unwilling to accept an outsider like my Constancia, even with a grand fortune."

She hooked Faith's hand in her arm and patted it in a motherly fashion as they wove their way through the restaurant. The doors opened, and the evening breeze blew in to greet them. A conveyance would soon arrive for Mrs Gedge. She would have made arrangements for Faith too, and no doubt that meant being conveyed back to Lady Vernon's.

But Mrs Gedge's unkind assessment hung heavily in the air. This was not how Mr Westaway was. Faith knew that, yet how much did Mrs Gedge really know him?

"So, Faith, tomorrow you will attend the ceremony to publicly honour Mr Westaway. You will be the shining star at his right hand, and you will be fêted and lauded. But that is not the path to freedom, Faith. You're clever enough to know that. Only you have the power to chart your own course. And, Mr Westaway's affections will be transient. You know that, also. He will not forgive your past and your lie. No love is that strong." She looked fondly at Faith as her carriage drew up. "So that is why I am confident you're going to visit me for that very large cheque I am looking forward to giving you."

Mrs Gedge raised her chin and adjusted the fur stole about her neck, no doubt as much to block out the cold as to hide the crepey neck which gave away her age. She squeezed the tips of Faith's fingers lightly.

"Enjoy your last evening together with this young man. Make him wring every last drop of joy from it, too. I shall think of you both... and the happiness that my Constancia might have enjoyed had she not died."

A vision of the crimson-red rose petals drifted across Faith's mind. It was Mrs Gedge's way of calling forth the last image Mr Westaway would have had of her. She realised that now. In a bath filled with the blood that pumped from the wrists Miss Constancia had sliced.

On the top step outside the hotel as the wind ruffled her hair, Faith finally understood why Mrs Gedge wished for vengeance against Mr Westaway and why she'd chosen Faith.

It had been Faith who'd shown Miss Constancia Gedge the secret entrance to the guest room that Mr Westaway would be occupying that weekend. Faith's reward would be Miss Constancia's gold and garnet bracelet. Miss Constancia had promised.

Faith had known nothing of any of the guests that were spending the weekend with the Gedge's, though she'd suspected Miss Constancia had lost her heart to someone on the invitation list. Why else would she ask Faith to help her to slip into a gentleman's bedchamber wearing nothing but a diaphanous, cream silk peignoir?

Faith was unaware of the extent to which her mistress was unhinged by her romantic entanglement—her unrequited feelings.

But when Miss Constancia had been rejected, she'd killed herself in Mr Westaway's own bathtub.

Mrs Gedge was already heading towards the carriage, the doors of which had been opened by the footman standing at the bottom of the stairs.

"Come along now, Faith," Mrs Gedge exhorted her, and Faith moved forward reluctantly, realising the older woman wished her to take a seat inside the carriage beside her.

Patting Faith's hand as they rounded the street corner, and the horses set off at a more even trot, the older woman said upon a sigh, "You must have guessed by now the association between my daughter,

Constancia, and Mr Westaway. That I have sought to use you to avenge his poor treatment of her that led to her death."

Faith said nothing as she stared into the darkness, turning her head slightly to observe Mrs Gedge's sharp-featured profile as she listened to the crackling of a piece of parchment the American drew out of her reticule and held up as they passed the glow of a street lamp.

"I do not need to see to read the last words he penned to her." Her tone had grown tighter, and there was a bitterness in the delivery that had been absent in her former breezy manner towards Faith.

"I know your daughter's death was a great blow, Mrs Gedge." Faith chose her words with difficulty. "But she died by her own hand." It was not the moment to declare that Mr Westaway was blameless. Mrs Gedge's trust in Faith depended upon her belief that Faith would follow through with the long-held agreement between them.

"My daughter believed she could do nothing else when her honour had been compromised to such a degree, that public shame and humiliation were inevitable after Mr Westaway reneged on the pledge made between them."

Mrs Gedge held out the letter for Faith to take while she began to relay its contents.

"First, he told Constancia that she was charming, every man's dream, but that he had intended marrying his childhood sweetheart upon her twenty-first birthday, which was four years hence. That is, a few months from now, Faith."

Faith tensed at the sympathetic hand Mrs Gedge placed briefly on her thigh before she went on. "When Constancia and Mr Westaway first met, it was like a flame was ignited in both of their hearts. I never wanted Constancia to marry an Englishman. At least, not one who had relatively few expectations and no title, when I knew that with Constancia's fortune, she could have married a Rockefeller back in America or an earl at the very least."

She sent Faith a scornful look. "But Constancia was not one to listen to reason. No, not my beautiful, wilful girl. The two lovers had become far too inflamed by their feelings for one another and their intention to run away together before…I don't know what happened." Mrs Gedge's face was a mask of derision now. "Perhaps his ardour actually did cool overnight. Perhaps he was contacted by his childhood sweetheart and persuaded to adhere to a previous, more compelling promise which prompted this letter." Snatching it back from Faith, she tapped it with a gloved finger. "But his words scored grooves of the deepest despair in my Constancia, and she, who obviously knew how to gain secret entrance to his chamber, and you will attest to that, Faith, I know! went there to persuade him otherwise. When he remained unmoved, she did what a young woman will do who is compromised, embarrassed…ruined." The word was a whisper, a half hiss, a half choke, while Mrs Gedge's face was a mask of malice. "She slit her wrists in his bathtub. Yes, Mr Westaway returned to find his former lover dead…by *his* hand."

Faith didn't know what to say to this. She remembered that night as if it were written in indelible ink upon her brain. Mrs Gedge had come upon Faith picking up Miss Constancia's bracelet in the young lady's bedchamber and gazing at it with indecision. Miss Constancia had promised it to fifteen-year-old Faith in a hurried whisper if Faith could help her gain admittance to a young man's bedchamber. There had been several young men staying at the house for that particular Friday to Saturday. Faith had not seen Mr Westaway, for she surely would have remembered him.

Now, Mrs Gedge was declaring, not only that Mr Westaway had once been a faithless lover to her daughter, but that Mr Westaway had all but forced the young woman's hand in taking her own life.

"Why did you not tell me this before you instructed me on what I must do with regard to Mr Westaway?" she asked.

"I felt that if you held him in such aversion, the naturally occurring mutual interest might be inhibited. You knew, of course, that he must be sacrificed, and you were a willing accomplice in this."

Faith hated knowing this was true. As much as she hated being so receptive to the woman's words, right now. A fire was raging in her breast. Had Mr Westaway really seduced and then abandoned an innocent young woman?

"So, Faith, I cannot have a similar fate befalling you, can I?" Her tone was concerned. "Not the girl I've nurtured all these years. My own proxy daughter."

Faith blinked. This was hardly what she supposed Mrs Gedge considered her. Mrs Gedge might have paid for an education, a wardrobe of fine clothes, and a roof over her head, but that had all been for her own self-interest. She'd never made a secret, from the beginning, that Faith was nothing more to her than a means to an end—a method of betrayal.

The way Mrs Gedge now laid out the supposed facts was far more disturbing than Faith might ever have thought.

If she'd truly thought about it at all.

THEY WERE OUTSIDE LADY VERNON'S LODGINGS NOW, AND THE DOOR to the old dowager's house was being opened by a servant. Light spilled over the portico as Faith was helped to disembark, swishing her pink and black swathed skirts behind her.

She wondered what she'd wear when, tomorrow, Faith stepped out on Mr Westaway's arm to a no-doubt rapturous welcome from an adoring public.

Would she quiz him about the letter? About everything Mrs Gedge had told her surrounding his relationship with Miss Constancia? Or would she follow through with their own escape plan, trusting that this time Crispin really was in love with her, and that he would be waiting when it was time for them to slip away? What of this childhood sweetheart? Was she still lurking in the wings? Or was she a figure of Mrs Gedge's imagination?

Yet, she had seen the letter briefly, when there was enough light to persuade her that it was Crispin's handwriting. And she had read the sentence that mentioned Constancia.

Faith's heart was heavy, and her mind was in turmoil as she climbed under the covers of her bed that night.

But as she drifted off to sleep, she was comforted to recall the light in Crispin's eyes when he had bid her farewell. And all the other times when he'd gazed upon her with a look that was so real and so intense, she could not entertain a shadow of doubt that he truly loved her and meant every promise he'd ever made.

Well, tomorrow he would have to make one final pledge for her to believe him. If he truly loved her, he would not promise to run away with her only to then leave her in the lurch.

If he agreed to run away with her in order to be secretly married before he departed for Germany, she'd know his heart was true.

CHAPTER 21

"Mrs Gedge organised for me to wear this?" Faith stared at the exquisite white and silver gown laid out on the bed in her chamber in Lady Vernon's house, adorned with swathes of white velvet bows, and compared it to the plain finery she'd worn previously. Wondered, also, if she'd have to give it back.

But Lady Vernon, who was smiling for a change, said, "Mrs Gedge recognises when a job has been well done. This is your reward. To step out in style so you can compete with the most well-endowed heiresses. Mr Westaway won't be able to keep his eyes off you. Or his hands." She sent Faith a beady look. "No doubt he'll find a way to spirit you away into a back room for a short while. And no doubt you'll relish the opportunity."

Lady Vernon's mind was like a gutter, Faith decided, though refrained from saying so.

"It's your chance to entrench what he'll miss for the rest of his life. For you will leave him shortly afterwards, and he will forever wonder why. You will break his heart."

"While I go on to enjoy the happiness that is my reward, bolstered by a handsome cheque from Mrs Gedge? It's a fair exchange." Faith tried to summon enthusiasm as her mind whirled over how she might make her own escape.

"After tonight, when he is happily thinking of your glorious years ahead together, you will be spirited away to somewhere he can't find you." Lady Vernon chuckled at Faith's blank look and traced a fingertip reverentially down the front of the gown upon the bed. "Ah, I wore a gown such as this, once. Many years ago." Her expression softened. "It earned me a marriage proposal, too." She looked up at Faith. "You surely didn't think we'd simply abandon you, my dear girl. After all you've done for us and knowing that Mr Westaway has no intention of keeping true to any pledges he might have made you. He would not have followed through. Indeed, he would not. We are looking after you, as you deserve, and we have a place for you to hide while poor Mr Westaway wonders what has become of you." She straightened and clapped her hands. In an instant, her dresser had materialised, and Lady Vernon put her hand on the doorknob.

"You will be a sight for sore eyes, my dear. Tonight will be a special night, indeed."

"One could tell she was a beauty when she was floating in that lake wearing what might be mistaken for a nightdress, but look at her now."

The chuckle that followed the young reporter's comment was the first distinct piece of conversation Faith heard as she passed in a seeming daze through the packed reception hall.

Crispin disengaged himself from his conversation with Miss Eaves and Sir Albion, intercepting Faith a few feet away.

For a second, they halted and stared at one another while the crowd pulsed around them.

"I have never seen a woman as stunning as you look tonight," he whispered, his eyes raking her with unbridled admiration. "And all too soon I have to give you up to all the other people who want to similarly compliment you and be seen with the latest toast to London town."

Faith glanced about her and saw they were garnering a good deal of interest and that his words were true. If they were ever to succeed in slipping away together, she'd better not allow him to be too singular in his attentions.

"People are looking," she whispered. "Oh Crispin, we won't have a moment to ourselves this evening, and I'd so wanted to talk to you." Her chest tightened, and the knot of worry grew.

"And I to you, my dearest. We must get married before I leave for Germany. You are so right, and I've been caught up in this...frenzy, fielding probing questions from father who is hardly delighted, I'm afraid. He threatens to come down to London before I depart for Germany when that had not been the plan." He glanced about him, his frown creased. The reception hall was a sumptuous location for an event like this, but there were no antechambers where they might be private.

Faith saw Sir Albion's wife turn from her conversation with her husband. She was bearing down on her, when Crispin said in a rushed whisper, "Your chaperone seemed only too happy to give us licence to be alone together, before. Is it possible?"

His words trailed off and Faith tugged his sleeve, urging him to finish his sentence. The suggestion had to come from Crispin. Faith could not be seen to be too desperate.

He raked back his hair, smiled at the advancing woman and whispered, "There is an inn not far from here that I know can be accessed from a side street so that you might be completely unobserved in entering. The Green Whistle. Could you possibly meet me there when tonight's proceedings are finished?"

"Do you mean...we'd run away together, tonight, Crispin?" She was fairly certain he didn't mean this, but he needed to give her some idea of his plans on the timing of their elopement.

"I'm not in a position to do that yet, my darling. One more day, and everything will be organised to my satisfaction."

"What is so important to organise tomorrow?"

"I have interviews; my photograph will be taken, and there are many wonderful things that will happen to entrench my reputation as an artist that have been planned for tomorrow. Oh Faith, you have no idea." His voice caught with emotion, and Faith understood the enormity of achieving one's life's ambition. Wasn't she within a hair's breadth of achieving hers?

Yet…

"I'm sorry, but we can't do it tonight, Faith." Concern wiped away his ebullience, and he leaned forward slightly. "It's too soon, though you surely can't imagine I'm prevaricating because I'm not sincere."

She shook her head, though she wasn't sure what to think. "I shall be at The Green Whistle later tonight. Somehow, I'll contrive it."

"Tell the servant who lets you in that you have room bespoken in the name of Mrs Emily Hardwicke." He glanced at her hands as if he would whisk them up and kiss them with an ardour to match that that was in his voice.

And then Lady Vernon was upon them; her gushing praise of Crispin's prodigious talent bringing their conversation to an end.

THE SOIREE SEEMED TO LAST FOREVER, WHILE FAITH DID HER BEST TO conduct herself appropriately. She was a shy debutante with a modicum of intelligence, as far as the rest of the world was concerned, and her efforts to project that image were aided by Lady Vernon, who made an apparent attempt to draw Faith out of her shyness.

"Answer Miss Eaves's question, Faith dearest," she said with contrived gentleness on one occasion when Faith was faced with a volley of queries on her impressions of London.

"It can feel overwhelming to a country girl," Faith said, glancing at Crispin on the other side of the room, in earnest discussion with a group of gentlemen. Her body throbbed at the thought of being alone with him in just a couple of short hours.

"And you have brothers and sisters, I gather. A few of them. What do they think of your success? What a shame they could not be here." Miss Eaves's pencil sped across the page.

"Everything happened so fast with the announcement of Mr Westaway winning such a grand prize they did not have time to make the journey." Faith was careful to avoid mentioning anything that might indicate even the location of her family. They were sunk in rusticity and never heard the London news until the greatest events were at least a month old. They certainly would make no connection between their Faith and the glorious creature she'd become.

The gathering began to disperse towards midnight, and Lady Vernon took Faith's arm, drawing her towards the door after they'd said their farewells.

"You have arranged a final assignation? The moment to cement what you are to him? To exact the greatest revenge when you are whisked away forever tomorrow?" Her beady eyes roamed over Faith's expression as if she were looking for guile. She gave Faith's wrist a squeeze. "Ah, but I'm sorry that it had to end this way though there really was no other, was there? The young man is enjoying his greatest moment of glory, and your secret visit to him will fill his heart with triumphant joy. He thinks he is on the cusp of life, the pinnacle of attainment, but that is how Mrs Gedge planned it. There is no more acute suffering than to have reached such dizzy heights before such a crushing fall."

Foreboding sliced through Faith. Was this really all Mrs Gedge had planned for Crispin? Was the extent of her loathing for him so great that destroying his happiness was her only plan? Or did she intend Crispin's descent to be an even greater one?

She forced a smile. "He will be distraught," she murmured. "For he loves me greatly. I have done everything Mrs Gedge would have me do. He is enslaved."

She had to believe that.

For if she couldn't count on the security of his love, she had nothing.

But in the private room at The Green Whistle, Crispin's ardour and sincerity could not be in doubt. Instead of swooping upon her with words of enthusiasm as to the astonishing reception he'd received that evening, his words were all for her.

"I couldn't have done it without you, Faith! You were the most glittering star in the firmament, my exquisite girl." He swept her into his embrace and covered her face and neck in kisses. "Because of you, I'm where I've always wanted to be in life. My work…my painting has been more important to me than anything. That is, until I met you." He cupped her face and stared into her eyes. "You think I'm not sincere about running away with you?" He dropped his voice. "We both have good reason to marry in secret, though I believe mine is greater." Then a smile tugged at his mouth. "I don't care about your family hounding me for what I can do for them, financially or otherwise, for I would gladly do it. I would do anything that would please you, Faith. But my father would put everything in my way to prevent me marrying you, Faith, and that's the truth. He's always wanted me to marry the daughter of his best friend, our neighbour, and there was a time when I thought I could do it. But my heart was not engaged."

"And the young lady? Is she in expectation of a marriage proposal?"

"No. We've known one another since we were children, and a match between us was once considered desirable by our parents. I'm sure she's as relieved as I am that the idea has not been mentioned for several years."

"So, there've been no other young ladies who've…entranced you?"

Crispin laughed and set her at arm's length. "I suppose you need to get the full measure of me before you make your final commitment to becoming my wife. All right—the truth…" His expression was suddenly serious. It was as if all the joy had drained out of him.

"Oh Crispin, there has!" Faith cried, but he pulled her back into his arms, shaking his head, fiercely.

"There was a young lady with whom you might say I was unwillingly involved a few years ago." He hesitated.

Lord, was he referring to Miss Gedge? Faith froze in his arms and willed him to go on without prompting questions that might seem odd to him.

But he seemed inclined to talk.

"She was a lovely girl. Bright, golden hair, a little like yours though she had not your serenity, your beauty. In fact, there was nothing serene about her. She was determined to make a catch, and she was… what is the term? Brash?"

"So, not a shy and sweet young thing from the provinces."

"Oh no, she was an American heiress looking for a title. She could have done better than me. Her mother hoped she would. But she fell for me, and it took very little on my part to make her believe we were destined to be together forever."

"So, you gave her hope?"

"Oh Faith, you know I'm not like that. I never believed I did at the time. But then she started writing me passionate love letters. I didn't know what to do. I told her that I was going to marry my childhood sweetheart. That my father had arranged it years ago, and this is how matters went in our world. I tried to make it less wounding and put the blame on me, but she was persistent."

Faith felt him shrinking away from her until he gently extricated himself from their embrace and went to the window. Softly, he said, "She killed herself because of me. You need to know that, Faith."

Faith ran to him and wrapped her arms around him, more joyful than she could show, for she believed he was nothing but truthful in his portrayal of the affair with Miss Constancia Gedge. It all made complete sense, now.

"If it's so painful to you, please, say nothing more, Crispin." She squeezed him tight and Crispin kissed the top of her head, tilting up her face to say with concern, "You're crying, Faith. What is it?"

"I haven't been entirely truthful with you, Crispin, and if you truly love me enough to want to run away with me, then I need to tell you something."

She felt him freeze, before the inevitable thaw, because of course he loved her, and that meant he trusted her…

Only, would he still love her when she had come to the end of her confession?

"What is it you want to tell me, Faith?"

The tone was encouraging, loving still, but for how much longer?

She took a breath, struggling for the truth she owed him. "I'm more than just a penniless debutante looking to make a good match."

He registered this with a squeeze and a murmur. "No, you're so much more than that, Faith. Of course, I know it."

She heard the rattle of a wagon on the cobbled street below the window and waited for silence. "My family origins are obscure. Far more obscure than I've led you to believe. Yes, I have nine brothers and sisters, and parents who will indeed touch you for every penny you might have and that's because they have nothing. They're yeoman, country stock. Some would call them peasants, and I would be one of them had it not been for a rich benefactress who gave me an education when I was in service."

She pulled away and looked at him, tortured by the extent of what she'd divulged to no one else. What would he think, not only in view of the fact he'd been lied to, but that she was so very humble?

He looked surprised. His frown and the way he was chewing his bottom lip were not signs she liked.

"You lied to me, Faith? About this? About your family?"

Faith twisted her hands together. Oh lord, if he were upset about her lying about this, how would he react to everything else?

Trying not to cry, she whispered, "When I got the opportunity to be your model; when Lady Vernon persuaded you to paint me, I never thought it would lead to this. I had the right credentials for that. For an artist's model. I could be silent; I could be enigmatic. What did it matter what else I was or wasn't? You'd made it so very clear that even if I'd had the slightly more elevated background I'd told you I had, I still could not be considered suitable in your father's eyes, and therefore not in yours." She pulled her cloak about her shoulders and began to pace. Would he send her away? She thought she'd die of a broken heart if he did. Quietly, she went on, "I didn't trouble myself about telling you the truth, because I imagined that if I were to be given more work for other painters my real background would play against me. But then I fell in love with you, Crispin, and you loved me back. I pressed you into showing your real feelings, and then pressed you even more to run away with me."

Leaning against the wall, she dropped her head. "I don't expect that, now. I'm not here to beg you to run away with me because the truth changes everything. I've lied to you, and I am not the woman you thought me."

A barking dog outside; a quarrel between a couple on the pavement, and the crackling fire were the only sounds as Faith waited for Crispin's response. When she glanced at him, his sloped shoulders and bent head as she stared into the flames suggested he was as deeply aggrieved as any man could be.

But when he turned suddenly to face her, there was a glow in his expression that was so at odds with the dire scenario Faith had conjured up, that her heart leapt with hope.

"Do you love me, Faith?"

She clenched her fists. "More than I love anything on this earth." And it was the truth.

"And you would marry me if *I* had nothing? Nothing, that is, other than prospects. I mean, would you love me if I were disowned, for example? If my father cut me out of his will?"

Faith hadn't considered this possibility, but it honestly didn't matter for the fact was, she would. She'd grown up with nothing, and while her expectations had been altered by the events of the past three years, she didn't suppose Crispin meant that living in a hovel was a likely outcome.

Nevertheless, she'd do even that, if she had to.

But she said, "As long as you had enough to feed me...and our family, it would be enough for me."

Tensely, she waited.

Then in two long strides, Crispin was holding her tightly in his arms, and his mouth was on hers as he communicated so very thoroughly the extent of his love.

CHAPTER 22

He had nearly everything for which he'd ever dreamed. His hard work, conducted for so long in secret, then put on hold while he obeyed his father's strictures, had now made him a sensation.

And his love for the woman who inspired his creative impulses, and filled him with joy and the greatest desire to protect her from anything at all unpleasant in the world, was returned.

So, when he received news that his father intended travelling to London the following day, Crispin should have felt in a strong position to defend his decision to pick up a brush and paint.

Unfortunately, he had every fear that his father would question at what cost to his real career this ten-day hiatus had taken.

As he directed his valet on what to pack in the trunk that would go ahead to Germany, his chief fear was that his father was about to burst into his townhouse in his usual bombastic manner and do his best to destroy his hopes and dreams.

He would not succeed. No, Lord Maxwell would not destroy Crispin's future happiness. Crispin's future was his own to decide.

Which was all the more reason to make tonight the night he whisked Faith off, so they could be secretly married in advance of whatever objections Lord Maxwell might have to his son's choice of wife.

It would not be a marriage that could be publicly disclosed.

Well, they were both in agreement on this point. They'd travel on the same packet, but not as husband and wife. Crispin would take up his posting, and in the weeks that followed, they'd contrive an excuse whereby she could be introduced as a suitable contender for his suit.

He'd been dismayed by her revelation; there was no doubt about that. She'd portrayed herself as someone she wasn't, and yet the essence of her was pure and true, and that's all that mattered to Crispin right now.

Now that he thought about it, perhaps it was better that she had divorced herself so completely from her peasant roots. She could pass as the finest lady in the land, and that's what was required if she were to be accepted by society as a diplomat's wife.

Besides, having such a fine actress might very well suit Crispin's purposes, he thought as he nodded for the first trunk to be sealed shut. It was pushed against the wall of his bedchamber and, like a dozen others currently stored in a spare bedchamber, it would travel ahead and be in situ when he reached the handsome dwelling in Leipzig that had been bespoken on his behalf.

Crispin moved about his room, staring at the familiar objects that made it so masculine. He imagined a lady's dressing table by the window; its mahogany surface littered with feminine objects. A silver-backed hairbrush like the one Crispin had already bought for Faith. A row of little bottles whose contents he couldn't begin to imagine though he could imagine the setting. He'd like to paint the beautiful Faith seated at her dressing table, having her hair done, perhaps.

A surge of great affection edged with desire made him straighten and try to cast his mind back to what he must do. The fact that Faith's apparent shyness concealed a sharp intelligence and keen observation powers might indeed make her the perfect helpmate.

He certainly had no doubts about the wisdom of marrying her. However, with so much to do in so little time, he had to put aside his desire to spend every moment possible in her arms.

"Benson, do you suppose my father will go riding before he gets in his carriage to come down to London and give me a verbal whipping?"

"That would depend if he wants to take the edge off his mood, sir."

Benson could be relied upon to be honest.

"And do you suppose this mood you speak of will be predominantly prideful or…not?"

Benson rose having secured the strap buckle. He gave the wooden trunk a firm pat for good measure.

"Knowing his lordship, sir, I'd say the latter were more likely. Not that it'll be of consequence, for soon you'll be departing for foreign shores, so there'll be little more that your father has to say that will greatly impact you, sir." He gave a short bow. "If that'll be all, sir."

"No, that is not all, Benson. I need your opinion on whether I will cut a more sartorial figure in the green or burgundy striped waistcoat."

"If you wish to impress the gentlemen, I would suggest the burgundy."

"And if it is not the gentlemen I wish to impress?"

Benson smiled a little. "Then I shall lay out the green waistcoat for you this evening, sir. What time will you be going out?"

This time it was Crispin's turn to smile. How could he not as he contemplated the happy outcome of this evening's wilful escapade—certainly wilful in his father's eyes. For the first time in a long while, he felt ridiculously confident that Faith would win over Lord Maxwell.

When the time was right.

"I shall leave here at eight this evening. Don't wait up for me." No, he and Faith would want a leisurely time to consummate the marriage-to-be that he had absolutely no qualms about contracting now.

"Very good, sir." Benson bowed and backed up a few steps to the doorway where Crispin was surprised to see Carter, the butler, hovering in the passageway before the older man moved on. Crispin moved back to the trunk, turning to glance back through the open door, for the two servants remained outside, apparently conferring with each other. He was on the point of returning to his work when his attention was caught by the expression on Carter's face.

Carter was the archetypal impassive retainer while Benson, the younger man, enjoyed a bit of levity.

There was no sign of levity on Benson's face now, however, as Carter whispered in his ear. In fact, in terms of disgust and horror, it very much resembled Carter's.

And that's when he noticed what had occasioned such altered behaviour as he straightened and took a few steps towards the door.

The two men had their heads bent over a newspaper.

"I think, sir, you ought to see this." Benson cleared his throat as he stalked past Crispin and placed the newspaper upon his writing desk.

The man couldn't seem to meet Crispin's eye and as Crispin moved forward, a great premonition sweeping away his initial perplexity as he glanced at the headline—*The Elaborate Ruse of the Painter's Muse.*

Dear God, someone had discovered the fact that Faith was not the penniless debutante society believed her to be. The truth was out, and now those well-upholstered society matrons who decided who was acceptable, would be conferring right now as to whether to allow a former servant into their rarefied domains.

He felt sick. Faith had so perfected her role as a well-brought-up lady, that she could have been accepted, without question, anyway.

And now this.

He put his hand over the newspaper article and looked at Benson. "I don't need to read it for she has told me of her past," he said gravely. "Nevertheless, I refuse to hold it against the lady, or to judge her harshly, though I've no doubt my father will."

Benson blinked. In fact, his mobile face betrayed such surprise at Crispin's words that Crispin was angered. He'd not thought the young Benson would be so easily shocked.

"I see you have your own opinion," he said, drawing back his shoulders. "Yet I would suggest you judge her over harshly when she is guilty of no more than your own sister."

This brought a sound of such apoplexy from both Benson and Carter that Crispin's ire was fairly whipped up, but before Crispin could speak, the young servant burst out, "With all due respect, my sister does not even know that…such establishments exist, and if she did, she'd hardly be one to step across the threshold—with all due respect, sir." Benson's nostrils flared and his colour heightened. "And considering your father's long-established enmity with Lord Harkom...well, I can't imagine what he's going to say!"

"What on earth are you talking about, Benson?" Crispin was more confused than angered by the young man's feisty response. "And what's Lord Harkom got to do with any of this?"

Crispin had no doubt Benson's sister had stepped across the threshold of many a dwelling as humble as the one in which Faith had been brought up.

And yet even as this thought registered, so too did a kernel of fear that he had missed a fundamental piece of what was under discussion.

Carter cleared his throat and tapped the newspaper. His bald pate was sweating. "I think, sir, that as you clearly have not read in its entirety the published facts, it is not my place to acquaint you with what will come as a great shock and perhaps disappointment." His Adam's apple bobbed up and down, and his breathing was laboured. He looked nervously at Benson who said, in halting tones, "Given the fact, sir, that I surmise the green waistcoat was to have been worn to impress the lady in question." His elegant finger tapped the newspaper article that Crispin now pulled more closely towards him, while he considered whether to reprimand Benson on such an appalling impudence as Benson went on, "I think we should perhaps retire and allow you to…digest what has recently come to light.

Clearly, Benson was outraged by the fact that Miss Montague had insinuated herself so thoroughly with the rich and titled.

But Lord Harkom?

Crispin had little liking for Harkom, whom he considered a devious, self-serving creature, and the fact that Faith's name had obviously become mixed up with his to the extent that it had made it into print, was deepening his concern.

"Like my sister I, myself, *naturally* have not stepped over the threshold of this...this..." his colour heightened "...Madame Chambon's, and nor am I suggesting that you know anyone who has, sir." He sent a pointed look at Crispin. "But that a...creature...who has been indentured to the woman who owns such an establishment, who has carried out her evil designs in order to entrap a good man such as yourself...should have insinuated herself into your good offices and become your muse, well, sir, I cannot bring myself to utter the extent of my horror and outrage." His shoulders rose and fell as he struggled to control his feelings while Crispin stared at the two men, confounded, as Benson went on, "But she has been exposed. She and Harkom will no longer be able to carry out the devious plan they no doubt were hatching to cause you ill. Yes, I would go so far as to suggest that you were her quarry from the very beginning, sir. In fact, it is Mr Carter's opinion that this was her very plan, hatched in concert with this...Madame Chambon *and* Lord Harkom, no less. Why, the photograph of the two of them together in that very house says all that needs to be said."

And indeed, after Crispin had pushed away Benson's hand in order to properly make out the photograph that went with the text so damningly summed up by his valet, a great pounding in his ears left him with a feeling akin to being shaken by a monstrously large and glossy cat whose meows of self-satisfied relish indicated his lowliness in the great order of things.

There was his Faith, wearing the simple gown she'd worn when he'd first met her those few short weeks ago, in the arms of a gentleman who looked as if he would like to devour her on the spot. It was little consolation that Faith was looking serious. As if she wanted to be elsewhere. Lord Harkom, as Crispin could now distinguish him, was leering, proprietorial. Like he'd come to the house—yes, Madame Chambon's nunnery—in expectation of securing a great conquest.

And he'd secured Faith.

"You may go now, Benson," Crispin said, tracing the picture with his forefinger, lingering on the damning title of the article which had been penned, he now saw, by Miss Eaves.

Meddling, interfering Miss Eaves, who'd come to London to establish her future at the expense of Crispin's.

The fact that Faith had been ruined in the process was, at this very moment, immaterial. For, in the intensity of this moment of discovery, the enormity of her crimes was laid so bare as to reveal the fact she could have had no real feelings for Crispin.

And that she probably never had.

THERE WAS ROOM FOR ONE MORE DRESS IN HER CARPETBAG. NOT THAT Faith had many that would be appropriate for the life she'd soon be living. How would the wife of a diplomat, a future British envoy, be expected to dress? Something modest would be appropriate in the interim, but after that?

Well, Faith was excellent at research. She'd researched everything that would make her beguiling and differently exciting in Mr Westaway's eyes. Fortunately, it hadn't been hard to find herself excited over international politics while she'd had to stop herself from overdosing on intrigue. The relationship between Germany and Great Britain at the moment was volatile, to say the least, and she was confident she could be a great asset to Crispin.

She could hear Lady Vernon issuing orders to a servant in the passage. Faith dropped in her tooth powder and brush, a thrill of excitement rippling through her. Lady Vernon planned to whisk Faith away later this evening, but by then, Faith would have been whisked away by someone far more exciting. Yes, Crispin had accepted the truth of her altered situation in his eyes. She'd told him the truth of her humble beginnings, and he had still accepted her.

"Mrs Gedge is looking forward to handing over the cheque you so deserve, Faith." Lady Vernon stood in the doorway looking like a smudge of something unpleasant, thought Faith as she glanced from the grey-pallored creature with her yellowing teeth, to the smooth line of her own fashionable princess-line pelisse.

"I'm sure she is. I've done her bidding thoroughly. Mr Westaway will be bereft." Faith's gaze didn't linger on Lady Vernon's face. She returned to her packing and wondered why Lady Vernon still lingered in the doorway. Was she Faith's gaoler now? Faith tried to keep her face impassive. If Lady Vernon wasn't going to let her out of her sight, then Faith would have to climb out of her bedchamber window in the middle of the night to escape. She would do whatever she had to.

"I believe you still have a few gowns and pieces to collect from Madame Chambon's."

Surprised, Faith looked up to see Lady Vernon studying her with interest. "I would be careful of crossing that threshold in daylight. Or any time, for that matter. Perhaps you should send for your possessions."

Faith pretended to consider the option. The term possessions really encompassed only a few trinkets and a ring given her by her grandmother. In total, they were worth very little, but they were all she had to remind her…of a past she wanted to forget.

The only reason she'd especially want to visit would be to say farewell to Charity. The only other real connection she'd made in her life was with Crispin.

He'd opened her heart and poured music into it. She'd become the person she'd always wanted to be: alive, interested, allowing her intelligence free rein.

However, if she were being allowed to leave the house alone to go to Madame Chambon's, it was greater good fortune than she could have hoped for.

"Yes, of course I'll be careful," she said. She glanced through the window at the sun dipping in the blue sky. Before nightfall, Faith would be out of here. Away from Lady Vernon and her life of pretence and subterfuge.

Soon she'd be with Crispin and, if he entertained any doubts, she'd prove to her new husband that a girl brought up in poverty truly could be worthy of a respected diplomat and a celebrated painter. She relished the challenge. She would be the best, most devoted, most educated wife he could wish for.

A little later, Faith stood up from her chair and faced Lady Vernon across the three feet of Aubusson carpet that separated them in the old lady's spartan townhouse.

"It's growing late. Perhaps I should make a quick visit to Madame Chambon's now." Her trunk was packed in her bedchamber, ready to be carried into the carriage that would be called later this evening to take her to Mrs Gedge's, and thence on to an unknown location for an unspecified waiting period. Faith hadn't asked too many questions for she'd never intended travelling that route.

Lady Vernon's change in plans, in that she was no longer visiting a friend and was now going to remain indoors, meant Faith would have to arrange to have her trunk collected later. She had a brush, a change of linen, and a few necessities in a small carpetbag so this would have to suffice.

"Send my regards to Madame Chambon." Lady Vernon looked up from her tatting. "And don't be too long, my girl."

Faith shook her head. This would be the last time she'd see Lady Vernon. And what a relief that was.

"Oh, do give her this now that I've finished with it. It might entertain her." Lady Vernon brandished a newspaper as Faith passed her chair. "Don't stay talking too long. Half an hour is the limit. You're to come right back, for at eleven o' clock tonight you're going on a different journey."

"Yes, Lady Vernon." Faith took the newspaper and hurried out of the room and up the stairs, snatching her carpetbag from her bed and shoving in the newspaper as she pushed aside the curtains and saw her hackney waiting in the cobbled street below.

Freedom.

It was exhilarating. Crispin would be pacing the floorboards at The Green Whistle at nine o' clock, as agreed. They'd parted with regret but excitement too, eager for the new adventure that awaited them both.

With the coins Lady Vernon had given her, Faith paid the driver and pulled her veil down over her face as she entered the premises through the back entrance. Her heart clutched as she remembered the last time she'd come here less than 48 hours before. The night of loving she and Crispin had shared had helped her survive the impatience to be with him.

"Crispin," she whispered, as she slipped through the open door and into what turned out to be an empty parlour.

She was too impatient to sit, so she went to the window and stared down at the traffic below. London had overwhelmed her when Mrs Gedge had brought her here as little more than a child. She'd grown used to it, though, and come to like the anonymity.

What would Germany be like? She couldn't wait to explore it with Crispin.

Catching sight of her reflection in the mirror above the mantelpiece, she saw the tenseness in her eyes. Little wonder. She'd put her future in Crispin's hands, and given up her opportunity to find independence through what Mrs Gedge would have been willing to pay her had she chosen a path of revenge rather than love.

The clock on the landing struck the half hour.

Where was Crispin?

Worry niggled at her as she walked restlessly to the window and back. She'd seek occupation in tidying her hair perhaps. Scrabbling in her carpetbag for the ivory comb, she encountered instead the newspaper she'd forgotten she'd taken to give to Madame Chambon. That would divert her.

She pulled it out and lowered herself on a spindly chair at the round table by the window where she could supplement the fading light by lighting the reading lamp.

It was a respectable newspaper, but as Faith glanced at the front page, she decided it must be filled with enough scandal to entertain Madame Chambon.

The old bawd would be titillated by such salacious pickings as the story behind the scandalous young woman who'd clearly been featured on the front page for parading herself as something pure when her heart was full of sin, if the headline was anything to go by. Faith did not even consider a parallel until Crispin's name caught her eye.

She put her hand over her mouth and gasped. Crispin? What connection did Crispin have to a woman clearly reviled in the press as someone shameless?

And then, as a sensation of stepping into an icy bath passed over her, Faith realised that it was she, herself, who was the subject of the article.

Faith Montague, named and shamed, by a major newspaper. Not only that, photographed in the arms of none other than Lord Harkom. The photograph had been lined up beside a photograph of Crispin's painting of Faith.

She thought she was going to be sick.

It was the picture taken just before Lord Harkom had tried to force himself on her. Just before Faith had been all but forsaken by Lady Vernon for her failure to win Crispin's affections before Mrs Gedge had given Faith her reprieve.

Regardless of what Faith might have been, there was no mistaking the kind of company she kept. The revealing costumes of the other prostitutes at Madame Chambon's proclaimed it brazenly to the world.

Hunched over, she read the article more closely in all its tawdry detail. It detailed her supposed life in scathing detail. Faith had come to London as a penniless country girl; beautiful and cunning. She had fallen quickly into vice, but her exceptional looks and talent for mimicry had earned her the interest of Lord Harkom, who had made her his mistress and, when he'd given her her congè, seen her taken under the wing of a female benefactress who'd set about equipping her with the skills needed to insinuate her way into Mr Westaway's heart.

And all for what?

For revenge.

Revenge for the loss of a daughter whose death this so-called benefactress laid squarely at Mr Westway's door.

So close to the truth, in fact, but so far in its most essential details —Faith had never intended to follow through with a plan that would destroy Crispin.

And Faith had never taken up with anyone before she'd met Crispin. Her beloved Crispin had won her entire loyalty. She'd given up her only chance of independence to be with him.

Panic swirled about her as she digested the implications.

She placed her palms down on the newspaper as if to obliterate the pictures and the content while she stared about the room that would remain empty—but for her.

Crispin had read this. Lady Vernon had given it to her as a sign.

What could Faith do now? She was exposed.

She rose quickly and shoved the newspaper into her carpetbag, hurrying to the door and pulling down her veil once again.

Where could she go? She couldn't return to Lady Vernon's. The woman had had a part in all this. She'd betrayed Faith. But what about Mrs Gedge? She'd invested heavily in Faith's education for three years. What would she think to know that her minion, Lady Vernon, had betrayed her too?

Only, Faith had no idea how to contact Mrs Gedge directly. They'd only ever met at Claridges Hotel for tea once a month.

She glanced up at the star-studded sky and shivered in the chilly night air.

She was about to hail a hackney but realised she'd not have the funds to pay for it. She'd used the only coins she had, the ones Lady Vernon had given her, to get here.

So, with heavy footsteps, she began to walk.

In the direction of the place she'd called home for three years, and which she'd sold her soul to leave.

"FAITH, WHAT'S BROUGHT YER BACK 'ERE," SQUEALED THE TWEENY, Lizabet, who opened the door to her. At least one person didn't know, she was glad to note.

"Just here to pick up a few belongings and see a few friends. And Madame Chambon."

"You really want to see 'er?" Lizabet grimaced as she led Faith through the gloomy passageway to the salon at the back of the house.

It was early for business, but a handful of the girls lounged about in varying states of dress and undress.

A couple whispered as Faith entered, but Charity straightened with a smile of genuine pleasure as Faith caught her eye.

Faith crossed the room and lowered herself onto the seat beside where Charity was pulling on a stocking seated in the informal sitting room.

"What have the girls been saying about me?" she asked her friend in a whisper. "Tell me the truth."

Charity shook her head as she glanced about, perhaps to see that Madame was nowhere about. "Oh Faith, it's a bad business, and I don't know how much is fiction, but the fact is, the photograph is damning enough. What will you do? Will you come back here to live? I'm sure Madame Chambon would take you in. She'd probably consider the notoriety would make you more valuable. And it would, don't you think? See, there's always a silver lining."

"I hardly call that a silver lining and no, I have no intention of—" She broke off at the honeyed tones of her former mistress.

"Ah, Faith, what a pleasant surprise, though I always knew you'd return."

Madame Chambon loomed over them, a frightening and imposing figure in a gown of lavender and lace, the russet hairpiece intricately interwoven with coils of fake and real hair, her beady eyes gazing at Faith through wire-rimmed spectacles.

"A short visit only," Faith said, her throat so dry she felt light-headed. Her legs felt lacking the substance needed to stand up. And yet she needed to leave this place as fast as she could.

"Oh?" Madame's look of enquiry was tinged with scepticism. "And where could you possibly be going at this time of night? Oh yes, Lady Vernon's, am I not correct? She had plans to whisk you away in order to complete the terms of Mrs Gedge's arrangement with her."

Madame Chambon straightened, patting her large bosom and emitting a waft of cloying patchouli perfume. "But a great deal has changed in the last couple of hours, Faith." Her brow creased. "Events have fairly run out of control, and...I think you must come to my office in order for me to acquaint you with everything to do with Mrs Gedge and Lady Vernon, whose authority is superior to mine where you are concerned, my dear. Charity, please excuse us."

Charity's concerned look made it plain that she understood the menace behind Madame Chambon's words.

"And please, Charity, do make a little more effort with your appearance tonight. I know you're tired, but if you can't attract the gentlemen like you used to, you will have to find somewhere else to lodge. I'm not a charity." She gave a sudden, short laugh as if only then realising the play on words.

What could Faith do but follow Madame Chambon along the gloomy passage and step into the opulently decorated office, where the brothel madam entertained a range of business associates from her fellow bawds to young gentlemen negotiating a contract to relieve Madame Chambon of one of her girls.

Or a woman like Mrs Gedge, though Faith was certain Mrs Gedge had never set foot in these Soho premises.

"Now, sit down and tell me what has brought you here when I was almost certain you'd run off to be with your lover; the charming Mr Westaway." Madame's nostrils flared. "You thought Lady Vernon very credulous if you truly believed you could hide from her the state of your heart. You are a strong-willed young woman, Faith, and Lady Vernon is a sharp-eyed—"

"Gaoler and snitch!" Faith spat.

"Those are singularly unkind terms for a noblewoman who has fallen on hard times and is simply using whatever resources she can to keep a roof over her head." Madame Chambon twisted in her chair in order to locate a decanter of sherry on a shelf behind her. "When nerves are being tested, I think a little fortification is in order. Faith, a glass?"

"And risk being drugged?" Faith shook her head, and Madame raised one eyebrow.

"I'd be careful of making unfounded accusations, Faith, since I think you have precious few options but to come back here." Madame settled herself in front of Faith and shook her head slowly, her look one of great tragedy. "I never thought it would come to this when Mrs Gedge brought you here, a wide-eyed country girl, though of course the fact that a bit of stealing wasn't beneath you augured well. I don't like it when my girls enter my doors with too many scruples. They are the difficult cases, I will admit. But you, Faith, were just perfect for what I had in mind, and to be sure, you have not disappointed me. It has all come to pass exactly as I had hoped." Her smile stretched to encompass her sharp, yellow eyeteeth. "Mrs Gedge had scruples, though." She shrugged. "To begin with, that is. And then she met Lady Vernon during the depths of her grief. A fortuitous meeting, indeed."

"I have never stolen in my life, nor will I," Faith said softly. "And I will *never* sleep with a man I do not love. So, I will profit you nothing if you force me to remain here for even one night."

She rose. "Mrs Gedge might have believed I stole her daughter's bracelet, and she might be filled with bitterness over losing Miss Constancia, but she cannot blame me for that." She shook her head. "No, she cannot be so evil that she'd see me sold into slavery because of what happened three years ago. Because I chanced to be holding up the bracelet that Miss Constancia promised would be mine if I helped her enter Mr Westaway's bedchamber. I was barely fifteen years old. I'd never seen something so valuable. I'd never ever laid eyes on Mr Westaway. I only discovered that Mr Westaway was the man Miss Constancia had killed herself over when he told me so himself." Faith shook her head again, her desperation rising. "It makes no sense. It's out of all proportion for a woman like her to do something like this."

"Like what, Faith? You're looking around my office in a very disdainful manner. Almost as if you felt yourself my superior. Or were the wife of a diplomat. A person who would never deign to step over my threshold. In fact, who may not know what comforts a house like this offers a husband like the one she'd surely neglect if he failed to give satisfaction. Very easy to do when one has such high expectations."

Faith struggled to breathe. "Mrs Gedge would not have paid for my education for three years, and a roof over my head, and food and clothes…all very great expenses…merely to see me forced to work in a…brothel!"

"What a terribly unsavoury term to use for my high-class establishment. However, you're quite right, Faith. Of course, Mrs Gedge never embarked upon a singular scheme against a blameless country girl. And nor did she. She was very willing to hand you a handsome cheque seeing Mr Westaway so unhappy, but matters took a surprising turn. Indeed, we were all taken aback: Lady Vernon, myself, Mrs Gedge who, as a token of her goodwill, insisted that I give you this."

Faith was halfway to the door when she turned, and her horrified gaze fell upon the glittering bauble Madame Chambon was holding out to her.

"You'd realise, of course, that the stones are really not worth much, though no doubt at fifteen you imagined the piece a king's ransom." Madame dangled the pretty piece of jewellery enticingly in front of her as she looked from Faith's mutinous expression to the bracelet that Miss Constancia had promised her three years before.

"You can keep it," Faith muttered, her hand upon the doorknob.

"Oh, my dear, that's very kind of you, but I would hate to fall foul of Mrs Gedge…or Lady Vernon, for that matter. And they have insisted it be a memento for you to keep…to remind you of their generosity towards you these past years."

"I'm not staying here, and I don't want it."

"Well, that's your decision, of course, Faith. You are perfectly at liberty to leave." She smiled sweetly. "So, you're going to seek refuge with your young man, are you? Or with one of your many friends? Perhaps your family, though I'd gained the impression there was little love lost between you. Nevertheless, your room is made up for you, and there are a few fine gowns hanging in the wardrobe that I anticipated you'd need. And I'll give this to Charity for safekeeping until you change your mind." She rose. "Good night, Faith. It's been a lovely little chat, and I'll be sure to pass on any messages that come for you."

CHAPTER 23

"Some may call it talent, but look where your intransigence has led you?" Lord Maxwell sent a derisive look at the half-finished painting upon the easel in Crispin's study. At this time of day in the city, the location offered the best light.

The fact that the painting was a study of Faith in languid repose, her resplendent hair framing her exquisite face, only shored up his father's argument. Unsurprisingly, no sooner than the news had broken back in his home village, Crispin's redoubtable pater had leapt upon his horse in order to cover the distance to London in a fraction of the time it would have taken him by carriage.

Thus, Crispin had had no warning of his lordship's arrival, which too quickly followed his own discovery of the day's damning news splashed across the newspaper which Lord Maxwell now brandished.

"You have been made to look a credulous fool!" his father now shouted, when Crispin made no reply to a statement that could not be refuted. "You were set up from the start, my boy. The cunning plan of a procuress and her sidekicks is providing society with unimaginable titillation. Just as you're about to step onto the world stage supposedly as a diplomat, a figure synonymous with tact, cunning, and strategy. Christ, boy, but you've disappointed me!"

He slammed down the newspaper and began to pace, while Crispin remained in the chair behind his desk where his father had found him contemplating a world that had quite literally shattered about his ears.

"I've always disappointed you, Father," he muttered. Strangely, uttering this particular truth was not nearly as painful as learning the extent of just how greatly he had been set up by Faith and Lady Vernon; two seemingly artless women he'd invited into his house. Women to whom he'd offered friendship and...

Love.

He'd offered Faith his heart, and he'd honestly believed in her sincerity when she'd claimed to have reciprocated. Maybe she *had* grown fond of him, and maybe she *was* saddened at the way matters had gone. That was the best he could hope for since there was nothing anyone could say or do to refute the cold, hard, indisputable facts. Faith had been one of Madame Chambon's girls, and Lord Harkom, his father's arch nemesis, had been her protector.

His father ignored him. He was muttering as he paced the floor, and for the moment, he looked entirely absorbed in his own thoughts until he swung around and ground out, "I'm damned if I know how we can paint this in a way that doesn't make you appear a complete idiot, boy! Yes, an idiot! I wouldn't be surprised if the position for which you've worked so hard all these years is withdrawn, and you never set foot in Germany to make the mark that—"

"That *you* have so longed for, Father," Crispin interrupted him with more energy as he raised his head. "Yes, you! This has always been what *you* wanted. My desire to paint was nothing as far as you were concerned, and yet I've just won a prestigious art prize, and my talents have been recognised—as I have always wanted them to be."

"Ha! What value is that when you were set up to win! Yes, I know that part is not yet confirmed, but who is this mysterious benefactor, eh?" He nodded fiercely to corroborate his theme. "No one knows, do they? Suggesting that this was the very means by which you have been made a laughing-stock. Yes, a laughing-stock on all counts. Why, you've succumbed to every lure cast your way. And yet, you are to be a diplomat! Yes, and you will be!" His father went on, hastily, "Because there is nothing else you can do. Your art certainly won't bring you the financial rewards you need to live the life of a gentleman. I don't know of any suitably connected, well-dowered young lady who would want anything to do with you for a few years. No, my boy; the only thing for you is to go quietly off to Germany with your tail between your legs, and pray that the press isn't having a field day in Leipzig as they are over here!"

A knock on the door interrupted his angry tirade, and Carter put his head around the door.

"Young lady here to see you, Mr Westaway."

"Unaccompanied?" Lord Maxwell barked before throwing back his head with a laugh. "My, my, what a brazen little piece your jezebel is. Persistent, too."

"Please leave, Father."

"Certainly not! I shall stay quietly here in this chair in the shadows by the window, and you can introduce me when it's timely. Carter, bring the young lady in."

Before Crispin could move out into the passage, Carter was ushering Faith through the door, and Crispin's heart was in a tumult he could not begin to explain. He'd thought rage and disappointment would be his chief emotions, but longing trumped them all.

A waft of lavender heralded her entrance, and he longed to clasp her to him.

"Crispin, I'm so sorry! Not everything is the way it's been portrayed in the newspapers!" She hurried forward like a breath of spring sunshine and gripped his hands, and he couldn't help holding them as he ground out, "Faith, how can you refute the fact that you lied? You targeted me in order to set me up. Isn't that the truth?"

Tears glistened on the edge of her lashes as she tipped her face up to his.

"I lied to you at first, but I confessed. Crispin, I never meant to hurt you. I certainly never meant to humiliate you or damage your career."

"But that's what you've done." He dropped her hands and turned his head away, acutely conscious of his father in the corner whose expression communicated his disgust. Faith, who had her back to him and so had not noticed they were not alone, went on, "Crispin, I have never been one of Madame Chambon's 'girls' as the newspaper claims. Nor have I ever been…kept! Not by Lord Harkom, not by any man! I was a…a virgin when I gave myself to you."

Perhaps she could see that he was not as moved as she'd wish. As he might have been had his father not been present.

Her voice took on a greater note of desperation. "Crispin, you must at least believe the truth of that! Why, the evidence was there. Whatever my sins might be, the fact is that I swore I would never give myself to a man I did not love. And then I met you. Yes, I fell in love with you, even though it was against my better judgement. Even though it was not as others would have wished it. I would confess all, if you would only say you still love me. That you want to still love me. I can prove the lies that are in that newspaper. Please, Crispin!"

There was nothing Crispin wanted more than to hold Faith against his chest and at least hear what she had to say. But a movement from his father suggested this would not be wise. Lord Maxwell would make the situation so much nastier if he made his presence known and Crispin had to protect Faith from that, at least. He'd hear her out when they were alone.

But for now, he'd have to show his father that he was not susceptible to her pleas. Perhaps there really was some explanation that could paint her in a less damning light, though, God help him, the picture of her in Harkom's arms surrounded by a group of harlots could hardly be explained away.

Still, she deserved an audience.

Alone.

"Faith, you've said all you need to." Putting his hand upon her shoulders, he turned her towards the door, careful to block any view she might have of his father. "I'm sorry." He lowered his eyes, careful not to look at her trembling mouth for fear he might lose control and just kiss her with all the disappointed passion that still burned within him. "Goodnight, my dear. I'm sorry it's come to this. I wish you well for your future."

A soft chuckle from Lord Maxwell was his reward when the door had closed behind Miss Faith Montague—the only woman he'd ever loved.

"Hardly masterful, my boy, but I'm glad to see you're not a complete slave to that soft heart of yours, which was always going to be your downfall." He rose and pointed to the desk with its pile of papers. "Now, read this latest report on the situation in the Black Forest. Meanwhile, I shall go and see what I can do to minimise the damage your foolish exploits have done to your reputation."

"No passionate leave taking? Or did you decide not to stay with Mr Westaway, after all.? Why Faith, it's barely eleven o'clock." Madame Chambon was waiting in the shadows when Faith returned to the house in Soho. She couldn't look at the woman; her defeat was so enormous. A great sob threatened to reduce her to a quivering wreck at Madame Chambon's feet, unless she could make her escape and throw herself onto her bed in the privacy of her room.

Her old, hated iron bed with its aged, dusty quilt. It represented so much that was wrong with her life, but right now, she had nowhere else to go. Lady Vernon would not be welcoming her back in a hurry. No, Faith had outlived her usefulness to the old termagant; Madame Chambon had made that clear.

She was about to pass Madame Chambon on her way to the stairs when she hesitated. It had taken her a long time to untangle the few facts she could about her altered situation.

"Mrs Gedge didn't hate Crispin Westaway as much as she hated me, did she?" She swallowed painfully. "Why? I never hurt her? I never stole from her? And yet…yet everything she's orchestrated has resulted in *my* ruin. Granted, Mr Westaway's reputation has suffered, but I…*I* have been ruined so much more effectively."

Madame Chambon put her hand on Faith's shoulder and walked

her to the bottom of the stairs. For just a moment, she sounded as if she sympathised.

"There's no room for sentiment in this business, Faith," she said. "Money is the only currency, and everyone has to pay their way. I don't think Mrs Gedge set out to destroy you, Faith." She brightened. "And, when all is said and done, she has endowed you with so much you would never have had as an ignorant servant."

"As I stand, I am in her debt." Faith began to tremble. "But after tonight? What happens to me then? Would…would she take me back as a servant? Would that satisfy her? For I would do anything rather than stay here with all that entails."

The pressure of Madame Chambon's fingers increased, and her smile became cloying as she steered Faith along the corridor. "I suspect Mrs Gedge would be unmoved by your loyalty, Faith. To have you under her roof would only remind her of everything she has lost. Do you not think that, perhaps, her feelings for you changed as she saw you grow into the beauty you have become…while her daughter lies mouldering in her grave?"

Faith suddenly understood. Jerking herself from Madame Chambon's grasp, she picked up her skirts and was about to take to the closest flight of stairs, when a masculine chuckle by the door of the drawing room made her whip her head around.

"It's been too long, Miss Montague." Faith recognised the voice before the face. Panicked, she searched for escape, but Madame effectively blocked her way to the stairs or the door to the street.

"Come, Faith, no need to be churlish." Madame's fingers dug into her arm as she propelled her towards one of the private entertaining rooms. She opened the door and pushed her in, Lord Harkom following close behind.

Now, Faith was standing opposite his lordship was turning the key in the lock. He stood facing Faith, arms akimbo, a speculative smile upon his thin lips.

"Let's get down to business, Miss Montague. My intelligence has it that you're all alone without husband *or* protector." He closed the distance between them and took both her hands in his, raising them to his lips. "So, I am here to offer you a solution."

Faith felt like a trapped canary. No one would come running to her aid if she screamed, but violence might be the result if she offered resistance.

Forcing herself not to reveal her terror or revulsion, she regarded him steadily.

"It is true; you have caught me at a disadvantage," she admitted, gently extracting her hands and making her way leisurely to the sofa in front of the fire. "Perhaps you'd pour us both a drink," she suggested, indicating the decanter on the sideboard as she sank against the cushions. "I do not come cheaply."

"You are not actually in a position to make too many demands, my dear," he reminded her as he poured them both a brandy before seating himself beside her, so close that his thigh was pressed against hers.

Faith managed not to flinch. "Thank you, Lord Harkom," she murmured, taking the brandy from him while she sought desperately for a means to play her cards so that she was not his victim—his plaything. At his mercy in any way. "Mr Westaway knows that to his cost."

Lord Harkom let out a bark of laughter. "Who played who for a fool? No, don't even try to make me think that you ever had the upper hand in that little affair, Miss Montague. Faith." He stilled and, with his eyes fixed on her face, ran the forefinger of his right hand gently around the edge of her décolletage. It was such a bold, proprietorial, and insulting action but Faith dared not move. She could not risk insulting him when she had no idea how to play this game. Lord Harkom was dangerous. One misstep on her part and he'd tumble her here and now. He'd force himself on her, and not a single person would come to her aid. Not only that; the whole world would consider she deserved it. That was perhaps the most painful reflection of all. She had not a single person she could depend upon. No friend. No lover. No family. No one would defend her honour. Everyone believed she was a liar and a whore.

"Mr Westaway paid a high price to enjoy me." She stared back at him, steadily, trying to still her breathing and keep her bosom from rising against his wandering fingers. "What price are you offering me, Lord Harkom? I do not work on a one-night, rotational basis. And while I have always brought value, I don't come cheaply. As I said."

Two small lines appeared between his eyes as he seemed to weigh up her words. Perhaps see her in a new light? As less of the victim than he'd come here believing?

"I don't know what Madame Chambon has told you, but this plan to humiliate Mr Westaway has been three years in the making. Do you know what care and consideration goes into achieving such a public fall from grace? Yes, two days ago he was society's darling for the talent that saw him carrying off the greatest prize money ever offered in an art competition. Now it's been revealed he was set up from the start. Brought down by the beautiful muse he fell in love with and was going to run away with. And that the art competition was rigged!" A tremor of self-disgust ran through her to even utter the words, but he seemed to be paying attention.

Good. She needed him to redress the power balance, even just a little. She needed all her wiles and cunning; all that intelligence about strategy and human behaviour that she'd honed over the past three years, to come to her aid.

"Why are you here, Lord Harkom? Surely not for a quick rutting to enjoy the spoils for just one night only. I thought you were playing the longer game. Given the enmity between your two families, I thought you'd come here to offer me something that I would consider attractive, and that would strike at the heart of Mr Westaway and his father's ability to enjoy peaceful nights."

Oh, Faith was sure Lord Harkom had considered both and that the longer-term proposition would follow naturally upon the immediate gratification of his carnal desires right here and now. But Faith had to show herself as a woman of business.

She drew her shoulders back and increased the space between them, just a little. Thank God he'd removed his hand as he clearly contemplated what she was saying.

She smiled at him, her confidence growing. "Have you made an agreement with Madame Chambon? I need it in writing, Lord Harkom. A six-month contract with an exclusive residence for me. If I am to be kept, it will be by a rich man who does not stint when it comes to showering largesse upon his most treasured possession—the woman who brought down his enemy."

Yes, she'd sown the seed. He'd probably had something in mind that would involve keeping her as his mistress in order to rub the noses of Crispin and his father more thoroughly into how they'd been played. But Faith's plan suggested she'd come more willingly, and play her part more convincingly, if he met her part way. And that could only be to his benefit.

When he didn't speak, she rose. "Well, perhaps you and Madame Chambon should speak together right now, Lord Harkom." She sent him another sweet smile and offered him her hand before indicating the door with a nod of her head. "Lady Chambon's office is just down the corridor, as I'm sure you know. Meanwhile, I need to change into something a little more…appropriate." She glanced down at her gown then moved towards the door, pausing with her hand on the doorknob. "When an arrangement is in writing, you know where to find me."

He did not stop her. Clearly, he took her at her word and would, most likely, follow through with a meeting with Madame Chambon to nut out the details, knowing, as Madame Chambon had probably told him, that she had nowhere in the world to go.

For she didn't.

Unless…

It was a forlorn hope but there had been someone who had treated Faith kindly.

THE STREET WAS DESERTED WHEN FAITH ARRIVED AT THE SMALL cottage by the river where she'd been conveyed so many times during the past three years. She'd been utterly terrified going by foot, carrying a carpetbag with one simple, old gown she'd snatched from her wardrobe together with the few possessions she had that might be worth anything.

It took several bouts of knocking before there was any response, and she nearly wept with relief when it was opened by a frightened-looking scullery maid.

"Mary, can you tell your master that he has a visitor," Faith exhorted her as she pushed her way past the child and into the familiar space.

The girl blinked open sleep-laden eyes. Faith suspected she'd been sleeping in front of the kitchen fire. Indeed, that's exactly where Faith hoped she might find some rest for the few hours that remained of tonight.

"Master's been long abed," the girl protested mildly though she didn't look as if she'd outright deny Faith. She was too young for that. And not as desperate as Faith to have her way, for the master was not an unkind man.

Faith waited nervously in the small back parlour where she'd spent so many hours at her lessons during the past three years.

Her first thought was that Professor Monk *must* receive her. Well, she was certain of that, at least. But what if he was part of Madame Chambon and Mrs Gedge's evil plan?

No, surely not. Not the kindly professor who took such pride in Faith's intelligent answers when he quizzed her on world diplomacy and the historical relations between countries.

But if he was not part of the evil plan, he must surely know what had happened to her since all of London could talk about nothing else, it would seem.

What would he say when she told him she had nowhere to go? That it was her own fault she'd fallen the way she had? Would he say that he was a man of learning and moral rectitude and their past association meant nothing to him?

Everyone else in Faith's life had forsaken her. The few friends she had were in no position to help her. Professor Monk would be like the rest of them—filled with moral outrage that would require her to pay for her sins.

Instead, his greeting was fatherly, and his first words suggested he'd not even heard what all London had been talking about.

"My dear Faith! Has your carriage broken down? Is Lady Vernon injured? Oh, dear me, I can't think why else you'd be on my doorstep all alone at this hour of the evening."

He was such an innocent guileless old man Faith knew he honestly did believe only the options that would put her in the most favourable light. Being faced with kindness and concern was so at odds with everything else she'd encountered this last terrible day, that she let out a great sob.

"My poor girl, come closer to the fire. You're in shock, surely? Oh, I do hope nothing terrible has happened. Truly, I wouldn't know what to do. Indeed, all I can think to do right now is to offer you some brandy."

"And a bed for the night?" Faith looked up at him, pleadingly, warmed by the light pressure of his hand on her shoulder. So different from the menace communicated by both Madame Chambon and Lord Harkom.

He blinked in surprise as he turned back from ushering Mary out of the room to fetch Faith a small draft of something "strong and medicinal".

"Please, Professor. I've been turned out of the house where I lodge. There was…an argument."

His kind eyes grew a little sterner, but before he could say anything Faith hurried on, "I was pressured to…accept the offer of a man whom I know to be unkind and…*bad*. Yes, bad."

"Forced to wed against your will?"

Faith nodded as she covered up the lie with the words, "I was told I had to accept this man's offer, or I would have nowhere else to go."

"What man? What man would force you into such a bargain, Faith?" The professor looked truly concerned, and with a sigh, Faith whispered, "Lord Harkom." For if she offered part of the truth, it was something, surely.

To Faith's surprise, the professor's eyebrows shot up. "Dear me,

Faith. Was Lord Harkom proposing *marriage* or…" He stopped abruptly."

Sadly, Faith shook her head. "No, Professor, that's why I came here. When I refused him, I had nowhere else to go."

"You have a benefactress who has paid my fees for three years, and yet I've never met her. Would she not offer you lodging?"

"Mrs Gedge." Faith shook her head. "No, I cannot go there either, for she too was insistent that I…" She finished on a sob.

"What about your chaperone? I briefly met Lady Vernon on one or two occasions. Why are you not staying with her?"

"I told you. They wanted me to accept an offer from Lord Harkom." She hung her head. "I'm not that sort of girl."

He blinked, owlishly, and stared at her as if she were suddenly a different creature.

Faith stood up. "Please don't condemn me for what has been out of my control. I want only to do what's right, but I have nowhere to go. No one to turn to. I only wanted shelter for the next few hours until the dawn. That's all I ask of you. Please, Professor. I'll sleep in the kitchen and leave before light. Just let me stay here where it's safe. Just for tonight."

"What then, Faith? What will you do then?"

"I'll find work. Anything. I'll be a servant. I could work for you, Professor. Could I?"

She stared hopefully at him, but he shook his head. "You can't waste your talents, my girl, and I won't employ you to scrub floors when I cannot have you under my roof in any other capacity. Let me think."

He rose and began to pace, scratching his whiskered chin as he began to mutter, for he always did this when deep in thought. As if he had to verbalise every possibility.

"You say you have been used, girl. Educated to be the intellectual match of any man when it comes to diplomacy, strategy. For that's what I did when I was instructed to give you a rudimentary understanding of the relations of the world stage. To make that the key focus of what I taught you. Why, I find this very difficult to understand."

"It was not because of Lord Harkom but an enemy of his. A man who is going to be British Envoy in Germany. I was used to make him look a fool, and then suddenly Lord Harkom was paying his addresses in a most alarming manner, and I had to escape. Perhaps…perhaps you know of a position where I could go. A place I could act as governess?"

"It was the very line of thought I was following." He gave a decisive nod. "But where? What family do I know?"

"I don't care. Any will do. Anywhere I can do an honest day's work and have food and a roof over my head. I don't require much. I just have to get away from London."

"My poor Faith." He regarded her sadly. "I never expected this when I agreed to teach you all those years ago. You are my most gifted student. A great beauty, indeed, now that I perceive you in a better light. And I fear a great evil has been perpetrated against you, though I cannot begin to fathom why. Of course, I will help you. Mary will make up a bed in the spare room, and tomorrow I will send you on your way, but not alone and friendless. I promise I will do what I can to help you, little though it may be."

CHAPTER 24

One Year Later

"And all that pink means it belongs to the British Empire." Faith put her finger on the map on the table in front of them and traced the borders, while her two charges stared dutifully with downcast heads, though their eyes kept straying to the trees and sunshine outside the schoolroom window.

Little wonder now that the sunshine had swept away two days of rain and the swathes of beautifully scythed lawn beckoned for a game of cricket.

"Is it teatime yet?" asked George, the eldest, sighing and wiping his nose with the back of his hand.

"I want a butter sandwich," said seven-year-old James, George's younger brother by two years.

Faith pushed back her chair and stood up. She could hardly blame them. The weather was glorious, and the little boys had been angels. They were good children for the most part; sweet and obedient, and they loved her. It warmed her heart to know that.

Which surprised Faith for she was not used to being loved. Not in such an innocent, overt manner by two little boys who spontaneously hugged her and did not even have to be exhorted to say goodnight every evening at seven—whereupon she'd receive a freely given kiss on the cheek by each.

Even after all this time, it brought a lump to her throat for she hadn't realised there were people in the world who did things for others without expecting payment of some kind.

Faith patted each boy on the head. "Enough geography. Time to stretch your arms high, boys, and take deep breaths," she said, leading the way. Like them, she didn't want to think about the British Empire and have to trace the borders of Germany one more time today.

"Close your eyes. Arms up high." She stood on tiptoe and thought, as she often did, of Crispin. He'd been one of these types of children once. A rare breed who acted out of the pureness of his heart which might, perhaps, account for why she'd lost hers so thoroughly.

And why her heart remained ever loyal, for she understood that, in the end, there'd simply been too much evidence circulating to blacken her name in his eyes.

"Ah, Miss Montague, I wondered if you could ask Ellen to have George and James in their pyjamas a little earlier tonight." Pretty Mrs Heathcote, the boys' mother, stood in the doorway smiling fondly at her boys, both of whom showed more delight than was warranted when she asked them if they'd enjoyed their afternoon lessons.

Having a mother as kind and maternal and interested as Mrs Heathcote was a great part of why George and James had such open hearts, Faith surmised. Did kindness and thoughtfulness to others really breed a child who would in turn grow into a kind and thoughtful man or woman?

It didn't necessarily follow, of course, that a child followed in their parents' footsteps. Crispin's father was cold and demanding, while he'd lost his mother young.

Yet he was sensitive, kind, artistic, thoughtful.

Faith liked to think she fell into the category of those who could change into someone better once they had good reason to, or were shown how.

"Of course, Mrs Heathcote." Faith smiled back. It would mean she had an extra half an hour to herself this evening, too. Not that she had much with which to occupy herself. She'd have dinner with the rest of the servants, but she'd not stay to sew and talk beyond half an hour after that. While the servants were decent enough people, they liked their own chatter and Faith's presence constrained them. She'd overheard the cook, once, saying something along those lines, and while Faith felt accepted as one of the household, and certainly suffered no unkindness at the hands of anyone, she simply wasn't 'one of them'. Not one of the family of four who lived upstairs in their very elegant country manor house, or one of the seven servants who toiled below stairs.

Duly, at half past six, Faith had the boys ready for bed and brought them down to say goodnight to their parents, who were entertaining a small number of people for their regular Friday-to-Monday.

The party was assembled in the drawing room, the three gentlemen and Mrs Heathcote sitting in front of the fire, while one of the female guests sat at the piano and the other stood at her right-hand side, turning the pages and singing in a sweet soprano.

Faith stood in the doorway, holding the hand of each boy, and gazing at the companionable grouping while she waited for the women to finish providing the entertainment.

The two ladies, fashionably dressed in low-cut evening gowns with elaborate bustles, looked to be in their early thirties; their husbands, or so she could only assume, handsome men sporting impressive moustaches. Turning a little, she noticed a third gentleman she'd not seen before, half hidden behind a large urn. His face was turned, but what she could see of his expression bore the signs of a pleasant disposition and a fair amount of appreciation as he listened.

She was about to sweep forward with the boys, when the gentleman swung around to face her, and a shocked breath caught in her throat; just as her own recognition must have registered on her face, for he raised his eyebrows and his eyes widened.

Mrs Heathcote stood up in a rustle of silk, now that the music had just come to an end, and swept towards her children, saying over her shoulder, "Lord Delmore, here are the boys, come to say goodnight."

The other two gentlemen were busily complimenting the ladies on their fine rendition, and Faith stood, frozen, barely able to force her mouth into the requisite smile, as Lord Delmore patted the boys on their heads and said he'd heard many good things about their attention to their studies.

Beyond a short, sharp look at Faith, and a murmured good evening, he said nothing, and after Faith had returned to her bedchamber, after handing George and James over to their nursemaid, she sat, trembling on her bed, and wondered how soon she would be exposed.

And yet, Lord Delmore had been a kind man she reflected, as she took a shawl from her wardrobe and wrapped herself in it to stave off the shaking. Would he really reveal her identity?

He might, if he believed she'd contaminate the children of his friends. A whore could be accepted nowhere in society.

Only, she wasn't a whore. She'd just happened to live amongst a house full of them.

She rose and went to the window, staring out at the moonlit lawns and neat gravelled pathways that wound amongst the trees.

A masculine cough sounded by the shrubbery beneath, and to Faith's surprise, she saw that Lord Delmore had gone outside to smoke a pipe, and that he was walking very deliberately around the terrace, coughing at various intervals.

Several times he glanced up, but of course he'd be unable to see which was Faith's room—Faith was certain he was trying to communicate with her—before he finally set off on the path towards the river.

Faith ran to her wardrobe and put on her one dark, serviceable coat, which might be considered acceptable wear for a walk in the gardens on a moonlit night without occasioning comment.

There was no question about the fact that she needed to be able to speak to him in private. She needed to find out what Lord Delmore intended to tell the Heathcotes. He might condemn her and expose her, but she suspected he'd tell her, first.

The light crunch of gravel beneath her hasty footsteps made her arrival to within his orbit known.

"Rather a surprise to see you here, Miss Montague." He didn't turn from his contemplation of a curious nodule on a trunk of willow tree when she came up to him by a small inlet half hidden by bulrushes, out of sight of the house.

Her insides quivered as she waited tensely for his next words. They would reveal something of his intentions, surely. Just running the short distance between the house and the river, Faith had thought only of how important it was for her to keep this job.

If she were dismissed, she'd have to return to Madame Chambon's.

And if she had to return to Madame Chambon's, she'd rather die. Yes, death would be preferable than having to give herself to a man, or men, in a transaction that took no account of the heart.

"Your name was on everyone's lips a year ago, Miss Montague... and then you disappeared."

Faith shifted position as she stared at his back before he turned to face her. "My old tutor arranged for me to work for the Heathcotes when I had nowhere else to go." She swallowed. "If you tell them what the newspapers printed about me, I'll lose my job."

"And do you like working here? Looking after two little boys? I imagine it's very different from what you are used to."

Faith shrugged. "I had nine brothers and sisters growing up. That was not a lie. And then I was strenuously educated for three years. So, what I do now is not so different from my realm of experience. Loving what I do is what's different."

"Ah, Miss Montague." He shook his head, his look sorrowful. "I am placed in a difficult position. My loyalty is towards the Heathcotes. They are old friends of mine. Good people."

"And I am not?" Faith bristled. "But of course, that's what the papers printed, isn't it? And there was a photograph."

"Of you and Lord Harkom, yes; a man who is no friend to Mr Westaway." Lord Delmore took out a handkerchief and mopped his brow. He looked a little older, but his eyes were still kind beneath their bushy brows. "I'm sorry, Faith. I want to believe that you've been ill done by and indeed, I do see that you have taken the path of redemption. Otherwise, no doubt, you'd still be..."

He hesitated, awkward suddenly, and Faith ground out, "Not with Lord Harkom! I've met him only twice, and that was two times more than I would have liked. He is not a good man. I never had any association with him other than accidental. It's nothing like the newspapers printed."

Lord Delmore frowned. "Yet you have a letter from him. Did you know that? Yes, it was delivered to my house after one of your… friends…came in search of you and found the residence where you'd spent last summer empty."

For a moment, Faith had no words. Finally, she whispered, "Lord Harkom wrote to *me*?" The thundering in her chest was almost painful. "Why, it makes no sense at all. Who brought the letter? Where is it?"

"I can't remember the young lady's name. Only that she couldn't write, so she dictated some words to my maid, Sarah, when she delivered the letter. The young woman was in the district, visiting a family member who, by coincidence, lived nearby, she said."

"When was this?"

"Only a few weeks ago. And, my dear, I'm not sure if I tucked the letter into my portable writing desk or left it in my bureau at home. But naturally, I shall forward it." His eyes raked her with a look of the old appreciation with which she'd become familiar. "I simply had never expected our paths to cross again."

"I don't want it if it comes from Lord Harkom." Faith sighed. "And it sounds as if I shall have to start looking for another job if your conscience will smite you for not telling Mr and Mrs Heathcote who I really am." She clasped her hands together. "And yet, I may still hold out hope for they are decent people. They, at least, would give me a hearing to decide whether I was a good person on balance, rather than condemn me for what five inches of editorial declares is the truth with no refutation from me."

Lord Delmore stepped forward and touched her arm. "I shall keep my silence for now, Faith. But only if I am assured that nothing you do will harm or embarrass this family."

The censure in the man's normally kind face cut Faith to the quick.

How easily people judged on the basis of nothing more than hearsay printed in a periodical. What about the presumption of innocence? She was just a woman, she supposed. A woman from a poor background with too many enemies.

"Of course, Lord Delmore." She inclined her head and turned.

There was no more to be said.

EXCEPT THAT LORD DELMORE HAD INDEED TUCKED THE LETTER HE'D received all those weeks ago into his portable writing desk, and when he found it the next morning, he delivered it straight to Faith as she was walking the boys along the gravel path by the river.

"It's not from Lord Harkom," she told him in relief after she'd ripped open the envelope before scanning its contents.

But her relief was short-lived, and by the time she'd come to the bottom, she was breathing heavily and wished she could sit down.

"What is it, Faith?"

She shook her head and glanced between the man standing opposite in a copse of trees by the river, then up to the house. "It's not from Lord Harkom, but it's *about* Lord Harkom, and it only confirms his evil reputation. Poor Mr Westaway."

Lord Delmore straightened his tie as he smiled. "That's the first time you've mentioned his name. I wasn't sure if you ever spared our talented painter, or should I say, diplomat, a thought."

Faith stared at the man before her and shook her head, unable to fathom the insinuation that Faith felt so little for him. "My lord, he is *all* I ever think about. That is, when I choose to dwell on the few good things in my life."

"And what does the letter say about Lord Harkom? What does your friend know that the rest of society does not? Oh, Faith." He looked profoundly saddened. "What got you into such a calling? Perhaps I should never have given you a letter if it re-establishes your connection to this dreadful life you once lived."

Faith knew she couldn't expect him to understand. Defending herself would be beyond useless, also. "My lord, we all have to survive, somehow." She glanced behind her. George was calling her, and he was too close to the river to make her easy. She began to walk towards the boy, saying over her shoulder, "And sometimes we don't have very many choices. But what we choose to believe about *other* people—provided we have done our due diligence—certainly is up to us."

THE LETTER HAD BEEN PROFOUNDLY DISTURBING. CHARITY HAD SPOKEN of vague ramblings and claims Lord Harkom had made after he'd consumed a great deal of whisky and was sufficiently pleased with the way Charity had performed in bed.

Faith wondered whom Charity had corralled to write such things, for although Charity was intelligent, she'd never been able to form her letters in the right order to make into words anyone could understand.

Clearly, Charity had been sufficiently alarmed by Lord Harkom's claims to want to tell Faith, even though she did not know the specific nature of the correspondence Lord Harkom claimed had unexpectedly come into his hands, and that would ruin Crispin Westaway if it were made public.

The letter, Charity was certain, was contained in an unlocked chest in his bedchamber, but Charity had had no opportunity to look for herself. She'd simply been told the litany that Mr Westaway would never continue in his current diplomatic role after this letter was made public, and all that stood between Westaway and ruin was Lord Harkom's good nature.

Charity wrote that his mood had turned ugly, and he'd told her that if she knew where Faith was, she should pass on the message that Crispin Westaway's future was entirely in her hands. Yes, Lord Harkom demanded a warm welcome from the woman who'd shown so little gratitude towards him for his generosity the last time they'd met; that Faith had an opportunity to rewrite their history, and in return, Lord Harkom would ensure Westaway's dark and ruinous secret never came to light.

Of course, in the months since their separation, Faith had followed Crispin's progress like the girl in love she was. It delighted her when she heard news that he'd impressed his superiors. When the newspapers had finally stopped making reference of his humiliation over the art prize that had been shown to be a ruse in order to entrap him with a common prostitute, a great weight had fallen from her shoulders. At last that was considered old news, and now, both of them had new lives to forge.

Except that Crispin's was filled with promise, while Faith felt that hers was like a dull continuum, punctuated by terror that she'd lose even that through exposure.

All she wanted was security, food, and shelter without having to sell her soul for it.

She hoped to remain with the Heathcotes until George went to school at Eton, like his father, after which Faith would find another position. Indeed, that was the best a governess in her position could hope for.

And Faith no longer had high hopes for anything.

But the letter had jarred her out of the quiet life of acceptance she'd been living. It reintroduced danger into her life, and reminded her painfully of the future she'd thought was within reach. The one that had been based on honesty and trust and hope.

In her bedchamber, she scoured every line for a hint from Charity as to what she thought Faith should do. Did Charity believe Lord Harkom? It would be easy to manufacture falsehoods in order to lure Faith back to him.

Yet, why would Charity go to the extremes of travelling hours into the country, if she didn't think Lord Harkom really did possess dangerous information that he'd not scruple to use against Crispin? Perhaps his information was not dangerous to Crispin, personally, but the policies Crispin endorsed. The policies that ensured Britain keep the peace amidst the turbulence of world politics.

Just a few words were all it had taken, but Charity apparently knew when a boast contained more than the kernel of truth that threatened to blow up a man's career like a powder keg.

Pillow talk. How many men had been brought undone by pillow talk? Perhaps without even knowing it, for they were all too liable to underrate the intelligence of the females they used for their pleasure.

Nervously, Faith addressed Mrs Heathcote after the boys had had their breakfast the next morning. The guests had left, and her mistress seemed in a particularly satisfied mood for all had gone well and now peace reigned again.

"My poor Faith. I'm so sorry to hear your mother is dangerously ill. Yes, of course you must go to her." The young matron looked up from the bench where she was making preserves with one of the maids in a small dark room in the back of the house. Her expression was genuinely sympathetic, and Faith wished she'd not had to lie in order to gain a few days. Yet what could she do if Crispin were in danger? If she could have avoided ever seeing Lord Harkom again, she would have.

"I'm sure we'll manage for five days without you. My mother can pay us a visit and spend all the time she wants to with the boys without worrying that she's interrupting their education. There! The matter is settled, and you must think only of what you can do for your family. Family is everything, I know."

Mrs Heathcote looked so pretty and so innocent as she stood above the marble countertop, spouting what she knew based on her own fortunate experience of life.

Faith bobbed a curtsey and thanked her, relieved to have got over the first hurdle so easily.

What would follow surely had the potential to be diabolical.

CHAPTER 25

The road outside Madame Chambon's house was painfully familiar, but Faith wasn't going to step across the threshold, even via the kitchen, so she waited nervously in the narrow side lane. Fortunately, Charity was soon out to greet her, having been sent a message by the bootboy.

"Faith! I never expected to see you again! You got my letter, didn't you? I hope I didn't alarm you, only I thought you might find it important considering what Mr Westaway was to you." Charity looked striking in crimson, her red-gold hair gleaming as it rippled down her back. Her evening gown was of the finest silk. Yes, Charity had become the reigning favourite during the year Faith had been away, and Madame Chambon saw the advantages in dealing well by those who brought in the greatest names, titles, and, of course, money.

"I'm so glad I was free to come," she went on, after a quick hug and a nervous look over her shoulder. "Though I have to meet Lord Stanford in five minutes." Her mouth curved up and Faith stared, incredulous as she asked, "You don't mind?"

Charity shook her head. "I mentioned him before. He's a regular, and I truly believe he's going to speak with Madame to release me."

"And make you his mistress in your own establishment?"

"Well, he's hardly going to offer to marry me!" Charity laughed before her expression grew serious, and she returned to the matter which had brought Faith to London.

"Lord Harkom's speech alarmed me greatly. He mentioned enough specifics to make me believe he truly had something to use against Mr Westaway, and yet I have not the slightest idea what it could be. Only that all Lord Harkom's correspondence is contained in a small leather chest which he keeps under his bed." Charity touched Faith's shoulder. "I didn't want to put you in danger, but I knew you'd want to know."

Faith stared at Charity's gown, and asked, "May I borrow a dress, one of your finest, for just one night?"

"And a governess doesn't have such confections in her wardrobe?" Charity's smile was rueful. "If I had the learning, I once thought I'd prefer to be a governess, though whether that would satisfy me now, I don't know." She smiled again, clearly thinking of Lord Stanford. "Of course, I'm happy to offer you my finest gown for the night, but I would urge you to reconsider seeing Lord Harkom in person. He was very angry with you, and vengeance is his natural response. I only told you because I couldn't hold onto the information. It sounded dangerous."

"Lord Harkom will agree to see me, at least." Faith raised her eyebrows. "If vengeance is his first inclination, I shall be ready to meet him on equal grounds."

Crispin wasn't expecting to be interrupted. During his two short weeks back in England, he had a great deal to do. Right now, he was preparing for a meeting with several ministers, so when he called "Come!" he was expecting the maid to announce Lord Grinwald with whom he would be conducting delicate negotiations.

Instead, he was surprised but pleased to find himself greeting his old friend and neighbour Lord Delmore. It had been a long time. More than a year, in fact, and as their acquaintanceship had been limited to the time Crispin spent at his aunt and uncle's home, and it was known that Lord Delmore's fondness for London was minimal, the gentleman's arrival was highly unusual.

"What brings you here? My short tenure here in London is not widely known." Crispin ushered Lord Delmore to a seat and called for tea, not liking to recall when they'd last been in company together.

Should he bring it up? It would only revive a time long past when Crispin had shown himself the foolish stripling he'd once been.

"I've heard good reports of your progress through the ranks, and not just from your father." Lord Delmore seated himself and glanced about the room: at the hunting scenes, the plaster busts, a suit of armour by the fireplace.

No flowers in vases. No lace doilies. No sign of any feminine touch.

He didn't ask the question though. Merely waited until the maid had placed the tray upon the table, poured them both a cup of Darjeeling, and retired.

"I saw Miss Montague last week."

Her name struck home like a well-placed blow to the solar plexus. Crispin hoped he didn't betray himself. Not by the fiery reddening of his face, which he tried to obscure by taking a judicious sip of his drink, nor by the clearing of his throat, which must surely denote discomfort to a keen observer.

There were a thousand questions he wanted to ask, but he didn't know where to start. Didn't know if he should ask anything, in fact.

He settled with, "Indeed."

"She looked very demure as one might expect. She's a governess, you know."

"Good lord!" This was unexpected.

"Yes, one would have imagined she'd have capitalised on her notoriety and made herself a fortune while she could. That was my initial thought, too."

Crispin put his cup down carefully. It was still too full to risk holding it when his hands were shaking. Strange. He'd found himself quite self-contained during these past months. His father's disgust, followed by the harsh tutoring he'd received at the hands of his pater had, he thought, cauterised all feeling.

Except shame.

And it was curious how that could be wrapped up and put away when hard work was all consuming.

"I wouldn't be surprised if she plans to see Lord Harkom. I don't know when, and that is why I'm here. I think you should stop her. Talk to her first, before she does something rash."

If everything that had gone before had been surprising, this was the most surprising of all. Crispin was glad he'd not been taking another sip of tea for even without, he still choked on his shock.

"Lord Delmore, I can't imagine why her…decisions and way of life should be your concern. They certainly are no longer mine."

"I thought you felt a *tendre* for the young lady. I thought she'd engaged your heart to the extent you were prepared to go so far as marriage, even when you believed her penniless."

Crispin shook his head and put up his hand, and Lord Delmore went on, "But it's not because of your feelings that I sought you out to tell you this." He sighed heavily. "Lord knows, I'm a man who likes the simple life. The skulduggery that's your domain now that you're in the thick of delicate continental diplomacy is not for me. I'd far rather be mouldering away in the country with a good book than breathing in London smog for a good cause."

"I'm your good cause? Or Miss Montague? I'm sorry, Lord Delmore, but I fail to understand you at all. You know what Miss Montague was revealed to be. I can have nothing to do with her —*especially* now. Besides," he muttered, "I thought she was with Lord Harkom in a capacity that made visiting him hardly a reason for you to come rushing down to London to tell me about it."

"I'd have thought the same had it not been for a letter my maid took, or rather transcribed, on behalf of one of Miss Montague's friends. Yes, one of those ladies of disrepute who are so desirable to the likes of Lord Harkom. It seems he's been highly indiscreet with a little ladybird who is far more intelligent than he gave her credit for. Even if she's illiterate."

Crispin rose, more to alleviate the difficulty of sitting still when his agitation was so great he didn't know what to do with himself. He poured them both a brandy and, without asking, handed one to Lord Delmore.

"So, what does this little ladybird suggest Lord Harkom has that could be of such interest to Miss Montague?"

Lord Delmore took a thoughtful sip. "She mentioned something about a letter. Or a couple of letters. I don't know, exactly. Just that these letters were potentially damaging."

"Damaging? To whom?" Crispin shrugged. "I have nothing to hide, yet you obviously give credence to whatever matter of grave import these letters contained. Anyway, why should it concern me? Why should anything Miss Montague does concern me? You know what I risk should it be revealed I have any association with her."

Lord Delmore worried his lip as he sent a dark look towards his younger friend. "When I look back on my life, I have far more regrets about the things I *didn't* do than those I did. Now, it's true that I don't know what these letters contain. Nor would it appear, does the, er, fair Cyprian who made the journey to find Miss Montague. She was simply worried enough by the suggestion of damage Lord Harkom hinted they could do to you, that she felt the need to travel a great distance to alert Miss Montague."

"I'm sure there's nothing further about my private life that can be disseminated to the public that would further embarrass me or discredit me," Crispin ground out.

His painting career lay in tatters. His personal standing had taken a very great hit. Thank God, he'd been able to remove himself from London almost immediately afterwards while his father had worked hard to pass it off as less than it was.

Certainly, less than it was to Crispin. Yes, Lord Maxwell's boy had been caught up in a vile scam that was to have won him a bride from the ranks of the impure through means of a bogus art competition.

After the shock and outrage, the sniggers had followed. Crispin had left the country at this point.

Now he'd returned to commiserations and bolstering affirmations that he'd had a lucky escape. He'd been clever enough to have seen through the young lady in time.

So, Crispin's reputation was intact, and he'd recovered his social standing.

But the state of his heart and his sense of trust would never recover.

"But what if it's not about your private life, Crispin? What if it's more than that? Yes, I know that a year on you still are wounded by what you see as Miss Montague's betrayal. Nevertheless, she *was* in love with you."

"Everything about her was a lie."

"Except, as I've just said, her love for you, Crispin." Lord Delmore's tone was patient. Crispin eyed him suspiciously, staring into the fireplace as he said darkly, "You sound like my father might have sounded if he'd ever chosen persuasion before threats. You are not my father, you know."

"But I'm an older man with more experience of matters like these. I have two grown-up sons and a daughter, all of whom are, in fact, older than you. Forgive me if you think I'm patronising you. That certainly was not my intention. But I do sense something sinister at play. I'm not suggesting for a moment that you go in search of Miss Montague. But do, I urge you, find her friend and hear what she has to say. I believe that trouble is afoot. Lord Harkom has an axe to grind. And we both know he's no friend of yours or your father's."

CHAPTER 26

The busyness of the small newspaper office and the professional air of the two young women bent over their desks, writing, took Faith by surprise after she'd been led up two flights of stairs to this unconventional scene in the attic above a barrister's premises.

"Can I help you, miss?" The younger woman, who was sitting at a large wooden desk beneath the window, raised her head to look enquiringly at Faith. Clearly, she did not recognise Faith as she halted her work, her pen poised above the paper.

"You're a proper lady journalist, now, Miss Eaves? Isn't that what they call you?" Faith looked at the various newspapers and magazines that were strewn about the tabletops and which lined the walls, some framed. "You achieved your dreams, after all." She hesitated as her eye was caught by the glaring front page of an issue published on August 15th, 1878. She didn't need to go any further to confirm the date, for the headline alone clearly depicted Faith's spectacular fall from grace. Even from a distance, the grainy photograph of Lord Harkom holding Faith in a waltz hold, surrounded by a group of women who were clearly not ladies, made Faith shiver with revulsion. "You've achieved your life's ambition."

Two furrows appeared between Miss Eaves's eyes, but as her gaze followed Faith's to the newspaper before returning to Faith, it seemed she finally reconciled the demure governess before her with the woman whose life she'd turned upside down.

Miss Eaves squared her shoulders.

"Miss Montague, why did you not say you were coming?" She glanced at the older woman who was still working but who was clearly also listening, and said, "Mamie, please would you leave us alone for a few minutes."

When Mamie had left the room, Miss Eaves invited Faith to sit, and when Faith said she didn't have long and would rather stand, Miss Eaves stood too and regarded her, still frowning, from the other side of the room.

Faith straightened. "I was hardly assured of a warm welcome in view of what you'd said about me in the past, so I thought the element of surprise might play in my favour." She moved to the window embrasure and found that she was suddenly far more nervous than she'd expected to be. She fiddled with the curtain tassel but kept her eyes on Miss Eaves, who straightened and said calmly but with a note of defensiveness, "It's the job of the journalist to tell the truth. The facts. I'm sorry if my article revealed you for what you are, or were, Miss Montague. I was seeking the truth and I laid it out for the public, as they deserved. It was nothing personal."

"But for me, it *was* deeply personal, Miss Eaves. For me, it was the ruin of my life." She swallowed, finding this even harder with every word, which was strange when she'd spent so many of the last months existing in a state of semiconsciousness; unable to properly feel anything, really. "You fed my dreams and ambitions into the furnace to feed your own."

"Why, Miss Montague, what a lovely way you have with words. Surely, you are in the wrong calling." She glanced pointedly at Faith's demure clothing and said, "Or have you seen the error of your ways and turned to another means of earning your living."

This was not going the way Faith had hoped it would. Miss Eaves, for all her emancipation, knew nothing of the desperate choices a woman had to make, daily, when she had no resources.

"You are very fierce in your determination to forge your own way in the world, Miss Eaves. I see you have your own office. And a secretary, even." She nodded, approvingly. "You must be paid well for your writing to manage the rent and wages since I know your uncle was very much against his niece working."

Miss Eaves pushed back a lock of chestnut-brown hair and her pert nose twitched. "I do work hard, Miss Montague. And the provision of a bit of space in a building that my uncle has no use for accounts for very little, and is only temporary until such time as I can properly establish myself and be completely independent."

Faith nodded. "That is generous of your uncle to give you such patronage. You must have won him around with the excellent reporting you did on last year's art prize. I daresay, after your hard work at the office—in space supplied by your uncle—that you go home to sleep in a bed and eat food that is supplied purely through your own endeavours. Or, is your food and lodgings supplemented too?" Faith couldn't seem to stop fiddling with the curtain tassel, but she glanced up to see Miss Eaves's reaction as she added, "Well, at least, only until such time as you make sufficient earnings through your writing to completely support yourself."

Miss Eaves flushed, but she kept her composure. "I resent the criticism, Miss Montague, though I understand your feelings at having been exposed for living a lie. I am a fierce advocate for furthering the opportunities of the fairer sex, but women will only ever be taken seriously, especially as newspaper reporters, if we are not afraid to speak the truth, however unpalatable."

Faith closed her eyes. "I don't disagree with you. But I cannot begin to explain the risk you run in ruining reputations, not least your own, if the truth as *you* see it, is only the partial truth."

Miss Eaves leaned against the table, and her fingers drummed an agitated tattoo. "Photographs don't lie. There was the truth, Miss Montague, and I told it. I'm sorry if it destroyed your marital chances, but the whole of society can breathe a sigh of relief that you did not insinuate yourself into their ranks once you were shown to be—"

"To be…what, Miss Eaves? The mistress of Lord Harkom, because that's what was suggested by the photograph? To be a prostitute, because the camera showed me standing in a room surrounded by women who certainly weren't dressed like ladies and so that was the assumption?" Faith shook her head. "That photograph was taken minutes before Lord Harkom attacked me, wanting what I refused to give since I had never traded my body for money or anything else—and I never have or will, which is why I work as a governess." She indicated her clothing.

"Please, Miss Montague; it is very easy to don a garment and pretend to be what you are not."

"It is, Miss Eaves. And that is what I did for three years as I was groomed to entice Mr Westaway to fall in love with me once I became his muse for the art prize which a wealthy woman—also American—established in order to wreak her own warped vengeance. I lived at Madame Chambon's, but I was not one of her girls. And I have never traded my body for money or material gain. Not with Lord Harkom or anyone else."

"This is sounding more and more like a Penny Dreadful novel, Miss Montague." Miss Eaves swatted at a fly and began to pace. "You can't expect me to believe a word of what you say."

"Of course, because words can twist the truth, yet photographs can't? That photograph was staged. So much of what you *inferred* was untrue."

"My inferences were endorsed and expanded by someone who knew very well the lie you lived."

"Indeed? And who was that? A woman who was jealous? A man whom I'd refused? Whoever it was, was certainly no friend of mine, though I might begin to guess."

"Lady Vernon came to see me. Yes, the dowager duchess. She'd discovered your true identity, and was incensed that someone like you should become the darling of the town when she knew what you really were."

"And had done since the moment she deposited me at Madame Chambon's three years before, and on every occasion she escorted me to my tutor in Bethnal Green, or to take tea at the Claridges Hotel with Mrs Gedge who established the art prize with just this outcome in mind. Yes, the millionaire American woman who wanted to kill the joy in Mr Westaway, the man whom she held responsible for her daughter's suicide, but she wanted to destroy me in the process because she couldn't bear that I was alive and beautiful, while her daughter was cold in the ground. An eager, gullible female reporter played very nicely into her hands."

Miss Eaves raised her chin and looked squarely at Faith. "I'm sorry I'm unable to offer you tea, Miss Montague."

"No matter, since I would not have accepted." She sent a pointed look at the newspaper in its frame upon the wall that had dissected her life as its front-page story. "It's so easy to believe that what one sees constitutes the truth. So much more so when you choose to believe that higher rank constitutes a greater propensity for delivering the truth. I'm afraid I have to go now." She ran her hands down the sides of her serviceable gown. "It's time for me to change into something more appropriate for this evening."

"Well, I'm glad you still have such evenings to look forward to then, Miss Montague, though I daresay I won't be seeing you at Lady Ridgeway's Masked Ball tonight. You had quite convinced me that I was the architect of the ruin of your entire life." She sniffed.

Faith faced her proudly. "I would never lay that at anyone's door, Miss Eaves. And nor do I look forward to this evening in the slightest. I simply hope that the risk I take will advance the safety of those nearest and dearest to me." She narrowed her eyes. "Unlike you, I like to do a little more research to ensure that the facts disseminated to the world are based entirely on truth."

CHAPTER 27

The looking glass was very complimentary. Or perhaps it was the dim lighting. Or the pale pink ruffled gown that clung to Faith's curves, accentuating her slim hips, flat belly, and generous breasts. The fashions of the day could be most suggestive, and a young lady who wore them as well as Faith did, was sure to come in for a great deal of generous praise.

Which was why it was important that Faith make her exit from Madame Chambon's without having been noticed.

She'd dressed in Charity's room, helped by her friend who'd acted as lady's maid, pulling in her corset until Faith could barely breathe. Charity was slighter than she was, and Faith had not worn fashionable, constricting corsets for a year.

When her coiffure was complete, a riot of curls rippling down her back, secured by a braid that held her fringe back, and a pair of sapphire earrings dangling beneath her ears, Charity's gasp of admiration was the first step needed to bolster the confidence that was fast being eroded by fear.

She'd always feared Lord Harkom. Right from the moment she'd noticed the wild gleam in his eyes when drinking with the other girls when she was a fifteen-year-old and made to peek from the top of the stairs to observe how the ladies used their attractions to lure a man into spending more. There was not a trick Madame Chambon missed and even though the gentlemen complained, they still tipped handsomely for their drinks as a prelude to the other pleasures they'd come to enjoy.

"I'm sorry you had to entertain Lord Harkom," Faith said, turning in a slow circle to ensure she'd not missed anything that could be improved upon. How different from the usual routine of dressing merely in order to bring a little learning to two little boys at the Heathcotes.

"There's far worse than him, but he isn't a...generous lover." Charity shrugged. "Still, he didn't hurt me as he's hurt some of the other girls. Maybe he wasn't as drunk—though he was drunk enough to be surprisingly free with his speech. Oh Faith, I hope I haven't done wrong in telling you something which now has the potential to see you in grave danger. I know I can't talk you out of this, but you will be careful, won't you? Don't let him..." Her words trailed off as if she didn't know what to say, ending finally, "You've never been one of us. I can't bear to think of you being used like a common—"

"Don't say it!" Faith turned upon her almost angrily. "You do what you have to do to save yourself from starving in the gutter. What man wouldn't do the same if the roles were reversed and women ruled the world?" Putting a hand to her forehead, she willed herself to be calm. She needed a clear head, and her corset was decidedly constricting when it came to growing emotional.

Drawing back her shoulders, she said quietly, "I will be careful. I have planned this well. I will never give myself to a man I do not love, and I would rather die than allow Lord Harkom to take that which I would only willingly give." She tapped the pendant around her neck. Upon it hung a tiny silver vial, hollowed out with a tiny stopper. "When Lord Harkom invites me to drink champagne, half the contents in this will see him lose consciousness, while I help myself to the information I'm sure he can't help boasting about."

"But Faith, that is far too dangerous! If he catches you, he'll punish you dreadfully!" Charity looked like she was going to cry. "He'll torture you! He did that to Anastasia, and it took her three weeks before her face was healed. Imagine what he'll do to you!"

Coldly, Faith said, "I won't let him. The entire contents of this vial are enough to kill someone my size. I'm prepared to take my chances, Charity." She smiled suddenly. "But I *won't* fail. I won't let Lord Harkom be the cause of my destruction for a second time."

SHE DID NOT FEEL SO BOLD BY THE TIME SHE WAS ADMITTED TO Mistress Kate's dancing rooms later that evening. Faith had it on good authority that Lord Harkom was going to be in attendance, having spoken to the ageing courtesan earlier in the afternoon to ensure she'd be received.

Once she'd made it clear that she was not here to poach any of Mistress Kate's long-term, favoured Cyprians, there'd been no opposition.

"Lord Harkom, is it? You're welcome to him," Mistress Kate had said with a curl of her lip. "I should pay you for the service you'll be rendering me this evening if you take him off my hands."

Her words did nothing to increase Faith's enthusiasm in her venture, though it did firm her resolve. Lord Harkom was a man who'd traded with impunity on his lineage for far too long. The fact that Faith intended ruining his reputation in a professional rather than private capacity gave her far greater satisfaction.

Now, Faith arranged herself on a chaise longue beneath a window in one of the smaller reception rooms, with the agreement that Mistress Kate would ensure that Lord Harkom came upon her at some stage during the evening.

A chance meeting would be far more effective to her plan than otherwise.

Of course, she'd also be vulnerable to other visitors, but she'd have to navigate those complications as they arose.

The room was thick was the scent of perfume and powder, and overwarm from the fire and the many people who occupied it. Faith gazed around her and wondered at the fact that Mistress Kate's had remained so popular for so long. It had been established by Kate in her youth, but even as she'd aged, she'd retained the loyalty of the many gentlemen she'd pleased during her career while ensuring an eager turnover of girls.

No, not eager. What girl would wish for a life so uncertain?

Nervously, Faith ran her finger around her low neckline. Lord, but it was difficult to play a role so alien to her natural inclination, but she had no choice if she were to achieve anything of value in her short, worthless life.

The room was growing even warmer as it filled with more perfumed, heated bodies. Behind her fan, Faith recognised several regulars from Madame Chambon's. But they were men she'd only seen from afar. Other than the night she'd been photographed, she'd never been on display. And surely a grainy photograph in a newspaper, and a painting that had briefly titillated society a year ago, would not reveal her tonight.

Only Lord Harkom would recognise her sufficiently to stop.

But, of course, the effort to which she'd gone to shore up her natural assets attracted the attention of those on the prowl. And the fact that Faith was here, in this room, proclaimed her as the whore she'd sworn she'd never be.

Nor would she, though she inclined her head and answered demurely when a couple of young blades on the town lurched up to her.

"What blessed charms has Mistress Kate served up to us tonight," declared the darker one, swaying dangerously as he looked from Faith to his friend. "Why, perhaps you'd care to dance, miss. The orchestra has just tuned up, don't you hear?"

"I like my men to be steadier on their feet, though you are very kind, sir." Faith simpered at him from over her fan. "And taller. Yes, I like my men to be taller. And even darker than you."

The gentleman pushed back his shoulders. "Why, you do have a discerning eye, don't you?" He sounded aggrieved. "Perhaps you never do get up and dance if you set your standards so high."

Faith made a pretence of sighing deeply. "I've spent many an evening languishing here," she said. "Disappointed. Waiting." She fluttered her eyes and raised them to the ceiling and was in the process of returning her gaze to the disaffected young man before her, when she beheld the very reason she was here.

And her heart did a frantic lurch to the top of her ribcage before settling like a stone.

"For a gentleman like me," supplied Lord Harkom, easing himself into her orbit and elbowing Faith's original admirer and his friend out of the way. For a long moment, he stared at her; a calculating gleam in his eye.

As if he'd run her to ground.

Faith turned her head, a frisson of fear making her mouth tremble.

All to the good. Let him see her fear. It would make him believe all the more powerfully in his mastery over her. He'd think he'd caught her by surprise.

He took a step closer. "Well, well, well," he murmured. "Miss Faith Montague. Who would have thought to find you…here."

Faith raised one shoulder as if in defiance and part self-protectiveness. She saw his gaze brush over her bare flesh, and the desire leap and dance in his coal-black eyes.

Oh God, she did not want to do this. And yet, she had to go through with it. Had to make him believe in her fear, her reluctance. It would stoke the abusing monster within him to act.

"Lord Harkom." Her tone sounded husky and inviting. She swallowed. "Good evening." What else could she say?

He settled himself beside her, his thigh pressing against hers on the love seat as he called to a waiter to bring them both brandy.

She took the cut-glass tumbler she was offered without a word, but was forced to answer when he remarked, "It's been some time since we last met. Since you reneged on the agreement we had, in fact. I wondered where you'd gone. Yes, I've often wondered that." He looked at her enquiringly, a note of menace in his tone.

"I found a friend who was good to me. Very good to me." She took a sip of her brandy and allowed a note of sorrow to creep into her voice while her eyes rose heavenward. "Sadly, all good things come to an end."

"So, you were quick to find a replacement for young Westaway. And me. Glad to know you weren't brokenhearted all this time. But you're at a loose end tonight, I can see." He stood and put his hand on her shoulder, his fingers playing with the light fabric that edged her shoulder strap. Faith shivered, and he ran his hand down her arm and gently gripped her elbow, as if feeling its smoothness, its composition.

"Ah Faith, you and I have some unfinished business, don't we?" With both hands on her shoulders, he drew her up. The familiar notes of leather and sandalwood filled her senses. She'd been too close to the smell of him before. "Come home with me and I'll show you I'm not the man you thought you feared."

Faith stared up at him and shook her head. "I don't want to go home with you, Lord Harkom," she murmured. "You can offer me nothing that I want."

His lordship glanced about the room. "You think there's someone here who can? Perhaps those two striplings who were courting you earlier?" Drawing her closer, he dipped his head and whispered, "I'm a rich and powerful man, and I think you know that I want you. Let bygones be bygones and I'll show you how kind and...generous I can be."

Faith stood her ground. "No, Lord Harkom." She shook her head. "The first time I met you, you tried to take what I was unwilling to give. You would not take no for an answer."

"A mere misunderstanding." He gave a gentle laugh. "Your procuress sanctioned more than a little persuasion to break you in. Encouraged it, in fact, since she said you'd never learn what you had to do otherwise."

"You were not gentle with me, Lord Harkom." Faith's trembling was real. "I have been fortunate to have enjoyed the protection of a man who was nothing but kind."

"It was not kind to leave you, Faith." Lord Harkom encompassed their surroundings with a sweep of his arm.

"He died unexpectedly, Lord Harkom. And left me with but a little provision. Not enough to tide me into my old age. I need to shore up my future while I can, while I am young and still—"

"Beautiful." He dipped his head to breathe in the scent of her hair and murmured it again. "So beautiful, Faith, and you have taught me the lesson of valuing that which I want so very much." Lightly, he placed both hands on her bare shoulders. "See how gentle I can be when it's worth my while? I want you, Faith. Not just for tonight. Come home with me, and I promise that I will treat you like a precious China doll."

Faith took a faltering step, her reluctance so from the heart, but at the same time furthering her purpose. Before they'd reached the doorway, she stopped. "You must woo me, take it slowly, treat me like a lady, if you are to enjoy me beyond tonight. If you think tonight is for settling old scores or teaching me a lesson, then that will not further your interests, Lord Harkom."

"My, my, Faith. You've learned how to negotiate and dish out threats. How very sweet." He laughed. "And intriguing."

"So, you promise you will deal with me kindly? Yes? Then I shall tell Mistress Kate who I am going with tonight. That will be my insurance, Lord Harkom."

She let him lead her through the throng, to stop to say a word to Mistress Kate, then out of the doors and into the street.

"Mind the step, Faith. I wonder if my offer of brandy was such a good idea. You want all your wits about you if you're to enjoy what I have in store for you."

"I hope you're not accusing me of overindulgence, my lord." Faith looked up at Lord Harkom, blinking as if to clear her head. "And I'm not sure I want what you have in store for me."

"Yet you're coming with me, aren't you, Faith?" He flagged down a hackney carriage and helped her in. "All the way to my beautiful home where I can make you feel like the princess you are. The princess I could make you. You are intrigued, aren't you? You want to know what kind of man I really am?"

Faith settled herself into the dark interior, sighing deeply as she dropped her head onto Lord Harkom's shoulder. At least feigning sleep for a few minutes would give her time to think and dispense with the need for conversation.

When the hackney halted outside his townhouse, she straightened, rubbing her eyes as she stared at him in the light of the gas lamp on the pavement.

He jumped out and opened the door, but she remained on the cushion.

"I'm really not sure this is such a good idea, Lord Harkom."

"Why, my dear? You considered it an excellent idea not so long ago."

She looked mutinous. "You helped ruin my reputation. And you and I have never been friends."

"But there is so much potential for us to be much more than that, eh Faith? Besides, I had nothing to do with the publication of the photograph, I assure you." He took her hand and helped her out, while she went unresistingly. Like a lamb to the slaughter. Except it wouldn't be hers. She was determined upon that.

When he put his arm about her, taking advantage of his close proximity to caress her breast, she slapped his hand away.

He laughed. "Oh yes, there are certain pretences to be kept up. I think that's part of your charm, Faith. Now, let me help you up the steps. That's a very tight skirt you're wearing. Very daring but very delectable. I shall enjoy seeing the mechanics of how you get it to cling so alluringly to that lovely body of yours. Yes, I'm quite the lover, but quite the engineer too. One is never just the one thing, don't you agree?"

"I don't promise I'll stay, Lord Harkom," she warned him as he led her through his sumptuously decorated townhouse. "You shall have to work hard to persuade me that there is any advantage in furthering our…acquaintance. If you do anything against my will, you will regret it; I promise you."

"Oh, I do love being threatened by a beautiful woman."

His chuckle chilled her to the bone. Faith sent him an arch look as they passed along a dim corridor lined with family portraits. "Don't think you can treat me as you treated me before when I was naïve and vulnerable."

She dismissed his inevitable scepticism at her words with another warning. "I'm neither of those things though, of course, I won't pretend I'm not looking for a protector. I doubt it will be you for more than this one night, but given time I shall find someone to my liking. Someone worthy of me, and someone who will punish you if you dare do wrong by me. Do you understand?"

Still chuckling as he nodded, he escorted her through the door, closing it behind them, catching Faith off balance as he pushed her against the wall, pinioning her like a butterfly as he covered her mouth with his.

Faith brought her knee up with enough pressure to break the contact without hurting him excessively, saying brightly, "Too soon, my lord. What did I tell you? A little wooing to break me in is required, I thought I'd made that clear. Perhaps some champagne? My head is starting to clear and, increasingly, I think that coming here was a very bad idea."

To her relief, amusement replaced the scowl that she'd feared was the precursor to greater menace.

He swept her an elaborate bow. "Of course, my dear, let's bring out the champagne before we get down to business, if that's what you want." He gripped her forearm and led her towards the dining room where he pulled out a chair for her, before ringing the bell for champagne.

Faith took the bottle as he was about to open it, her mind reeling with the risk of doing what she was about to suggest, rather than staying safely here.

As he sank into the chair beside her, she tickled his cheek with the feather in her headdress. "We don't *have* to drink it here, my lord." Her tone was teasing. "I only wanted to make clear that I don't expect to be hustled into any congress without the necessary preliminaries." Rising, she pointed to the glasses before them. "Why don't you take those, and I'll take this, and we can remove ourselves from the proximity of the servants. We can partake of a glass while you compare me to the stars and the moon and the sun, and if your words are pretty enough, and I've consumed enough to make me insensible to the terrible mistake I know in my heart of hearts this really is, then we can proceed from there. How does that please my lord?" She looked playfully at him, astonished to see the transformation. Charity was right. He truly did like being ordered about by a woman.

But, of course, he'd got ahead of himself, and Faith could only hope she was able to reel him in, for once in his bedchamber, he marched her to the bed and tossed her down upon the counterpane, looming over her to kiss her throat and the swell of her breasts. Faith wriggled out from beneath him and stood with her hands on her hips.

"Really, my lord; it's all or nothing with you, isn't it?" She moved unhurriedly towards the small sofa in the centre of the room where she settled herself, tucking her feet beneath her and waving the uncorked bottle towards him.

"Now you can do the honours. I need a drink, Lord Harkom. Probably two if I'm going to enjoy what you have in store for me."

"But not so much that you'll be in danger of not remembering such delights, my precious," he murmured.

Faith hiccupped as she took it, tossing back a long draft as he was in the process of sitting down.

"There's no danger of that, Lord Harkom, though I will need you to top me up." She waved her half-empty glass in the air while indicating the champagne bottle on the sideboard adding with a suggestive look, "I'm referring to my drink, as I'm sure you understand."

He hesitated then visibly relaxed. Perhaps he liked what her double entendre suggested—that she was growing drunk and malleable, and he'd soon have her where he wanted her.

"Well, well, you are in a delightfully pleasing mood tonight and very different from the last time we met, Faith," he remarked, his back turned to her for the few seconds she needed.

The less than two seconds it took for her to uncap the tiny vial around her neck and tip the contents into her glass.

"Having London's most beautiful woman in my bed was beyond my expectations when I set out this evening." He brought them both a glass of fizzing liquid before settling close beside her on the sofa, placing his free hand on her thigh.

She'd ignore it for now. The hand of a man on her person. A man she despised. It was intended as foreplay, but as God was her witness, Faith would do whatever was in her power to avert what Lord Harkom had in mind.

She studied him over the rim of her glass. Did he suspect anything? Or did he imagine that her desire for material goods could overcome the deep loathing that he'd whipped up in her when he'd manhandled her so roughly a year before?

It was a shock to realise that his experience must have seen the return of women whom he'd abused so that Faith's behaviour tonight was not aberrant.

And yet, to her it was so very aberrant.

But then, wasn't she the consummate actress?

For a year, she'd played her role as demure governess so well she'd never been suspected for the fraud she was. For the woman of notoriety she was. For three years prior to that she'd been trained in the arts of seduction. She knew how to whip up a man's desire, how to spur him on when he might have second thoughts, how to pleasure him in bed. In an academic sense, only, of course.

And how to take control if a situation suggested danger. This was where her energies were being channelled now, for she had no intention of doing any of the former.

She'd rather die than have to practise those bedroom skills she'd silently sworn would be reserved for the man she loved.

Crispin.

But did she love him enough, after all this time, that he deserved the ultimate sacrifice?

Their love had been brief, passionate, and sincere. She still believed that.

But how quickly he had dismissed her.

Lord Harkom's hand crept further up her thigh as he bent to refill their glasses at Faith's mumbled direction.

"When we've finished the bottle, we can begin the grand finale!" she declared.

"Or the first act," he responded with a throaty chuckle.

Lord, neither if Faith's plan came to fruition.

But dutifully, and as her role required, she giggled, nibbling his ear as she leaned into him; distracting him with her pretence of embracing his overtures.

"Oh, but you are killing me with anticipation, my love," he muttered, twisting his large body so that he suddenly seemed in danger of crushing her as he trailed kisses along her jawbone.

"Let's drink to that!" she declared with a raucous laugh, raising her glass high, offering it to him with an impish look while she relieved him of his empty glass.

Obediently, he drained the contents of the glass before finding himself in possession of another glass filled with fizzing liquid while Faith declared with false joy, "Yes! Drink to tonight's wild congress."

And without questioning, Lord Harkom drained that glass, too.

CHAPTER 28

Crispin had never desired visiting Madame Chambon's when it was lauded amongst his set as a place of high revels.

And certainly not after he'd learned it was Faith's lodgings, for by then his heart had been eviscerated by her faithlessness, and Madame Chambon's represented everything he despised. It had hothoused a woman who'd learned tricks to trap and entice a man when he'd thought himself so clever in sniffing out artifice.

He'd thought Miss Montague so uniquely innocent and unaffected by the world around her; a fragile rose without thorns, and he was to have been the gallant who would rescue her and gently teach her the ways of the world.

Now, surrounded by the far-from-innocent young women from whom he presumed Faith had learned the tricks of the trade, he felt out of place and deeply uncomfortable.

Lord Delmore had placed him in an impossible position. Crispin had no wish to delve into the overinflated mysteries that an imaginative young Cyprian had been hinting at, for surely they did not endanger him, and surely she was merely fishing for Crispin's involvement for reasons unknown?

He suspected these reasons unknown had a very clear and calculating agenda.

"Charity?" he asked, when an elfin-faced creature sat on the arm of the sofa he was sitting on, her chestnut hair brushing his cheek as she leaned towards him.

"I heard you were looking for me, sir. Come along, shall we?" She took his hand and he rose, silent as she led him along a corridor and up a flight of stairs to a bedchamber on the first floor. "Now, where shall we begin?" Her smile was pleasant and helpful as she waved him towards the large iron bed that dominated the room. A lamp upon the side table bathed the room in a soft glow, and the red-velvet counterpane and plumped-up pillows filled his senses with unexpected desire.

Not for Charity, who'd dropped one shoulder of her evening gown and who seemed pretty and pleasing enough.

But for Faith.

For all he knew, she was still here, and this was just the prelude for finding himself in the right bed.

Her bed.

Yes, he'd weaken if he saw her again. He knew he would.

And he despised himself for it.

Taking a seat on the edge of the counterpane, he said, "I want you to tell me what you know about Faith Montague." He made no move to adjust his clothing, while Charity by this stage was hitching up her skirts to kneel on the bed beside him, one hand already insinuating itself inside his shirt.

She withdrew it as if stung. "Good lord, you're Mr Westaway, aren't you?"

With a scramble and a tugging of her clothing to appear more decent, she took up position at the end of the bed and regarded him, curiously. "I never thought you'd come *here*?"

"Where else might I find her?" Amusement swept away his discomfort. She seemed horrified to be in the company of a gentleman he hoped Faith had painted as not using women in such a cavalier fashion.

"Certainly not here!"

"But this is the only address I have for her."

"She's not lived here for a year. And before that, she never lived as one of us. You do know that, of course."

Before he could make any remark to this, she indicated the bed. "Faith lived in the attic like one of the servants. She didn't have a bed for entertaining."

"But she lived here for…how long? Three years?" He didn't care what she made of his scepticism.

"Yes, Madame had instructions to teach her how to entice a gentleman, but Madame was instructed that she was to be kept pure." Charity sighed. "It was difficult for Faith. Some of the girls were resentful of her because she was so beautiful, and because she didn't have to do the things they had to do for money. They saw that she had lovely clothes, and that she was given learning from a tutor, and that she went to tea at Claridges once a month. She didn't have many friends."

Crispin held up his hand. "*Who* made these instructions concerning Faith?"

"Mrs Gedge. I remember the name only because Faith made up the saying that rhymed, "Working for Mrs Gedge was like living on a knife edge."

"Mrs Gedge." Crispin rolled the name over his tongue as a bitter taste filled his mouth. "What did she look like?"

Charity shrugged. "I never saw her. I only heard that she had bright-red hair. One of the girls saw her when she came in her carriage with Lady Vernon."

"Lady Vernon came *here*?"

"Often. Though she always came in disguise. Sometimes she'd bring girls to Madame Chambon."

"Good lord." He looked about him, horrified. "Lady Vernon brought girls here?" He couldn't begin to imagine the humpbacked dowager stepping foot in a place like this. "And one of these girls was Faith? When was this? When did Lady Vernon bring her here the first time?"

"About three years ago. I wasn't here, then."

"But *why* was Faith brought here?" Crispin stared at the counterpane which must have seen so much action, then through the windows at the church spire outside, and tried to assimilate his thoughts. "If she wasn't one of you, and if she lived in the attic, what possible reason did she have for being here?"

Charity settled herself more comfortably on the end of the bed, tucking her knees beneath her chin as she looked at him. "You do ask a lot of questions. I hope they're going to help Faith." She raised her eyebrows and went on, "Faith had been a servant for Mrs Gedge, who accused her of stealing. She hadn't, of course. Faith was always honest; I hope you know that. Always true to her word. But when a fine lady accuses a servant of something, whose word is going to be believed? So, after Mrs Gedge accused Faith of taking her daughter's bracelet, she brought Faith here because she said Faith had to work off her debt to her."

"What proof did this Mrs Gedge have against Faith?"

"None, of course. She simply found Faith holding her daughter's bracelet in her daughter's bedchamber, and when Mrs Gedge challenged her, Faith said the young lady had promised it to her for showing her a secret passage into a gentleman's bedchamber." Charity shrugged again. "Being here wasn't all bad, of course. Faith got a good education, and she loved her lessons in art and in history and politics. She used to teach some of us more interested girls, both because we liked to learn, but also because it helps pass the time with the gentlemen who don't always want to do things in bed. And, then Faith got to go to smart places. Like I said, sometimes she'd take tea at Claridges with Mrs Gedge."

"Did you say Mrs Gedge was American?"

Charity nodded. "It's hard not to miss an accent like that. I never heard her but Grace, one of the girls here, said she heard an American accent coming from the carriage the night Faith was brought here. And Faith said the lady she'd worked for was an American."

"Do you remember Faith ever talking about Mrs Gedge's daughter?" A tingle of apprehension ran all the way down Crispin's legs as he thought of the life of indenture Faith must have lived within these walls.

"Yes, but the girl died. Killed herself, Faith said. Not that she knew her well as Faith had only been working for Mrs Gedge, or rather, Miss Constancia, for a little while before this grand house party."

"So, Miss Constancia asked Faith about a secret doorway?" He'd always wondered how the young woman could have slipped into his room without him knowing it.

Then slipped into his bed.

Lord, he'd never forget his horror. He'd overreacted though. He saw that, now. But to find a young woman, naked in his bed in the middle of the night in her own house, had been beyond traumatic.

Charity sighed. "And then the young lady did herself in with the young gentleman's razor in his bathtub. They found her in the bath. Not a sight one would forget, I imagine."

No, it had not been. Crispin's stomach churned at the memory. But he'd hardly known the girl. Met her on only a few occasions before she'd set her cap at him.

Crispin rose. It was too difficult to have to think about, though the vision of a young woman floating dead in his bathtub, her red-gold hair spread out about her, her face serene and deathly white in contrast with the blood-red water, often returned to haunt him.

"Mrs Gedge was not only Faith's benefactress; she was the anonymous benefactress of the grand art prize."

The prize that was to place Faith under his roof with instructions that she must make him fall in love with her.

Why? So she could break his heart, of course.

And what choices other than to obey would be available to a vulnerable young girl with a threat of prosecution hanging over her head?

"Where will I find her?" he asked, and Charity cocked her head.

"She's gone to see Lord Harkom, of course. I thought you knew. But, I suppose you had to be told that Faith's not the girl you thought her, otherwise you'd not want to rush over there now. Which you really ought to do."

"She's with Harkom? By God, I ought to—!" He raked his fingers through his hair. "She's with him...*now*, you say? Why not tell me this earlier!?"

"I just told you, Mr Westaway. You came here believing Faith used you as an opportunity to better herself. You didn't believe she loved you, which I assure you, she does. Otherwise, she'd not risk herself with Lord Harkom in order to salvage those letters he says are so damaging to you."

Crispin shook his head. "I have nothing to hide. No love letters that I've ever written which run the risk of sullying my reputation. I can't imagine what Lord Harkom thinks he can hold over me. Unless...!" He moved quickly to the door. "Unless he was using it as a ruse in order to lure Faith to him. She refused him before so..."

Charity fidgeted with her necklace. "Lord Harkom doesn't like to be turned down; it's true. So maybe what you say is right. But nor would it have been right for me to say nothing if there really was something to those letters."

"But why wait so long? Why did you not write immediately, if that was your fear?"

"I'm not stupid, sir, but the letters do have a way of mixing themselves up before my eyes. And no, Faith was careful that no one knew where she was so as not to put me, or her friends, in danger. Besides, I was hoping I'd see you myself so I could tell you about Faith. Like I'm doing now."

"How unlucky I missed her if she was here earlier tonight!" He strode to the door. "Thank you, Charity. I shall go there now. I just hope to God I'm not too late."

FAITH LOOKED AT THE PRONE FORM OF LORD HARKOM WITH satisfaction. Sprawled on the sofa, arms outstretched, legs splayed, he did not look the kind of specimen she'd consider worthy of her, for all he was handsome in a cruel, effete kind of way. And rich.

He would have set her up, nicely.

If she were that kind of girl.

Carefully, she assessed her opportunities. She could only trust that Charity had been right.

She hurried to the large bed and went down on her knees to scrabble underneath. The light was too dim to see, so she rose and quickly carried the lamp to aid her search, going down on her belly to feel about in the dark.

Perhaps Charity had mistaken the chest for something else?

Perhaps Lord Harkom had moved it?

Lord Harkom made a loud snoring noise and his body convulsed, making Faith jump, too.

But as her arm swung wide, it found the handle of an object which, drawing it towards her and into the light, turned out to be a small, neat chest.

With no lock.

Her hands were trembling so much, and her heart beating so fiercely she felt sick, but time was not on her side, so she set to her search with as clear a head as she could.

The letters were arranged in bundles, and the top few seemed to be correspondence from various women to Lord Harkom. Tied up in ribbon, they all seemed similar she decided as she slipped each from its envelope and read the first couple of sentences. Mistresses and spurned lovers. There seemed a lot of those.

As she neared the bottom, her spirits fell. Perhaps she was looking in the wrong chest for there was no sign of anything that suggested an interest in Mr Westaway.

Until she reached the very bottom and found the only envelope not addressed to Lord Harkom or from Lord Harkom.

Faith rolled back on her haunches and closed her eyes a moment. Could this be the letter she was after? Her fingers seemed not to work as they should, and it was difficult not to tear the cheap, single sheet of paper she pulled from its envelope before quickly scanning its contents.

Lord Harkom groaned in his sleep, and Faith's fingers went slack. She stared at the letter, its words a jumble in front of her face. This must be how Charity had felt every time Faith had tried to teach her the alphabet.

But it wasn't that Faith couldn't understand the contents. There was nothing ambiguous about the information, or about the demands for satisfaction or else public disclosure would follow.

Putting a hand to her bosom to try and still the rapid rise and fall, she closed her eyes. Her stomach churned. This wasn't what she'd expected to find. Not at all.

But it clearly was what Lord Harkom had alluded to when he'd told Charity he had correspondence that would damn Mr Westaway in the eyes of the public.

She was just tucking the envelope into her corset and about to close the lid of the chest and rise, when the last three letters of a very familiar name caught her eye.

"Christ, but my head hurts!"

Faith jerked her head up, snatching blindly at the letters and stuffing three, indiscriminately, down the front of her bodice before pushing the chest back into its hiding place and taking up the lamp as she rose to her feet.

"Faith, is that you? What are you doing?"

Faith waved the lamp. "Oh, Lord Harkom! I was so worried and about to fetch help. I…I thought perhaps you might have had a seizure."

When she saw the top of a letter poking out from her corset, she put her hand down her front to push it out of sight and gave her décolletage a little tug, as if righting her clothes.

She leaned over him and put her hand to his cheek. "Goodness, but you are dangerously hot to the touch. You need some water. Instantly!"

Before he could grip her dress with his grasping hand, Faith nimbly eluded him and glided to the door. "I'll be back with a servant and something to drink as soon as I can!" she lied.

When she'd finally escaped into the corridor, she picked up her skirts and ran for her life.

CHAPTER 29

"Lord Harkom, my apologies for intruding at this late hour!" Breathing heavily after his sprint from Soho to the more salubrious environs of Mayfair, Crispin stood in the doorway of his lordship's bedchamber and eyed with dispassion a clearly dissipated Lord Harkom, who was lying in an alarmingly abandoned state.

The two empty champagne glasses did not augur well. Not with the dishevelled state the other man was in, his evening clothes rumpled, though fortunately, the counterpane didn't look too disturbed.

Still, the chaise longue was a comfortable affair, and it was clear Harkom had been entertaining female guests. Crispin could tell by the lingering fragrance of peonies. Faith liked the scent of peonies, though he didn't care to think too much along those lines.

Had she really come here? Had she ventured into the lion's den in order to safeguard Crispin's reputation? How would he know if these were just more lies? Charity seemed sincere enough, but, like Faith, she'd been trained to act a part.

Harkom blinked and rose, stiffly, from the chaise, running his hands through his rumpled hair and gazing blearily about him before focusing on Crispin.

"Gad, but that was some sport, and I don't wonder you've elbowed your way in looking for your piece of the girl. I knew you'd come sniffing her out, but she's gone now." Harkom laughed and lurched to the cabinet where he kept his brandy.

Crispin eyed him beadily. He seemed addleheaded yet not drunk. Surely, he should have been more aggressive and demanding as to how and why Crispin had found his way to his room. A servant certainly wouldn't have led him there.

Indeed, Crispin had been very creative in gaining admittance to Lord Harkom's townhouse with none of the servants the wiser.

With an unsteady hand, Lord Harkom poured them both a measure and handed one to Crispin, who put it down on the nearest surface. He was not about to drink companionably with the possible violator of the woman he loved.

"What did you do to her? She didn't come here willingly." The anger started in his spine and was like a slow burn to his brain. He didn't know if he'd have the self-control to behave as he ought, for physical violence would get him nowhere. Finding Faith to ensure she was safe was his primary concern.

Harkom blinked, with difficulty it seemed, as he turned back to Crispin. "Oh yes, she hooked her little hand into the crook of my arm and all but begged me to look after her. I found her at Mistress Kate's." He smiled, nastily. "Terribly sad. Her previous protector had died, and she had no other offers of a roof over her head. Of course, it was music to my senses. It's rather well known in some circles that she's become my little obsession."

"But she's not here now." Crispin tried to hide his nervous distraction as Lord Harkom leaned against the sideboard. The man was holding his hand to the side of his head and swaying.

He seemed to be having trouble concentrating on the matter at hand. "No, I can't imagine what I was thinking, letting her go like that. Still, she'll come back. And if she doesn't soon enough, I know how to make her."

"I'll get to her first." Crispin's voice was a dangerous growl.

Harkom blinked. For a moment he looked surprised, then his face took on its habitual sneer. "Oh, the fact you had her first was a great pity to me, but I intend to *keep* her. With your name about to be so sullied, you'll wonder how you never knew before now that you had no friends."

Crispin bit into his bottom lip. "I have done nothing of which I am ashamed."

Lord Harkom chuckled and began to count on his fingers. "No past dalliances with married women; no secret babies foisted on well-bred young ladies." His voice was becoming increasingly slurred, and he seemed to have difficulty standing straight. "It's true enough, what you say. Sadly, you had no say in this little matter, though if you ask your father if your mother was an innkeeper's daughter, you might be a little disappointed by his lack of conviction when he tries to deny it."

Crispin blinked stupidly at the other man. "What are you saying?"

Lord Harkom sent him a long look, though he blinked rapidly throughout, as if trying to keep Crispin in focus.

"Never wondered why you look nothing like your father?"

"I take after my maternal line."

"So that's what you've been told? By your fond pater? Or your anxious aunts?" The older man laughed. "Of course, it's what you'd want to believe, but what about if your mother was barren? Or believed she was barren after ten years being married to your father yielded no heir for poor desperate Lord Maxwell?"

"This is an outrageous claim. No one will believe it! On what basis can you even suggest such a thing."

Lord Harkom's lips stretched wide, and his nostrils flared. "Only from the woman who delivered you, asking me for money in return for a letter she'd kept between your father and the poor unmarried woman whom he paid to relieve her of her baby." He examined the half-moons of his right hand.

"Anyone could have made such a spurious claim, but where would it get them? It's a forgery, of course! What possible reason would she have to contact *you*?"

"Because she also found the love letters your mother and I

exchanged before your mother was forced to marry your father, a much older man she could not bear, by the way."

"You lie! My mother would never—"

"How would you know? You were only an infant when she died. You don't even remember your mother."

It was true, but it did not bear up Harkom's claims. Crispin shook his head as if to clear it. Lies! And yet, an uncomfortable kernel of possibility had taken root. Not only did Crispin look nothing like his father, or indeed, the portrait of his mother that hung in the dining room, Crispin's temperament was as different from his father's as it was possible to be.

Harkom shrugged. "Your father married the woman I loved and blamed her for being barren when clearly the problem lay with him. But he needed a son, didn't he?" He chuckled. "You only have to read the letter to find out how he managed it. Why, your father *bought* you, believing you were his, when in fact the girl was already pregnant when she allowed Lord Maxwell to lie with her. Pregnant by a farm labourer!" He burst out laughing. "I can't imagine where you got your delicate hands from and your fine, painterly sensitivities. Anomalies arise where one least expects them to, don't they? But yet, it's all in the letter."

Crispin shook his head. "No, I don't believe it. Show me the letter. Or don't you have it? Perhaps Faith succeeded in retrieving it, after all. It's the reason she came here after she learned from her friend, Charity, whom you visited at Madame Chambon's, that you had information that was damaging to me?"

Lord Harkom jerked as if he'd been stung, and his eyes glanced to a location somewhere near the base of the bed. Regaining some composure, he said, "Your Faith proved most faith*less* when she aligned her star with mine. I promise you; she was not thinking of you, or retrieving letters, when we made love this afternoon. I've never been with a woman so eager!"

"How dare you!" Crispin clenched his fists and strode over to Lord Harkom, gripping the man's collar and forcing his head up. "You lie!

Faith has a pure heart and pure motives. She would never have come to you and put herself in danger unless it was to help…me."

It was a sobering thought. Whether or not it would prove true, was another matter. But yet, it's what he wanted to believe.

To his surprise, Lord Harkom's head lolled, and he slumped even further down the wall. Crispin was not met with the aggression he'd expected.

As for the story he'd just told Crispin, it was so far-fetched Crispin couldn't begin to assimilate how there could be a grain of truth in it.

And yet, he'd never felt he belonged in the home he'd grown up in. His father had always seemed distant and alien, though wasn't that normal?

"Show me the letter," he demanded once more in a low voice. It couldn't be true. A father who was a country peasant, and a mother who was an innkeeper's daughter? Common yeoman stock?

Perhaps Lord Harkom acceded because he was concerned at Faith's reasons for coming to his room. He certainly would not have done it on Crispin's account. He took a couple of staggering steps towards the bed and dropped to his knees, pulling out a small wooden chest.

Two narrow furrows between his eyes grew deeper as he shuffled the papers and his breathing increased. He appeared not to see Crispin when he turned his head in his direction, his eyes glassy as he muttered, "By God, the wench has taken it." He thumped his hand on the lid. "The wench has stolen the letter. Why did I not think that might be a possibility?"

"One might not have thought it necessary to lock a cupboard or a chest containing incriminating documents if peddling lies is such a commonplace event." Crispin moved towards the door, then, on second thoughts, changed direction and took a few steps towards Lord Harkom. "I was going to leave like a gentleman, but in view of the fact that apparently I am a man of no breeding, let me give you this for your treatment of Faith and all those other poor women you treat like playthings."

Striking out with a sharp uppercut, he watched with satisfaction as Lord Harkom crumpled to the floor.

WITH THE LETTERS BURNING A HOLE IN HER BODICE, FAITH MADE HER way to Madame Chambon's as quickly as she could, entering through the back door and arriving in Charity's bedchamber to find it mercifully empty but for Charity.

"Oh, my dear friend, I was so worried for you," Charity wept as she threw her arms about Faith. "Did Lord Harkom hurt you? Did Mr Westaway find you?"

"Mr Westaway?" A thrill of longing travelled through Faith at the sound of his name, but disappointment followed for the fact she'd not seen him. "He really went after me? I mean, he took the trouble…not through vengeance?"

"Lord, Faith, must you be so suspicious? I'm not and look at the life I lead." Charity indicated her room with a sweep of her arm. "So, you found what you wanted from Lord Harkom and he didn't hurt you?" The fact she was so anxious about Faith's well-being made Faith want to weep on the spot.

Also, what she'd learned upon reading them.

"He didn't hurt me, no. And I have the letters.

"So, now you know the truth? Or was Lord Harkom nothing but hot air?"

A tear forced its way out of Faith's eye as she put her hand to her bodice. "It wasn't what I wanted to be the truth, but I do have the incriminating letters—and Lord Harkom doesn't. That's the main thing." A spasm of fear made her reassess as she turned towards the door. "Please don't ask me about it now, Charity. Look, I really should go. I can't subject you to danger. Now I need to find Miss Eaves. Perhaps she can help me."

"Miss Eaves!" Charity scoffed, calling after her friend as Faith ran to the door, "Come back, Faith. I'm perfectly safe. You know Madame Chambon guards us like a wolfhound, and the only reason Anastasia got hurt was because Madame thought she needed teaching a lesson. Please tell me why you want to seek out Miss Eaves? She's no friend of yours. Unless you want her to print the letter you found!"

"Dear God, only one of them." Faith swung around, her jaw set. "I'll never breathe a word about the other letter, and so I'm not even going to tell you what was in it. But Charity, when Anastasia got hurt, didn't she leave shortly afterwards?"

Charity nodded.

"Do you know where she went?"

"No, I don't, Faith. She moved on to another life. That's how it is with girls like us. No need to look so concerned."

"She left with Lady Vernon, didn't she?"

"I don't remember exactly—"

"Please try." Faith gripped Charity by both forearms and looked into her friend's eyes. "Try and remember who took Anastasia away."

Charity looked puzzled, and then a look of understanding crept over her face.

"Yes, I don't have time to tell you more, Charity, but this is the reason I need to find Miss Eaves. She might not be the one who can reveal this to the world, and although she's been no friend of mine, she does have connections, both in the newspaper world and in society. And it's because of her belief that she really was telling a truth the world needed to know, that she printed what she did about me, that I think she's the person most likely to help me now."

"But Faith, you don't even know where she lives!"

"No, but I do know where she'll be tonight." Faith turned and hurried back, a thought occurring to her. "Charity, I need your masque. The one on a stick. Indeed, it's fortuitous that Miss Eaves will be attending Lady Ridgeway's Masquerade. I'm sure she'd not want to talk to me unless we were in disguise."

CHAPTER 30

Crispin didn't care that he was damp with evening mist by the time he'd walked to Madame Chambon's. He needed a bracing walk to clear his head, and he wasn't going anywhere afterwards. Not after he'd located Faith. What he'd say to her, he wasn't sure.

And how she'd react to seeing him after all this time, he had no idea.

Would she consider he'd let her down? He hadn't found her in a whole year though it wasn't for want of trying.

Was there any truth in Lord Harkom's claim, earlier, about what he'd done to Faith?

Not *with* Faith.

He couldn't believe that, and not after Charity's claims that Faith had gone to see him because of her concerns over Crispin.

Her *concerns* over him?

What? About the letter regarding his parentage? Or were they other concerns?

Had Faith read the claims espoused by Harkom? Were they indeed written down as allegations? Letters? Faith had the letters, he suspected, but could there be any truth in them?

His throat felt dry, and his head was sore. The street lamps looked hazy like his surroundings. Was his father's coldness predicated upon the fact that Crispin was not his natural-born son? Could he have suspected that he'd had someone else's bastard foisted on him?

By an innkeeper's daughter?

Crispin swallowed. No, this was Harkom's way of extracting the maximum from the situation. It couldn't be true.

By the time he reached Madame Chambon's, his outerwear was slick with wet, but he didn't care. He just wanted to find Faith and sink into her arms. If she could forgive him, it didn't matter if Harkom's allegations were true or not.

Of course, if Harkom's allegations were given credence, then that was a different matter. But he didn't want to go there yet. He just wanted Faith.

"Oh, Mr Westaway; you just missed her." Charity was lying on her front on her bed, when Crispin entered after knocking briefly and being invited in. She rose onto her knees, her face a picture of delight as her silk peignoir fell away revealing the mounds of her full white breasts over the top of her corset. "I'm so glad it's you though," she added, as she covered herself. "I mean, that *because* it's you, you don't want any of my pleasuring." She blushed, and Crispin could see the flare of colour was real. He was sure he blushed too, as she went on, "I mean, it would be so wrong to be pleasuring the young man whom my best friend is in love with."

Crispin felt a stab in his chest cavity and tried to ignore the words that resounded in his head...*the young man whom my best friend is in love with.* Could that really be true? "Please, Charity, I don't think I have much time and I need to find her!"

"She's gone to Lady Ridgeway's masquerade," Charity told him.

"I can't believe I was too late!" He raked his hands through his hair. "Was she…all right after her encounter with Lord Harkom?" He could barely push out the question, though it seemed odd that Faith would make her way to further revelry if she were not.

"She didn't say. She wanted to find Miss Eaves. She had an important letter to give her."

He blinked. "Miss Eaves? She's going to give the letter to Miss Eaves?"

Could she really have hated him so much?

All the hope and expectation he'd built up drained out of him.

Charity slipped to the floor and went to her dressing table where she began to pin up a curl. "Well, *one* of the letters. She wouldn't tell me about the other one. But the letter she was going to give Miss Eaves was the important one, she said."

"The one she found in Lord Harkom's chest?"

Charity nodded, looking at him in the mirror. "Well, she found them both there. But this one is the one she hopes is going to put things right."

"But…Miss Eaves destroyed Faith's reputation. Faith's not…planning revenge, is she?"

Charity turned as she let out a surprised laugh. "What a masculine thing to say. Revenge? Faith would never resort to revenge to harm anyone." Her forehead wrinkled as she reassessed this statement, looking more closely at Crispin as she added, "I mean, she never intended wreaking revenge on you, Mr Westaway. That was Mrs Gedge's idea, and you do know that Faith was entirely powerless in that woman's hands. Just as I'm powerless in Madame Chambon's. Do you think I like doing what I do to earn a living?" She shrugged. "I simply have no other choice open to me."

This was not the time for Crispin to delve further into these murky depths. When he found Faith, he intended asking her a good many questions about her motivations, but there was too much at stake now for him to tarry.

"Yes, make your way to Lady Ridgeway's, and I hope you find Faith. And that you'll be good to her, for I fear what she's found puts her in very grave danger."

"You know?" Crispin moved forward and gripped Charity's shoulders, forcing her to look at him.

Charity's large blue eyes suddenly filled with tears which she brushed away, saying with a shaky laugh, "I try to pretend there's nothing happening under this roof, and that we're all safe as long as

Madame sees us as bringing in the money, but the truth is, a girl is never safe here. One wrong action and Faith could be next."

"Surely you can't mean it." He didn't know what to say. "Are you suggesting there is something more sinister at play than Mrs Gedge's plan for revenge against me?

Charity nodded. "It was in a letter Faith found. I think the letter was from Lady Vernon to Lord Harkom, but Faith wouldn't tell me. She said it would put me in danger to know."

"What do you think it's about, Charity? I need *something* to go on."

"I think it's about a girl who disappeared from here a few months ago. A girl called Anastasia. Lord Harkom was very cruel to her. He hurt her. And then she disappeared."

"And Lady Vernon's involved?"

Charity nodded, her lower lip trembling. "Please don't ask me anything more, Mr Westaway, because it would all be guesswork. It's only after Faith left that I really began to puzzle it all out. And this is my conclusion. I think Lady Vernon and Lord Harkom are in some evil business together. And unless Faith is very careful, she could find herself in some extremely hot water."

Faith's attire was perfectly suited to the evening's entertainment, while Charity's demi-masque on a stick provided the necessary anonymity. Her identity would be discovered in due course, but initially, Faith might be able to mingle enough to search out Miss Eaves before she was asked to leave.

She found the young woman in the midst of a group of ladies all talking about hats.

Only Miss Eaves was not sufficiently interested, so her eyes were scouring the room in search of greater diversion when Faith dropped her demi-masque and caught her eye.

Miss Eaves's mouth fell open, but a subtle crook of her finger had Faith following her into the shadows.

"Well, well, Miss Montague. I see you are back at your trade." The young woman's eyes raked Faith's ensemble with obvious censure, for the figure-hugging ensemble, while fashionable, was risqué. "I just wonder how you have made your way inside without being recognised. You know you have no place here."

Faith had no time to defend herself or try to alter Miss Eaves's opinion. The young woman had clearly become a great deal more polished and sophisticated since the first time Faith had met her.

"Read this and tell me what you think." Faith thrust Lady Vernon's letter into Miss Eaves's gloved hand and waited impatiently as the other slowly began to read—with obvious reluctance.

Finally, she handed it back. "White women snatched from a London brothel into slavery? Sold to a sultan in Constantinople? Really, Miss Montague? You expected everyone to believe you a fine lady when you were nothing but a yeoman's daughter caught for stealing. A very clever one, obviously, to have entrapped Mr Westaway as you did. But this?" She tapped the letter with her forefinger before handing it back to Faith. "A forgery! You want me to print this as a front-page story so I can be sued for libel?"

"Only if it were proved untrue."

She gave a brittle laugh. "I'm sorry, but I can't indulge your wild fancies, Miss Montague. Not tonight, or any other night." She turned, but Faith turned with her, gripping the sleeve of her expensive evening gown.

"Please, Miss Eaves, you're the only person I know of with connections that might be able to bring justice to Lady Vernon and Lord Harkom."

"How convenient. The very people you claim are the architects of your demise." Miss Eaves's smile dripped scepticism.

Stung, Faith dropped her hand. For a long moment, the two women stared at one another. Faith looked away first. She had no more time to waste.

"Then I'll find Lord Delmore. If you won't believe me, he will. I should have gone to him in the first place." Angrily, Faith swept past her, the crowd parting as she made her way to the double doors.

CHAPTER 31

The inclement weather did nothing to aid Crispin's evening. Although his evening clothes were damp, they were passable enough for him to excite little attention when he entered Lady Ridgeway's ballroom a little later that evening.

He managed to bow and nod with sufficient politeness, that his anxiety and hurry to find Miss Eaves and, hopefully Faith, were not too apparent.

A year had passed, and he'd given a good account of himself in Germany. Society tended to forget a young man's transgressions and, in time, regard with amusement the fact he might have been hoodwinked by a beautiful girl in order to paint her. If he'd distinguished himself in his consular post, and besides, was ensconced somewhere on the Continent where out of sight meant out of mind until the matter was more or less forgotten, then all to the good.

So, Crispin found himself nodding and forcing a smile and a greeting to all manner of unexpected past acquaintances of his father and himself as he pushed through the throng.

How long would that last? he wondered with a stab of discomfort, and then was surprised that the depth of his shock over his own possibly lowly origins didn't overwrite his fears over Faith to the extent he'd have imagined they would.

And wasn't this because, being on more of an equal footing, so to speak, she'd suddenly become so much more accessible to him?

Of course, it wasn't as easy to spot her when most people carried a mask on a stick, although in many cases, this was dropped due to the late hour and amount of champagne consumed.

A pink gown. That's what Charity had said she was wearing, but none of the women in pink gowns were Faith, and none could hold a candle to her, besides.

But there was Miss Eaves, her dark-brown hair and ruddy face instantly recognisable as he closed the distance between them, arriving right before her as she turned away from a group of ladies discussing, he could just make out, hats.

"Mr Westaway!" She seemed to lose her composure for a second before she added, "We have not seen you for some time, though I hear you have distinguished yourself. I hope your father is well."

"I'm flattered that you have followed my career and take a concern in the family." He genuinely had not intended it to sound so ironic, but rather than let it rest, Miss Eaves flushed and said, "I told only the facts as they presented themselves, Mr Westaway. I'd imagined you were thankful for your lucky escape. No one wants to be taken for a fool or enter into a lifetime contract against their will."

"Which is exactly what happened to Faith. Have you seen her, Miss Eaves?"

Miss Eaves sent a longing glance towards the circle in which she'd earlier been ensconced before answering, with a shrug, "She was here earlier."

"Good lord, then she has given you the letter?" He felt his shoulders slump. "She came here with that express purpose."

"I heard an outlandish story of women being lured into some kind of unbelievable slavery to the Ottoman sultan. All the product of a disordered mind and only a forgery to substantiate it."

"Then you saw the letter?" Crispin felt himself come to life. "Faith was going to give you the correspondence between Lady Vernon and

Lord Harkom to verify the truth of this. She's taken an enormous risk to uncover the truth, managing to extract it from Lord Harkom. I've just come from there."

Miss Eaves pressed her lips together. She seemed unable to answer.

Crispin could barely keep still. "Miss Eaves, you must tell me how long ago she left! Miss Montague is in great danger. I'd heard whispers that suggested such a thing was happening, but there was nothing to substantiate it until tonight. The letter is no forgery, Miss Eaves. Surely you could tell that for yourself!"

"Mr Westaway, I…" She bit her lip, her confusion apparent. "I don't know what to tell you except that she told me she was going to find Lord Delmore."

Crispin turned on his heel. "If you see her again, detain her," he said, over his shoulder, his tone urgent. "Persuade her not to go anywhere unless she is accompanied."

He was about to slip into the crowd when Miss Eaves detained him with a hand on his sleeve. When he looked into her frightened face he noticed her skin was very pale and there was a tremor in her voice as she said, "Miss Montague left the room about half an hour ago. I followed her, when my uncle called me over to meet a new arrival just as Miss Montague was descending the front steps." She pressed her lips together and rolled one shoulder, and Crispin felt a stab of very real terror, justified as Miss Eaves finished, "Lady Vernon seemed to be waiting for her from just inside the carriage that had drawn up. I caught only a glimpse before Miss Montague was inside. And…" she hesitated "… in the glow of the lamplight, I believe I saw Lord Harkom. Certainly, at the time I believed it was Lord Harkom, for I returned thinking with such scepticism of her renewed defence that she'd ever had a willing association with him."

Crispin was already heading towards the door. "And nor has she, he said angrily. "Miss Eaves, if you see anything or hear anything that could help this case, please send a message directly to my lodgings. Dear God, I just hope and pray I find her in time."

CHAPTER 32

The blindfold was cutting into Faith's eyes painfully by the time she was released. When she stumbled, she realised it was as much due to the fact the flooring was unstable as that she was disoriented.

The cry of seagulls and the smell of brine and tar made it clear that she was on board a boat.

Or something larger, for the room was commodious with a large porthole that looked over the ocean. Dawn had broken, and the fact that her head hurt unconscionably compounded the realisation that she'd been drugged.

She swung around to confront her captors, and was not surprised to see Lord Harkom's golden hair lit by the late-afternoon sun that shone through the glass and, seated upon a chair at his side, the hunched, crow-like form of Lady Vernon.

"My, my, Lady Vernon; it's been a long night for you," Faith remarked drily. "You're not usually an early riser, so I'm sorry to put you through such discomfort."

Lady Vernon grimaced which Faith took to be a smile. "I was not going to be denied the pleasure of seeing you go where you deserved.

My goodness, but you've caused us a great deal of trouble, Faith. Finally, you'll be getting your just desserts."

Faith looked towards the porthole where the choppy sea was partly obscured by the crew in striped jerseys leaping from the rigging onto the deck. She could hear voices. Shouts that at first she thought were in French, before she realised some of them spoke a language she didn't recognise. "You won't get away with this, Lady Vernon. Nor you, Lord Harkom. Your activities have been exposed."

"On what evidence, my dear Faith?" He looked satisfied as he paced back and forth across the room. "Whatever correspondence you found is now back in my possession. Besides, who might you have told who would actually believe you? A liar and a whore."

Faith shivered as she imagined the groping that must have been involved when she was unconscious. She swallowed, her fear obviously showing before Lord Harkom said, "I haven't violated you, if that's what you're worried about. There'd be little pleasure for either of us in doing that if you were not awake to enjoy it." With a glance at Lady Vernon, he added, "All good things must wait, and I have a special parting gift for you before the boat sets sail. I'd have liked to have kept you, my dear, in the style you could have enjoyed, had you been a little cleverer. In fact, I had thought you came to my residence to negotiate a special agreement with me." He sighed. "However, your quick mind and ability to master the politics of a situation will stand you in good stead when it comes to learning a new language. Turkish, in fact. Yes, you have an eager patron a few hundred miles north of Constantinople waiting for you. He's paid a king's ransom for a girl fitting just your description, and since I have decided you're more trouble than you're worth, I'm taking you there, myself."

"Or face capture, yourself, in England!" Faith shot back.

"Oh, the passage of time and the fact there is nothing to connect me with any wrongdoing will stand me in good stead."

She'd managed to keep her fear under control when she was speaking, but having to listen to him spout his evil, unleashed the shivering she'd kept in check until now. She clasped her arms about herself for she had no opera cloak or other means of warmth, and her evening dress was very bare about her bodice.

"So, Faith, have you anything to say for yourself?"

The light from the porthole spilled in a luminous circle in the centre of the room, and into this Lord Harkom stepped, as if he were a golden prince rather than the Prince of Darkness she now knew him to be.

"She's not going with you, Harkom."

Faith turned with a start; the familiar voice so unexpected and so welcome. A tall, brown-haired gentleman in evening clothes, with tired eyes, high cheekbones, and a sensitive mouth, locked eyes with her.

Crispin.

She'd thought of him so often during these past twelve months. Too often, in her imaginings, their welcome was curt and full of recrimination at the way each had failed the other. But now, as he stepped into the full beam of light to stand face to face with Lord Harkom, he looked every bit the handsome hero of her dreams.

"It's over, Harkom." He turned to Lady Vernon with an exaggerated bow, following a brief smile of encouragement for Faith before he went on, "Your activities have been revealed. Thanks to Lady Vernon's correspondence, we've been apprised of your involvement in the trade of friendless young women from English shores to the Ottomans. You will shortly be in custody, and Miss Montague will be leaving with me."

He took a step forward and, with hope and happiness flooding through her, Faith moved towards the hand he offered.

"A little peremptory, I think, Mr Westaway." As Lord Harkom spoke, the boat gave a shudder and a jolt which sent Faith stumbling briefly into Crispin's arms, before her nemesis snatched her against him, pressing her face against his shoulder with one cupped hand. "Well, well, this is unexpected. It would appear we've already set sail for foreign shores. Sorry, Lady Vernon; just a minor disturbance to our plans. I'm sure you'll find your sea legs soon enough."

Faith, after a brief struggle, realised it might not be a good time to vent her outrage. Lady Vernon, for her part, seemed equally outraged, for she drew her bony frame to its full height and sent a querulous look towards the door.

"I have hardly prepared for sea travel, Lord Harkom. Go and see what's happened! We can't have set sail yet."

"Oh, I very much fear we have, Lady Vernon." Lord Harkom shook his head with a look of feigned regret. "I didn't think it would come to this. I'd very much hoped it wouldn't. But I'm not a man to leave anything to chance."

"Except that your stupidity invited this whole debacle." Lady Vernon pointed at Faith before turning to Lord Harkom. "Lord only knows what you were doing when you invited this conniving creature into your bedchamber, and with an unlocked chest, too! That's what's behind all this." She began to shake as her fury mounted. "We have the letter back. The two letters back. Originals, and the only evidence of our involvement. We've been so careful. I've been so careful. This was not necessary. I want to go home now. Give the orders that we are to turn back." Her arm trembled as she pointed at the sea through the porthole.

Lord Harkom gave Faith a squeeze and lowered his face to put his cheek against hers. "All in good time, Lady Vernon; all in good time." He dropped a kiss upon Faith's brow. "I want to enjoy this one first. I want Westaway to feel the pain I felt when his father married the woman I loved."

"What do you want from me to guarantee that no harm comes to Faith? That she is granted her freedom." Crispin spoke softly but clearly, and Lord Harkom barked out a laugh.

"It's a bit late for that, don't you think? You've been resting on your laurels a whole year, and you clearly didn't give poor Faith here a second thought."

"Faith is very good at hiding her tracks," Crispin said pointedly. "I searched for you, you know." The fact he spoke directly to her made Faith's heart beat wildly as she held her breath and kept eye contact with the striking man before her. "I'll admit that after we were parted,

I was angry and disappointed. My father told me it was what I deserved. What I should have expected."

"Just as we expected he would," Lady Vernon said, on a sniff. She'd walked to the porthole and stood staring dolefully out at the white-capped waves that surrounded them, turning to say over her shoulder, "A brothel is hardly the environment a gentleman such as he would like to think nurtured his son's intended."

"But more than he deserves," Lord Harkom ground out. "Did your father suffer to see his only child so horribly compromised? I hope he did. Has he been disappointed by what he was dealt? I'm sure he has. After all, what can one expect of the son of an innkeeper's faithless slut of a daughter and a country yokel."

"You've concocted this story without a shred of evidence." Crispin held himself proudly. "Meanwhile, the two of you are clearly guilty of a crime that would see you rot in prison. You've been soliciting girls and selling them into slavery." He regarded Faith with a sad smile. "Faith was lured into doing what she never would have done of her own volition."

"And she has served our purposes well." Lady Vernon gave a short laugh. "The only fly in the ointment was Mrs Gedge. She wanted to be kept updated regarding Faith's progress at every juncture. She wanted reports that she actually was getting her lessons; that she was being turned into a lady. Yes, she wanted Faith to be every bit as accomplished and desirable as her own Constancia had been so that she could entice Mr Westaway with her charms."

"Not that that went very well, initially," Lord Harkom resumed. "I'll admit I was mightily taken by the girl's beauty when I spied her at Madame Chambon's, but it was only after I learned that there was any connection to Lord Maxwell that she became of such interest to me."

Faith gasped. "That's why you tried to take me, unwillingly! After I returned from being painted at the end of the first week. The first painting." She swung around to confront Lady Vernon. "You decided that I'd failed in my mission to Mrs Gedge, so you might as well make use of me by selling me to Lord Harkom."

Lady Vernon sniffed. "And then, all of a sudden Mrs Gedge was offering me more money to make a final onslaught for the second painting. Suddenly, she'd elevated the prize money, and my reward, and you, Faith, were becoming too interested, yourself, in the young man you'd initially intended to seduce and leave. Ah yes," she sighed. "It was becoming very interesting and filled with possibilities. I could collect from Mrs Gedge—spectacularly, I might add, after the newspapers obligingly ran their story—*and* claim a reward from Lord Harkom who had his own particular vendetta against Mr Westaway."

"So, Miss Eaves was part of this, too?" Faith couldn't believe she'd been so gullible, but Lady Vernon dismissed this notion. "The silly little thing lives to tell the truth. Women who deceive and are otherwise immoral deserve to be revealed for who they are so that men can respect the rest of the fairer sex. Yes, she ran that story believing it was in the interests of advancing women's rights. And that such apparent transparency was needed in the interests of maintaining the integrity of the arts world. Oh, she was delightfully sincere and oh, so obliging."

Lord Harkom laughed. "An unexpected piece of largesse, that was. As was discovering that Westaway surely had fallen in love. With you, Faith! The woman who'd been recruited to break his heart. And, that not only had you broken his heart, you'd made him a laughing-stock, severely damaged his career prospects, and thoroughly damaged his relationship with his father. Why, you were just perfect. But then you disappeared. You were good, Faith. No one could find you, and I'd almost given up hope when suddenly, here you are." He turned. "And here Westaway is. Ready for the final reckoning." His nostrils flared, and he patted his pocket before drawing out a small pistol. "The crew are disinclined to tie you to the masthead, and the captain maintains the fact that this is a regular sailing. But just be aware of what you risk if you try to overcome me, Westaway. Your father killed the woman I loved, and I am more than happy to kill you."

Crispin shook his head. "You lie. What could my mother possibly have seen in a cruel and twisted madman?"

Lord Harkom ignored him. "Yes, he snatched her away from me

and, not being satisfied with that, he broke her heart and then he killed her."

"My mother died of fever," Crispin countered.

"The woman you believed was your mother. The woman who agreed to travel to France, pretending to be in the early stages of pregnancy, so that there'd be no questions asked after she returned with the brat that was foisted on an innkeeper's daughter by Westaway senior. The bastard he thought was his, but who was cuckolded when the child—you—arrived a good month earlier than you should have done. Yes, your *real* mother, the innkeeper's daughter, was already a month gone to her country yokel lover when she agreed to be a broodmare to your father. It solved a very great problem for her, no doubt. Yes, she garnished her pocketbook and lived very comfortably, until the money ran out and she wrote to me informing me of the situation, after having been apprised of my vendetta against your father." He pointed the revolver at Crispin and shook his head. "Look at you, Westaway. Parading about in those clothes like a gentleman. It's a joke."

Crispin didn't seem to heed him. He neared Faith and held out his hand. "Let her come to me for now," he said, smiling at Faith. "You can torture us later. I've been waiting for this a long time."

To Faith's surprise, Lord Harkom released her and she ran into Crispin's arms. She barely registered Lord Harkom's desultory clap. "What sport the two of you will provide as we proceed to tear young love asunder. Yes. Hold her, kiss her, enjoy her for this short time, while my heart breaks to think of such a lovely thing being so tarnished by what I have in store. Yes, when we reach shore you'll be parted, never to see one another again." He looked through the heavy doors and then outside at the raging seas. "For the next two days, you are my captives and will be completely beholden to me. So, you may have a few minutes under my watch to remember the closeness that you once apparently enjoyed. After that, I shall enjoy tearing the two of you apart once more—just as your father did to me and your mother."

❄

FAITH LAY ON HER BACK UPON THE COVERS OF THE LARGE BED IN THE stateroom to which she'd been assigned and stared through the porthole at the choppy seas beyond. Her cheeks were damp from tears, but there was no point in wiping them away. More would simply join them.

It had been a long time since she'd wept. Her upbringing had made her strong. Her father punished softness. And that meant tears. Faith had never enjoyed closeness to either parent or, in fact, her siblings. They'd bickered and lashed out at each other, and she'd seen her removal from the family home to work in the big house as a reprieve from such pettiness.

She'd not even cried when she'd been falsely accused of stealing. Injustice was a natural part of her experience.

Her education at the hands of a man of kindness and ethics had given her a new realisation of life and human beings. Perhaps it had set her up for unhappiness by making her realise that even she had prospects for it. Professor Monk had given her enough examples of people from humble beginnings who had changed the world and received their just rewards to give her hope that she, too, might find a meaning for her life.

Now, as the boat was lifted and tossed upon the waves of the English Channel, Faith imagined the worst that Lord Harkom had in store for her. He might even make Crispin watch.

She shuddered, and a sob lodged in her throat.

"Faith."

Terrified, she half rose, ready to fight with everything she had at her disposal.

It was Lady Vernon, her gimlet eye trained on Faith.

"You're to get yourself ready to receive Lord Harkom this evening. I've brought you a change of clothes and a few other necessaries to clean yourself up. You're hardly looking your best."

"He can take me as I am," Faith muttered, but the prospect of clean water for washing and a change of linen and new gown was too enticing. She felt dirty and unkempt.

"So, Lord Harkom keeps women's clothing and ivory brushes on hand for such contingencies?" Faith asked Lady Vernon, as she'd worked on her coiffure and changed into the dark-blue confection with its ruffles and ribbons that was presented. It did not require a corset, and nor were there combinations. It was the perfect item for easy divestment, she thought cynically. Lord Harkom wouldn't need to do much work to have her where he wanted.

Lady Vernon didn't answer as she appeared to be on the point of leaving. Faith detained her. "I need to go outside for some fresh air. I shall be sick, otherwise, and Lord Harkom won't want that, I'm sure."

Fortunately, Lady Vernon didn't seem too troubled by the suggestion, saying, "I suppose there's not far you can go." So, Faith found herself on the forward deck with the wind ruining the smoothness of her newly brushed hair, hurrying towards the railing while Lady Vernon remained just inside the doorway, protected from the cold.

"Faith!"

It was Crispin. She turned, her hands shaking as they gripped the railing before Crispin covered them with his own.

"I am so sorry for putting you through this." His voice tickled her ear and sent tendrils of warmth through her.

"You aren't responsible," she returned, shocked he should even think it. "I was given the mission of breaking your heart. I accepted."

"Did you have a choice?"

Seaspray weighed down her eyelashes and dripped onto her cheeks as she raised her eyes to look at him.

"Oh Faith, you were young. A child, when you were taken by Mrs Gedge. You were slotted into a life for which you were completely unprepared, but you used everything you had to survive. Look at you!" There was admiration in his eyes. "Your beauty was an advantage. Of course, it was. But you had a mind that was agile, a clever wit, and a love of knowledge that was fed; however extraordinary those circumstances were."

"And now you are a captive at the hands of your father's arch nemesis; a man who is clearly mad, and who thinks that destroying you will punish your father in the way he wants to." Faith squeezed Crispin's hand. "You're here because of me, and for that I'm truly sorry."

Crispin smiled down at her. "I'm just as responsible for being here. I'm culpable for not having been able to better look after the woman I love. Don't think I haven't thought about that all these many hours I've had to suffer the rocking of this boat, and know that soon a time will come when Harkom exerts his vile power and makes us both suffer."

He glanced towards the doorway where Lady Vernon was sheltering. Perhaps she wasn't planning to intervene because of the discomfort and the cold. Perhaps it was under Lord Harkom's orders. After all, the greater the bond forged between Faith and Crispin now, the more they would suffer later, when Lord Harkom decided it was time.

"I'm afraid," Faith whispered, nestling against him. "I've only ever been with a man I love. When I saw Lord Harkom earlier this evening, I was fired up with zealous rage because I thought I had nothing to lose. I drugged him, and I succeeded in my mission. But now he has triumphed."

"Because I have failed you."

"Not you!" Faith twisted in the circle of his arms and raised her own to cup his face. "Why would you have behaved otherwise? Miss Eaves printed a story that looked very credible. So credible that *she* believed it because, as we know, she is a young woman who is driven by principle—on the surface, at any rate. The photograph told a compelling story. The villains were people of standing in high society. I was revealed for what I am. And people like me are never believed above people like Lord Harkom and Lady Vernon and Mrs Gedge."

Crispin wrapped her more closely in his arms. "You know I will fight to the death to protect you from Harkom when he comes to you, this evening."

"Oh, don't waste a good life when I am what I am," Faith said, trying to smile. "It's what I was trained for. It's what Charity endures numerous times every day. I've been living in a cloud. Don't be foolish on my account, Crispin. We are very effectively Lord Harkom's prisoners, and I would be happier if you saved your energies for a surprise attack rather than when he is expecting it. For you know that is his plan."

"Lord, but you do know how to read a man."

"I've been trained in the science for years. I applied it very skilfully to you." She couldn't help smiling. "If I made you love me, though, it was at my expense. That was where I failed in my mission."

"Oh no, it wasn't. That was where Lady Vernon and Mrs Gedge must be congratulating themselves. They were able to destroy you at the same time as my reputation. A double win. Mrs Gedge couldn't bear the thought that her beautiful Constancia should be dead while you, a worthless creature in her eyes, should only grow more beautiful; accomplished. Everything she'd have wished for her daughter." He stopped, gripping her forearms as he asked, "But Faith, do you still love me? After all this time, and all the hours you must have run over in your mind how I'd failed you. Forsaken you."

"I thought about you every day, Crispin. I wondered how I could still love a man I knew thought the very worst of me. Because you did, didn't you?

He nodded. "There was no piece of evidence I could find to exonerate you. Not until yesterday and…" he looked up at the tall mast and rigging, the sails flapping loudly in the wind, "a lot has happened since then."

They were aware of Lady Vernon coming towards them.

"I suppose Lord Harkom would want you apart, now." She sounded distinctly out of sorts. "I wish to go to my cabin and I can't leave you here."

"Where is Lord Harkom? Not retching his guts out, I trust?"

Lady Harkom's nose twitched. "I gather that's exactly what he's doing, but I'm sure he'll recover soon enough. He has grand plans for you, Faith." Her mouth twisted.

"I never liked you, Lady Vernon, but I had no idea I had such good reason to trust my instincts." Faith stared her down. "Your evil knows no bounds, does it?"

"We all do what we must to survive. A title is no guarantee of a comfortable life. I've not wished for much, and I'm hardly extravagant. Not like his good lordship." She indicated the innards of the boat, and presumably, Lord Harkom, with a jerk of her head. "Without supplementing my meagre allowance, I too would have been placed in your situation, Faith. Only...I don't have quite your assets. So don't play the moral high ground with me."

"You and Lord Harkom make strange bedfellows," Faith countered. "I hope he makes this line of business worth your while. You do know what awaits you when you return to England."

Lady Vernon shrugged. "Don't threaten me, girl. You'll be long gone, and I intend to be safely returned to England before too long. I hadn't factored in this trip across the channel, it's true, but Lord Harkom and I can come to some agreement over that. So, don't worry yourself over my future, Faith. Enjoy your nabob in the delightful harem seven hours' camel ride from Constantinople, or wherever Lord Harkom has arranged for you to go. There were several options. He may be planning to auction you, for all I know. And I don't care a jot. You were always more trouble than you were worth. I never understood Mrs Gedge's need to play so fairly by you."

"Indeed, I admire your trust in Lord Harkom," Crispin remarked. "He's hardly renowned for dealing honestly with anyone."

"Come on, Faith." Lady Vernon ignored him. "I'm going to lock you in your cabin now where you can expect a visit from Lord Harkom as soon as he's feeling up to you. As for you, Mr Westaway," she shot him a look as if unsure what to do, then shrugged. "I daresay I can't order you to your cabin, and these sailors apparently won't take orders from any but their captain, so enjoy your view of the high seas. I'll be glad when land is sighted. Like Lord Harkom, I was not made for boat travel."

There was only so long that Crispin could spend in the biting wind. When he went in, he tried Faith's door, but it was securely bolted. He tried Lord Harkom's door and found that similarly bolted from the inside. However, instead of the silence that had greeted him when he'd knocked lightly for Faith, he could hear retching and a drawn-out groan from the other side.

On the quarterdeck, he located the bosun, the only crew member who could speak English it appeared, and asked him if Lord Harkom was in need of assistance.

"Like the ol' woman, the seas ain't the thing fer 'igh-born stomachs. All 'e needs is ter put 'is two flat feet on summat that doesn't move."

"Is Lord Harkom *so* seasick?"

The bosun sniggered. "Can't drag 'imself from 'is bunk."

"And how is the young lady who is locked in her room supposed to eat her dinner?"

"I'll take summat to 'er. The gennulman gave me orders ter see she were well attended."

"If his lordship is so indisposed, perhaps you'd allow her some fresh air at the same time she takes some refreshment."

"I can do that fer 'er if it's worth me while." The bosun offered him a gap-toothed grin, and Crispin obligingly dug into his pocket and withdrew a pound note. The bosun's eyes grew large. "She can 'ave all the time an' all the vittels she wants, sir," he said, taking the note with a shifty glance to ensure he'd not been observed by any of his fellows.

Crispin glanced about him. "Then let her go, now," he ordered but the bosun shook his head. "Not wiv others about wot'd see me disobeying orders." He sent Crispin a sly look. "Why don't you go and get yerself some rest. I'll let you know when the coast is clear."

Crispin went to his bunk and lay down.

He presumed they were not going to dock within the next few hours, perhaps longer. And it had been a very long day already. But how could he sleep after Lady Vernon's ominous words?

Lord Harkom was involved in the white slave trade, and Faith was his next victim.

He'd learned that she'd been ready to consume a vial of poison and kill herself only a few hours before. What might she contemplate doing now? The thought terrified him, but he was powerless to help her. Yet again, he'd failed her.

Despite his best efforts, sleep claimed him at last, and when he woke at the sound of his door being slowly opened, he was refreshed enough to have a weapon ready. The candlestick was clutched in his right fist, and Lord Harkom was going to receive the full force of a hefty blow until, in the darkness, he heard Faith's tentative voice.

"Crispin. Can I slide in next to you? There's not much room, is there?"

Her words sounded so ridiculous under the circumstances that he laughed as he drew aside the covers and brought her close against his side.

She rested her head on his shoulder, and he stroked her face, staring into the darkness.

"The bosun forgot to bolt the door when he took me my food." She laughed. "Can you believe that?"

"I can."

"Of course, it was you, wasn't it? And here I am." She snuggled in closer and hooked one thigh over his, partly to stop from falling out of bed, he supposed, while a tremor of longing shook him to the bone.

"And Lord Harkom is terribly indisposed. He hasn't left his stateroom since he spoke to us." She sighed. "Maybe he's afraid of being accosted by you, Crispin."

"A terrifying proposition." Crispin felt his inadequacy. "Harkom is a champion pugilist, and I'm hardly fighting material. No, he knows he holds the upper hand. As soon as his strength returns, he'll carry on as he pleases." He began to stroke her cheek. It was soft and smooth, but also hot to the touch. In the darkness, he imagined its flush of colour. He'd have liked to have been able to see her. He was a painter, after all. But simply touching her filled him with a deep peacefulness. "He may also choose to stay in his room because he realises he's miscalculated. He's on a boat that wasn't prearranged for nefarious dealings. The crew will answer only to the captain, and the captain has no interest in breaking the law. Harkom realises this, I think."

"Then we could enlist the captain's help?"

"I've tried. The captain says his orders are to take us to Rotterdam, and that's all he'll do. He's not taking sides.

"Will you kiss me, Crispin?"

"It might be dangerous."

"I like danger."

He found her lips easily in the dark. She'd been waiting for him, and she drew him into the kiss with a light hand upon his cheek.

He'd not been exaggerating when he'd voiced concern about the danger. The simple touch of his lips against hers ignited him from within. The feel of her breasts pressing against him, harder with each rising breath, became a conflagration that threatened to consume him.

"I love you, Crispin," she whispered, shifting over him so that her body covered his and his hand came in contact with her naked thigh when he sought to hold her as the ship pitched.

"And you, Faith. I love you, too."

She wriggled a little, and suddenly she was positioned directly above him, and he was straining to keep his basest impulses in check. But her hand was on him, her little fingers working the buttons of his trousers, and he was in no doubt what she wanted.

There were no words to be said. No doubts or fears to be allayed. Their time was limited and their need for one another all consuming.

He skimmed her smooth, moist thighs until his hand was on her heated mound. With a sigh, she cupped his cheek and kissed him more deeply.

The need to protect her was uppermost in his mind, but so was his need to communicate his real feelings for this brave and beautiful young woman.

She wanted him. She was ready for him. She made that clear enough as she felt for him.

Another pitch of the boat, and he was as one with the woman for whom he'd sacrifice everything.

THEIR SLEEP WAS SHORT, BUT DEEP AND REVIVING.

When Crispin awoke, it was to find Faith gazing down at him, her eyes luminous in the gloom.

"Lord Harkom will come for me soon, and you won't be able to stop him. I don't want you to die in some fruitless attempt to save me." Her voice was determined; her mouth clenched.

"And fail you a second time? Lord, Faith, we were so nearly man and wife. How different things would have been if the timing had been in our favour. We might not be bound before the law, but I feel as if we are."

"You didn't fail me before. Circumstances conspired to put us both in an impossible position." She hesitated. "I don't blame you for believing what everyone else did. And nor do I blame you for not following through on a marriage that would have bound you to a woman who would surely have ruined your career."

"Oh Faith, my career is not as a diplomat, I see that now." He stroked her cheek. "You made me see that. This last year has been anathema to me. I thought following the path that would make my father happy would earn me his approval. But, here with you..." It was difficult to put his feelings into words. "You're what's important, Faith."

"Because of that letter? Because you think that you're no better than me after all?" She twisted within the circle of his arm and looked down at him. "How can it be proved?"

Already, Crispin's mind was turning on what the immediate future held for both of them. The question of his origins seemed almost unimportant when he very much feared he'd not ever make it home to England. If Harkom really planned to spirit Faith away using a distribution ring that had yielded success and financial rewards in the past, he'd not scruple at disposing of a man he not only hated for personal reasons, but who had the power to see him face the noose.

Faith seemed to grasp this at the same time for she gripped his arm tighter. "Crispin, what are you thinking? That it doesn't matter? But it does. It matters because you *will* escape. You will return to England, where you'll prove that you're every bit the son your father would be proud of. I'm sure he is very proud of you, even if he doesn't show it. I couldn't bear it if I were the reason you'd have to make a choice between your father's wishes and your own."

He held her tighter and felt a stab of pain for what she must have experienced to have been so belittled by a man Crispin felt less and less affiliation with, regardless of his true parentage.

What he had, now, was what he had to fight for. Faith was his responsibility; his true love. If they survived their ordeal, he'd sacrifice everything for her.

"As long as I have breath in my body, I will fight for you, Faith," he vowed.

"I will not be a burden." She pressed her lips together. "Love does not survive when it means sacrifice and duty at the cost of what's truly in your heart. I pushed for you to marry me—quickly—because I was afraid for my future. Yes, my future. I didn't think about yours, Crispin; only that I believed I could make everything up to you by making you happy...pleasing you during the years we had together as man and wife. I've been taught how to please men. Yes, listen to me and don't shy away from the awful truth. When I met you, it was by design. I'd spent three years groomed in how to entice *you*. You owe me nothing. You certainly don't owe me your life!"

He felt her tears raining down upon his chest, and tenderly brushed her wet cheek with his fingertip. "My dearest Faith. Because of you, I feel more alive in this moment than I ever have. I owe you everything!" He kissed her again. And then, because he was afraid of her wilfulness, he cupped her face as he angled himself over her, and said softly, "Your place is by my side. While you are here, I will do all in my power to protect you. I would give my life to see you safe, Faith. You need to know that."

AND FAITH WAS VERY MUCH AFRAID THAT THIS WOULD BE THE COST Lord Harkom would extract.

She also knew the time would come, sooner rather than later, when her nemesis would recover sufficiently to make his overtures.

When she was sure Crispin was sleeping, Faith quietly climbed out of their shared bunk and slipped out of the room.

Breathing in the fresh air on deck, she spied land and her heart sank. On board the ship, they had the protection of the crew who, although they'd offered little in the way of overt assistance, nevertheless refused to lock them up.

And, with Lord Harkom so indisposed, Lady Vernon had not enforced Faith's prisoner status. But soon matters would come to a head.

She tapped softly on the door. "Lord Harkom, it's me, Faith. I'm alone, and I want to speak to you." The sound of footsteps made her cringe, and hurriedly she added, "I have a crew member with me so don't try to take advantage. I just need to speak to you." She glanced over her shoulder at the Frenchman who showed no understanding, but who stood implacably nearby, as she'd requested.

"I'll go with you willingly if you'll release Crispin," she said, leaping back with a squeal when he flung open the door.

He looked ill and haggard, his appearance not improved by the ironic curl of his lip. "Do you think that'll please me, Faith?" He laughed. "To have you submit to me, meek as a little lamb." This time he threw back his head and indulged in his mirth even more. "Why, what did Madame Chambon teach you? Certainly not how to tread carefully with men of my proclivities which, I daresay, is all to the good. Now, where's your Mr Westaway? I was feeling mightily indisposed a few minutes ago and certain I'd not have the strength to crawl from my bed, but your delightful little proposition has fired me up."

Faith darted back at his approach, but he gripped her shoulder to stop her fleeing and barked out the order, in French, to the seaman behind her, to fetch Mr Westaway.

"I'm already here," Crispin announced, arriving behind Faith and attempting to pull her to his side.

"The little wench has offered herself to me, Westaway, so hands off, thank you." Harkom waved a pistol in his face.

Tendrils of dismay curled around Faith's inards to see the expression on Crispin's face, and to realise how badly she'd compromised both their safety.

"Yes, she came here, of her own volition, and offered herself to me if I'd allow you to return home safely. Isn't that sweet? Especially considering the way you treated her all those months ago. Now—" With a jerk of his wrist, Faith found herself in the circle of Harkom's arm, before he'd pinned her by her neck, his other hand holding the revolver.

"How easy to claim self-defence for your death, Westaway," he snarled. "But that would be letting you off too easily. No, you can come in and watch your beloved debase herself at my command. And you will die, knowing that her fate is to do the same for the pleasure of the various Far Eastern nabobs who are willing to pay a high price for an English princess with the treasured golden hair and white skin."

Unable to move, Faith shuddered as he caressed her cheeks, sliding his hand the length of her neck to skim her décolletage.

"Stop!" Crispin lunged forward but was halted by a sharp crack as Harkom fired in the air.

"Yes, loaded, in case you thought otherwise. Now, would you kindly step inside, Miss Montague. I've been waiting for this a long time now."

Faith screamed and gripped the lintel as Lord Harkom proceeded to pull her inside, slamming the door in Crispin's face.

"You can listen to her wail and beg, Westaway!" he shouted. "Unfortunately, I can't do what I have to do *and* keep my pistol trained on you."

RAISING HIS LEG HIGH, CRISPIN KICKED AT THE DOOR, BUT IT HELD FAST. He could hear Faith's whimpers within and the sound of Harkom's harsh laughter, before the thud of a body landing on the ground.

Again, he tried to kick in the door, but it was solid, and locked.

"Faith! Are you all right! Harkom! For God's sake! You don't need to do this to have your revenge on me. You can shoot me now if it'll please you! Let her go!"

Another muffled cry from Faith was too much. With a howl of rage, Crispin hurled himself against the door, but still it would not yield.

"You might have more luck if you had a key, Mr Westaway."

Crispin turned at Lady Vernon's silken tones. She looked like a crow of ill portent as she hovered at the end of the corridor, her back to the light so Crispin could see only her illuminated form. And then he heard the clink of keys, and saw she held up the keyring upon which a dozen keys dangled.

"No! Don't, please don't!" Faith's cry from indoors was tortuous, but Lady Vernon seemed unaffected.

"Don't try to take it from me or I'll cast it overboard," she warned as he began to stride towards her. "I'll give it to you on one condition." The sea was only a few feet from her. She could throw it over her shoulder with ease, and he would never have it.

"What is your condition?" There wasn't much time, but if he could save Faith from Harkom's final assault he'd agree to anything.

"I fear we're being followed." With a jerk of her thumb she indicated a schooner much closer than Crispin would have believed. There was no time to investigate further, but it seemed to be heading straight for them. "If we are apprehended, you'd better swear on your life that you'll say Harkom took me captive, as Faith's chaperone. Do that, and not only will you have the key, you'll have my testimony as to what he's been doing. Otherwise," she shrugged, "I can't see there will be any case for Harkom to answer. Not to mention there's the matter with the letter from your fond, cash-strapped mother. Your real mother, that is."

"Give me the key and you have my word."

And then it was in his hand, and Crispin was striding back down the corridor, inserting the rusty key, and thrusting open the doorway upon a scene of vile degradation.

❄

Faith knew there was no point in struggling, and yet she could not do otherwise. To submit without a fight went against any grain of survival instinct she had, while the hope she could cause Harkom damage made the penalty she'd pay worth it.

"You are more a fighter than I gave you credit for, Faith. I'm sorry I didn't try harder to break you in," he panted as he caged her body with his.

"I'll die fighting, Lord Harkom," she vowed, jerking her head upwards to try and bite his ear.

He slapped her then, and she yelped with the pain, her world hazing into red and black for a moment before her consciousness became refocused on what he was doing with his other hand.

She tried to wriggle free for it was now beneath her skirts, while his other was busy unbuttoning himself. She felt like a moth in the maw of a giant, deadly spider, and her efforts were futile.

Crispin was just on the other side of the door, but it was solid, and he was as helpless as she. If she could only lie still. Stop herself from reacting and it might be better for all of them. Harkom might lose the ability, even, if he were confronted by meek passivity.

It would certainly be better for Crispin who'd be tormented by what he was helpless to remedy.

"You'll die, any way I take you. You'll die in a Turkish harem far away from here, unmourned by any, Faith, for you gave up your right to respect a long time ago."

"And you did not, Lord Harkom?"

"Ah Faith, but you are a fine sparring partner. Why did I not make you my mistress when I could have set you up so nicely after Westaway forsook you?"

"I never forsook her!"

Suddenly, the door was open and Crispin's tall, straight form was silhouetted in the doorway for a split second before he hurled himself onto Lord Harkom.

It was enough to knock him off her and, taking advantage of her reprieve, Faith rolled out from beneath him, finding sanctuary half under the bed.

Crispin's eyes were trained on Lord Harkom, while Lord Harkom's pistol was trained on Crispin.

"You'd die for her?" spat Harkom. "Gutter scum? You're more of a fool than I thought. A pretty face that will corrode soon enough, and then what will it all have been for? Well, it doesn't matter, does it, for you'll be dead!"

And then there was another commotion, outside, followed by the sound of splitting wood before the boat was jolted as if it had been sideswiped by a much larger vessel.

Faith screamed as Harkom's weapon discharged.

CHAPTER 33

Faith screamed and threw herself upon Crispin's body, just as the boat was boarded and newcomers had spilled into the room.

More evil was about to render her more helpless.

If Crispin were dead, she wanted to die too. What was left for her if she was dragged home and forced to fend for herself, yet again? Her only refuge was Madame Chambon's, and who knew how involved she was in the evil trade plied by Lady Vernon and Lord Harkom.

So, she simply buried her face in Crispin's neck, sobbing as she felt his weakened hand upon the back of her head; sobbing even more when she heard his whispered, "I'll make sure you're looked after, Faith."

How could he look after her? The bullet wound to his chest had caused a spreading stain that she'd tried to staunch with her skirts, but still the blood oozed. He'd die from loss of blood before he died from anything else, and Faith would be watching, unable to do anything.

Her mind was so focused on Crispin's needs, she gave no thought to Lord Harkom until she heard a masculine voice she could not place —although she was sure she'd heard it before—bark out a directive to someone else, and then the pounding of feet before a groan of pain.

"Harkom! That's enough!"

Turning her face only so she could observe what was happening out of the corner of her eye, she saw a stocky young man bending by the prone figure of Lord Harkom, who gave a yell of pain as he was rolled over and his arms were tied behind his back.

"Christ, I'm not going anywhere! Can't you see I've taken a bullet?"

And indeed, a spreading pool of blood near his shoulder bore testimony to the claim.

But he was not mortally wounded as Crispin was. If Faith wasn't focused so wholly on protecting Crispin from evil, she'd have hurled herself on her violator and clawed his eyes out.

"Faith? Faith, are you all right?"

With an effort, she turned her head, blinking dazedly to find herself staring right into Lord Delmore's eyes.

"Crispin's been shot," she wept, the tears starting to flow. "Lord Harkom shot him." With the emotion unleashed, she found she could not stop, and as Lord Delmore put his arms about her to draw her to her feet, she still could not stop. "He's dying," she whimpered as she pressed her face against Lord Delmore's chest.

"We're going to do everything we can to help him; make sure that doesn't happen," soothed Lord Delmore standing above them. A light salt-tinged breeze ruffled his overcoat. He smiled encouragingly before gently pushing her away in order to kneel beside Crispin.

"I've seen men worse than that come off the battlefield, and live. Come with me, Faith. The boat's waiting." He beckoned to someone just out of sight and, shocked, Faith locked eyes with the last person she expected to see on a boat so far from home.

But as she allowed herself to be led by the woman she blamed for causing her downfall, she realised too that Miss Eaves must have acted swiftly and boldly to have effected the rescue that had just taken place.

Miss Eaves sent her a level look as an array of emotions flitted across her face. "I had access to a much faster vessel than the one Lord Harkom enlisted to take you away," she said as she helped Faith across the deck and to the railing, where a sleek schooner was moored beside the leaky tub they inhabited.

"It's my father's. He's sailing around the world and happened to have come into port just two days ago, so was available to take us on this little jaunt when I woke him last night having enlisted Lord Delmore's help." Her smile broadened as she released her grip on Faith's arm so that Faith could take the hand offered by a waiting crewman who stood on the rocking deck of the *Clever Amy*. "Yes, I do want to make it as a newspaper reporter and a woman on my own terms, but it does help to have well-placed connections; I admit it."

"Your father?" Faith gaped as she took in Miss Eaves's words before a strident American voice made her turn, and she was confronted by a tall blonde man built like a wrestler wearing a crisp, cream suit. He was shouting orders to the crew to bring the wounded and bound Lord Harkom down the ladder, but at the same time there was an air of life about him that suggested he was enjoying himself enormously.

"Miss Montague?" Coming out of a barked command to one of his crewmen, he offered Faith a deep bow. "I'm Ellison Eaves; pleased to meet you. My daughter didn't do you justice when she described you, my dear girl. What an ordeal you've been through! Amy gave me the barest of details so you'll have to fill me in on the return journey. I look forward to it, though I promise you, it'll take half the time that old leaky sieve took to get you this far."

Faith was saved having to answer by the arrival of the captain of their vessel with whom Mr Eaves dealt very cordially, before Amy's father pulled out a fist full of notes, which he proffered to the captain with the instruction that if he were called upon to supply further details, he'd be sure to remember who the real villain of the piece was, indicating pointedly the form of Lord Harkom who was being carried, groaning, along the gangplank.

Faith stood forlornly at the railing, as she watched Crispin being carried with a great deal more tenderness than his lordship, out of the cabin and across the deck. Gripping his hand as he passed, she was relieved to feel the gentle pressure in return, and she released it to follow the group into one of the commodious cabins where, to her surprise, Miss Eaves appeared, saying, "Stay here with him, if you like. We're about to set course for England, so make your appearance in the dining room whenever you're ready. There'll be a good dinner laid on, and I'm sure you could do with a fortifying brandy." She ran the back of her hand across her forehead. "I certainly could after the events of tonight, though I'll have to keep a clear head in order to write my story." Then, to Faith's surprise, she took her hand and shook it energetically. "I can't thank you enough, Miss Montague, for providing me with the copy I need to keep my name front and centre. This time, though, I hope I can go some way towards making up for the last article."

Faith clenched her jaw. "I really don't care what you print, Miss Eaves. All I care about is Crispin." Despite starting so strong, her voice dissolved as she added, "I don't think I could bear to lose him a second time."

"Nor will you!" came Ellis Eaves's robust tones as he appeared behind his daughter like a well-dressed hulking giant. "Can't you tell the difference between a mortal wound to the heart and when a feller's only been winged? Sure, there's lots of blood to make the women squeal and despair, but it's hardly mortal. Lord Harkom, though. Well, it's touch and go with him, I'd say."

"And Lady Vernon?" Faith swung around and searched for her amongst those milling about the deck of both boats. She'd not seen her since glimpsing her through the doorway after Crispin had hurtled in and torn her from Harkom's suffocating onslaught.

"Lady who? Lady Vernon? Ah yes, I remember the name, but can't say I've seen other ladies about the place other than you and Amy."

CHAPTER 34

"A deep breath for courage…all right, Faith?" In the corridor outside his father's study, Crispin took Faith's hand and gave it a squeeze. "Remember, nothing he says can make a jot of difference to the fact that you and I *are* going to be married."

He'd thought he'd suffer nerves in the lead-up to this historic confrontation, but for the first time, he felt a lightness of being he'd never experienced before.

And when his father issued the command to enter in his usual stentorian tones, he did not quake or wish himself a hundred miles away. Instead, he sauntered in and said, "Father, I want you to meet my future wife, Miss Faith Montague. We're getting married at St Margaret's on Saturday next and hope you'll do us the honour of attending with your blessing."

"Miss Montague…" Lord Maxwell drew out the pause. "I'm pleased to meet you." He rose from his chair at his desk and indicated the cluster of seats by the fireplace. "You seem to enjoy the bright lights though I can see they might seek you out."

Crispin was surprised to see the flare of admiration in his father's eye.

"You and your compatriots made quite a sensation in bringing to justice one of London's most surprising villains. Yes, involved in a grubby scheme we shall not mention for delicacy's sake."

"Faith's actions were heroic."

"I heard yours were too, Crispin. But I wonder..." He came out from behind his desk, and although he smiled at Faith, the furrow between his eyes didn't augur well. "Have you truly considered the ramifications of this hasty marriage? Marrying between the stations, no matter how distinguished the behaviour of each party, is bound to lead to unhappiness."

"So you truly believe one's status should be shackled by one's origins? One's birth?" Crispin watched his father carefully as he went on, "Lord Harkom received a letter from...let us say that she was not a lady but a woman who purported to be my real mother. Outrageous, of course! Unless you believe it invites investigation rather than condemnation?"

Lord Maxwell blanched and held his son's look for a long moment until Crispin broke the silence. "Or do you think it's the *learned* behaviour and ability to conduct oneself appropriately in the social sphere to which one is to be elevated that defines a true lady or gentleman?"

He smiled to see his father's internal battle. Crispin's own shock at the discovery of his likely parentage had been replaced by acceptance. So much had happened between learning the information, and now.

"For if that's the case, then Faith and I were made for each other. Don't you see, Father. Each of us has been elevated from our humble origins. Each of us has been taught how to behave in the sphere our benefactors intended for us—as one of the top ten thousand."

Lord Maxwell had recovered himself. He did not even refute Crispin's insinuations that he might believe his parentage was more humble than he'd believed. He began to pace, his hands behind his back.

"You've proved yourself a finer diplomat than anyone expected." His voice was gruff. "You need a wife who can adapt to the restrictions and the expectations...the loneliness of being in a foreign country, even. I see that. I see how loneliness for you, my boy, can be a danger."

"So, this is the basis on which you would sanction my marriage to Faith?" Crispin was careful to spell it out. "Because she knows how to behave, she's decorative, she'll keep me occupied and, in Germany, she'll be out of the glare of inevitable interest."

Lord Maxwell stopped and inclined his head. "These are not inconsequential considerations."

"But you are not disposed towards withholding your endorsement?"

"I am not…on condition you continue in your current position."

"You know of my love of painting."

"Of course, I do, boy, but there's a time for everything. You need to put food on the table. So, have your wedding, leave the country and, in a year or so, if you still wish to paint, then I shall give you my support."

This was more than Crispin had expected. But would Faith understand just how momentous this was? He swallowed. The kernel of doubt that had been initially motivated by fear of his father's reaction turned to doubt that Faith would consider this an acceptable compromise.

He turned to find her gazing up at him, a faint smile about her lips, her beautiful eyes filled with understanding.

"I think what your father proposes is very wise," she said, putting her hand on his arm.

"You do?"

She nodded. "Sometimes we need to make sacrifices simply to keep a roof over our heads or to satisfy those upon whom we depend."

Her understood her meaning. It was the only way she'd survived.

But there was more.

She gave his arm a gentle squeeze. "Your father has only your best interests at heart. He wants to see you succeed. No parent wants to see their children make a mistake that can destroy their lives and that can never be undone."

"I won't give up…" He'd nearly said 'my painting' but then he'd long ago realised that his painting was not the most important thing in his life. "You, Faith. I won't give you up." The words sounded impassioned, even to his own ears but he didn't care.

Faith smiled. "Your father's not asking you to do that and, besides, even if he did I'd ensure I was too forceful for that to happen."

"It would not be necessary, I assure you," he murmured, longing to kiss her.

"No, I think I'm confident on that score," she replied with a soft, happy laugh. "But your father is right. You need a profession until you are established as a painter." She paused, "And if what I've heard from Miss Eaves is true, her uncle is very keen to offer you all the patronage you need from that quarter."

Crispin looked from his father to Faith and could hardly believe his good fortune. He had the backing and the love of both. He had the loyalty of the woman he adored while a promising career as a painter beckoned.

"I think I have everything I could wish for," he said, feeling bemused, quite suddenly. "What about you, Faith? Is this what you want?"

Faith gazed up at the man who promised her more than she could ever have dreamed of.

It was almost too much to take in. Within seemingly a few heart beats she suddenly had security. She had freedom and respect.

And she had love.

The love of a man who had proved he had the courage of his convictions. Crispin had set out to protect her when he still believed the worst of her. But his loyalty to what they had once shared had driven him on. What else would account for his actions of the recent past?

"You are what I want, Crispin," she said, softly, so only he could hear. "I don't care if you're a diplomat or a painter, I just want us to be happy together."

"I think she'll be good for you, my boy." Lord Maxwell must have heard for he looked approvingly at both of them. "Just make sure you really are the man she thinks you are."

Faith recognised how his gruff words might be interpreted by a sensitive young man as doubt edged with criticism. She'd rarely encountered a kind word, herself, until she'd met Crispin.

"Have no fear on that score, Lord Maxwell," she said, gripping Crispin's hand, tightly. "If you could have seen the heroic way he faced down Lord Harkom who was holding a gun, you'd be agitating that he receive a medal of valour." But as she tipped her face to Crispin's, her words were only for him.

"We will be good for each other, Crispin. And I promise I shall never let you down."

"I know you won't, just as I know my own mind, Faith." His eyes glowed with feeling as he took both her hands in his, ignoring his father behind them. "I didn't realise how much I wanted to keep painting until I met you. But with you as my wife, I know I'll spend the rest of my life trying to do justice to your beauty and your goodness with more than just a paintbrush."

Still holding her hand he gave a sharp tug so that she had no choice but to stumble after him, through the open door and into the passage where he pinioned her against the wall and kissed her soundly.

"And that's just the beginning," he promised, cupping her face, his expression adoring.

Faith sank against him as she twined her arms around his neck and closed her eyes.

"The beginning of a grand new life," she whispered as a great weight lifted from her shoulders. The secrets and lies had been exposed and Crispin still wanted her. But the kiss had unleashed something hard to control and her body ached for him. Spirals of desire were shooting up her spine. She tightened her grip around his neck and pressed herself against him, her voice hoarse as she whispered, "If you really want to show me that your father has no hold over you, then kiss me again." She laughed softly. "Prove that this really is a new beginning."

THE END

WEDDING VIOLET EXTRACT

Wedding Violet (Book 4)

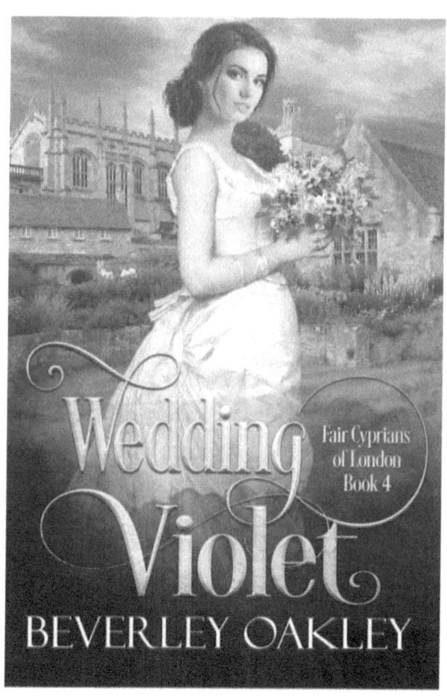

There's a new girl at Madame Chambon's. Her name is Violet Lilywhite and she'll do anything to escape - especially if it involves a sham marriage to a very handsome and charming viscount.

Read Wedding Violet to see how that goes.

Wedding Violet

Abandoned at the altar, Max, Lord Belvedere believes he's evaded family obligation in favour of a life of adventuring in Africa. But his ailing Aunt Euphemia has other ideas.

When Max finds himself in the delightfully diverting arms of Violet Lilywhite while visiting London's most prestigious House of Assignation, he happens upon the perfect plan. A sham wedding to a 'penniless shop girl' should fulfil Aunt Euphemia's romantic dreams without losing him his newfound liberty.

Violet agrees to the deception with no hesitation. Lord Belvedere is certainly the most charming and surprising of all her male consorts but she has no illusions about a shared future. She wants only to escape the clutches of infamous Madame Chambon.

The plan is perfect.

Until Max and Violet fall in love.

Read an Extract...

"By Gad, that was the best tupping I've ever paid for, my lovely Victoria!"

"Violet."

Lord Belvedere swept back his fringe with an elegant, long-fingered hand. Reclining in all his youthful glory upon the satin-coverlet of the iron four poster, he regarded Violet with undisguised satisfaction.

Through the thin walls of Madame Chambon's infamous House of Assignation sounded the thumps and cries of the night's trade. Strange that this had become normal to her now, Violet thought as she sat at the end of the bed, her knees beneath her, untangling her long fair hair with her fingers.

"Actually, it's the first tupping I *have* ever paid for—and worth every penny, my exquisite Violet." Belvedere made sure to get her name right this time. He grinned as he met her look, then reached forward to draw her down beside him. "Where *did* you learn those tricks?"

"I could ask you the same, my Lord," Violet replied, gently disengaging herself from his embrace to sit on the edge of the bed and look for her stockings. For once, it was more than lip service. It *was* the best tupping she could remember from her strange, sordid year.

Unfortunately, she was going to have to cut short this surprisingly pleasurable encounter if she wasn't to anger her most reliable and high-paying customer, Lord Randolph. He'd probably be pacing the length of the drawing room downstairs like a caged tiger by now.

With an extremely satisfied sigh, Lord Belvedere put his hands behind his head and crossed his ankles. "And I would answer that pleasing a woman has always been a favourite pursuit of mine. He continued to regard Violet with appreciation. "Now, let's finish it off with a bottle of champagne and bring out the checkerboard, shall we?"

Violet flicked a quick glance at him as she bent down to roll on one of the fine, white stockings she'd found hanging over the iron bed end. He really was rather a delicious specimen with his soulful caramel eyes that could easily disarm a girl. And that beautifully curved mouth was as accomplished at kissing as it was issuing quips that made her laugh. This last hour they'd done all that and more as they'd rolled about on the pink satin counterpane in Violet's attic room with its view of St Paul's being its most redeeming feature. There weren't many other redeeming features at Madame Chambon's.

Lord Belvedere looked in no hurry to leave. He stretched languidly and Violet tried to hide her interest in assessing his unashamed naked form. She'd never experienced feelings, other than revulsion, for any of the men she entertained in order to keep a roof over her head.

"Yes, champagne and checkers is just the thing, I say!" He sat up, clicking his fingers as he joined her on the edge of the bed.

"I'm afraid no one is going to come running at your summons, my lord." With a dampening smile, Violet turned and presented him with her back, holding up the long laces of her corset in a clear implication that she needed his help. "Regrettably, our time together is at an end and I'd appreciate it if you helped make me decent. I presume you have done this before?"

"Naturally." But instead of the tug of laces, she felt his arms go over her shoulders to fondle her breasts while he pulled her against him and nuzzled her ear. She could feel the swell of his erection against her behind while the whisper of his breath against her ear stirred her insides into an unexpected state of excitement.

The acknowledgement of this sensation of physical enjoyment was troubling.

"Nevertheless, I have no intention of leaving before we've ended matters in a civilised fashion." He kissed her shoulder and turned her to face him. "I realise there are men who consider it civilised, or within their rights, to pay an unseemly amount for sex and then leave the moment they come." He smiled pleasantly at her as he stroked her cheek. "I, however, am a gentleman and I like to reward good value. You, my dear Violet, have given excellent value."

Violet blinked, surprised at the pang of regret she felt at his impending departure until she remembered how important the no doubt hideously impatient Lord Randolph was to her long term goal of escaping Madame Chambon's House of Assignation. Or Bordello, Nunnery, Brothel or whatever term it went by in the lexicon of the gentlemen who crossed its threshold in pursuit of London's most sought-after companions. Ladies of the night. Lightskirts. Fair Cyprians. She'd been called many things but she rather liked the way 'my fair Violet' rolled off young Lord Belvedere's tongue. Just as she'd liked what young Lord Belvedere's tongue had done to her in a myriad of other unexpectedly erotic ways this evening.

"Madame Chambon will be most pleased," Violet murmured, extricating herself from his grasp.

"I have no interest in pleasing Madame Chambon."

It seemed Lord Belvedere was not going to be easily persuaded to leave. He cupped Violet's chin, turning her head slightly so that she was forced to look at him. "If I'm cutting into the time of your next highly anticipated customer then perhaps Madame Chambon will be pleased if I double your rate just so we can drink champagne and play checkers together for half an hour. I trust you can play checkers. It's hardly a complicated game."

Violet considered him. She made no secret of it as her eyes roamed the length of him: his long, muscled thighs lightly dusted with the dark hair from which his manhood sprouted; further up, his well delineated chest with its delicate nipples suggesting the first possibility of vulnerability. His mouth was the second. And it really was a lovely mouth, his lips soft though his jaw determined; as determined as his eyes as he stared back at her.

He indicated the bell that sat on her side table. "Surely you need only ring that and a servant *will* come running to do our bidding?"

It was true. If Violet was creative enough, her next customer would be given the necessary excuse that would see him offered any of the other exceptional young women for whom Madame Chambon's establishment was renowned.

"Unless you would, in fact, prefer to be entertained by your next customer rather than drink champagne with me?" His voice was lower by several notches. Caramel and persuasive. Like his eyes.

No, Violet had no desire to entertain Lord Randolph but nor did she want to anger him. Lord Randolph was well on the way to making her that offer of exclusivity which every girl at Madame's craved.

She licked her lips as she stared back at his lordship. She'd happily drink champagne with him. Heavens! She'd happily roll about on the bed with him for another session, which was unheard of.

Violet contemplated her options. Perhaps denying Lord Randolph tonight might be just the ticket for hustling him along the road to setting her up in her own little ladybird's lair so Violet could shed this hated life and plan her next elevation.

Without a word, she picked up the little bell and sent the message for which his lordship was so eager. Champagne and a board game. What a perfectly delightful way to end an evening.

"Clever move, lovely Violet. You're as inspiring on the chequerboard as you are in bed."

Predictably, they were once again back on the pink satin coverlet, Lord Belvedere stark naked, Violet in only a peignoir, but he'd been true to his expressed desires. It seemed he really did want to end their session with some rivalry on the chequerboard and some lively conversation rather than once again demonstrate his prowess as a lover.

Violet watched his lordship toss back his champagne. His cheeks were flushed and there was an air of excitement about him, or suppressed emotion, that she'd not noticed before.

With a gusty sigh he set down his glass and sent Violet a long and level look as he leaned back against the pillows. "Definitely a moment to celebrate. A lucky escape, if ever there was one."

Violet shook her head when he reached for the bottle on the bedside drawers and tried to top up her glass. "And what have you escaped, my lord? A marauding tiger? The firing squad?" She tried to sound relaxed as she ran her forefinger over the smooth surface of the white chequer she was waiting to move once it was her turn. She could see an opportunity that she suspected he'd missed.

"Not quite, though, either way, my fate would have been equally unhappy." Lord Belvedere leaned over, picked up his black, and neatly moved to take three of her checkers. "You thought I'd missed that, my love. But I'm not so stupid. Nor are you, for that matter." Then, in a more robust tone, "I was to have got married tonight. Can you believe it, but three hours ago I was all dressed up and standing at the altar in my very finest."

"You were to have been…married?" Violet felt her first flush of panic for the evening as she tried to discern if the beautiful…*naked*… man before her was in earnest.

If he was, then—what had she done?

Sensing her discomfort, he patted her wrist. "I waited at the altar for more than an hour for the wretched female." For the first time this evening he looked grim. "Lord, I certainly had everyone's sympathy by the time we all realised the game was over."

"I'm sorry." Violet plucked at the silken folds of her peignoir and thought how strangely different men were from women when dealing with crises of the heart. Recalling the moment of realisation that the man she'd loved had let her down so terribly still sent ice through her veins, nearly two years later. But her first recourse had hardly been sexual diversion. A wave of self-revulsion engulfed her. Oh no, that had come much later. Though hardly at her behest.

"Lord, you can't imagine it! I'd arrived at the church feeling sick to my stomach with nerves but determined to do the right thing."

She searched for any sign of remorse on Lord Belvedere's part for having assuaged his wounded pride in the arms of a...lightskirt – oh, how she did suffer at the terms that indicated how far she'd fallen.

But she could find none.

He glanced at her, then looked away, stroking the glossy tops of the marble checkers as he added, reflectively. "Of course, I got what I deserved. The whole debacle was, after all, my fault."

"What was your fault? That she didn't arrive?" Violet tried to imagine what scenario might have prevented an eager bride-to-be from making such an important appointment. Her self-recrimination of a moment before was replaced by a surge of anger towards the man in front of her. Somehow, she suspected, Lord Belvedere had evaded a marriage he didn't want. Perhaps he hadn't waited long enough. Perhaps he'd ensured his bride-to-be was detained on purpose. Oh, Violet knew of many underhand ways a man could slip and slide out of his obligations.

Yet, was she any better? If she were made of sterner stuff and lived by her principles she'd point at the door and tell him to get out right now. No young woman should ever have to go through what Violet had gone through.

Just as quickly, the emotion drained away. Why should she expect any better from a client? Clearly Lord Belvedere, for all his charm and winning ways, was as morally deficient as all the rest.

And, besides, one only had to see how far Violet had fallen than to know that she was the last person alive who could criticize another for their morals.

Lord Belvedere shook his head, unaware of her changed feelings towards him. "No, it was my fault for asking her to be there in the first place. For asking her to marry me when I knew she didn't want to. Standing there, in the silent vestry, feeling the sympathy of the wedding guests while my own shame nearly felled me... well, it was just divine punishment." He took another sip, then kissed the tips of his fingers in a careless gesture of gallantry towards Violet.

Violet sought for a response. She was hardly about to exonerate him if that's what he wanted. "That sounds like an excuse to me. She wouldn't have accepted if she didn't want to marry you. What if she was in an accident and that's why she was delayed?" Her outrage grew. What a *terrible* thing for him to have done? Gone straight from the church to Violet's bed. Why, that made Violet implicit in causing an innocent young woman pain she did not deserve.

"Believe me, there was no accident. Mabel cried off at the last moment. She realised what I should have realised: that she should never have accepted me and that she'd be making as big a mistake as I by trying to please our families rather than ourselves."

His face softened as he extended his arm and stroked Violet's shoulder. "No need to look like that. No harm done. Best thing that ever happened, in fact."

Violet frowned. She couldn't decide whether his cavalier attitude hid a broken heart or whether he really was as overjoyed to be free as he made out.

"Your father must have been dismayed to say the least."

"Pater's been dead a long while. Mother the same. No trouble from that quarter." His smile broadened.

"So...the poor young lady's decision to cry off has left everyone happy? What a strange state of affairs."

"Well, not everyone was happy. My grandfather was irate, to say the least, as was hers. They share adjoining estates and thought the idea of forging the next generation to create a mighty union a capital idea." Lord Belvedere sighed and, for the first time, looked regretful as he toyed with the checkers. "My great-aunt, alas, is inconsolable."

Violet wasn't sure how to navigate such strange territory. "I suppose it's better if one doesn't get married just to please one's grandfather...or great-aunt," she said slowly while also thinking of the many women who married to please everyone in their families other than themselves.

Suddenly he became brisk. "Now, where were we? Your turn, I believe?"

Violet studied the checker board and made her move.

"Got me! And I didn't see it coming!" Lord Belvedere took another slug of champagne.

"That's either because you wanted to redeem yourself by playing the gentleman and letting me win or because your wits are addled."

He laughed as he moved one of his chequers three places. "I like to think of myself as a gentleman. I've not found myself in an establishment like this before. And as to my wits being addled, it is not, in fact, a sensation with which I'm terribly familiar. I like operating with a clear mind. Tonight is an exception."

"That would make you an anomaly amongst your set." Violet sent him a wicked smile across the top of her glass as he raised one eyebrow and clearly pondered a response. She wondered if he were the kind who was quick to anger when their manliness or any other apparent prowess was questioned, despite his assertions that suggested the contrary.

"I *am* an anomaly amongst my set, apparently." He gestured his surroundings with a sweep of his arm. "Yes, it's my first visit to a place like this and I don't know why I allowed Bletchley – that's my best man – to persuade me to come here though when I set eyes on you all objections died on my lips. But, do you know, I recognised three gentlemen. Married men, too." He shook his head. "Now, coming to a place like this when one is married is not, in my opinion, the mark of a gentleman."

Violet shifted position, uncomfortable with his talk. "Some of these men do not enjoy the comforts of home that they—"

"Feel entitled to?" he interrupted. He shook his head, his expression uncompromising. "Sorry, but that doesn't wash with me. They should have been wiser in their choice of wife."

"You do not recognise a double standard? I hardly believe you are practising as you preach, Lord Belvedere. Sorry if I sound sceptical but don't you think you'd have soon been back through those doors to see me as a married man if the woman you wed proved unsatisfactory in bed?"

He sent her a level look and shook his head. "No."

"No?" Violet tried for her most artful smile in an attempt to lighten the mood.

To her surprise, he remained serious. "No. Honour and freedom are the codes by which I live. I was ready to follow the honourable path and do what grandfather wished of me for the sake of the family. I'd have accepted my responsibility and I'd have been faithful, regardless of what it cost me. But when Mabel bolted, I was overwhelmed by the prospect of being, suddenly and unexpectedly, free." He relaxed, his beautiful smile transforming him into the most handsome man Violet thought she'd ever seen.

"My, but I am glad it was you who came to my rescue, sweet Violet. So much so that I'm truly sorry to leave you, knowing that I shan't be back."

A pang of regret ripped through her. Violet couldn't believe it. She actually wanted to welcome this man back into her arms and was telling him so? What's more, she meant it, for while she'd said similar words to Lord Randolph, that had been paying her most valuable customer the necessary lip service. Survival talk.

"You'd be very welcome," she said softly. And he would. In all the time she'd been at Madame Chambon's, Violet had never met a man as charming as Lord Belvedere.

"Ah well." He began to neaten the checker board, placing the scattered checkers in their rightful places. Violet couldn't keep her eyes off his hands. They were long-fingered and gentle. Well, gentle when needed, and very successful in whipping up her long-dormant sexual impulses, too. She swallowed, hoping he didn't notice the blush that brightened her cheeks as she recalled the clearly mutually enjoyable exploits that had so recently played out upon her bed.

He looked up. "Lightskirts are forbidden in my code of gallantry and tonight will be a single lapse before I pick myself up after the tumultuous events of this afternoon and forge ahead as the gentleman I propose to be."

Violet ignored the taunt to her calling. "I think you are more upset about being jilted than you would allow."

"My pride was dented, it's true, but I am more excited about the freedom ahead of me than I am downcast at losing face."

Violet held out her empty glass, then raised it in a toast as the foaming liquid spilled over the edge. "Here's to your freedom, my lord. Go forth and make the most of it for not many of us know what freedom is."

He raised his eyebrows as if her words surprised him, stopping with the glass poised at his lips. "And what is freedom for you, my lovely Violet?"

"Choosing the man upon whom I bestow my favours." She regretted the words the moment they were out and hoped one of Madame's spies didn't have their ear to the wall. Gentlemen paid a fortune to come to this house in order to feel they were the centre of the universe.

"Ah, so that's why you're so pleased I'm here since you invited me back and it's clear we like one another." In one swift movement, he placed his glass upon the chest of drawers and pushed her back onto the mattress, kissing her thoroughly on the mouth while one hand skimmed her thigh.

To Violet's astonishment, her body responded with a skittering of pleasurable anticipation right the way up her spine while her womb pulsed with desire.

Until, to her equal surprise, her pleasure was replaced by a sense of desolation when he rolled off her and stood up, casting about for his shirt which he began pulling over his head.

"You have been utterly beguiling, sweet Violet," he said, as his head emerged and he positioned his stiffened collar before reaching for his trousers. His light brown eyes sparkled. He truly did look like a man who was both satisfied yet regretful to be leaving.

But surely he'd come back?

"And, dear girl, you deserve all the freedom you desire."

"So, freedom for you is simply not being married to Miss Mabel?" Violet couldn't let him go without knowing more. "Is that all?"

"Freedom for me is adventuring across the seas to foreign lands. I was supposed to be heading off on my wedding tour to the Continent as we speak but I've a notion that Africa will suit me far better." As he worked to slide his cufflinks into place his expression took on a faraway look. "Yes, Africa. There's gold and diamonds to be discovered there. Perhaps I'll invest in a gold mine. And shoot some lions and tigers. Why, I'm free. I can do anything I want. You have no idea how wonderful it is to say those words out loud, Violet. *I'm free.*"

Violet watched him in silence. Already he was leaping forward in his life, envisioning all the marvellous opportunities that lay ahead. She felt like weeping at the vast chasm between what each could hope for from their respective futures. Instead, she murmured, "There are no tigers in Africa."

He stopped as he slid the second cufflink home, his lips trembling with suppressed amusement. "Not only beautiful, you are also clever, sweet Violet. I was testing you, of course. Though what would you know about tigers?"

A great pounding in her head made her close her eyes. *What would she know about tigers?* More than he'd ever find out, she thought, painfully.

"A little," she ventured. But he was too occupied with tidying himself to attend to her properly. Finally satisfied with his appearance, he turned and put his hands on her shoulders.

"Farewell, my lovely Violet. Thank you for this evening. You brought me back from the brink."

"But now you will never think of me again. Or visit?"

Why had she said that? It sounded bitter and that was something she'd sworn she would never be. Not like her grandmother who revelled in it and who'd ensured the orphans thrust upon her would never know what it was like to be carefree as their punishment for being born.

He was halfway to the door but he turned, a myriad of emotions flitting across his face. What a handsome man he was, his well-cut suit highlighting his broad shoulders and long legs, his smile boyish and heartrending. In two strides he returned to sweep her into his arms and kiss her deeply.

A long, languid, thorough kiss that left her shaking and desperate for more when they both came up for air.

For a moment they remained clasped tightly in one another's arm, the only sound their heavy breathing.

After a moment he whispered, "No, I will not return, alas. But I've enjoyed what we shared." He held her away from him, and gently touched her lips with his forefinger. "It was a … particularly satisfying intimacy I could never engage in with a young lady I'd only just met."

"You just did."

"With a marriage prospect, then." He cleared his throat and seemed to try for a brisker, more light-hearted tone. "Well, now, my lovely Violet, it has been an absolute pleasure meeting you." He dropped his hands and made for the door. "I wish you all the best for your life. You never know, perhaps I'll send a postcard from the Sudan or Cairo, for I don't expect I will forget you in a hurry."

"Address it to Miss Violet Lilywhite," Violet murmured, wanting to imprint it on his brain. "And you can always ask for me by name if you choose to return."

His smile was genuine but regretful as he put his hand on the door knob. "As I said, I shan't be back, but I'll certainly recommend you to the more discerning of my set. Decent fellows. A girl like you deserves the best."

[End of Chapter One]

Is this the last encounter Violet has with her most attractive customer? **Find out in Wedding Violet.**

ALSO BY BEVERLEY OAKLEY

The Daughters of Sin series follows the intertwining lives and sibling rivalry of Lord Partington's two nobly born - and two illegitimate - daughters as they compete for love during several London Seasons.

With Hetty and Araminta both falling for men on opposing sides of a dastardly plot that is being investigated by Stephen Cranbourne, now a secret agent in the Foreign Office, there's lashings of skullduggery and intrigue bound up in the central romance.

What Readers are Saying About the Series:

"...lies, misdeeds, treachery, and romance. What an impressive story! Ms. Oakley has a unique way of telling her stories, bringing unknown heroes/ heroines into the spotlight, as they navigate a world of espionage, and intrigue, all while trying to survive and find their HEA. Magnificent and mesmerizing!" ~ **Amazon reader**

"Full of secrets, murders, intrigues and you feel you know the characters and want to strangle some of them, especially Araminta!!! I have since read all in the series and can't wait for Book 5... This is a series I will read again and again." ~ **Amazon reader**

Below is the order of the books:

Book 1: Her Gilded Prison

Book 2: Dangerous Gentlemen

Book 3: The Mysterious Governess

Book 4: Beyond Rubies

Book 5: Lady Unveiled: The Cuckold Conspiracy

GET A FREE BOOK

You can get Her Gilded Prison - Book 1 - for FREE by joining my newsletter. Just visit: www.beverleyoakley.com

Four very different sisters compete for love during an exciting London season: a celebrated actress with a heart of gold, a shy yet daring wallflower, and the artistic, illegitimate daughter of a nobleman. Caught up in a high-stakes game of intrigue and deceit orchestrated by their sister, the ton's reigning beauty, each must play their part to bring a dangerous traitor to justice while finding a man deserving of their love and special talents.

Buy the complete series as a Box set and save.

ACKNOWLEDGMENTS

Thank you, Facebook, for unexpectedly reconnecting me with my old high school school friend, Nina Campbell, after more than twenty years. Her excellent judgement and enthusiasm have been a tremendous highlight in my long writing journey.

And a Lexi Greene, another beautiful writer and human being whose romances make my laugh and cry. Thank you for being with me on this fun ride from the days before we were published - that's fifteen years!

Another big shout-out to my editor, Bev Harrison, and my cover designer Dar Albert of Wicked Smart Designs. I always feel confident putting out a book when you both are involved.

And, finally, big thanks to Cliff and Corinne, readers whose kindness and attention to detail really helped polish the final work.

I couldn't have done this without you all.

Beverley

www.ingramcontent.com/pod-product-compliance
Lightning Source LLC
Chambersburg PA
CBHW032006110726
47901CB00004B/985

* 9 7 8 0 6 4 8 4 0 5 9 3 1 *